A WORLD SLOWED

The Jared Chronicles - Book One

RICK TIPPINS

DOOMSDAY
PRESS

TO MAHSA

Chapter 1

JARED SAT AT A TABLE, sipping a cup of tea, staring out a window, and taking in the expansive campus of his employer. He and his fellow employees were not for want while at any of the numerous campuses scattered throughout Silicon Valley. Jared's employer provided catered food trucks, laundry service and even a designated nap area. Jared always felt this was way over the top and took away from what he was trying to achieve in his chosen field of work. If his employer redirected those millions of dollars into his projects, he would be light-years ahead of where he was now. The problem was all the people who worked alongside him demanded these things that bled the company of funds it should have used for research and development.

Jared exhaled as he watched a woman ride past on one of the bicycles the company kept stashed all over its campuses. The bikes were used instead of walking since some of the campuses' buildings could be quite a good distance from one another. Jared knew where the woman worked, and although he wasn't sure of her exact yearly compensation, he knew the company's pay scales well enough to know that she could afford several bicycles of her own. Jared never wanted to be part of the problem, so he brought tea bags from home and only took hot water from the company.

He watched as the woman rode off, thinking he didn't even know her name. Why would he know her name? Although they'd been to the same meetings on countless occasions, neither had ever spoken a word to the other. The fact was, Jared didn't speak to many folks at the company. He wasn't socially screwed up; he was simply focused on his tasks at the company and didn't have time to be hanging around the break room making idle chitchat.

Jared turned away from the window, looking at the wall-mounted television tuned to CNN and spewing nonstop news. Jared cared little for the news unless it had to do with the tech world or weather, the latter serving more as a guide, letting him know if he should wear flip-flops or sneakers, a T-shirt, or a T-shirt and a sweat jacket. The news anchor spoke about violence in the Middle East. He rolled his eyes, thinking CNN could have simply looped the same video footage and gone home for the next five years and no one would have been the wiser. The story switched gears to POTUS and the fight on global terrorism. Jared had voted for the current president, as had many in the company. The company had also donated to the president's campaign. Jared wished he could make time to research all the candidates, but he was not able. Consequently, he voted his party, which was Democrat.

While sipping his tea, Jared sat silently watching the people outside, his mind immersed in thoughts of his current project. Jared was irritated with the issues preventing him from completing his current project, which was a small piece of a much larger venture. The issues with the project reminded him of the wasted funds being used on frivolous expenditures. Making matters worse, other people assigned to the project were holding him back.

He knew he would be staying late tonight, working on things that no one else would do. *I need my own project assigned only to me. A project with a reasonable budget and realistic deadlines. No group of people to have to placate during my creative process, no boss breathing down my neck, wanting to be cc'd on every single project-related email. A project that will test me.* He hated working in the company's so called "project groups." The concept made him feel like being an Olympic athlete and being asked to run a relay with old fat, people. Jared could not understand why the company failed to recognize the obvious, cut the fat, and work more efficiently. Finished with his tea and his internal gripe session, he stood and headed back to his desk.

The September sun continued to bask the Bay Area in its waning warmth well after 6:00 p.m. At 7:21 p.m., Jared's computer abruptly shut down and all his office lights went off. This happened instantly and at the exact same moment. He rose and walked to the doorway, peering out into the empty hallway. Nothing, the campus was shrouded in an eerie blanket of powerless silence. Down the hall, Jared saw two people step into the hallway from their offices, searching for the source of this interruption, just as he was doing. Jared ducked back inside, not wanting to be trapped in a conversation about the power outage. He returned to his desk and sat down, figuring he'd wait for the backup generator to restart the building's power. He sat there for several minutes before looking at his watch. The screen was blank.

"Give me a break," Jared blurted out loud, immediately fishing his phone out of a pants pocket and depressing the home button. Nothing happened. He pushed the button again and a third time before getting back to his feet and returning to the doorway. He looked down at his watch and then to his phone before stepping fully into the hall. The same two people were quietly conversing about thirty yards down the hall, as they repeatedly depressed buttons on their own cell phones.

Jared could tell they were experiencing the same glitch from which he found himself suffering. They looked his way then went back to their discussion.

Jared ambled back to his cubicle, still perplexed by the sudden loss of power to the campus, his watch and his cell phone. He stuffed his phone back in his pocket then stopped and stood like a statue, halfway between the door and his desk. He couldn't work without power, and he had things to do. Truth be told, no one waited for him at his home in Belmont some fourteen miles north, so he would work late into the night in order to get these things done.

He decided to go outside and check the other buildings. *If the power's off everywhere, I'll head home and start up again tomorrow morning,* he told himself. Jared knew this meant he would have to stay late all week and more than likely come in on the weekend, which wasn't completely out of the ordinary for him. He grabbed his Cal Berkeley zip-up sweat jacket and headed out the door, purposely turning in the opposite direction of the two who were still standing in the hallway like a couple of zombies, unable to make a decision.

Jared burst out the front doors of building 43 and again stood extremely still. Instantly, he noticed the lack of artificial light and an eerie absolute silence. He surveyed the campus, taking in the silence and the absence of manmade light along with several other people milling about. The people were clustered near the buildings on the campus as if discussing some important companywide project. Jared looked at the bicycle rack and quickly pushed away the urge to use one for the rather lengthy walk to where he parked his car on the far northeast side of the property.

Jared walked with his head down, avoiding any eye contact with the clusters of people as he made his way across the campus grounds. No one attempted to speak to him as he walked. The campus was usually full of people who walked with earbuds inserted, for all intents and purposes in an alternate world. Today was different, no one had earbuds in and people were actually talking to one another, so he kept his head lowered and just walked.

Jared arrived at his car, pulling his key fob out and depressing the unlock button. Nothing happened. He pressed it again, moving closer to the car, but still it seemed the fob refused to communicate with the vehicle. Jared flipped open the key, inserted it in the lock, and pulled open the door. He lowered himself into the vehicle, pushed the key into the ignition, and turned. Nothing happened, not even a dying battery click. He turned the key in the ignition several more times, then checked to make sure the car was in park and hadn't somehow slipped into drive, which would have caused the vehicle to fail in its starting sequence. There were no dash lights, no clicking sounds; the vehicle was dead.

After his car failed to start, Jared returned to building 43, where he saw more utility workers than regular company employees. Where in the hell did all these guys come from? He'd never seen this many on campus and pondered the idea that maybe they stayed hidden somewhere and only came out like firefighters when something needed fixing.

He returned to his desk, where he sat down and thought about what was going on. Had someone on the campus done something that had knocked out the power and damaged everyone's personal electronics? If so, they would be finished, unless the company could find a way to make money with their mistake.

As Jared sat thinking of what to do next, he realized a landline sat directly in front of him. He'd never used it in all the time he'd been at the company. Although it had rung quite a lot in the first few months of his employment, he never answered it, and people soon grew to understand that if you wanted to reach Jared Culp, you'd better have his mobile number. He snatched the telephone receiver from its cradle and put it to his ear. He heard no dial tone. Jared just held the handset for a moment, trying to process the last few sequences of events. Slowly he returned the handset to its cradle. He didn't know for sure how much time had passed since the outage, but he figured it had to be about an hour or so.

He returned to his office's doorway again, peering down the hallway; this time it was empty. He stepped out farther from his cubicle and scanned the campus outside, seeing all the bicycles were now gone from the rack. He could see security moving around along with the utility personnel. The company, although it had many faults, took great care of the employees and was probably already putting together some sort of plan to get everyone home safe. Busses, cabs, or maybe a town car— somewhere someone had to have a working vehicle. Jared wished his phone worked so he could call an Uber and be done with this mess.

"Hey, you there," a security person said after spotting Jared and starting toward him from outside building 43. The man seemed agitated as he waved his hands and yelled several times.

Jared moved toward the front door and met the man near the now empty bicycle rack. The man appeared amped up and out of breath.

"What's going on with the power?" Jared asked before the security man could start in on him.

"Dunno, man. Just know that we're clearing and securing every building on the campus." The man moved past Jared and entered building 43.

"Hey, my car won't start, is the company going to get us home?"

The security man shot a look over his shoulder, stopped, and turned back to face Jared. "Are you serious? Take a look around, man. All the power's out, your car won't start, and there's a small plane parked in the east lot because it lost power and had to make an emergency landing."

Jared looked, but couldn't see the plane from building 43.

"So no, man, I don't think the company is going to give you a lift home." With that, the security man turned and moved into building 43, calling out to any stray employees.

Chapter 2

DARKNESS FORCED JARED BACK to his car, the only place he could think to go at the present time under the present circumstances, whatever they were. Once seated in his car, Jared locked the doors. He didn't know why but he just knew he felt better with the doors locked. At this point, he found himself hungry, confused, and getting a little scared. He looked at the hulking outline of the other cars in the darkness and couldn't tell if they also harbored evicted residents of the company buildings.

His surroundings appeared pitch black, and Jared couldn't remember being in a darker place in all his life. Jared's eyes began to adjust to this new kind of darkness as he sat alone in his vehicle. A short time later he began to make out shapes in the inky blackness. Nothing was moving or making noise in the parking lot as the car began to feel stuffy. Jared turned the key and depressed the window button before being reeled back to the present reality, which didn't foster power windows. Jared cracked the door open and was nearly scared into a premature grave when a man's voice erupted from the darkness directly to the rear of his vehicle.

"Yo, you got room in there?"

"No, we're full," Jared blurted out as he pulled the car door closed, locking it with trembling fingers. *Where did that guy come from?* Jared turned in his seat, staring into the black night, tracking the shadowy figure as the man checked car doors and called out to people.

Jared reached back and started to put on his seatbelt, but stopped short, letting the belt return to its taut, unused position. He was more than a little rattled right now, and that guy had done nothing to calm his deteriorating nerves. He felt vulnerable, thinking nothing he'd done in life had prepared him for spending the night in his car with no power, no cell phone, no food, no water. Jared glanced over his shoulder at the more spacious back seat of his car. With more effort than he would have thought necessary, he climbed between the two front seats and into the rear of the little car.

Finally, Jared began to drift off into a less than deep slumber when he was literally ripped from his troubled dreams by a woman's bloodcurdling scream. He didn't move a muscle except to open his eyes. Jared laid absolutely motionless for nearly five minutes before slowly raising himself to gaze out the car's windows into the black and seemingly inhospitable night. His body was like an overtightened piano string, the stress began to affect his ability to form any likeness of a clear thought.

Had he really heard a woman scream, or had he dreamed it? He was pretty sure it had been real, but began to doubt himself, just a little. Either way, it had woken him, causing even more chaos in an already hectic night of broken sleep, hunger, and thirst along with an unhealthy dose of instability in his world. Slowly the fatigue won over and Jared slipped back down in the back seat, his breath deepening and his muscles relaxing just a hair as he drifted into a fitful sleep, dreaming of shadowy figures and screaming women.

Chapter 3

SUNLIGHT STREAMED in across the dash as Jared sat bolt upright, jerked into consciousness by the emerging day's light. His mouth tasted like he hadn't brushed his teeth in a week, and he was both hungry and thirsty. He looked around the parking lot and saw nothing but empty cars. Slowly he shifted his gaze skyward and took in the many different sources of smoke on the horizon.

"What the hell?" he muttered as he sat fully upright, opening the car door. He stumbled out of the car and stretched before turning three hundred and sixty degrees, taking in all the smoke drifting across the skyline. What was going on? What was burning and why? Jared could hear no sirens and, come to think of it, he hadn't heard a single siren all night. In fact, the day was void of all the normal ambient manmade noise usually assaulting one's senses in any urban setting. Jared could hear birds chirping and that was about it. No, wait, he could hear insects. He could actually hear bees, or some other flying insect, humming about the parking lot.

Jared struck out across the parking lot towards building 43. He had a toothbrush and could freshen up while he figured out what was going on. He again tugged his phone out of his pants pocket and depressed the home button—nothing, *fuck*. He returned the phone to his pocket and glanced at his watch, which was also in a state of disobedient hibernation. Once Jared reached building 43, he found the doors locked with no indication of life inside. He walked the campus, looking for open doors to other buildings, and found none.

As Jared made his way back towards his car, he saw a security man walking across the campus. Jared hesitated and then, simply out of desperation for an answer, waved at the man. Jared adjusted his course to intercept the man just before the guy would have cut between two campus buildings. "What's going on with the power, man?"

The security man stopped and looked Jared up and down before answering, "Don't know." The man turned and gestured back the way he'd come. "Everything went down last night, and the boss says to button it all up and keep everybody out till they can get it fixed."

"Yeah, you guys kicked me out of 43 last night and I had to sleep in my car," Jared said, with more than a little edge to his voice.

"Don't know what to tell you, man. Can't find the boss today, and I slept in some cat's cubicle in 45 all night. Worst night's sleep I ever had." The man suddenly looked tired as he continued, "I'm tired, hungry and I'm going home. Gonna walk, I guess."

Jared was incredulous as he spoke. "That's it, that's all you know? I can't accept that, the company has to provide rides, food, water. Where is everyone?"

The security man threw his arms in the air. "Man, I don't know. They left, rode the bikes home, walked home, your guess is as good as any." Dropping his arms, the man nodded out past the parking lots. "Something bad has happened, heard a lot of gunshots last night, and I heard a woman scream."

Jared nodded. "I heard that too."

With that, the man turned and walked off across the grounds towards the city streets beyond the safety of the campus.

"There any bikes left?" Jared called out.

The security man turned, but never broke stride. "What?"

Jared stared at him for a long moment, then dropped his head. "Nothing."

Chapter 4

THE SUN WAS MUCH HIGHER in the sky now, raising the temperature to the point where Jared returned to his car, seeking refuge from its relentless rays. That was the dumbest thing he'd done so far, the car was twice as hot inside as the weather was outside, so he climbed out, locked the vehicle, and began walking west. He planned to find an open store or a cop or anyone who could get him a ride home and tell him what in the hell was going on.

He trudged along, thinking through his route, realizing that when he drove home, there was a completely different thought process than walking home. He had the roadways memorized, and it didn't really matter if the routes weren't exactly direct or took roundabout ways to get him to his apartment. Just as long as he wasn't adding a half hour to the commute, he would do what everyone else did: drive, listen to the radio, and maybe do some light texting or make a call with his hands-free gear. Walking, on the other hand, was a completely different animal; direct routes were a must. Jared had no plans of walking any extra miles, so sticking strictly to the roadways was out of the question. He would have to cut time by hopping a few fences, cutting through parks, and maybe even some yards, although deep down he knew that probably was a bad idea.

Jared cleared the parking lot and entered the surface streets surrounding the campus. The streets were empty, no cars, no people, not even a dog. He walked west along Rengstorff Avenue, passing a self-storage and a couple of businesses that showed zero signs of life and appeared locked. The air was filled with a thick acrid scent of smoke, while the road was littered with stopped vehicles, as they too had lost power in the middle of their daily routines. Some were stopped perfectly in the road as if the driver had simply coasted to a stop, never deviating from their lane at the time of...*At the time of what?* he wondered. *Power outage*, that was what he was calling it; power outage was far less scary than the unknown.

Many of the cars were pulled haphazardly to the curb as if the drivers had attempted to park before their forward momentum was lost. This was one of those life things where what you saw did not paint an accurate picture of life. The vehicles left perfectly in the lanes belonged to people who didn't have the common sense to take some sort of action after a loss of power and were content to stop in the middle of the road and wait for help, while the drivers of the cockeyed half-curbed vehicles had actually taken action, attempting to guide their stricken steeds to the safety of the curb line, where not only would they be safe, but the general motoring public would also not be impeded by their presence.

Jared wondered how long the drivers in the perfect cars had sat waiting for help. He immediately scanned the cars, searching for any occupants who might have been dumb enough to simply sit and wait for help. Jared remembered himself sitting huddled, scared and cold in his car the night before, and felt a pang of embarrassment at his judgmental thought process.

Suddenly it dawned on him. What was going on here, why

had all the cars stopped, why had his phone stopped, and why was the sky filled with smoke?

He sat on the curb and withdrew his phone. He attempted to power the unit up without success before turning it over in his hand. It was an Apple product and he knew a few people who had developed its technology. Heck, he knew the man who had come up with the design for the shape of this phone. The guy had come up with dozens of designs, and this had been the one chosen.

Jared pulled out his car keys and used a nail clipper attached to the ring to open the phone, exposing its internal workings. The process took some time, and Jared knew the phone was a total loss, as he had damaged it during the opening process, which included some pounding and a lot of prying. When the phone was open, he gently removed the tiny motherboard, inspecting it closely. He was familiar with the tiny board; he always sought to learn through what others were doing and how they were applying new tech to current products, like Apple always seemed to be doing.

Jared froze as he brought the little electronic board near his face, inspecting it. His mind raced over everything he had ever learned about electronics and the things that affected them. He stood, dropped his key fob on the ground, and crushed it with his foot. He picked up the tiny electronic component and closely inspected it. Jared was stunned as he struggled to wrap his brain around what he was seeing. Both electronic components showed signs of an overload, their weak links burning in place, rendering them useless for their intended purposes, no longer able to allow the unrestricted flow of data, energy, or anything for that matter. Jared recognized the damage as being permanent, making both items unusable. If this had happened to all these cars, his phone, and his key fob, what else had been affected?

His eyes drifted to the sky, where the smoke from far-off

fires still wafted across the calm blue sky. Planes, he knew people who worked for companies that supplied parts for most of the world's airplane builders and, nearly without exception, the equipment was electronic based. *Did all the planes fall out of the sky yesterday? Is the smoke from the burned wreckage along with human bodies?* Jared remembered hearing somewhere that the Bay Area was one of the most congested areas in the world in terms of air traffic. How many planes would be in the air at any given time, he didn't know.

Jared's personality lent itself to looking at a project, identifying the problems, prioritizing, and then slowly coming up with solutions to said problems. This approach had rewarded him with success since grade school, and he had excelled at his job using it. Jared started that process now, but not knowing the cause left him without a jumping-off point, which he badly needed in order to effectively initiate progress. Although Jared didn't know the cause of his current situation, he already had the core problem identified. It was just so far outside what he thought was possible, he simply could not accept that all these electronic devices were no longer functioning, sustaining his world as they had his entire life.

Jared stood there on the side of the street, staring at his cell phone's stricken guts and smelling the smoke in the air, his mind swimming with uncertainty. He slowly relaxed his hand, the phone dropping to the concrete, bouncing next to the shattered key fob. He had to get home, sleep, and wait this thing out. Once he got home, time would sort the whole thing out, the government would send help, but in the meantime, he would be safe inside his apartment while it all played out. Jared took one glance at the shattered fob and phone, then turned and started walking.

Chapter 5

SOLAR FLARES HAVE BEEN KNOWN to man since the 1800s and have been studied in order to understand how they emit energy, what types of energy are emitted, and what fallout comes with exposure to these emissions. The harmful energy emitted during a solar flare reaches Earth in 1 to 4 days, leaving mankind little time to react. As in many of Mother Nature's endeavors, mankind can only watch and try to compensate as the event is happening or after it is over. Floods, droughts, storms and temperature extremes are just some of the tantrums Mother Nature forces mankind to endure.

When the sun experiences a buildup of magnetic energy to the point of release, it emits radiation in the form of nearly the whole of the electromagnetic continuum. This includes hard X-rays along with gamma rays emitted from the sun in volumes equal to millions of one-hundred-megaton hydrogen bombs. These solar flares can last as short as a few seconds and as long as hours. Most solar flares, while large in comparison to Earth, are not large enough to have many adverse effects on its inhabitants. A larger solar flare could and would have devastating effects on the current earthly population. After a large solar flare, Earth would have 1 to 4 days before the different types of energy slammed into the population and its technology. Satellites would be the first manmade objects to be disrupted and, when the energy reached Earth's surface, it would damage any and all unprotected electronic equipment.

On September 9, the day Jared slept in his car, one such solar flare reared its ugly head. The flare, although most likely not the largest in our planet's history, was by far the largest ever recorded in the last hundred years. It caught the Americas dead in its sights, knocking out the lights of the United States, Canada, Mexico and South America.

The United States leadership realized within seconds the country had been radiated back to the Stone Age and, in an act of self-preservation, launched an attack against key targets on the opposite side of the globe with its own version of a solar flare, the EMP or electromagnetic pulse weapon. The United States fired on China, Russia and the Middle East. Known only to key people in Washington the United States also sent missiles to countries like England, Germany and Israel.

Surprisingly this was not a decision made at the time of the solar flare, but one made years before in a strategic planning session which had studied an event that could take the United States off the table as a superpower. The leadership agreed if the United States couldn't be a superpower, no one could. This decision was made after it was decided even allies like France and Germany would take advantage of a floundering United States' position in the world's power scale. The United States would not be able to defend itself from an invading force and would be forced to invite foreign countries in to prevent the extinction of her population, in the form of humanitarian support.

Studies done on the aftermath of either an EMP attack or an equivalent solar flare was that the US population would be reduced significantly within the first six months without humanitarian aid, but would suffer a catastrophic loss of identity were the country to allow a foreign military to position itself on American soil. The study concluded that the United States would not have the military might to force an occupying military to leave, and would soon after be subjugated. After the United States let fly its missiles, those countries intended as targets launched their own counterattack. The result was catastrophic as mankind undid hundreds of years of technology, crippling the entire planet in less than two hours.

Although these studies were theoretical in nature, they were done by intelligent men and women who understood the infrastructure of the United States and its delicate balance in regard to supporting life within its borders. The first to die would be the elderly and those with illnesses necessitating routine medical assistance to survive. Diabetics would be without insulin, just to name one group. The professionals who cared for these people would no longer have the tools for proper care and would in most cases choose to abandon their patients, returning to their homes to care for and be with their own families. Patients with survivable ailments, but no daily care, would catch staph infections along with a myriad of other formerly treatable complications. Millions would die from illnesses completely treatable in the world of old.

Most heavily populated metropolitan regions of the US have about three to five days of food in grocery markets at any given time. This was under normal conditions and not in the conditions that would follow an event like an EMP or massive solar flare. People would loot and, in doing so, they would stock up, taking more than they ever would have on a normal shopping day. This was viewed as having little effect on the population-reduction timeline, as some people would have food and others wouldn't, meaning some would live a few days longer than others, but not a significant number of days. Within a month, starvation would be a real thing in all the heavily populated areas of the world.

As starvation spread across the globe, people would try to leave the built-up areas and move into more rural areas. Crime would skyrocket, and millions more would die in their attempts to leave the cities. There were few people left in the world prepared to walk more than a few miles at a time. The United States government studies theorized that most of the deaths would occur within the first 120 days and would be mostly the old and sick, followed by starvation- and dehydration-related deaths.

After the first 120 days, there would be people who had stocked up on food, water and weapons. They would likely not be folks found in the built-up urban areas, but country people, used to surviving and providing for themselves. They would provide zero assistance to those seeking help with food, water or protection. The people who had taken the time to prepare themselves usually didn't have much use for the city types, who, in their eyes, were against everything the country folks held near and dear. The folks who would come streaming into the countryside would be many of the same Americans who tried, year after year, to ban guns, limit hunting, tell the ranchers how to raise their herds, and tell farmers how to grow their crops. No, these two groups would not be friends and would collide like bodies of raging water.

The loss of life during this time would be there, but not big enough to play much of a role. Thieves found stealing crops or animals would be shot on sight as ranchers and farmers began taking the law into their own hands. Eventually the land would stabilize itself; the death rate would slow as the last of the world's weaker humans passed on. It would be the Great Depression times a thousand. You either had a skill, were an asset to a community, or you died.

Very few could live outside a community and survive

indefinitely. A hundred years ago there were many men who lived off the land, but now there were precious few men or women who understood enough about Mother Nature to take from her bounty in today's day and age. She did not allow just anyone her life-giving nectar, it had to be earned. A man could earn it within a community, or he could earn it on his own, hunting and fishing and sleeping on the ground. Communal and solitary life both had their pros and cons, and the survivors would either overcome the cons, or they would die.

It was the plan of the United States government to emerge from their hiding place after six months and begin an outreach program using Special Forces, like they had in Afghanistan and a dozen other third-world countries in decades past. Reaching out to whatever communities had survived or risen from the ruined world. Within a year the government hoped to have repopulated the coastlines, opened ports, and started trading with other countries in an effort to rebuild the country of old.

The power grid would have been the first thing the government started to rebuild, but they were met with a sizable snag before the end of the first week. America was attacked from within; Russian and Chinese agents who had been living in America for decades were activated by the event. They had very specific orders in case of this type of situation, and they acted like a well-oiled machine.

The White House was attacked by sixty-five Chinese agents and burned while every single occupant was murdered where they stood. This went on around the capital and, to make matters worse, Air Force One crashed trying to land at JFK International, killing the President and many of his staff. After the attacks, the Russian and Chinese agents withdrew and simply became victims like the rest of the population, but the damage had been done. America's leadership was either dead or unable to muster due to the complete collapse of the communications and transportation component of the country.

The Chinese and Russians were not the only ones with a plan to cut off the head of their enemies. The US also had agents in place across the globe, and they wrought havoc in much the same manner as was done back home on US soil.

Man had made himself vulnerable with his dependency on technology. If mankind had used technology for things like flights, telling time, and simple nonessential matters, he could have survived with a much lower death rate. Mankind had not done this and had integrated technology into his water and food sources, making the delivery of both dependent on a functional power grid, and now this was gone. Mankind had also set the table with all his weapons poised to strike at his neighbors on a moment's notice.

Mother Nature is a peculiar animal in that she always fixes herself and, after the last century in which man had scarred her badly, it was time for action. She had only to deliver one savage blow, step back, and watch her problem take care of itself. Of seven billion people, only a few hundred million would likely survive the first year. Many of those who survived would be people who hadn't left a very large footprint in the first place.

They would be in the mountains of Afghanistan and the rain forests of South America, and they most likely would not even know there had been an event. News would eventually reach them, and they would go on with their lives, uncaring and unaffected. Mother Nature had hit the reset button and she would survive. The question was whether mankind could do the same.

Chapter 6

JARED HAD no idea at the time that his "wait at home" idea was going to be about as effective as Air Force Once's landing had been. He walked west towards the El Camino Real, which he planned on taking north to his apartment. He saw folks in their front yards with camping gear, barbequing meat and drinking beer like it was a holiday weekend. Some folks gave him a wave while others had a look of fear on their faces; these people neither waved nor smiled.

Jared walked and walked. His feet hurt as he stared at the sneakers he had on, thanking God he hadn't opted for flip-flops the morning of the event.

Up ahead Jared spotted two side-by-side duplexes, the occupants out front, sitting on the grass socializing, three women and three men. They appeared to be normal hard-working blue-collar types, and they acknowledged Jared as he approached.

"Want a beer, man?" one of the men called out, hefting a Coors Light in the air. "They're warm, but everything's warm right now with the power out and all."

Jared stopped in front of the man. "I'm good, but if you have some water, I'm dying of thirst."

The man reached in a cooler and tossed Jared a bottle of water. "You walking home?"

"Yeah," Jared replied, opening the bottle before nearly draining it in a single draw. "Thanks, man." Jared caught his breath, readying himself for another go at the water. He hadn't realized how good water could taste when one was thirsty. He took another long draw off the bottle before looking at the group. "You guys know what happened?"

Most of the group shook their heads before the first man replied, "No one knows anything around here. Usually you'd see the cops or the fire department, maybe PG&E running around trying to fix whatever was wrong, but we haven't seen anyone with a uniform." He gestured to the cars on the road. "We woke up this morning and all those cars had people sleeping in them. Some folks wanted to sleep in our house— that didn't happen. Then a few hours after the sun came up, they pretty much all left. We seen a couple of folks like you walking, but no emergency-type people except one guy who came by wearing those pants cops wear, the wool kind, but he had on a jacket to hide the top. We all knew he was a cop and even asked. He denied it and hurried off like he didn't want anyone to know or something."

Jared stared at all the cars in the street, wondering if there was food in any of them. "You guys know if there's any place to get food around here?"

The first man shook his head. "No, we really haven't left except to go down to the corner store, and it was open last night, but only taking cash. The ATM, credit card machine, everything was down."

Jared nodded. "Your cell phones work?"

The man smiled. "I wish. Everything that plugs in or takes a battery is dead."

Jared thanked the people for the water and moved on down the road, keeping the empty bottle in case he found a water source he could refill at. It had started, the little voice somewhere in the far reaches of his brain, telling him to hoard, conserve, stockpile and survive.

He walked two blocks and came to a small neighborhood store, probably the store the man who gave him the water had spoken of. The doors were open and a very tired-looking Middle Eastern man was sitting in a chair in front of the business. As Jared drew closer, the man stood, and Jared could clearly see the man was armed with a pistol in a holster on his right hip. The sight was so foreign to Jared, he was neither alarmed nor shocked, just curious as he stayed on course for the front doors of the business. The man disappeared into the business ahead of Jared and stood waiting behind the register as Jared poked his head into the dark interior.

"We take cash only," the man said in heavily accented English.

Jared felt in his pockets for the cash he always carried. Forty dollars, in the form of two twenty-dollar bills. He pulled the twenties out and held them up so the man could see. The man seemed to relax just a hair, but eyed Jared as he made his way around the store, picking through the granola bars. In the end, he bought six energy bars and a bottle of Smart Water. The man claimed he had to have exact change, so the whole lot cost Jared a twenty-dollar bill.

Jared walked out of the store and pocketed all the bars except one, which he opened and promptly devoured. He washed the last of the bar down with some of the water, then ate another bar.

After eating, he continued down the road, reaching the El Camino Real about ten minutes later. Jared knew the El Camino Real, or ECR as it was referred to, would take him all the way to San Francisco if he stayed on it. He only needed to use it to get to the little town of Belmont. He'd walk through Palo Alto and then on through Menlo Park, both very affluent cities and safe for a person like Jared to be on foot in. The next town wasn't so safe. Redwood City was a little dicey to be on foot in, especially after dark, so Jared needed to hurry. Jared had driven through Redwood City many times and, as long as he was in his car, he felt comfortable. There was just that little stretch where he would see what he thought were gang members driving and walking about the streets, and he felt a pang of fear stab at his chest when he thought of this area.

ECR was littered with cars, even more than the other streets had been. It was a heavily traveled alternative to the 101 highway, and someone on a bicycle would have had a hard time picking their way through the mess left on the road. Jared stayed on the sidewalks and walked past the array of vehicle corpses blocking the street for as far as he could see.

Somewhere in Palo Alto, Jared saw an elderly man sitting in a Tesla sedan, just sitting and staring out the windshield. Jared ducked down and peered in at the man as he walked by, but the man never moved. Well, whatever had happened, it seemed that a Tesla was not the car to have right now. He moved on, the old man's face burning itself into his mind, expressionless, or was it hopeless?

As Jared hurried north on the ECR, the sun began to hang lower on the horizon, and Jared knew he wasn't going to make it home before night blanketed the sky. He took a deep breath and looked around, realizing he was almost to Redwood City, but still in Menlo Park. He walked, ate another energy bar, and drank some water. He thought about his job and the project he had been working on. He wondered if whatever had happened had affected the company's servers, hoping none of his work had been lost.

Chapter 7

ONE THING about the Bay Area and San Mateo County is it has some of the priciest real estate in the world, but it also has some dangerous neighborhoods within a baseball toss of these real-estate gems. Atherton is filled with multimillion-dollar properties, but it borders Redwood City's neighborhood, which is a Northern California narcotics hub. East Palo Alto and Palo Alto border each other and could not be more different.

One could be driving and in a matter of seconds leave Palo Alto, one of the most affluent cities on the West Coast, and be in East Palo Alto, one of the most violent cities on the West Coast. Jared walked past the "Welcome to Redwood City" sign, continuing north, all the while looking behind and ahead as if expecting trouble.

It happened two blocks later; Jared saw them, five young Latino men wearing white t-shirts and dark-colored jeans. The men were standing over a figure who laid crumpled on the ground next to a car. The men were yelling, cursing and threatening the figure. Every now and again, one of the assailants would lean in, delivering a vicious punch as the figure cowered and attempted to protect himself. One of the men kicked the figure, causing the poor wretch to curl into a tighter fetal ball.

Jared stood frozen, like a deer, not moving for fear the movement would attract their attention.

"Down here, get down here."

Jared heard the voice, close and raspy. His already over-wrought nerves nearly sent him fleeing blindly into the surrounding neighborhood. The man was homeless, dirty and unshaven, huddled down off the sidewalk where a small path led to a creek. Jared hadn't even noticed the small bridge spanning the tiny creek.

"Move before they see you," the man hissed, his voice laden with urgency.

Jared had been so thoroughly startled he hadn't moved a muscle except to direct his eyes in the direction of the man on the path. Jared glanced back at the Latino men, who had resumed beating and kicking the fallen man, before slowly side-stepping to the edge of the concrete and gingerly stepping down into the tall grass and weeds.

The homeless man turned and scurried down the slippery trail towards the creek. Once he reached the creek, he turned and picked his way through trash, vegetation, and who knew what else, heading up under the bridge. Jared followed, slipping, tripping and scrambling in an effort to keep up with the filthy man. The homeless man stopped high up under the bridge, where the earth and the concrete of the bridge met.

A homeless encampment was set up with pallets of wood, a sleeping bag, and some plastic containers the man had food and other items stored in. Jared stooped low and stopped short of the pallets as the man turned and sat on the sleeping bag.

"That was a close call, man."

Jared nodded, taking in the encampment and the smell—the smell was of wet body odor and rotting food. Jared tried not to show the welling sensation of nausea that had begun to wash over him. The man moved to one side, making room for Jared on the pallets. Jared held fast, acting as if he didn't realize the man's intent.

"Sit, sit, my man," the man said, patting the filthy sleeping bag.

"I'm all right," Jared lied, his back already starting to ache from the stooped position.

"The name's Bob," said the bum, thrusting out his blackened hand.

Jared had no idea why he did it, but he reached out and took Bob's damp, cold and grimy hand. Bob pumped the hand and smiled a less than toothpaste model smile. Bob held Jared's hand and kept pumping away as his smile began to fade.

"Well, what's your fucking name?" rasped Bob.

Jared's mouth opened as he tried to gather himself. "Jared, my name's Jared."

Bob released Jared's aching hand and nodded. Jared's back was killing him now, so he moved closer to Bob, smelling the rancid odors emitting from the man.

"Mind if I sit?" Jared asked.

Bob nodded and Jared moved onto the pallets, moving the sleeping bag aside with his foot. He felt it was better to sit on the wood than on the putrid fabric of that sleeping bag. Jared sat with his legs pulled up under himself, arms wrapped around the front of his knees, feeling very much like he needed a hot shower, some food, and maybe a good microbrew beer.

"You live down here?" Jared asked.

"Yep, been down here for ten or fifteen years, ever since I got out of the Army."

"Ten years, here, under the bridge?" Jared queried incredulously.

Bob nodded his head vigorously. "Probably fifteen years, I can't remember exactly. I get eight hundred dollars a month for my disability, come up, get my check, grab supplies, and come right back down, where it's safe. I watch all the people from the weeds where I saw you. I know everyone in this neighborhood, and not one of them knows me. Good for you I was up top watching, or you'd be getting the stuffing kicked out of you."

Jared smiled wryly and stared at his feet. "Thanks. Why were they beating on that guy?"

Bob shifted in his seat and stared back up the trail. "They rob folks from time to time, but something isn't right up topside, 'cause they've been at it all day and I haven't seen one cop since yesterday. I seen 'em rob and beat probably six people just today."

The light was starting to disappear as the two sat under the bridge, a world away from what was happening up on the streets.

Jared gestured at the trail. "They ever come down here?"

"Naw, they rob folks with things of value. I ain't got a pot to piss in, man."

Jared just bobbed his head in agreement, then shifted his weight, staring up and down the creek bed, the water being the loudest thing he could hear. The yelling had subsided above him on the street, and he shivered at the thought of the poor wretch lying, beaten and bleeding, less than a football field's length away.

Was the man dead? Had he gotten to his feet and stumbled off into the neighborhood after the men were done with him? What had they taken from him? What did Jared have that the men would want so badly that they would beat and rob him for it? He stared at his wrist, where he wore a thirty-dollar Casio watch, which was the most valuable thing he possessed at the time, and it didn't even work now.

It was getting dark now, and Jared could hardly see the brackish waters of the small creek from where he sat.

"You drink that water?" Jared asked, gesturing towards the babbling water's edge.

"Yeah, I drink it, but you'd better not unless you want to shit your pants for the next four or five days."

Jared squinted through the darkness in the direction of the water. "What's in it that would cause that?"

Bob shrugged his drooping shoulders. "Dunno, some damn parasite or something."

Jared was thirsty again, and the water bottles he saved from earlier were empty. "What happened the first time you drank the water?"

Bob looked incredulously at Jared. "I shit my pants for five days, dude."

Jared grunted, nodded, and stared back at the sound of the creek.

"If you have to drink creek water to survive, I guess it's like a rite of passage," Bob continued.

The two sat in the darkness, listening to the cheerful noise of the creek. For a moment, Jared relaxed and, other than being a little cold, felt totally at peace in the world. He couldn't remember the last time he had felt so absolutely relaxed and detached from the rest of the world. No humming computers, no nagging boss or co-workers. He still had deadlines on projects back at work, but they would assuredly be pushed forward until after this power-outage mess was resolved.

It was almost like an unexpected vacation, an escape from his rat race of a life. He almost laughed out loud at this thought as he sat under a bridge, with a bum, not a hundred yards from where a man had just been robbed and beaten nearly to death, while contemplating drinking from the roiling waters of a parasite-infested creek. *Wow, is my life such a gong show that this is a break from it?*

Gunshots rang out, five, six, maybe seven; Jared couldn't count as fast as the shooter was pulling the trigger. He rolled off the pallet, cowering in the mud. He hadn't moved to a better position of concealment or cover; he had simply felt the need to move and had done so without thought. Bob sat still as a statue in the exact spot Jared had left him, not moving except to turn his head and stare dubiously down at Jared.

"You've never been shot at," Bob stated matter-of-factly.

Jared's eyes were wide with fear, the shots sounded like they had been right next to them, and what kind of thing was that to say to someone? Of course, he'd never been shot at.

"They shooting at us?"

With this, Bob laughed softly into his hands, muffling the sound and rocking back and forth for a full thirty-seconds before composing himself. "Boy, you'll know when they're shooting at you, you'll hear the bullets, and you'll see me running like there's no tomorrow." He laughed quietly for a little longer while Jared stared blankly at him.

"You've been shot down here?" Jared asked after a short time.

Bob composed himself again, looking seriously at Jared and shaking his head. "I ain't been shot here, but I been shot at plenty." Bob lifted his disgusting clothes, exposing his white chest and belly. There was a long scar on Bob's chest and several smaller scars on his torso. Jared was taken aback by how white Bob's flesh appeared, as if the filth of living under a bridge in a muddy creek bed had no effect on his body, only his hands and feet.

"How many times were you shot?" Jared queried, still transfixed on Bob's snowy white undercarriage.

"Once. All the other holes are from surgeries I had after the fact." Bob dropped his clothing back into place and adjusted the soiled layers until they were just right.

Jared slowly got to his feet and returned to the pallet, sitting with his knees drawn up close to his chest, trying to keep what little heat he had corralled within his chest.

"It hurt?" he finally got out, almost embarrassed he had even asked the question.

Bob again gave him a look. "Hell yeah, it hurt. Damn thing missed my heart by an inch and tore a hole in one of my lungs. Almost suffocated during the helicopter ride back to base."

"Like a military base?" Jared interjected.

"Yeah, like a military base. I was in Iraq when I got hit, and that was the end of my military career."

"Did you say you were in the Marines?"

"No, I was in the Army, infantry, thought I'd spend a career there, but then, bam, some sorry fucker sneaks a lucky shot in and I'm out of the Army, hooked on painkillers, and shortly after that"—Bob gestured with his palms up to the surrounding scenery—"I'm living under this bridge, not in a van down by the river—I'm living under the fucking bridge…down by the river."

Bob turned to Jared, who had been listening intently. He looked long and hard at Jared until the young man turned away. *Who is this guy who nearly walked into a beating? How can someone be so out of tune with their surroundings that they would willingly walk right into the lion's den and be eaten without ever seeing it coming?* Bob guessed the world was full of these folks, walking around the streets with their heads buried in some electronic device, oblivious to their environment, talking to ten folks over text, but wouldn't so much as say *hi* or *excuse me* to a real human.

This Jared guy seemed like the rest of them, but also seemed different. He actually asked about the gunshot wound and asked if they'd been shot at. He had come down into the creek and sat next to Bob and, although Bob could tell the man was repulsed by the conditions, he hadn't commented on it. Bob decided he liked this Jared guy, he couldn't put his finger on why exactly, but there was some quality about the man he liked, an innocence, a pure soul, or maybe it was Jared's wholesome naivety, Bob didn't know.

Bob sat contemplating his next move. Should he lend a hand to a complete stranger? Would the lost soul take Bob's advice, or would he be like so many other people were nowadays, and dismiss his ramblings as those of a deranged homeless bum? Words spewed from the liquor-laden lips of an addict, not to be trusted and certainly not to be listened to by educated, working and functioning people of society. There it was again, that feeling Bob couldn't place, the feeling that although Jared was just like every other Starbucks-drinking clown he saw on a daily basis, he had a different quality to him. Like right now the man sat in silence, not needing to fill the air with idle and meaningless chitchat. Bob made his decision.

"You're gonna die up there without help, you know," Bob started. "Most of you are going to die within the next six months, check that, the next three months."

"What are you talking about?" Jared asked, his face scrunched in confusion.

Bob held out his hand. "Give me all your electronics. Come on, I'll give 'em back."

Jared slowly pulled off his watch and handed the useless timepiece to Bob.

Bob held the watch up, inspecting it from several angles as if this would lend credibility to whatever he would say following his examination of the former timekeeper. "It's fried, along with all the other electronics. They're all gone."

Jared nodded.

"Seems like everything got caught up in some power surge." Bob pursed his lips tightly together. "One of two things happened up there. Either there was one heck of a solar flare, or we are at war and folks have seen fit to detonate some sort of electromagnetic pulse weapon."

"Wouldn't that have killed a bunch of people?" Jared argued.

"Nope, if it is what I think it is, they detonate a couple of hundred miles in the sky and, most of the time, you wouldn't even know something had happened."

Jared mused this over in the darkness, thinking about all his things that ran on electricity. Everything ran on it nowadays; every single useful thing in Jared's life ran off some type of energy source and had at least a small circuit board of some sort.

Bob leaned into Jared. "Man, are you putting this together? Everything is gone. This area has about three days' supply of food—after that, chaos." Bob licked his lips as he continued, "Man, all the trucks and trains that bring this food in are dead. No more food means people are gonna start fighting and killing each other very soon for the little bit that's left."

Jared's head was swimming as he listened to the homeless man.

Bob went on. "No cops, no firefighters, no nothing. You wanna go home, you walk or ride a bike, no more cars, bro." Bob swept his hands around his living quarters. "Even I'm going to have to get the hell out of here before they scavenge everything up there and then come down here to see what I have."

Jared shook his head. "No way, man, no way, not everything, not like that."

Bob nodded towards the street. "You hear any sirens since you've been down here?"

Jared shook his head.

"Hell no you didn't, 'cause there aren't no cops anymore. They probably all walked home."

Once again, the two sat in silence, each man pondering their very questionable future.

Jared was the first to break the silence. "I gotta get home and figure out what's going on and what I'm going to do." He rose slowly to his feet. He really didn't want to walk up and out of this creek bed and face whatever evil lurked in the darkness above. Once on his feet, Jared realized he was exhausted beyond words. Every joint, ligament and bone in his body ached as if he'd been run over by a truck.

"Sit down, Jared," Bob said, his voice low and soft like a father about to impart some valuable knowledge to a son. "You can't go anywhere around this place in the dark. They may kill you."

Jared shifted his feet in the muck. "I have to get home."

Bob smiled in the blackness, showing yellowed teeth. "You can stay here. It'll suck, but you won't get your ass beat up and robbed, and I'll give you some advice that may save your life."

Jared remained standing as Bob patted the dirty pallet with a dirtier hand. "Sit down, my friend, and listen."

Jared slowly succumbed to Bob's patting of the pallet, slumping to the ground next to the filthy, homeless former Army infantryman.

"What advice is going to save my life, Bob?"

Bob reached under the pallet and produced a bottle of cheap vodka. Jared stared at the label and could not say he had ever even heard of the brand. The bottle was plastic, which Jared figured could not be a good thing. Bob unscrewed the top and tilted the bottle to his lips, allowing the clear fluid to pour down his throat. When he was finished, he placed the cap back on the bottle and tightened it before reverently returning the bottle to its hiding spot under the pallet. Jared thought Bob's drinking of the vodka appeared almost like a religious ceremony. He almost stood and marched straight up the embankment and out onto the street, but the images of the men beating the hapless man danced across his mind's eye, and that was enough to affix his ass to the pallet next to Bob the bum.

"Jared, you're gonna have to ride this first part out in a hiding spot, with food and water. You need weapons, or a weapon, and you need to know how to use it and be willing to use it."

Jared shook his head. "I'm not really a weapon guy. Jared paused. "Plus, I'm going to my place; I have some food there."

Bob's eyes flashed with more than a little anger. "You're not getting the severity of your situation, man. People will come to your place and kill you for your food. That's gonna happen in about a week."

Bob droned on into the night, telling Jared about the need to find a weapon and figure out how to use the weapon. He told Jared about all the different types of guns that could be found in abandoned homes, and the importance of ammunition for these guns. Bob talked, only stopping to reverently pull the vodka out, unscrew the top, take a long draw, and then return the bottle to its berth.

Bob talked about Iraq and the things he'd seen while he was deployed. He told Jared he had been engaged when he left and found out his fiancée was being a little less than faithful when he returned, which soured Bob on women for years to come. Jared listened as Bob preached about the importance of getting out of the Bay Area sooner than later. Bob ranted about finding a hiding place where Jared could hole up while the population murdered and starved itself to death. He warned of an unfriendly welcome in the rural areas, where people would be struggling to survive just like everyone else.

"Country folk won't have much use for you city types. They got no use for someone who ain't no use." Bob talked about traveling at night once Jared cleared the city areas, and the importance of staying off the roads and using binoculars to check an area before passing through it. Bob lectured about getting to an outdoors store, and what things were important to take and what things weren't. He harped long and hard about the weight of the survival equipment Jared would need.

"You're gonna be on a bike or walking, so you can't take everything with you. Take only what is essential, and take the lightest version of it." Bob belabored the weight issue till Jared stopped him and declared he totally understood.

"Good shoes too, my man, hurt your feet and you're dead in the water. If you can't walk, you can't get food or water and you die."

Every bit of advice Bob gave ended this way: if Jared failed to follow said advice, he would die. Don't hide, die; don't get good shoes, die; and so it went for hours into the night.

Bob was adamant that Jared not drink any creek or lake water until a few months into the event. His reasoning was that the world was going to be most violent in the first few months, and Jared could not afford to be deathly ill for five days while everyone was killing each other. Bob's advice was to survive the first three months and then gather a weeks' worth of food and water, find a safe place to be a mess, and drink away. Once Jared's body had built immunity to whatever adulterants live in the waters of California, he could ditch the water-purification pump, making his gear even lighter. Bob was insistent on a good water-purification system early on in Jared's future.

"Get something tomorrow," Bob said.

Bob talked about all sorts of tricks for finding water, animals and plants one could eat, but mostly he stressed the importance of a weapon. Jared needed a pistol and a rifle, Bob said. The pistol was in case he was forced to fight in a confined space or getting to the rifle wasn't an option. Bob talked about finding a short-barreled rifle Jared could conceal. Bob felt people would shoot first when dealing with an armed person, and just maybe they wouldn't shoot at an unarmed man. This, he said, included robbers and landowners alike.

"They see you're armed and they intend to rob you, they're going to set an ambush and just kill your ass. They think you're not armed, they're more likely to try to suck you in with some ruse." Bob's lessons always had an element of tactics and maneuvering to place Jared at an advantage in all his scenarios.

After what seemed like hours of listening to Bob's tireless monologue, Jared simply stopped listening, closed his eyes, and was asleep. He never knew when Bob stopped or how many lesson plans Bob delivered that he never heard, but when Jared opened his eyes, the sun was up.

Chapter 8

BOB WAS PASSED OUT COLD, a white boney foot protruding from under the heap of rags he called his bed. Jared just stared at the man's foot for a long while, thinking about the last two days' events. He finally pulled himself to his feet and gingerly stepped over the man, quietly making his way out of the encampment.

Jared was stiff, sore, and felt like he had a hangover even though he had not partaken in the vodka binge the night before, which in hindsight had never been offered to him. Before he turned and started up the muddy dirt trail, he took one quick glance back at the comatose bum wrapped in filth, lying under a bridge, the world just starting to come apart at the seams above him. Jared still wasn't convinced the military or cops wouldn't come rolling into town at any second, so the moment only lingered briefly before he turned, clambering up to the street.

Jared didn't know what time it was, but he knew it was early. He saw no one in the streets and felt a wave of relief wash over him. Had he seen the men from the night before, he would have gone running back to Bob. Once Jared was on the

ECR, things started feeling normal and he relaxed, feeling a bit of the stress leave his tense shoulder muscles. He had been pushed to his limit the night before, but he felt better now. The sun was coming up, and the stiffness in his limbs was dissipating a little with each step.

Jared stopped at a house and knocked on the door. When there was no answer, he drank from a garden hose in the front yard until his thirst was quenched, then filled his water bottles before resuming his journey home. Every now and again, he would see curious faces peering at him from behind curtains, but no one was out on the street at that time of the morning. Jared finally reached the central area of Redwood City and felt even better. This area was safe, and the ECR was lined with businesses, none of which were open.

Jared had been walking for about forty minutes when he saw an overturned and burned-out hulk of a police car. The squad car was in the middle of all the other abandoned traffic. Not a single car had been molested except the police car. The vehicle had been flipped onto its side and set afire. The vehicle smoldered as Jared approached, cautiously looking through the shattered windows, holding his breath, hoping he would not see the burned remains of an officer. There was no officer and there were no guns Jared noticed. The racks where a shotgun and AR-15 assault rifle were kept were badly damaged, the locking mechanisms broken and hanging open.

Jared moved on through the cool morning air, his senses keyed up like never before. The slightest noise had him jerking his head around, readying himself for flight. A dog crashed out of a side yard and bounded down the sidewalk a short distance before stopping and sniffing something in front of a business. The dog became enthralled with what it found, so Jared crossed the street in order to maintain a comfortable distance from the mangy animal.

As Jared drew abreast the animal, he realized, to his utter

horror, the dog was gnawing on a human body. Jared froze in place and just stared at the body of a middle-aged woman only partly clothed and most assuredly dead by the amount of gore visible. Jared's mind was racing; it was racing to the point of breakdown if he didn't get it under control. A dead woman and no one had come out and taken care of the body. Worse yet, no one had probably reported it, so there she laid, half naked and being eaten by a dog. Jared was about to cross the street and drive the dog away when it occurred to him that he might end up the same way if he made any noise, so he took one last glance at the ill-fated woman and moved north, plodding up ECR into San Carlos.

A mile into San Carlos, Jared heard a large crowd yelling and seemingly upset, but not in a dangerous way. He turned into the downtown area, walking carefully towards the noise of the crowd till he came to what was obviously the city hall.

About a hundred fifty people were standing outside the front of the building, yelling at three very tired-looking people. One could have been the mayor, Jared didn't know. He was older, maybe in his sixties, wearing slacks and a button-up shirt, which was missing the tie. The other two were cops, the first cops he had seen in almost three days. The older of the two cops was wearing slacks and some sort of police jacket with the word "Sheriff" on the back along with sheriff patches on the sleeves. The last cop was maybe forty years old and was in full uniform, armed and looking a little more than haggard.

The crowd was angry and demanding answers the poor beleaguered three didn't seem to have.

"Why aren't cops out there watching for looters and thieves?" a man from the crowd roared.

The mayor looking guy raised his hand and then gestured to the older of the two cops. "Mark, can you answer the man's question?"

The older of the two cops looked like he would rather have

been anywhere else but there at that particular moment, but he stepped forward and addressed the man. "There are no cops, people. They went home to their families. The last of 'em left this morning, and the fact that they stayed for nearly three days should say a little something about their dedication, so how about giving us a break and going home."

The man in the crowd was incensed. "Give you a break? Give you a break? Give us a break. When are we getting power and some basic services around here? You guys are the ones in charge of all that."

Mark shook his head. "There is no power; there are no services. Go home and start thinking about what it is you're going to do for your family to get through this."

The mayor raised his voice above the din of the crowd. "People, we have nothing for you. We are in the same situation you all are in. Mark here lives in the East Bay and hasn't seen nor heard from his family, so we're all in this together."

Jared hung at the rear of the crowd, listening and watching the cops as the mob complained, then threatened, and finally turned, melting into the neighborhood. Jared moved forward as the three city officials began to walk towards the building.

"Excuse me," Jared called out.

Mark turned angrily on Jared. It was evident that whatever Jared was about to say had better not be a dumb question or a complaint. Jared stopped a short distance from the three.

"Jesus, what now?" Mark snarled.

"What happened? I was at work and everything just stopped, so I'm walking home, and I saw a dead lady down the ECR about a mile. A dog was eating her." Jared hoped that last part would buy him at least an answer.

All three men drew in deep breaths, and then their shoulders slumped in unison.

Mark spoke first. "Everything is gone, as far as we know.

State, federal and local assets are down, and no one is talking out there, 'cause nothing electronic is working."

The mayor joined in, "Try to get to a safe place and wait till the government can sort this mess out."

The three men stood for a long moment just staring at each other.

"So that's all you have right now?"

Mark nodded. "Yep, that's all we have. Now I don't mean to be rude, but I have a long walk home." The three men turned again and headed towards the city hall.

"Ride a bike home, Officer," Jared called out from behind the men.

Mark waved a hand in thanks, without turning around.

The door closed and the men disappeared into the building. Jared was about to turn and start walking again when the door opened and Mark poked his head out. "Come here, man, got something for you."

Jared cocked his head and then slowly walked to the open door. Mark showed Jared into the building and down several flights of stairs to a basement area, where there were literally a hundred bicycles chained up inside a giant chain-link cage.

Mark nodded to the cage full of bikes. "Most of 'em are real pieces of shit, but I got a pretty good one for my ride home and, I figured, what the hell, I can take your name and address and lend you a bike. When this blows over, you either bring it back or I come get it; either way works."

Jared smiled and dug out his wallet, ready to produce his license.

Mark laughed out loud and clapped Jared on the shoulder. "I'm messing with you, man. Nothing's getting back to normal anytime soon, and I've been trying to dump this pile of junk for months."

Chapter 9

JARED PEDALED ALONG THE SIDEWALK, making good time, feeling the breeze rush through his hair. He passed more than a couple of shops that had been broken into, and even saw a few looters carrying items from the stores.

One such encounter found Jared face-to-face with a father and his family. There were four of them: the father, mother, and two children. The children were a boy and girl Jared figured to be about eight and ten years old. The family was just coming out of a small convenience store, their arms loaded with food, when Jared encountered them.

The father looked up, shame clouding his face. He lowered his head, beckoning his family as he scurried down the walkway, disappearing to the rear of the store. Jared rode on, thinking about the family and the look he'd seen on the father's face. *Was the man ashamed of the looting, or not being able to provide for his family without stealing?*

The looters along with everyone Jared passed seemed content to avoid each other at this point. If Jared saw a group of male looters, he would cross the street and pass them on the opposite sidewalk, keeping a safe distance between himself and any foolishness like he'd seen in Redwood City. Things that just a couple of days before hadn't held much value in the world were now worth killing for. Jared knew how the value of a bike had changed for him, so he was careful to keep his distance from anyone other than women, children and families.

The sun was high in the sky when Jared dismounted in front of his apartment complex. He wheeled the bicycle to the secure gate and punched in the code. Nothing happened; he re-entered the code, nothing.

"Damn," Jared swore out loud. The gate was controlled by some sort of electrical mechanism. He wheeled the bike around the building and found the gate across the parking area stood halfway open.

"Score," he exclaimed, rushing through the gap, pushing the bike to his lower-level apartment. The apartment smelled like rotten food. Jared opened the refrigerator and was nearly knocked off his feet by the stench that belched forth, enveloping him like a rancid fog.

He staggered away from the disgusting array of smells flowing from his refrigerator. After nearly vomiting, Jared gathered himself, fleeing to the back of the apartment, where he grabbed a towel, wet it, and wrapped the fabric around his face before heading back to the kitchen.

Halfway back, Jared stopped short. The water was working —the flipping water had run just like nothing was wrong. He made his way back to the small bathroom and turned the water on, seeing it flow out of the faucet. Jared slowly turned the hot water valve on and the cold water valve off. He waited and, there it came, hot water, not scalding hot, but hot enough.

Jared slowly walked back towards the rancid kitchen, thinking about the water and the hot water. Water got to his house under pressure, not power, if he remembered correctly. Natural gas was also pushed to neighborhoods under pressure, but Jared was pretty sure there was an electrical component to the natural gas side. This meant Jared might soon not have hot water and would be taking cold showers. He didn't much like the thought of that, deciding to toss the contents of the refrigerator and then take a long hot shower.

Gagging and swearing, he dragged everything from his refrigerator and tossed it out in a dumpster. He returned to the apartment and, using some towels and hot water, cleaned the inside of the appliance. Jared removed the towel from around his face, looked at it, then threw it out as well.

After the hazmat cleanup, Jared stripped and took a long hot shower; the water felt like it was actually peeling away all the stresses from the previous couple of days. The water poured down his back and he enjoyed its warmth, hoping it would last.

The shower proved to help clear his head as he thought back over the last three days, mulling over what he'd seen, heard and come across. He slept in his car, slept under a bridge with a bum, and hadn't had anything substantive to eat in seventy-two hours. He'd seen a dead woman and taken a bicycle from the police evidence locker at the behest of a cop. He either walked or rode all the way home from work, which was a first. Come to think of it, there had been several firsts during the last three days.

Jared finished showering, changed into sweats, and laid down on his bed, where his head swam with everything going on outside his apartment. *Looters, dead bodies, what the hell happened?* Jared drifted off into possibly the deepest sleep he'd ever had in his life.

Jared's eyes flashed open as he came out of his comatose slumber, sitting upright in the darkness, senses searching for any sign of danger. Slowly he brought his breathing under control his eyes darting around the dark room. He couldn't see a thing. The darkness was so absolute, Jared could almost feel its touch.

He got out of bed, feeling his way to the front room, where he drew back the curtains, and examined the surrounding area. There was just enough ambient light to allow Jared to see the courtyard and some of the street. He knelt in front of the window, waiting as his eyes adjusted to the lack of light. He stared up into the sky and thought how utterly lightless the world was without electricity. Once his eyes adjusted, Jared stood and strode out the front door into the courtyard.

Jared had no idea what time it was as he walked out to the street and surveyed the neighborhood. Out of the darkness came the sound of breaking glass and scuttling feet. Jared crouched, searching frantically for the source of the disturbance. He saw nothing as the night returned to its quiet normality. In the distance, gunshots erupted—that was all Jared had to hear. He turned and ran to his apartment, slamming and locking the door behind him. He glanced at the front door to ensure the deadbolt was locked. It was, which helped him relax about one-hundredth of a percent.

All around Jared, people huddled in their apartments, just as bewildered as he was. Down the road, looters moved in and out of businesses, taking items of perceived value. One man carried a sixty-inch television on his back, struggling down the road, weaving in and out of the deserted vehicles on his way home, laden with an object that at the moment and probably the foreseeable future was about as useful as nuts on a nun. Family men and women looted food and water for their families, while younger and single folk looted items they thought were of value. Little did they know few material items would be of any value in the coming months, years, and most likely decades.

Jared sat in the flickering light of a single small candle only the sound of his breathing disturbing the stillness of the little apartment. He stared at the coffee table, saw the photo album on the lower shelf and reached for it. His mother had made the album and given it to him a couple of Christmases ago. It was a pictorial memorialization of his entire life.

He thumbed the album open and stared at pictures of himself as a young boy, his father and mother always a constant in the collage of photographs chronicling his adolescence. In one picture, his father stood next to him, Jared proudly holding up a small trout while his father's face beamed with fatherly pride. There were a great many pictures of projects he'd created throughout his youth. There was the fabled bed maker, which would have worked if it had only been properly funded. Then there was the quad toothbrush, whose only flaw was every mouth was a different size, so mass production never got off the ground.

There were more pictures of him and his mother, her helping him get ready for the prom, which assuredly had caused her to cry herself to sleep since her perfect child was attending the event alone. Although he tried, he knew she was hurt and, even though he truly didn't care or have the time to find a date, his mother would do what moms do and, when her expectations weren't met, she would suffer emotionally. Jared felt bad about the whole experience, but there had truly been nothing he could have done. He doubted he could even have found a girl to go with him. Had his mother known he couldn't get a girl to attend the prom, it would have affected her much worse than his excuse about not having the time to find a date.

He continued leafing through the book until he came upon a picture of Monica and himself standing at his college campus. His parents had visited from Florida and wanted to see where he attended school. Monica had come bouncing across the campus when she spied Jared with his parents and charmed the ever-loving pants off not only his father, but his mother as well. Jared remembered watching it happen and knowing full well he was going to be asked about this vivacious young woman for weeks to come. His mother did not disappoint. Monica had hardly cleared earshot when his mother turned on him and began an interrogation any American water-boarding CIA officer would have been proud of.

After the initial line of direct questions, which went unanswered, his mother had predictably shifted gears and began her motherly cajoling in an effort to extract the coveted information regarding this brilliantly entertaining young woman. In the end, Jared assured her, Monica was just a school friend whom he worked on projects with from time to time. His father had finally come to his rescue by gently suggesting his mother leave the lad alone. With a sideways glance, as if she wasn't done with the matter, his mother had dropped the Monica interrogation.

Jared felt suddenly very alone, holding the album, gazing at the pictures of Monica and his parents. He hadn't talked to Monica in a long time and only talked to his mother once every few weeks. He was so busy he rarely took her calls and, when she would text him to say she loved and missed him, he usually only replied with a short one-sentence text. Now, feeling lonely, he also felt guilty for not having taken the time to call her back and ask about his father and their lives in Florida.

He'd never even been to their new house. Jared missed his parents at the moment like he'd never missed anything or anyone in his entire life. He even found himself missing Monica, wondering where she was and what she was doing. Jared's longing turned to anger as he realized how utterly this little power-outage thing had cut him off from the only people in the world who even remotely mattered to him.

The following morning Jared woke, cleaned his face, and combed his hair. This part of his day felt as normal as any other day. It wasn't till he walked into the front of the apartment, would have turned the TV on, and grabbed something from the refrigerator that the gravity of his situation struck him with the force of a speeding bulldozer. Jared stood grim faced, chest heaving, the emotions cascading through him like a wild river. His legs weakened and he slumped to the floor, eyes moistening in preparation for the cry of his life. Jared did not consider himself a tough guy and had not cultivated a hardened guise by growing a beard and adopting some swarthy style of walk like many other young men did these days. On the flip side, he'd never been a sensitive guy either; therefore, he found little reason to be upset enough to cry much. He was simply himself and that was fine with him.

Now it was different. Jared started with clinched eyes, fighting the sensation in his chest, throat and head, but then it took control and he sobbed. Jared wept like never before. He moaned, and cried out to his mother, tears flowed down his reddened cheeks.

After an hour, Jared rose, exhausted and disheveled. He walked back to the bathroom, where he, again, combed his hair, washed his face, and then returned to the front of his apartment. He ate cold cereal with water, after which he devoured an apple. He was too wrung out to be upset, lonely or even scared. He just sat, ate and stared at the wall. Overwrought as he was, Jared had just enough of his wits to know that the cold cereal and water sucked a lot of ass in the taste department. He'd have to go out and find some food that didn't make him want to vomit, and he'd have to do it sooner than later. He'd thrown most of the food in his possession into a dumpster the previous day.

Chapter 10

THE WEATHER WAS warm and clear, blues skies marred only by the still-wafting smoke from fires content with burning themselves out in the absence of pretty much any and all first responders.

Jared rode the evidence bike up to the front of a darkened supermarket and stopped. The store was darker inside than he would have expected, his current self still clinging to his past self and those expectations from just a couple of days ago. He leaned the bike against a concrete pillar and stepped a few feet inside the front doors.

The place smelled awful and the store was in shambles. The area just inside the business and around the checkout stands was almost impassable due to debris and overturned food racks. Jared scrutinized the dark interior, allowing his eyes to adjust, all the while trying not to gag as the smell of decaying food bombarded his senses. He slowly pulled his shirt up over his nose and ventured deeper inside the structure. He carried two shopping sacks, intending to fill them with food, water and whatever else he thought he might need in the coming days. Next he planned on leaving a note with his credit card information at the manager's office in order to keep his conscience clear.

Jared began filling the sacks with nonperishable food items. He grabbed cold cereal boxes, dried fruit, and mixed nuts. When he came to the dairy department, he nearly vomited. Someone had opened the glass doors, realized the milk had spoiled, and then tore all the cartons of milk out of the refrigerator, leaving them broken and leaking on the store floor. Jared quickly moved past this area in search of other foods he could take without fear of spoiling. The store had been picked through already, but there was a fair amount of usable food left in the aisles, not all of it on the shelves, but Jared didn't really care at this point. While still in the rear of the store, Jared was about finished when he froze, adrenalin pouring into his bloodstream to the point of chest pain.

A man about twenty-five stood in the dark doorway leading to the storage area in the back of the store. He was about six feet tall and naturally thick, but looked a little unhealthy. Jared thought he had the look of a drug addict, the man's eyes and sallow face being the primary indicators.

"You're in my fucking store, fuck-face," the man hissed out of the darkness.

Jared stood frozen; he could not move. He thought about moving, running mostly, but he was actually frozen with fear. Part of his brain was thinking rationally and was amazed by his inability to move, while the other side of his brain had merely shut down, stopped working, unable to command muscles to engage, to flee, escape this threat.

Jared heard the scuff of feet behind him and finally was able to engage his neck muscles, turning in time to see two equally insalubrious men moving up an aisle to his rear.

Jared dropped the sacks. "I'll leave; I didn't know you guys were here."

The first man smiled, showing his yellowish teeth. "Don't

work like that, man. You gotta pay us if you come in here."

Jared held out his hands. "I'm here 'cause I don't have anything. What do you want me to pay with?"

The three men moved closer. Jared stood still, letting it happen. He knew deep down in some hidden and long-suppressed primal part of his brain that he should be doing something, anything to preserve his well-being, but he didn't. He stood fast until one of the men stepped forward, striking him in the head from behind. Jared sprawled forward, landing hard on the cold floor. The first man caught him in the shoulder with a vicious kick that glanced off his shoulder and the side of his head, nearly taking his ear off.

Jared instinctively curled into a ball and covered his face and head the best he could as the punches and kicks rained down from above. The beating lasted roughly thirty-seconds before the men transitioned from beating to searching Jared's pockets, grocery sacks and waistband. One man took his wallet and rifled through its contents, tossing them over his shoulder and tearing the wallet in half before throwing it violently at Jared.

"Get the fuck out. Next time I see you, I'll kill you," the first man roared, his chest heaving from the exertion of the beating he'd just administered.

Jared scrambled to his feet, staggering out the front doors, and burst out of the store into the bright sunny day, the light hurting his eyes. He grabbed the bike but stopped short when he heard the man behind him.

"Leave the bike, shit stain."

Jared dropped the bike and ran—he ran for his life, running the entire mile home. He stumbled through the half-open gate, making his way to his apartment. Once inside, he drew the curtains and fell onto his couch, panting and bleeding. As he sat, he thought about what had happened and how surreal the event seemed.

The initial blow from behind hadn't even really hurt. His knee hurt more from the fall than any other wound he received during his failed shopping spree. The worst part had been being scared. The beating hadn't been that bad although he could feel the soreness starting to creep into his body, and knew he was going to hurt like hell in the days to come.

After a bit, Jared hauled himself off the couch, making his way into the bathroom where he swallowed several ibuprofen, chasing them with water he palmed from the sink's faucet. Jared thought of all the hurdles ahead of him as he washed the clotted blood from his eyebrows, hair and face.

After cleaning his face, he bent over the bathroom sink allowing the water to cascade through his blood-soaked hair, chilling him to the bone. He waited for the water to warm up and, when it didn't, he realized the hot water was gone and wasn't coming back. Slowly, he pulled his head from under the faucet, wrung as much of the cold water out of his locks as he could, then turned the faucet handle to the off position. *No fucking hot water isn't gonna kill me, but it's going to sure make showers miserable,* he thought.

Back out on the couch, Jared started thinking about his predicament and how to problem solve the issues associated with the mess. No power—he didn't really have an answer for that, so he simply removed it from the list of problems he would attack. No food was going to be a big issue, especially with lunatics like the guys he'd met earlier in the day claiming stake to the stores. Jared came up with two approaches to the issue. Avoid them or deal with them, with avoid winning out after only a couple seconds of thought.

After several long minutes of thought, Jared stood, chose the largest wall in his tiny apartment, and tore every picture off it, tossing them into a corner. Next he took a black marker and began charting out what had happened and what he was going to do. He wrote the date and approximate time of the first event and everything he'd seen. He made a list of all the services missing, then added sublists of the effects the lack of these services had caused so far.

Police, missing; he'd actually seen what he thought was the last of the San Carlos cops packing up and going home. This was going to cause all sorts of problems, one of which he had experienced firsthand. His list memorialized the number of days since the event and how society was deteriorating as the days passed. In the end, Jared knew he had to leave his home and move east into the country, where he would try to find work on a farm just so he could eat. He figured the sooner he got out east, the less competition he would have for work. Although he had been an engineer geek, he had enjoyed and subsequently paid attention to some of his history classes. He learned about the Great Depression and how valuable work was; it allowed a person to make a living. Without work, families would go hungry, lose their homes, and much worse.

Jared authored a gear list, which included several things he would need to survive while traveling across California. He needed a water-purification pump, and light nonperishable foods he could carry. He would need a small tent, toothbrush, clothes, a bike…the list went on and on. Next Jared mapped out a strategy for obtaining the items on his list, possible locations, routes to and from, along with tactics he felt would afford him the best chance at getting what he needed without enduring another physical round of violence.

When he was done, the wall and half of another wall were covered in black marker. The tiny room looked like a cross between Jared's work conference room at the start of a new project and the walls of a madman's home. When he finished, Jared sat back, sore, swollen, and just gazed at his handiwork. It was the first feeling of accomplishment he had in what seemed like an eternity.

Chapter 11

JARED WAS A VERY practical man in his own environment, which was the electronic world. In the current world, not so much; he felt vulnerable, unsure what to do about his current situation, and more than a little scared. He glanced at the walls covered in all the information he would have usually have needed to make quick and decisive decisions in order to move forward. He sat trying to formulate a plan, thinking of ways, he could overcome what was happening.

Jared rose to his feet after a long, thoughtful, but ineffective thinking session and inventoried his food stores. He did this mindlessly and for no other reason than he hadn't really come up with any hard and effective ideas about how to get through this thing that was happening. This was easier to think about and not that hard to come to the conclusion that he had about a week's worth of food in his apartment if he stretched it, missed a couple of meals, and was careful not to overeat.

The water was still flowing, so he wasn't overly concerned about hydration, but he had started to hear more gunfire, and the occasional scream had evolved into a more common occurrence. He heard a human cry for help about every hour now, and it chilled him to the bone as he sat huddled in his apartment, waiting, planning, but in the end really only wasting time and precious resources. He knew he had to get out of the populated area, and he was fast realizing he had to do it sooner than later, before society completely caved in on itself.

The following morning, day four since the event, Jared opened his front door, surveying the courtyard. He watched as a Mexican family who lived three doors down loaded their belongings onto a red Radio Flyer wagon, using twine to tie the load down like a miniature covered wagon from some old western flick. Jared cocked his head and watched, wondering where they planned on going with two toddlers and using what amounted to be a child's play thing to haul their life belongings. It seemed absurd to him they would take the children out into the streets, until Jared noticed the father, with a large black pistol gripped firmly in his right hand. He looked determined to protect his family at all costs, willing to sacrifice anything for them, including his own life. *Holy fucking shit, the guy has a gun right the fuck out in the open.* Jared just stood there, mouth agape, watching the little family preparing the wagon.

People were getting desperate and it was only four days into basically what amounted to a power outage. How had society slipped so quickly into this abyss? Jared eyed the father, who was eyeing him back, pistol held low as he began pulling the wagon, quietly prodding his small family to follow closely. Jared caught the wife's eye briefly; she looked scared, but not in the way Jared was scared. The mother looked scared and uncertain, as any mother would be with two small children; she was scared for her offspring, for their future, and for their safety.

"Where you guys headed?" Jared called out.

The father turned, walking backwards, pulling the wagon. "Mexico," he replied, so matter of fact, Jared just stood there for a moment processing what the man just said.

"Mexico, with the kids, walking?"

"Yeah, walking," the father said flatly.

"That's like five hundred miles," Jared said, his mouth hanging slightly open.

"Closer to six hundred where we're headed," the father returned as he swiveled back in the direction he was walking.

Jared watched as the doomed family slowly walked out of the courtyard, turned south, and disappeared from his view.

He knew it was time to go. If families were willing to drag wives and children across six hundred miles of land on foot, pulling a wagon with what they hoped would be enough to survive the arduous journey then he needed to get the hell out of this town and go someplace he could scratch out an existence. Jared stepped back inside his dim apartment and took a deep breath.

This was going to be extremely difficult and even more dangerous, but he was going to walk or ride a bike or pull a wagon to Florida where his parents lived. His plan was simple: Make contact with as few humans as possible. Find a sporting goods store, round out his gear list with a tent, water-purification system, and several other essentials Bob had insisted he would need in to not die.

Jared wore jeans, a cotton pullover shirt, and a pair of sneakers. The shoes were great for walking around town, going to and from work if he drove, but he found that the walk home from work had caused him quite a lot of foot pain and even a couple of blisters. He'd have to replace the shoes, along with the small North Face pack he had stuffed with food, water and extra clothes. The pack was small, like the pack a college student would use, had a ton of pockets, and was the only pack he had. Jared packed the evening prior under the light of a small candle he found under the bathroom sink. He planned on bringing everything he felt would assist him in his endeavor to procure lifesaving materials.

Jared left the small apartment, using side streets and staying off the main roadways for fear of contacting any more unsavory folks like the ones he encountered in the supermarket. He figured people he came across in the neighborhoods would more likely be holed up in their homes with their families. He wasn't carrying much and didn't think he would look like a target worth pursuing; still, he worried about being accosted again. Jared walked in the shadows as much as he could and, whenever he was forced to cross a large intersection, would wait and watch, trying to determine if anyone was out there watching the intersection, waiting to pounce on some unsuspecting traveler.

During these stress-filled exercises, Jared saw other people slinking along the sidewalks, heads turning this way and that, always looking for signs of danger. *In just four and a half days—or was it five days, the days were starting to blend together at this point—the world had gone from a fairly safe and functioning place to a place where people walked around like deer, always on alert for danger.*

Jared continued to avoid all human contact as he picked his way across town to the REI he knew held some of the answers to his needs. It took him three hours to travel what normally would have taken five minutes in a car and maybe half an hour on foot under normal conditions. He was committed to not being a victim again even if it meant skulking around in the shadows like a rat. His face was still swollen and sore to the touch, from the beating he had endured at the Safeway a few days before.

Once he was within sight of the store, Jared scanned the surrounding area, looking for a suitable spot to wait and watch without being seen. He decided to approach this problem like he would have at work; he'd solve it through thought and planning. This would become the norm; it would have to be the norm if he planned on surviving. Most new projects were driven by the latest technology, and Jared knew all too well that if the proper research was not done, his project could have a faulty component that would likely render the entire project useless. He would test, research, and then retest before ever committing to any new unproven piece of technology.

Jared used the same approach before he committed to entering this store; he would know everything there was to know about the building and anyone associated with the store. He failed to do this research at the supermarket and nearly paid with his life. He wouldn't make that mistake twice. Jared rationalized that most people would not think of REI as a place they needed to loot. The store wasn't a place normal folks shopped for food, and REI wasn't known for its sixty-inch televisions. He silently wished he came here days ago before people were as desperate as they'd become.

Jared settled on a low row of hedges across the street from the front of REI, where he had a fairly unobstructed view of the front and left side of the large structure. There were no doors on the left side, while the face of the building had a large roll-up door for deliveries as well as double glass front doors. Both entrances were closed, the interior was dark, and Jared could not see more than a few feet inside the darkened business.

He was using a small pair of cheap binoculars he'd bought years earlier for baseball games and found they still performed poorly, making him regret not spending the money for a decent set. Jared tried the finest of adjustments on the focus ring in a futile attempt to see deeper into the darkened store. The more he looked at the front doors, the more he thought the glass might be missing; he just couldn't be one hundred percent sure. One thing was for sure: when he went into that store, he was taking a pair of binoculars, and they would be the most expensive ones he could find since he had little to no working knowledge of what qualified as good binoculars.

Jared laid in the hedgerow for an hour before making his way to the rear of the building, which took nearly an hour and a half. He had to keep telling himself not to cut corners, to slow down, not to just bolt across open areas, and to take his time because deliberate action would be his savior. If he was more patient then the other guy, he would avoid conflict or injury. Jared formulated a plan to climb the fence accessing the freeway, move along the east side of the building, using the drainage ditch for cover. Once he reached the northeast corner of the building he would wait and watch some more before making his approach, which would be well after dark.

Jared wondered how many minutes of patience would translate into a non-beatdown shopping spree. As the sun began to dip into the west, Jared decided to move closer. He got to his feet, and scurried across the street before he broke into a sprint toward the northeast corner of the structure. When he reached the building, he dropped to his belly and laid in the weeds, his gaze fixed on the building. Nothing had changed, yet he laid there panting, not moving another inch for fear each time he moved he risked being exposed.

His heart rate finally slowed and his fear subsided. The temptation to get up and just walk into the store to get the things he needed was now front and center in his thoughts. What was he going to do, just lie there forever, frozen in fear?

He ran his hand across his still swollen and sore face and quickly decided against that ill-advised tactic. He wasn't ten feet from Highway 101, which would have been a deafening place not days before, but now it was so absolutely quiet, spooky even.

Jared shifted his body on the hard ground and looked around his position, suddenly feeling very alone. He had been in the new hide site for about five minutes when he heard footsteps on the highway behind him. He froze before slowly turning his head, scanning for the approaching noise maker. Jared saw the culprits, a young couple in their early twenties and probably wearing the same clothes they had been clothed in the day of the event.

The woman was wearing sandals, jeans and a lightweight blouse, while the man was clothed in jeans and a T-shirt. They carried nothing and looked exhausted. Jared could tell the woman's feet were deteriorating by the way she limped along-side her hipster man. The woman's limp was further confirma-tion of his need for good shoes once he started his shopping spree. Jared made a mental note moving the procurement of shoes to the top of his list. He surveyed the couple, barely moving his head as they passed behind him, picking their way through the litany of cars marooned on the highway.

The two didn't even have a water bottle, as far as Jared could see. He wondered where they had come from and where they were going and how long before some family pet was feasting on their dead bodies. Jared quickly pushed the thought out of his head. That was too close to home, thinking things like that, being they were all in the same mess, and he wasn't much better off than the two miserable-looking souls passing him on the vehicle-littered highway. The couple passed without so much as a word spoken between them and never once glanced off the road in his direction, which Jared was thankful for.

As the day wore on, more and more people passed Jared on the highway. Some folks were by themselves, while others were in groups. Some appeared to be families, while it was apparent that others were most likely neighbors or co-workers.

One group that passed on the highway was the nefarious type. These people were not intent on where they were going, but instead went about looking into every stopped car. Occa-sionally they smashed a window and took an item they felt was of value to them. There were three of them, and Jared hardly breathed as they worked their way past his position. His heart beat so hard in his chest, he could almost hear it and half believed that if he glanced down, he would have seen puffs of dust emanating from under his pounding chest. He could definitely feel it and almost moved his hand to his chest in an attempt to quell the rapid beating, but thought better of moving a muscle.

Eventually, the recalcitrant men moved on, taking their thieving endeavors south into Redwood City's jurisdiction, not that there were jurisdictions any longer. Jared wondered if that word could just be erased from Webster's dictionary, along with a whole lot of other words like law and order, police, firemen, and a list a mile long he didn't even want to imagine.

Chapter 12

LATER IN THE AFTERNOON, the sun hung low on the horizon, elongating the shadows, seemingly stealing the heat from the air, eliciting a shiver from Jared's overwrought frame. He saw hundreds of people pass on the highway that afternoon, the number growing as the day went on. The sun sank lower on the horizon and, as night approached, the number of travelers slowed to a trickle.

Nighttime travel is dangerous, but why is it dangerous? Jared wondered. If folks were traveling during daylight hours, wouldn't it make sense for criminals to go out hunting during those times as well? Then everyone could sleep the night away and do it all over the following day, like that cartoon with the wolf and sheepdog. Jared pondered this, making a mental note to think more about the possibility of traveling at night in order to avoid roving gangs like the ones he'd been beaten by and the ones he'd seen breaking into all the stranded vehicles on the highway.

It suddenly dawned on him that the reason night had been dangerous in the past was due to criminals using the darkness to their advantage against detection from the cops. Now that the cops were gone, the darkness would only make acquiring victims more difficult due to reduced visibility and availability. Most people were still living life like they had before, staying off the streets at night and moving about in daylight. Apparently, the criminal element had already begun to adapt, coming out and hunting their prey in broad daylight. When it came to traveling, day was the new night.

There was just so much to think about; it was worse than any project he'd ever been a part of, mostly because failure to make the right move would likely result in injury or even death. Poor decisions related to a work project would, in a worst-case scenario, result in termination. That meant a three-month vacation, a severance package, and then a new job at a competitor's business. It happened every single week, and the people in his industry were not afraid of quitting or even being fired, knowing they'd have a new job before their replacement unpacked. Jared knew people who had been fired, then given three years' salary and sent on their way. These people usually left with some of the biggest smiles ever recorded.

Darkness finally blanketed the Bay Area, but still Jared laid in the grass, watching and listening. It seemed sound traveled even better at night after the event, or maybe the lack of night vision caused his ears to work more efficiently. Not one person had so much as entered the REI store's parking lot, much less entered the store itself during his observation exercise. This gave Jared a small dose of relief as he thought about being inside the store with no one watching his back. He had begun to make a new list of personal preferences in his life, like having an entire store to himself when he shopped.

Jared laid for a while longer, thinking about how lost and completely reliant on city, county, state and federal government assistance people had become. Yes, people had ravaged many of the stores where food could be found in abundance, yet here was a store that had nearly every essential item one could ever hope for in the current world situation, and not a soul had stopped or even peeked in the front windows.

Jared rose to his feet and scaled the fence, making his way along the northern wall towards the front doors. As he reached the doors, he realized they had not been broken out and that the glass doors stood completely ajar as if some employee knew people would need what was inside the store, leaving them open as a gesture of kindness to his or her fellow man or woman. Jared thought about the employee and wondered if the person had known the world was becoming a very hard place to survive in.

Had the person felt compelled to make it just a little easier on some poor soul? He wished he could shake the employee's hand, knowing that had the doors been locked, he would have had to smash the glass. This act alone would have made dangerous and unnecessary noise, most likely sending out an invite to unwanted guests.

Jared had to avoid all human contact until he figured out how to defend himself properly. Jared had never been one to wallow in denial, but in light of current events, he was fast becoming a true blood realist. He was swiftly beginning to understand he sorely lacked any skills needed in dealing directly with hostiles. He'd never been a fighter, never fired a gun, and pretty much avoided any and all conflict both growing up and as an adult. Self-defense was certainly the elephant in the room, and he knew it had to be addressed sooner or later. In fact, he hadn't even addressed it on the apartment wall back home, not because he was in denial, but because he hadn't the slightest idea how to address it.

Bob had talked about it along with everything else, but telling someone to purify water and telling them to learn to fight and operate a firearm were two very different things. It wasn't like he could run down to the local strip mall karate shop and get in a quick couple of lessons or go to a range and pay some retiree to teach him to shoot. All that was gone; he had to learn on the fly.

Once he reached the open doors, Jared laid on the ground next to the wall, only his head poking around the doorjamb to gaze into the inky blackness of the store's interior.

Not a sound emanated from inside the store as Jared laid motionless, feeling the still-warm concrete under his body. He stayed there for just a moment, feeling weirdly relaxed and at ease as the warmth penetrated his body.

Jared caught himself, shook his head, rose, and strode straight into the store. He went directly to the front counters and leaned down, closely inspecting all the gadgets placed near the checkout area. Finally, he found what he was looking for, a Cyalume light stick. He pulled the light stick from its wrapper and fished an old sock out of his pants pocket. The light stick was the perfect tool for what he was about to do, better than a candle by a country mile.

The light stick would last for twelve hours, radiated no heat, was not toxic, and could be slid quickly into the sock if he needed to extinguish its light. A candle was hot, messy and a fire hazard. Candles had their place, and Jared fully intended to take some tonight, but just not for this retrieval operation.

Jared walked slowly around the store, wishing REI had traditional aisles so he could just go up one and down the next, covering all the aisles, getting everything he needed and leaving. Instead the store was set up with some items being displayed in traditional aisles while other items were grouped together with what Jared thought resembled little more than jumbled disorder.

He made his way to the backpack area and chose a sturdy pack designed for weeklong backpacking trips. He sat down facing the front of the store and went through every feature the pack had. Once he had familiarized himself with all the pack's pockets, zippers, compartments and straps, he slung it onto his back and set off to find a sleeping bag.

Jared quickly chose the most expensive sleeping bag he'd ever seen. It was light and rated for temperatures rarely seen in California. He took the sleeping bag and dragged it around the store, filling it with the rest of the items he had come up with as vital survival gear. There were tiny stoves for cooking along with the fuel canisters that fed them. There was a very expensive—well, inexpensive—water-purification system and pills for purifying water. Since he wasn't paying, everything was classified as inexpensive as far as Jared was concerned.

Jared hadn't had the pills on his list and hadn't even known of their existence before seeing them next to the water-purification system. He grabbed light sticks, and he hoarded maps. He shopped for a tent and chose a two-man tent rated for three seasons. Jared went through the store, slowly filling the sleeping bag until he had everything on his list plus a couple of items he hadn't even thought of, like the water-purification pills and a small hatchet.

He took the water-purification pills because they were tiny, light and seemed like a good backup to the mechanical purification system he stuffed in the sleeping bag. He scavenged a flint for lighting fires for the same reasons, lightweight and a good backup to the stove. Jared knew the stove would only be useful as long as he had fuel for it. Failure to locate more fuel would mean tossing the stove and moving on to a more time-honored method for heating food or water. He continued his shopping spree, dropping a set of titanium cookware along with water bottles and utensils into the sleeping bag.

Next Jared moved to the men's clothing racks and quickly grabbed pants, shirts, and a jacket. He chose a light jacket and planned on layering his clothing in order to stay away from a larger style jacket that would be too hot most of the year. Jared slipped into the new clothes and headed to the shoe area.

He had no idea how many miles a pair of shoes would last, so he planned on taking two pairs of the same shoe. He tried on shoes, one brand after another, walking around in the darkness and wiggling his toes like any other time he'd bought shoes. He finally settled on a pair of rugged trail-running shoes made by Solomon. He liked how light yet supportive they were, and stalked around the shoe sales area, climbing up on one of the false rocks the store had for customers to test shoes on.

Jared didn't possess much knowledge about backpacking equipment so he often times chose the most expensive item hoping it would be the best. Shoes, on the other hand, were a little different. He felt they should be based on a combination of price along with fit and comfort. If they were expensive and hurt his feet, he'd have big problems. Jared crammed the extra pair of shoes into the sleeping bag, then dragged it towards the front of the store.

When he neared the front of the store, Jared slid the light stick into the sock, stuffing it into a pants pocket. He was about to exit the store when he looked at all the bikes lined perfectly up in four rows.

Why hadn't he thought of that? He had a bike already and used it to make the last part of his journey home, and there was the issue of---the thugs at the market who had brazenly taken it from him. He walked over to the bike rack and spied a bike trailer. *Who knew they had those, and how awesome for me.* He could haul four or five times the gear with a trailer and wouldn't have to have an uncomfortable pack on his back as he rode.

Jared carefully looked over several different trailers and chose one he felt suited his needs. Next he went through the rows of bikes until he found one he felt fit his size and weight. He attached the trailer to the bike and then loaded the bulging sleeping bag and pack into the trailer.

Jared pushed the bike towards the front doors, straining his eyes and ears for any sign of danger. Hearing nothing to cause him concern, he shuffled forward, out the doors, and south along the highway fence. He wished he could get the bike onto the highway and move away from the store, but the fence would have been too difficult to get over with all his newfound equipment.

Once away from the front doors, Jared climbed on the bike and began pedaling through the connected business parks located along the highway. He rode until he found a secluded area to the rear of a business that backed up to the highway. He dismounted, pulling his bike and trailer under a large mass of bushes.

Jared found he could nearly stand once inside the bushes without being visible from either the highway or the business's parking lot. He removed all the gear he took from the REI store, dumping it on the ground in the darkness under the bushes. He fumbled blindly in the darkness, looking for the tarps he'd taken.

Finding them, he strung them up inside the bush in order to block any light from escaping the bush and alerting anyone to his presence. Once he secured the tarps, he fished the sock out of his pocket and removed the light stick. He hung it from a branch and then began the tedious job of unpacking all the gear.

He first removed everything from the store packaging, separated the trash from the gear, and then organized it into piles. Food, cookware, utensils and stove in one pile, while other things, like the water-purification pills and system, were in another pile.

After Jared finished this, he began packing the backpack with items he felt were the absolute essentials for survival. His plan was to have the pack as an emergency and backup system to the trailer. If he ran into trouble and was forced to abandon the bike and trailer, he planned on having the pack furnished and ready to be grabbed, donned and carried to a safe place with enough provisions to sustain him for a week or more. Jared sat on the hard ground, packing, unpacking and repacking gear, trying to get the load out just right.

He thought about how fragile and one-dimensional his plan of survival was and how it relied on some very thin contingencies. Sure, he had water bottles and he had water-purification capabilities, but he could only carry enough water for a couple of days at most, but what good were water-purification capabilities without water. He had to find water sources along his route or he was dead in the water, so to speak.

Food would also be a gigantic issue in the future, and Jared knew this could be just as deadly, although much slower to affect him than the water issue. He knew he had enough food to last about a month, but after that he would have to find a food source. This concerned him greatly since he had no idea of what was ahead in the way of stores. Would they be ravaged, picked clean, would there be people along the way willing to trade or help out?

He didn't know and couldn't know until he was on the road and actually beyond any point of return. It was a little like being handed a parachute by a complete stranger and asked to leave the aircraft. He would find out how well the parachute worked and, if it didn't, he was dead.

Jared had never hunted and never had an interest in it until now. The problem was he didn't have a gun and hadn't the slightest idea where to even look for an animal to hunt. Even if he were able to bring an animal down, he'd never butchered anything other than a fish when he was younger, when his father had taken him fishing up in the Sierras. He hadn't liked it as a kid and doubted the feeling would change now, but his new mantra was slowly becoming "you don't have to like it, you just have to do it."

After rearranging the gear in the pack and bike trailer

nearly a hundred times, Jared spread out the sleeping bag and climbed in, exhausted from the day's activities. Wrapped in the sleeping bag, hidden inside the bushes with the tarps draped about him, Jared felt pretty safe, like a moth in a cocoon, insulated from the uncertain world outside his foliaged sanctuary.

Chapter 13

VOICES CUT through the crisp morning air, startling Jared out of a deep slumber. He didn't move, lying completely motionless in his sleeping bag. He tried reaching back into his sleep memory in a futile effort to determine the direction the invasive voices came from. He didn't have long to wait, as the voices again drifted across the cool morning air from the direction of the highway. Jared slowly moved his arms up and out of the bag, after which he slid his entire body out and onto the har, cold ground. He slithered on his belly to the edge of the bush fort he constructed the night prior, searching for those responsible for disturbing his morning slumber.

Jared spotted them, a man and woman, the man wearing a small backpack while the woman pushed a stroller. Jared squinted in the early morning's brightness, just able to make out two tiny feet protruding from the front of the stroller. The presence of a baby relaxed him a little as he laid back on top of the sleeping bag. He wiped his hand across his face, staring up at the morning sun, whose rays were stabbing through the branches of the bush and warming his exposed skin.

He waited until the couple passed before rolling over and

setting up his tiny stove. He placed a titanium pan on the stove, lit the heating system, and filled the pan with water. As the water came to a rolling boil, Jared reached over, cutting the fuel flow to the stove. He ripped open a dehydrated bag of eggs and bacon before pouring some of the hot water in and resealing the bag. He set the bag aside and prepared a small cup of instant coffee, which smelled absolutely glorious. *Today is going to be a better day than the last four days combined, and all because of this one little cup of java,* he thought.

After eating in absolute silence, Jared sat back and slowly sipped the black coffee until it was gone and his insides glowed with the hot fluid's heat. After allowing his breakfast to settle, Jared stowed all his gear in the pack and bike trailer. He rolled the tarps up and sat back, thinking about his next move.

He still needed some items if he wanted to start his journey. He needed a pair of bolt cutters to circumvent the many barriers modern man had seen fit to erect at every turn. To simply enter the highway with all his gear, he needed to either ride to an on-ramp or cut a hole in the fence. Jared didn't like the thought of being trapped on the highway with no alternative except to flee or stand and fight.

He felt fairly certain he would not be doing any fighting, which left fleeing. Jared realized it would come down to a simple race like ones he saw on National Geographic. If he were faster than those pursuing him, then he would live to see another day; if not, well, he didn't want to think about the "if not."

He did like the fact that he had seen a lot of people on the highway, and most seemed harmless and quite frankly too distracted with their own troubles to pose any real threat to him. They seemed like normal people just trying to get wherever they were going. Other than the car burglars the night before, he hadn't seen anyone committing any questionable acts of moral turpitude.

For the rest of day five, Jared rode the bike through the industrial area of San Carlos, looking for a pair of bolt cutters and a small tool set he could use to work on the bike with. He kicked himself for not looking for a bike tool kit at the REI, which undoubtedly would have been lightweight and had only the tools necessary for bicycle-repair-type operations. He kicked himself a second time for not grabbing a few extra tubes and tires as well.

As he rode, Jared passed people who seemed to be doing the same thing he was. Everyone was scavenging anything they felt bettered their odds of survival in this pitiless new world. No one bothered him, much to his relief, and he didn't attempt to talk to anyone, but instead avoided people as much as possible. When he observed someone ahead, he would cross the street or even turn down a side street, completely avoiding contact. People got the message, and nobody so much as called out to him.

By the end of the fifth day, Jared had all the things he felt he needed to start his trek across the country where he hoped to find his parents. He rode the bike back out to the highway and started pedaling south. He planned on getting to the San Jose area before nightfall, find a place to hole up, and start mapping out his route. It was September and Jared knew he might not make it through the mountains to the east before he was smashed with serious weather. Crossing the Sierras in October or November was something he would rather avoid. Any delays would put him closer to snow storms than he cared to be. He had formulated a loose plan in his head over the past couple of days that would take him south to warmer and flatter lands.

Jared wanted to stay a fair distance away from the Mexico border, feeling that the natural lawlessness of that country with the Cartels would exacerbate the current state of Southern California. He picked his way through the maze of vehicles, passing more and more people on the highway. Today was different from yesterday; the people looked just a little more desperate. The looks he got came from a bit wilder eyes than the day before. People surveyed his bike, trailer and gear with more calculating looks than they had the day prior. It was as if they were taking inventory of his possessions and evaluating the risk-benefit factor in attempting to seize his belongings. Jared felt less and less comfortable the closer he got to San Jose.

Jared heard gunshots in the distance on more than a few occasions, and as he pedaled across overpasses, he gazed down into the neighborhoods and could see looting, burning and utter chaos. People were beginning to panic, becoming desperate in their fight for the last of the supplies in their neighborhoods. Jared was sure that more than a few of these people would have come after him had they possessed the ability to move fast enough to catch him as he pedaled through the deteriorating wreckages of recently civilized neighborhoods.

After actually witnessing a man run out of a store, a second man in pursuit, guns in both men's hands, along with the subsequent gunfight that followed, Jared pulled over and tore open his map. He hadn't waited to see who won the gunfight. Instead he stood up and pumped the pedals till his legs burned like California wildfires. Jared pedaled hard until he reached a large line of bushes, pulled over, and secreted his gear.

Out of breath and completely terrified, Jared studied the map, knowing he had to bypass the city somehow. Passing directly through the city was likely to result in either his death or the loss of everything he gathered. The fights he witnessed so far had been over small amounts of food, small enough for one person to carry.

As he perused the map, seeking an alternate route, he considered the fact that he was dangerously one-dimensional, and this scared him. He was not confident in his ability to stand and fight, knowing full well his fight record was 0-1 after the market beatdown. He also was acutely aware he had no ability to keep anyone at bay due to his lack of firearms. This left running and hiding as his only defense, and it left him feeling impotent.

Jared studied the map a full fifteen minutes before deciding on a route that would take him down below the southern end of San Francisco Bay. Jared would use surface streets as much as possible, working his way over to Route 130. The map indicated Route 130 would take him through what appeared to be a very remote area heading east towards Highway 5. Once he reached the 5, he would continue using country back roads, making his way southeast, skirting the foothills of the Sierras. He would continue southeast until he reached the Indian Wells area, where he wouldn't be accosted by severe cold weather.

It seemed like an easy plan, with water being the only real issue Jared was constantly thinking about. He came up with a few water sources like pools, creeks, ponds, and animal water troughs. He hoped he would be educated along the way, resulting in his finding other water sources, but wasn't counting on it.

In the end, he realized he had to pick his way through San Jose; there was no other way through. Jared was a little more than nervous about it, but knew he would just have to be extra vigilant or pay the price.

Jared struck out again, pedaling along the surface streets, his map propped up on the handlebars. He kept close tabs on the streets he was on as well as the ones he was passing. Jared was deep into the city of San Jose and had heard a lot of gunfire along with other sounds to cause him trepidation. Luckily so far none of the sounds of violence had caused him anything but slight detours and high levels of anxiety along with what felt like gallons of adrenaline being dumped into his bloodstream.

As Jared crested a small rise in the road, he saw several men in the distance standing next to a makeshift roadblock. The roadblock was no more than two cars, a Tesla and a Ford Fusion, pushed together across the road along with some racks and other unidentifiable items that afforded the men both cover and a road-blocking component. Jared stopped and tried to back up, but the men had seen him and began moving into positions behind the two cars.

Jared scooted the bike back out of sight before returning to the rise, peering down on the very disturbing scene below. The men were pointing, and he could hear one man yelling instructions to another. Two of the men had what looked like wicked-looking assault rifles, and one of these men stepped forward, waving at Jared, calling out for him to come on down.

Jared wasn't about to do that and ducked back to where he felt he could still see the men, but they wouldn't have a good line of sight on him. That was when it happened; several snaps near Jared's head caused him to drop to the ground, panting, wrought with panic as bullets tore through the air near his head. A bullet smashed into the asphalt not two feet from him, kicking up debris, which splashed across Jared's face. The sensation on his face acted like a slap, waking him from his state of frozen indecision. He was being shot at, and the realization slammed into his already overtaxed brain like a freight train. *Holy fucking shit, why the fuck would they just open up like that?*

Jared turned, grabbed his bike, and dragged it down the small rise in the opposite direction of the gunfire. Jared did not know a thing about guns. He had no idea of a weapon's capability by looking at it and didn't know if a pistol was just as deadly as a rifle or vice versa. What Jared did know was he had seen rifles like these men had in newscasts he'd seen in the past. The rifles were black and looked just like the ones carried by the troops in the Middle East. That scared him just a little more than if he'd simply been attacked by pistol-wielding madmen.

Jared pushed the bike for a short distance at a dead run before clambering on and pumping his legs for all they were worth. The rise had been about forty yards from the roadblock and Jared remembered running a forty-yard dash in high school in somewhere around five seconds. He took the first possible side street in the event the men had rushed to the top of the rise, trying to get more shots at him. He rode for nearly ten minutes before making his way to the rear of a warehouse, where he dismounted and just stood there for a few seconds, shaking and nearly breaking into tears.

The men hadn't chased him. In fact, the men had seen some guy on a bike with no pack, and that wasn't worth the energy it would have taken to sprint half the length of a football field just to kill him and go through his pockets. Had they known that behind that bike was a trailer stuffed to the gills with food and all types of other pertinent gear, the men would surely have gone to great lengths to kill Jared and relieve his dead body of his entire worldly chattel. Sometimes it was better to be lucky than good.

The rear of the warehouse was bordered by a chain-link fence separating the parking lot from a small creek. Jared held out his hands and watched as they shook, his adrenaline-soaked system trying to stabilize like a stricken World War II bomber. Jared felt like the bomber's pilot trying desperately to stay the aircraft's uncooperative yaw and pitch. Jared's body was the aircraft and he was the hapless pilot, simply along for the ride at this point, a test pilot, someone not expected to make it.

It was quickly apparent the shaking was going to continue for some time, so Jared set about getting his bolt cutters out and slicing a large hole in the fence, shaking hands and all. Next he pushed the bike and all his gear through the hole.

Jared lurched down into the creek bed, shoving the bike and trailer to the ground under a cluster of overhanging bushes. Once the gear was hidden, Jared picked his way along the creek, trying to keep his feet out of the water as he scuttled along the bank.

He found a nice growth of brush along the shoreline and concealed himself under the foliage. He was hot, breathless and scared half to death. He could see back up the creek to where he had come down the embankment, and he waited, hoping and praying he would not see men with rifles making their way down into the creek bed.

Jared huddled in the brush for a very long time, staring back up the creek, barely able to breathe for fear of making any noise that might attract the attention of the men who had recently tried to kill him. What was the reason for the violent outburst? What was the reason for the roadblock? What authority did they have to be closing down streets? They obviously were not cops—none of them had been wearing uniforms and, although Jared was not an expert on police uniforms and grooming standards, he knew what a cop should look like, and these guys did not fit the bill.

They had been dirty and wore facial hair, and not the well-groomed beards seen in the beer-brewing industry. They had appeared more than a little desperate and had carried an assortment of weapons. The police Jared had seen on the news, handling major incidents, always seemed to be carrying the same type of guns. The black rifle he'd seen in all the overseas combat footage piped through the news channels ever since September 11, 2001, was their weapon of choice. Jared never paid much attention to California's nonstop war against the Second Amendment, but if this rifle was the weapon the politicians had been after, they had failed miserably in keeping those guns out of the hands of the men who had nearly killed him recently.

Jared reflected on the incident. Two of the men possessed rifles and had fired at him, while the rest of the pack had carried some sort of handguns. Either they were bad shots or Jared had been out of range; he didn't have a clue. He could talk intelligently about a lot of complicated things, but guns, their rates of fire, and effective ranges were not among them. Jared wished he paid more attention when his father had talked about hunting and fishing during his adolescence. It was too late for that now, so he had to make sure he was more careful going forward

Jared shivered, cold now after his sweat had done its job in cooling his overheated body. His legs and back were stiff from the exertion and then the sudden long-term yoga position in the brush. Jared figured he'd been in hiding for at least two hours when he rose and slowly made his way back to where he'd hidden his bike and trailer. He looked down at his gear, the bike and trailer, the life-giving food and water, and the water-purification system. This bundle of possessions—which every living human he came in contact with would want for themselves—would either save his life or be the reason he laid dead on some cold street somewhere.

It dawned on Jared that the men had no real interest in him; they were interested in what he had. They probably didn't even know he had food, water and shelter, and still they had tried to kill him just to find out. Had the world grown that desperate in just six short days? Had the population turned into savages in less than a week?

How could he keep dodging these people day after day if folks were going to turn into complete maniacs already? In two weeks, the area would be a war zone if people were willing to kill someone on day six just to see if they had food or water. By the second week, Jared figured the Bay Area would be a slaughterhouse, with men and women killing their neighbors for a mere morsel of food.

Jared shuddered as the thought assaulted his brain housing group, rattling him to the core. He wasn't built to deal with things like this, physically or mentally. Sure, he was mentally tough and could stay up for days, forgoing sleep in order to meet a deadline. If he had to run or otherwise exert himself, he would always stop when he felt the lactic acid begin to build in his muscles.

This new world was a place for those who knew things like how to fire a weapon, how to farm, and how to run even when your lungs felt as though they might burst. It was a new world, and Jared was a stranger to it all. Standing near his bicycle, he decided here was as good a place as any to call it a night, so he set about making camp in a flat spot alongside the little creek.

Despite the day's wild events, Jared slept like a corpse, waking only when the sun began to bake the side of his face. He lurched upright, feeling sweat trickle down his chest as he fought his way out of the overheated sleeping bag, slowly rising to his feet and completing a 360-degree turn, listening and looking for anything that could be a threat. *What have I turned into?* In his former life, he wouldn't be functioning at this level until well after his second cup of java.

Jared started what was becoming a new routine of preparing a light breakfast over a small gas stove outdoors. As Jared squatted next to the tiny creek, sipping coffee and eating a dehydrated breakfast out of a bag, his mind raced, thinking of his future and how best to survive the next couple of weeks without ending up in the middle of the road with dogs eating his rotting body. He shivered at the thought of the woman in San Carlos, despite the morning heat.

Jared went back through everything that had happened to him to this point. The supermarket beating was telling in that the men had not killed him, but were more protecting their goods. The men from the day prior had tried to kill him, but they might have done that because he fled, and that was their only option in stopping him from escaping with whatever meager assets he might or might not have had.

He pondered this for a moment, surmising this was both good and bad. If he dropped the bike and fled on foot, he had a pretty good feeling the men would have stopped shooting and simply taken his gear. Jared had no intention of leaving his life source behind unless it was a last resort.

He would need a smaller pack to carry on his back at all times. The pack would have the water-purification system and some food, just the essentials. If he was forced to leave the bike behind, he'd at least have something to sustain him for a short time.

Or maybe he was thinking about this all wrong, and the punks in the supermarket had not killed him because society had just begun to crumble, and the guys with the rifles had tried to kill him because they were part of this societal collapse at a much more advanced point. This scared the ever-loving hell out of Jared.

Jared knew he needed to find another sporting goods store before he left the Bay Area, and the thought troubled him greatly. He ate his breakfast in despair, finishing and repacking his cooking equipment. Once he was packed and the trailer loaded, Jared dropped back to the ground, staring up at the heavens, tears starting to stream down his face. He let the tears pour from his ducts, breathing, but not sobbing.

He simply leaked in despair, the sky offering no sympathy, but again posing no threat and, after a few moments, he wiped his face, rose to his feet, and was done. The cry had a cleansing effect, leaving him feeling refreshed and ready to tackle this next obstacle of locating a store.

Chapter 14

JARED FOUND the tallest building he could, hid his bike and trailer in some bushes, and set to watching the place. Over the course of two hours, Jared circled the building and thoroughly reconnoitered the immediate surrounding areas. The building was in an industrial part of town with no real food sources and, subsequently, Jared saw no other humans. As much as he hated doing it, Jared finally smashed the glass in the front doors with a rock

The building was an office building, four stories tall, dark and seemingly deserted. Jared entered the building, located the stairs, and wound his way up to the top floor, where he could scan the surrounding area with his binoculars. Jared moved from one office to the next, peering through his optics, searching the landscape below. His efforts were rewarded with the sight of a Target store about half a mile to the west.

Standing there in an empty office building, overlooking a dying society, Jared was nearly overcome with a longing for human companionship, which was quite the new feeling for him altogether. The binoculars drooped in his hands, and his jaw fell slack as he took in the city's landscape. There were some people in his field of view, but they were a long way out and seemed to be darting from one building to another. Fires burned all over the city, their tendrils thin and evident for the first few dozen feet before being wisped away by the light breeze.

Empires rose and fell all throughout history, Jared had seen a good portion of the current rise, but never dreamed he would be witness to the fall. Mother Nature did not like accumulation; man did. Mother Nature was not fond of monocultures; man was. Mother Nature was a tremendous force; man, not so much. Jared was witnessing Mother Nature reclaim control of her body, which was the Earth. She would wrest control from mankind, wiping him out if necessary; after all, he was the problem. Mother Nature decided it was time to diversify, and she was about to level the playing field across the board. Jared knew this meant the human race was going to be reined in, the population cut drastically. The days of billions of humans and less than a half dozen white rhinos roaming the earth were quickly coming to an end. He desperately did not want to be reined in; he wanted to be one of the half dozen humans left when this whole thing stabilized. Jared let out a breath and closed his eyes. Man had been killing the world for a couple of hundred years and that reign of ecoterrorism driven by greed was about to come to an end.

Jared turned and started back towards the stairwell

The trip to Target was without event, and Jared was able to find a great location inside a building out of the sun and across the street, with a great view of the store's front. Two hours into watching the store, Jared saw two teenage boys ride up on bicycles and enter the store. He held his breath, waiting for disaster to befall the two lads. Nothing happened, and silence was the only thing emanating from within the store.

Ten minutes later the two emerged pushing a shopping cart full of essentials like toilet paper, toothpaste and the like. Jared watched as the two placed the cart between their bikes and struggled to get going, each boy holding the cart with one hand and toiling away at the pedals while steering the bike with their other hand. Jared watched them through the binoculars and thought they looked like brothers.

The boys were a couple of hundred yards away, weaving back and forth, pushing the cart and trying not to fall, when three young men stepped into the street, seemingly out of nowhere, blocking the youths' path. The two boys were forced to a stop, and they relinquished their hold on the cart and simply stood straddling their bicycles, as young kids so often do when not pedaling. The three men approached, strutting confidently up to the youths.

Jared adjusted his position, watching intently as the three surrounded the two and began rifling through the cart. Jared could see the two brothers were scared as the three young men went about relieving them of their goods. Jared watched, frozen, as the three young men began pushing the cart up into an apartment complex parking lot, leaving the two boys standing behind without so much as a rearward glance. The two brothers stood for just a moment before leaping off their bikes and starting after the three. It happened so quickly; Jared tore the binoculars away from his eyes.

One of the three apparently heard the boys, turned, and produced a pistol, firing at the approaching boys, hitting his mark and dropping both kids to the ground, where they laid motionless. The man strode right up to the boys' limp bodies and, when he stood over them, he began firing again. The man's weapon stopped firing, and he held it up as if inspecting it, the slide locked to the rear, chamber empty.

He pulled something out of his pocket and performed what Jared could only assume was a reload, after which he simply turned and rejoined his friends before disappearing into the apartment complex. The man's face was burned into Jared's memory, hate and rage written across it as he had stood over the young boys, stealing the life from their innocent bodies.

Jared peered through the binoculars again, scanning the two lifeless forms lying on the sidewalk with dark red blood pooling out from under their bodies. Jared was breathing hard as if he'd been running. He felt sick, scared and more than a little angry. The boys could not have been more than fourteen years old, and this animal had murdered them both over some toilet paper and toothpaste. Jared also felt a pang of guilt for not helping these young boys. He felt claustrophobic as if the world were closing in on him.

All these human emotions were not meant to descend on a man at the same time. These situations were what caused a man to leap off a bridge, run naked down a public street, or put a gun in his mouth and pull the trigger. Jared needed to get a handle on himself before he descended any deeper into the abyss that seemed to have opened up and begun to swallow him.

Jared laid in his hiding place for the better part of an hour, trying not to look up the street at the two brothers lying in a heap like so much dirty laundry. As the fear began to subside, the guilt built, and this caused anger. Jared was not naturally an angry person, always striving to avoid conflict whenever possible, but this anger felt good somehow, strange and new as it was

Another hour passed and Jared simply felt wrung out, nothing left in the tanks, too tired to even pull the binoculars to his face and look at the carnage up the street. He thought about the tragedy he had just witnessed, and evaluated the incident like he would a project at work. The boys were outnumbered and outgunned, albeit they probably didn't know that at the time.

They had also been outsized by the older and more sophisticated males. Three things against them and nothing going for them—why hadn't they just let the guys have the toilet paper and gone back for more? Jared assured himself that would not be a mistake he made, and vowed to get that smaller pack and have it on his back at all times.

Something Jared had been avoiding was the gun factor. He hadn't cared for them as a kid, neither disliking nor hating them, he simply couldn't care less about firearms. He never had a use for them and therefore had never bothered to learn a thing about them other than what he saw on television or in a movie. It was becoming obvious to him that he would have a far better chance for survival if he carried and knew how to use a gun. He thought about this as if it were a piece of technology he'd never used in his old job and now needed for a project. He would seek out a weapon, familiarize himself with it, and that would be that. Deep down he knew it wouldn't be that easy.

Steering clear of the two dead juveniles, Jared scavenged a small black JanSport backpack from inside Target. After securing the small day pack, Jared pedaled a short distance before pulling off the road and moving into a large thicket. There he set about loading the smaller JanSport pack with what he felt were essential items for a short survival period in case he was forced to run, leaving his bike and trailer behind.

When Jared came near a strip mall or a grocery store, he would stop and watch. People were usually in and around these places, foraging for food and water. He would then pick his way around the area, trying to avoid contact, which worked fairly well for most of the rest of the day, but resulted in a very slow trip as he zigged and zagged his way around the crowds.

Once, Jared rounded a corner and came face-to-face with a woman carrying an armful of pilfered items. The woman's face contorted in fear as Jared stammered, "Excuse me," and pedaled past her. The woman stared straight ahead, never uttering a word. Jared even checked twice, but the woman never stopped, looked back or deviated her course. *What has society come to?*

On second thought, Jared was convinced society hadn't changed much on the public social interaction spectrum. Before the power went out, people would move about in public glued to a cell phone screen, not interacting with anyone around them. Now it was fear driving the wedge between human interactions. Maybe people weren't meant to socialize with others outside their tribes, and there would always be a reason promoting this behavior, whether it was a phone or fear itself.

Another thought flashed in his mind. He hadn't seen a single person in the last few days scavenging electronics like he'd seen during the first couple of days. People were realizing how dire their situations were and adjusting. This thought sent a stab of fear through his chest.

Jared pedaled his bike through an older part of San Jose, with not much in the way of strip malls or places to get food, so there were few if any people in his path. This part of town was of a more industrial nature with auto shops, shipping businesses and the like. In the distance, Jared thought he saw movement in front of one of these businesses. He quickly pulled off the road and laid the bike in some bushes before creeping out to the sidewalk for a better look with the binoculars.

A good seventy or so yards out, he could see an older man on a ladder removing the letters from the upper portion of the business's window. Jared squinted in the field glasses, wondering what in the hell this old-timer was doing, and then it hit him. He could see the remaining letters: ND AMMO. This was a gun store and the old guy was trying to make sure no one knew it was a gun store.

He was about to leap up when he realized the old man was armed to the teeth. The old codger had a pistol on his hip and one of those black rifles hanging on his back from some sort of sling. Running down there and getting shot was not how Jared wanted to end the day, so he went back to his bike, slowly pushing it out onto the street, where he stopped in plain view of God and everyone, including this gunned-up elder statesman.

Jared stood in the middle of the street, held his hands up, and whistled. The old man came down the ladder like a young sailor would negotiate a ship's ladder, moving like a panther to a cinderblock wall while bringing the rifle around to his front and training it in Jared's direction. This all happened in about one second, or so it seemed to Jared.

"Is it just you?" the man called out.

"Yes, I'm alone," Jared answered.

"Move closer so we don't have to yell," the old man instructed in a gruff, somewhat raspy voice.

Jared pushed the bike along the street, getting within ten yards of the old fella.

"That's close enough. Now what do you want?" he barked.

Jared stared at the half-disassembled sign, then back at the older man, whose steely eyes let Jared know without words that he was not fucking around.

"Things are going bad around here, and I was thinking I might need one of---" He didn't finish his sentence, instead just gesturing up at the sign.

The old man's eyes narrowed as he leaned forward menacingly with the black rifle pointed directly at Jared's chest. "One of what, boy?"

Jared shifted uncomfortably. "A gun, sir."

The old man's demeanor did not change in the slightest. "You even know how to use one?" he quipped.

Jared stared at the ground. "No, I never needed one till now."

The old man seemed to relax just a bit, gazing past Jared, looking at the trailer attached to his bike. The old man lifted his chin an inch moving his head about ever so slightly. Jared thought the old guy actually sniffed like a dog trying to catch scent of whatever was in the trailer.

Seeing the man's interest in the trailer, Jared turned, hefting his chin towards all his worldly possessions. "I have things to trade for a gun, food and stuff like that."

The old man pointed to the curb. "Sit down and don't move," he growled and, after Jared sat, he moved out from behind the wall, striding right past Jared and stopping at the trailer. The old guy inspected the trailer's contents carefully, almost respectfully, as Jared sat and stared, wondering what would happen next.

Did I fuck myself here by just walking up to this walking gun display? Jared sat there aware of the day pack on his back, with enough supplies for a week at most. If this guy was going to rob him, he was ready for it, well, not really, but at least if the old bastard was a bad shot and Jared got away, he'd have something to eat and drink for a couple of days. If the guy was going to just kill him, he was not ready for that. Jared started to talk and then thought better of it, remembering something his father had taught him about the older generations and their love of mute young people. The man finished his inspection before turning to Jared.

"Get up that ladder and pull the rest of those letters off that goddamn sign. There's a box of other letters up there on the ledge. Here's what I want you to spell."

Jared did as he was told, and in less than five minutes he was standing on the sidewalk in front of a gun store with a sign indicating the business fixed computers.

"Get your bike and all that gear inside the store, out of sight, before some damn assholes come along and I have to kill their asses."

Obediently Jared did as he was told, pushing the bike in front of the old guy, struggling to get through the front doors with absolutely no help from the cranky old man, who stood back, watching up and down the street with those narrow eyes set deep in his craggy old face.

Once inside the store, the old man drew the shades and motioned for Jared to move deeper into the structure. Jared stopped next to the cash register before a hallway and looked back at the old man.

"All the way back," the man ordered. He slung the rifle, his hands free, but Jared felt that if the need arose, he'd have a firearm in those old boney hands before he could blink an eye.

Jared walked the length of the hall and found himself in what appeared to be a fairly spacious workshop. There were benches with vises, a couple of huge safes, and a lot of other things Jared could not identify. Along one wall was an old leather couch, which the man pointed at and Jared understood to mean "sit the fuck down," which he promptly did. He sat awkwardly, still wearing the day pack.

"For Christ's sake, take that damn thing off. If I wanted any of your gear, I would have just killed ya out front." The old-timer shook his head in disgust. "I can't believe you've made it this long." The old man leaned back against a bench and eyed Jared closely. "Where'd you come from?"

Jared wriggled out of the backpack, placing it on the floor between his feet. "Belmont."

The old man threw his head back and gave a hearty laugh. "You rode that bike with that little piss-ass trailer all the way down from Belmont?"

Jared nodded and the man laughed even harder.

"You're lucky to be alive."

"I know," Jared murmured.

The man just stared at him for a long while, studying him like some sort of scientist would study a lab animal. The stare lasted a ridiculously long period of time, and Jared was about to get up and attempt to leave when the man spoke.

"I don't have but about a week's worth of food left here. I can't walk too far, but my water situation is alright with the creek behind this place. I propose a deal, a trade."

Jared cocked his head as the man went on. "You go out and set me up with some food and provisions. I know this area, so there'll be no searching; you'll have maps and know exactly where you'll be going. I, in return, will set you up with a pistol and a rifle. I'll even throw in some instruction," the man added.

Jared thought about the offer then asked, "How do I know you'll hold up your end of the deal?"

The old man's eyes narrowed, and Jared immediately wished he hadn't questioned the old-timer's integrity.

"Because I'm a man of my word, you little shit, and I don't fuck people over unless they need fucking over." The man leaned in close. "Do you need fucking over, lad?"

Jared shook his head. "No, sir, I'd prefer to stay unfucked over."

"Here's how it's going to work," the old man continued. "I'm gonna give you a pistol and ammo; then I will teach you how to use it. After that, you are going out to fetch my supplies and, when you get back, I will give you a rifle and teach you how to use it."

Jared was surprised; the deal actually sounded fair and, from what he'd seen over the last few days, fair was not a commodity that was readily available. The old man looked questioningly at Jared, who slowly nodded as he thought about all his other options, which were about two. The man stuck his hand out, and Jared got up and shook the man's hand. His grip was like a vise, and Jared tried not to visibly wince as the man pumped his pained appendage like a jackhammer.

"Name's Bart, and yours?"

Jared realized the man had no intention of releasing his

death grip until he got a name. "Jared," he blurted out, and his crumpled hand was released.

The old man actually broke into a warm smile, and Jared could see the man who had once been, before the world fell apart and people began killing one another over toothpaste.

"Well, Jared, it's sure nice to meet you."

"Likewise," stammered Jared.

"There's just a couple of house rules. If you're gonna be staying for a few days, you should know 'em," Bart said. "First off, there's a shitter in the lot behind this place, been there due to some construction next door. You can shit in it, but if ya gotta piss, do it somewhere else. I don't want that thing full and of no use to me. I know it's gonna happen, but better later than sooner."

Jared nodded. "Got it."

"Secondly, no sneaking around here at night, that's a sure-fire way to get your ass shot. If you gotta use the commode after lights out, get me and I will provide security for you." Bart scratched his chin, trying to think of another house rule but couldn't, so he elaborated on the commode rule.

"It'd be best if you did your business before dark, and any midnight potty breaks should really be done in your room. Make sure you got a bottle in there. Me, I use a Gatorade bottle with the large opening; it's what fits me best. I don't know what size equipment you're sporting, so I'll leave the make and model of your bottle up to you. Just try to get it right. Don't want piss on the floors if I can help it."

Chapter 15

THE NEXT TWO days found Jared learning everything there was to know about a Glock 19 pistol. Jared held the oddly square and futuristic looking weapon in his calloused hand.

"So, I guess there are eighteen other models of this gun?" Jared questioned.

"What the fuck are you talking about?"

"If this is nineteen, then are there eighteen other models?" Jared asked again.

Bart rolled his eyes, took a deep breath, and scratched his stubbly chin. "The gun's designer is named Gaston Glock, and he got a patent for his first gun way back when Christ was a corporal. It turned out to be the seventeenth patent he ever got, so he named the gun the Glock 17, fucking really creative guy, huh? So, as I understand the Glock folklore, the guns were then numbered or named in the order they came out. That makes this here little fucker the third gun old Gaston put on the market."

"Oh," was all Jared could think to say.

Bart raised both eyebrows. "Now can we get back to it?"

Jared dutifully nodded in the affirmative.

He learned everything, from the gun's history to how it worked. Bart taught him about the malfunctions guns were prone to experience, and explained in great detail what caused each malfunction and how to remedy these breakdowns. Jared handled the firearm until his hands were blistered, ached, and then Bart made him handle it some more. Not only did Jared sleep with the gun, he went to the bathroom and ate with it. He was never without the weapon, and Bart stressed the importance of keeping it on him at all times. Jared dry fired the pistol until he was blue in the face. Bart was always by his side, tweaking his stance, his grip on the weapon, and a litany of other deficiencies Jared had when it came to weapons handling.

At the end of the first day, Bart had Jared stow all his gear in a back room not bigger than most bathrooms. The tiny room was furnished with a cot and a small nightstand.

"You can sleep here while we get you ready," Bart said with no complaint from Jared. After setting up his gear and spreading the sleeping bag out on the cot, Jared found his way through the semidarkness to where Bart was stringing up his early warning devices. He strung several soda cans, which contained several shotgun pellets, on fishing line and placed them across every entrance to the store. Front, back and all the windows. Bart locked the shop and drew a security gate across the front of the store.

"By the time anyone was able to break through all this, I'd be up here giving 'em hell." The old fella chortled.

Jared did not doubt for a moment that Bart would give hell to anyone stupid enough to try to enter the store uninvited. Jared also realized all the windows in the store were covered over with foil, and wondered if it were to keep prying eyes out or light in. His answer came when Bart dropped a large piece of canvas over the entrance to the hall and proclaimed, "Let there be light," turning on a large gas lantern. He moved down the hall and into the workshop, Jared following him in, seeing he had set up a small circular table with two folding chairs.

"Sit down," Bart said, nodding to one of the two chairs. "We can play a little cards, have a drink before bed, take a load off, make you sleep better."

Jared found himself sitting in the dimly lit room with Bart, an old gun guy, playing Spades and drinking straight Kentucky Bourbon from small plastic cups. The scene was surreal, and Jared nearly pinched himself. He looked at the bottle as Bart poured a second helping for himself: Knob Creek and the label indicated the juice was 120 proof. He took a draw from the cup and felt the whiskey burn his lips, then his throat, and finally warm his belly. He took a second and much longer draw, swished the fluid around his mouth, then swallowed it. The effect was instant; he could feel the last few days melt away, his shoulders relaxing, his mind slowing. He suddenly felt very safe and very warm.

The two men drank and played cards; they talked and laughed and, at times, were just silent. Bart told Jared about his life, starting from when he joined the Army in 1966 when he was only eighteen years old. Bart told him how he'd gone to Vietnam, where many of his friends were killed, and how Bart was wounded and was in two separate helicopter crashes, surviving them all.

As Bart drank into the night, he told Jared how he got out of the Army after four years, came back home to San Jose, and worked for the San Jose Police Department for over thirty years before retiring.

Bart explained that after September 11, 2001, things changed for him. He married, but never had children. His wife passed away in 2003, and Bart had needed a hobby to take his mind off the void left by his wife's death. Bart explained how he had always put money into a second retirement, and he was able to use that money to lease this building and purchase his entire inventory in order to start the business. Bart went on to tell Jared how his connections with the police department came in handy in regard to his business, which boomed within the first year. Bart finished up with, "And the rest is history, as they say."

Jared sat staring at him as Bart grabbed the bottle and poured each man another two fingers, Bart's fifth. After the whiskey was poured, both men—one young and naive, the other older and full of experience—sat back and studied one another.

"So, what's your story, son?" Bart queried.

Jared looked at the cup in front of him, almost reached for it, and then thought twice. His body was already warm and humming with more than a good buzz. He thought back to his family and how he had come to be who he was.

He was born in a small town outside Seattle, Washington, to David and Shannon Culp. David attended Washington University and was on a trip to Vancouver with friends when he first laid eyes on Shannon, who was attending college at Camosun University, working on a degree in business. David made his intentions known right off and began planning for a life after college, when he would bring Shannon to the States and begin a family. The two were married a month after finishing college, and Jared was born ten months after that.

David always excelled in school and, although he played some sports, they were not the driving force in his life, as was the case for many of the children he grew up with. David started a hardware store in town after college, where both he and Shannon worked long hours together to make a decent living for their family. After Jared was born, the two parents worked so hard, they simply never had the time to plan for another child, so Jared had no siblings.

Growing up, he went to school and worked in the family business on the weekends. David would give Jared a task and later find him tinkering in the back of the store with some sort of electronic contraption that Jared would swear was going to change the world. David was a patient, hardworking family man who would artfully guide Jared back to the task at hand without crushing his explorative spirit.

David and Shannon worried about Jared on a social level, talking at length about the lack of friends and the time he spent by himself, working on all his projects. Brilliant as some of Jared's creations were, his parents were not only hardworking, they were social. They didn't understand and they worried about their son. When Jared was old enough, he would reassure them, telling his parents that what he did made him happy, and wasn't that what they wanted for him? Shannon and David couldn't argue with this logic, but still they worried.

Jared grew into an intelligent young man, joining several academic groups and making quite a name for himself with the teachers from several high schools in the area. Jared went to his senior prom alone, and his mother was beside herself. Jared consoled her by saying he was going because it was an expected part of high school, and he was going alone because he didn't have the time to court a young woman with all the things he had going on in his life with school and preparing for college.

The following year, Jared went to the University of California at Berkeley on an academic scholarship. He began at Cal where he had left off in high school, working hard and impressing the staff with his outside-the-box thought processes. Jared worked best when left alone, but in his junior year, he worked with a female student named Monica, who had many of the same personality traits Jared possessed. This, for some reason, worked, and the two would spend hours in the lab working out issues with whatever project they were laboring on at the time. Monica was from the Bay Area and had grown up with an academic-minded set of parents, who pushed her from the time she could hold her head up.

Her father told her a million times—no, more like a billion times—that Chinese and Japanese families were pushing their children harder than any American family could possibly comprehend. He told Monica these people would be the educated people in the country, and the result would be they would get the jobs while all the American kids who stopped their education after high school or went to a junior college would be left out in the cold. By cold he meant washing dishes and digging ditches. Monica knew no other way than studying and then studying some more.

Learning came easier than most to Monica and, although she had a few friends, they were neatly placed in her life so as not to interfere with her studies. During high school Monica had her friends organized into neat little groups. There was Nancy, her friend from biology, whom she saw every day during her senior year, but she didn't know a thing about Nancy outside of the biology world. Then after high school, Monica never so much as spoke to Nancy again.

Then there was Bradley, a nice boy from her junior year who had actually asked her to a dance, which she declined because it conflicted with her study schedule. What Monica didn't know was Bradly had gone way out on a limb as a young insecure sixteen-year-old to ask her out and, when she rebuked him, he was crushed, devastated and embarrassed. Monica never knew the devastation she caused him.

She had treated the invitation like a meeting: she checked her schedule, found she wasn't available, and even looked into rearranging an event or two, but her de-confliction efforts never came through, so she declined the invitation and that was that. No malice, no thought of the effects her actions had on the boy, and sadly no awareness of Bradley's change after the fiasco.

Monica was on a mission in life and directed zero energy towards anything that wasn't part of her mission. In college, Monica and Jared were a perfect couple who co-existed like two coins in a pocket; there was no human connection and no feelings for one another that weren't related to the other person being able to further a project. They would celebrate each other's lab success, but had no idea when the other's birthday was.

They both finished school and went on to a master's program, Jared staying at Cal and Monica leaving to attend school at the University of Central Florida in Orlando. Although they had each other's phone numbers, they never called. There was no reason to call, their studies were in different fields at this point, and the projects they worked on were in completely different areas of engineering exploration.

Since graduating and getting a job at the company, Jared had thought about Monica, which he found strange at first, wondering what she was working on, and he even contemplated calling her to see how things were going, but thought it might be a little weird to just call out of the blue with no real reason other than nosey curiosity, so he never called. He knew she lived in Orlando through friends at work who had gone to Cal and knew people who worked with Monica, but other than that, they had lost contact.

Jared finished telling Bart his story by relaying everything he'd seen and gone through since the event knocked out all the power. He told Bart about the dead woman and the dog, the cops who seemed indifferent about the whole affair, how he saw two kids murdered earlier that day, and generally how fucked up the whole world had become in less than a week. Bart sat silent for a long while before talking.

"You got your ass beat pretty good, it sounds like." Jared nodded and Bart smiled sideways. "Not as bad as you'd think it would be though, right?"

Jared thought for a moment then shook his head.

"Worst part is right before something bad is about to happen."

Jared kept nodding as Bart spoke, thinking to himself how unbelievably frightened he'd been. He'd been unable to move or react, frozen in place until it was too late and they were on him.

"The trick, my boy, is to control that initial fear. Problem is you have to take a few beatdowns before you realize this." Bart took a long swig from his cup. Jared stared at his own cup, then gave in and did the same.

"Once you've come to terms with these high-stress situations, they become easier to manage, and you, my friend, become a dangerous motherfucker. I see a guy getting ready to fight and he's hopping all over the place, I know I've already won. Now I see a guy standing still, chin down, waiting for an opening, well, that's a cat I'm gonna be extra careful with."

Again, both men sat in silence, Jared staring into the cup of brown liquid, thinking about being scared and trying to control it and all that bullshit Bart was talking about.

"Now getting shot is as bad as you think it is, my friend. Gunfights are fucking more than a little hectic. Just know that you have to overcome that fear, or you will get shot, and it will suck a lot of ass, and you probably will die, especially nowadays with no hospitals or meds to help you through those hard times." Bart finished his drink, stood up, capped the bottle, and stretched. "I'm about done here. I drink any more and I'll start getting all emotional talking about gunfights; they have that effect on me." Without another word, Bart turned and left, leaving Jared alone with his somewhat drunken thoughts of gunfights and God knew what else.

"Turn the lantern off when you're done," came Bart's raspy voice from the hallway as he sauntered off to bed.

Chapter 16

JARED FELT a little groggy the next morning as he sat up, holding his hands to his aching head. Coffee was what he needed and needed fast. He stumbled out into the hall and immediately smelled food and coffee. He found Bart in the workshop, sipping a cup of coffee, an empty plate resting on the table in front of him. Bart was reading a book, not just a book, but a romance novel. It was a novel by Jennifer Haymore called Secrets of an Accidental Duchess. Jared stood staring until Bart drew his pistol and laid it on the table without so much as a glance in Jared's direction.

"I don't want to hear a goddamn word," was all the old man said.

Jared pivoted wordlessly, returning to his room to forage for some breakfast packets. When he returned to the workshop, he briskly walked in, greeting Bart without making eye contact, and set about heating his breakfast on a small stove. When Jared finished cooking his breakfast, he moved to the table. The book was gone, the pistol secured in its holster, and Bart sat quietly sipping his coffee as if nothing had happened.

Jared glanced about the room for the book then caught

himself. He'd been beaten to a pulp once this week and didn't care to make it twice, so he dropped into a chair and dug into his breakfast, deciding to leave the Fifty Shades of Grey thing alone in the interest of self-preservation.

The rest of the second day consisted of a lot of the same training Jared had experienced the first day.

"Repetition," Bart kept saying as he ran Jared through drill after drill. "A man will always revert to his training in a time of crisis," Bart barked.

Jared didn't even fully understand what this meant, but nodded dutifully and kept at the drills.

Bart had converted one of the small rooms into a makeshift firing range. It was small, but most gunfights, Bart explained, happened within feet of one's assailant. After lunch, Bart took Jared to the firing range again, and they fired a few hundred rounds before setting to cleaning the weapon.

"Cleaning this weapon is the most important thing you will do. Keep it clean and it won't fail you in a time of need."

Jared nodded again as he scrubbed at the built-up carbon in the weapon's slide.

Bart took a step closer. "I'm serious about this, boy, this isn't one of those things you nod your head to and store the info somewhere in that pea brain of yours for later. A dirty weapon will get you killed."

Jared thought about this and tried to equate it to something from his old world and couldn't. If he didn't run updates at his old job, no one would die, especially him. He would get a nasty-gram from IT, and that would have been that. Bart had explained to him the difference between a deep cleaning and a field cleaning.

If Jared found himself in a prolonged battle and could get to a place of reasonable safety, he could down one of his weapon systems to give it a cursory cleaning before re-engaging the enemy. This was only in a long and drawn-out fight lasting hours or days. Bart emphasized that he was never to down both weapons at the same time and that the cleaning would have to be the fastest of his life.

What the hell am I doing here with this old guy? What has happened to the world and, more importantly, my little world? His whole world had revolved around the computer industry, and now that simply didn't exist. It seemed so unfair, like an Olympic sprinter losing both legs in a freak accident. Jared sat in silence, cleaning the weapon, looking at the parts, taking in the engineering genius that went into creating this firearm. It was really a very simple concept wherein the weapon used the ammunition to cause the action that reloaded the gun and kept it in a constant state of readiness. The springs were like the starter in a motor vehicle, and the exploding ammunition was like the engine. Combustion, it drove everything in this manmade world.

After the weapon was cleaned, Bart brought out a box and dropped it on the table. *He really is one for dramatics,* thought Jared as Bart stood looking at Jared as if waiting for a response to the presence of this mysterious box.

"Open it." Bart nodded at the box.

Jared leaned forward, lifting the top to the box, exposing two additional Glock 19 handguns. He looked up at Bart, with a quizzical looked etched on his face. "And?"

Bart grabbed one of the weapons and handed it to Jared. "And---it's an Airsoft version of the gun you've been shooting for the last couple of days, good for force-on-force training."

"Force-on-force?" Jared asked.

"Force-on-force, like you going against me using Airsoft to determine deficiencies in your tactics."

Jared hefted one of the Airsoft Glocks. "Do they hurt?"

"Fuck yeah, they hurt. Wouldn't be a damn bit of good if they didn't." Bart snatched the second gun from the box, sighting it across the room. "It's called positive reinforcement.

You fuck up, you get hit, it hurts like hell, and you stop fucking up in order to stop the pain, repeat if necessary. Today we work on clearing a building, getting into a room without getting killed, and basically learn how to survive inside a structure against an opposing force."

Bart spent the next few hours working with Jared on moving inside a building, teaching him how to search a room without ever stepping through the door. Bart slowly moved across the doorway, visually clearing the interior of the room as he went. Bart described a dynamic entry versus slow and deliberate entries. Bart stressed that Jared only use a dynamic entry in the most serious of situations.

The dynamic entry was fast and caused the person searching a building to process a tremendous amount of information in a split second. There was serious room for error, Bart said, and it was the way most of the guys in that business got shot. Dynamic entries were used for rescuing hostages in cases where the good guys had reason to believe the bad guys were intent on killing the hostages and therefore had to be dealt with swiftly in order to thwart the hostage killing.

Bart further explained how an operator could slip in and out of the two types of movements depending on the circumstances. Bart told Jared that he would most likely never rescue a hostage but would instead use the dynamic style in a situation where he was in a building running for his life. He'd have to clear corners of rooms as he traversed through them during an escape, and it was good to know how.

Bart's favorite way to clear a building was to do it slowly, using his pie method, as he called it. He would clear most of the room from outside by viewing the interior of the room from outside the doorway before setting up to enter the room. Once he performed his visual inspection and was ready to make entry to a room, he explained, there were only the two hard corners left that he wouldn't have seen from the outside.

When he entered the room, he would first focus on the two hard corners and then reinspect the areas of the room already seen from outside in the hallway.

Bart worked Jared as a solo operator and then taught him how to work in a team of two. The lessons Bart taught in the two-man work were based on not being in a position where you shot your partner by accident if all hell broke loose. Jared learned where his weapon should be pointed and how his feet should be planted. He learned to keep his finger off the trigger unless he was shooting. Stumbling or being surprised with a man's finger on the trigger was sure to end badly. He learned how to glide and not walk so he could shoot while moving. Bart explained that this little talent would separate the live guys from the dead guys.

"It's easier for a moving man to shoot a stationary man than it is for a stationary man to shoot a moving man," Bart said, and it was his experience that under stress, a trained man would miss a moving target seventy-five percent of the time.

After lunch, the two men began working with the Airsoft pistols, Bart placing stationary targets in the room at first and then transitioning himself into the aggressor role. All the morning's lessons were put to the test as Jared entered room after room and was peppered with the small but painful shots to various areas of his body. Bart only allowed him a light T-shirt, citing the pain would help Jared remember his mistakes. Jared found the slower he went, the less he was shot and the more he was able to shoot Bart. He liked this...a lot. By the end of the day, Jared looked like a leper, his flesh dotted with dozens of bruises.

The next few days found Jared either on the live-fire range or clearing rooms, trying not to get peppered by Bart's accurate fire. By the end of the fourth day, Jared was moving through the gun store, sometimes clearing the entire structure without Bart placing a single shot on him.

That evening they sat eating in silence, drinking bourbon for the first time since that first night, Bart having set a hard-and-fast rule that they would not drink on school nights, as he called it.

Bart broke the silence. "Tomorrow you go out and start getting my supplies. You're ready as far as being able to point that thing at something and hit it. I'm just worried about whether or not you can shoot a human being."

Jared stayed quiet as he looked up at Bart's very serious face.

"In this new world there will come a time when it is either you or the other guy and, if you decide you can't shoot a man, then it's gonna be you. There is no second place in a gunfight. As Ricky Bobby said, 'If you're not first, you're last.'"

Jared cocked his head, question written on his face. "Huh?"

"*Talladega Nights*, you never saw it, did you?"

Jared slowly shook his head.

"Jesus, mother, and Mary, boy, you should have got out more." With that, Bart threw his hands in the air, got up, and walked out of the workshop.

Chapter 17

THE FOLLOWING MORNING, Jared found Bart sitting at the table in his workshop, only this time, there was no romance novel. The romance novel had been replaced with maps and a notepad, which were strewn across the table. Bart looked up, went back to his scribbling, then laid the pencil down and stretched.

"I have maps and notes here detailing where you need to go and what routes to take. Once you're there, you can go off the list, load up, and pedal on back to unload, and go back out. Figure you can get three maybe four loads in a day. Once it gets close to sundown, we shut it down—too dangerous out there at night."

Jared took a deep breath, thinking this had all happened too quickly. He'd been swept away by the man, lost control of his life. He could simply take the gun and this crazy old man's list and ride off, never to return. He blinked and tried to clear his head.

"I'll go after I eat something." *Bart kept his end of the deal so far, so why am I thinking of just taking off and leaving the old fart here in this dank building with less than three days' food left to survive?* Jared doubted very strongly the old coffin dodger would allow him to leave with the trailer loaded with all his belongings anyway.

Bart sat staring at Jared before speaking. "You thinking of taking off on me?"

Jared nodded his head, he didn't know why, and he braced for the storm he was sure would come.

"Fair enough, I get it. I sit here and risk nothing holding up my end of the deal, while you gotta go out and possibly get killed. I get it."

"It's not that," Jared said. "It's like this whole thing hasn't sunk in. It's not real, and here I am living in your building, learning to shoot a gun, and now I'm about to go out and deal with who knows what."

Bart stood, spreading his arms out wide. "Want to call the deal off?" His arms fell back to his sides. "I'm pretty sure if we call off the deal, we will both die within the next couple of weeks. You will be murdered and I will starve to death."

Jared took a deep breath and started making coffee. "I'm going out for you, Bart, don't worry, I'm going out."

Bart sat back down and seemed suddenly frail, his shoulders slumped. "Good, I respect a man of his word. One last thing," Bart started, "I won't belabor the issue of moving out in the open since you were able to get all the way down here on your own, but I will say this, you have to know the difference between cover and concealment."

Jared nodded like he understood, even though he had no idea what the old guy was talking about, but he also knew Bart was going to tell him about this whether he liked it or not. It was Bart's way of ensuring his supplies made it back. So, for the next ten minutes, Bart explained that cover was something Jared could hide behind that would not only conceal him, but stop bullets, while concealment was something he could hide in or behind that would conceal his presence, but would not stop bullets

Bart droned on about always keeping a gunfight fluid, moving whenever possible to keep your opponent off-balance, making him constantly adjust to you and not the other way around. Bart explained how tall grass and bushes were great concealment, but were shitty cover should the bullets start flying. He told Jared how a car could be great cover as long as you positioned yourself behind the engine or a rim. The lesson lasted about fifteen minutes, ten minutes longer than Jared felt necessary.

After the cover and concealment lesson, Jared ate, had a cup of joe, was briefed by Bart...again, prepped his bike and trailer, rechecked the map, making sure he had the route committed to memory, and left out the back of the business. He pedaled hard for several blocks before slowing. He navigated to the first site, an REI, and pulled up in front and across the street. He set up his usual observation spot, far enough away to see but not too close.

Jared hadn't heard gunfire since he'd been with Bart, and chalked that up to the fact that he was in an area where people didn't live or scavenge for food. After an hour, Jared got to his feet and ran across the parking lot to the front doors of the store. He entered the dark store and cracked a light stick, using it to light his way to the sleeping bags section.

He hadn't only memorized the route, but most of the shopping list as well, getting right to work throwing items into the sleeping bag as he dragged it up and down the aisles. When he had everything the old bastard wanted, he crept back to the front of the store, shoving the light stick in his pants pocket before peering out into the brightly lit day. There was no sign of danger, so he hurried to the bike, loaded the trailer, and pedaled off towards the gun shop.

He arrived back at Bart's place without incident, rapping on the back door. Bart opened it with half a smile on his face. Jared pushed past him, moving the bike and its load inside, where he immediately felt safer, shedding the coat of tension that had clothed his body since the moment he left the gun store and this cantankerous old man.

By the end of the first day, Jared had completed three trips, one to REI, one to Home Depot, and the last to CVS. He was able to pick up most of the items Bart had on his lists, and the things he didn't get were due to the stores having already been looted. Bart took no medications before the event, instructing Jared to only grabbed health-related items like vitamins, nonperishable medications and ointments along with a truckload...or a small bike trailer load of bandages and other accoutrements related to the first aid family.

When Jared passed through the back door for the last time, he was spent. After the physical exertion combined with the high level of concentration it took to clear a building, he was exhausted, famished and a bit jittery. Bart had food ready and forced Jared to drink more water than he cared to drink at the moment, but the old son of a bitch just rolled in to some diatribe about staying hydrated and blah, blah, blah. While Jared quietly ate, Bart went about inventorying his new gear, which he stored in the workshop. The old man was meticulous about his inventories and how he stowed it all.

Bart finished what he was doing and turned to Jared. "You see anyone out there today?"

"A couple of people, but we both steered clear of each other."

Bart slowly nodded. "I don't mean to harp on you, but that last load you brought in, you had your shirt open and the pistol was exposed. Someone gets the drop on an unarmed man, they're more likely to be careless. If they see you're armed, they're probably just going to shoot you rather than risk a gunfight."

Jared took a deep breath and didn't argue.

"Yeah, I want you to get all my stuff, but whether you believe me or not, I don't want to see you get killed out there."

Jared turned back to his food and took another bite. This guy was the strangest man he'd ever met. He was sure Bart would kill him in a New York minute if Jared gave him cause, and now he was telling him he actually cared about his welfare, just flipping strange. Maybe the old guy was lonely, Jared didn't have a clue, but every day, Bart did or said something that contradicted his usual harsh exterior. Jared was sure the crusty old guy had not been the type to ever volunteer at a soup kitchen, but the more time the two spent together, the more Jared saw a slightly different side to the man.

"Tomorrow's a big day," Bart said. "You're going to a food source, and you are almost certain to meet other people—desperate people and possibly violent people. I want you mentally ready. Your mental readiness is ten times more important than your physical readiness."

Jared was too tired for any more speeches, opting to simply nod his head as he ate the last of his freeze-dried lasagna.

That night, Jared dreamed of the beating he'd taken in the Belmont store and was jolted out of a deep sleep, not by the dream but by the sound of gunfire. He heard Bart moving through the hallway and got up himself, moving into the hall. Bart had a rifle and was peering through the front of the shop.

"No lights," hissed Bart as he scanned. There was more gunfire and voices, men yelling. Some sounded in distress; others sounded like they were issuing orders. It all sounded very close as the two men stood frozen in the hallway, listening to what could very well be the killing of other human beings.

Jared's breath was coming in short ragged gasps, and he could feel the adrenalin surging through his veins, threatening to take over in the form of panic. He took a moment, trying to gather himself. He needed to control what was happening and to take stock of his body and how it was reacting to a threat that was real, but not necessarily imminent. The commotion was outside the gun store, close enough so Jared could decipher the voices as male and the language as English, but too distant to make out exactly what they were saying.

Bart turned slightly, looking over his shoulder. "You good?" Jared nodded.

"Where's your fucking weapon, man?" Bart growled.

Jared slipped sheepishly back into his room and grabbed the Glock off his bed, returning to Bart's side.

"Finger off the trigger," was all Bart said as the two listened to the voices as they faded into the distance. Bart stood at the front of the shop for another thirty minutes before turning to Jared. "Leave that pistol behind again and I'll duct-tape it to your fucking hand." Without another word, Bart stalked off to bed.

Jared couldn't remember having a worse night's sleep in his life. He tossed and turned, fell asleep and dreamed of the screams he heard that night, then would wake feeling fatigued and uneasy.

Not much was said the next morning as the two men ate, drank coffee, and got Jared out the back door and on his way. He was sure to keep his shirt pulled down, covering the Glock on his right hip along with the four extra magazines on his left side. The ammo was heavy, the tops of the magazines chafed his side if he wasn't careful, and the added weight had his back aching by three in the afternoon. Bart came unglued when Jared mentioned carrying the ammo in the trailer, causing Jared to quickly abandon the idea purely in an effort to stop Bart's barrage of curses and insults.

Jared knew today's route better than all the others, having mentally rehearsed all the turns and street names in his head prior to leaving. As he pedaled, his mind raced with all these thoughts, but he was also scanning the road ahead, looking for anything that looked like it wasn't right. Three blocks from the

Safeway store, Jared passed two dead men lying face down in a front yard. They were on the ground in a myriad of awkward positions, like puppets dropped by a child suddenly called for dinner. Jared wondered if they had been shot, and assumed they were leftovers from the previous night's festivities.

Jared pedaled on past the corpses, closing to within a block of Bart's designated Safeway. He dismounted the bike, pushing it along the sidewalk, all the while searching for a good spot to watch the store before going in. He moved to the rear of a business across the street from the Safeway, hiding the bike and trailer behind a dumpster. Jared found an old pallet and leaned it against the side of the building, climbing up till he could reach the rungs of a ladder that stretched up to the roof.

He grabbed the rungs and hoisted himself up the ladder until he crested the rooftop, where he transitioned into a slow crawl across the roof towards the opposite side. The roof was flat tar and gravel that played hell with his knees during the crawl. He reached the far side, swallowed hard, then peeked over the slightly raised edge towards the Safeway. Jared brought the binoculars to his eyes in order to scan the front of the deserted shell of a business.

The store was in a state of disarray, with shopping carts strewn about, the front glass on the business smashed, and the interior too dark to discern anything inside. Jared sat on the rooftop for what seemed like hours, nothing moving except his occasional shift to relieve aching joints. Birds flew by, the wind blew, and the clouds blotted out the sun's warming rays. The temperature had dropped and Jared was beginning to feel stiff. He was also aware of the time he was taking out of his day by watching the store. He would get maybe two loads at this pace, but he was more than a little apprehensive about simply strolling into this store and running down the shopping list.

Jared heard a scuffing sound and tensed, slowly pulling the binoculars from his eyes in order to widen his field of view. He didn't see anything, but he had definitely heard something other than the birds and the light breeze. Instinctively, he lowered his body so only his eyes peered over the top of the roof line.

The human eye is attracted to movement, and this little fact didn't fail Jared as he caught something in his peripheral vision, to the left of the Safeway. Slowly, ever so slowly, he brought the binoculars back to his eyes and stared down at the spot where he'd seen movement. He locked on the cause, and his blood felt cold running through his veins as he looked at the face of the very man he'd seen murder two young boys just days before.

Adrenalin surged through Jared's body, washing over him like a tsunami. His breath quickened and became shallow as he gazed upon the man's smiling face. The man walked with two others, most likely the same two he'd been with at the time of the murders, but Jared wasn't sure. He was focused solely on the cause of the boys' deaths, and he was staring at the same man's smug fucking face now.

Jared's mind wandered to an old man he knew and his words regarding situations like this very one. Let the rush be your motivator, let it strengthen you, don't let it weaken you, Bart had said. Bart had gone on to say Jared would never feel more alive than when he was face-to-face with death himself. It was like riding a giant wave: you could fight it and end up balled up on the ocean's floor, or you could ride it, feel the wind in your hair and enjoy the rush, Bart had chortled. Jared could feel the ill effects of this rush starting to take hold and, with it, a twinge of fear tightened in his chest.

He rolled over and took a deep breath, trying to steel his nerves. *Goddamn, that felt better.* He took two more deep breaths as he rolled back over and reacquired the murderous trio below. He felt a hell of a lot better being able to see them than when he rolled over and lost sight of them. He pondered this for a moment and decided to visit this little phenomenon at a later time, and he'd do it over a bourbon with the old man.

It was weird how he'd just done that. He'd gone from a mental fetal position to one of almost a predator. He watched as the men approached the front of the store, entered and were out of sight for several minutes before reappearing, each man holding a bottle of alcohol. The men were laughing and joking and drinking the liquor as they made their way to a set of tables and chairs outside the store. They sat on a table and continued drinking and talking. They didn't seem concerned about their surroundings as they drank and prattled on about who knows what. Jared was too far from the men to hear what they were saying, only catching an occasional word along with their loud laughter.

The men drank for what seemed like an hour before picking up and slowly moving up the street in the direction they'd come. Without thinking, Jared slunk to the roof's edge where he'd originally ascended, and dropped silently down the same ladder, landing lightly on the ground. He moved around the building until he had a visual of the retreating men. The men were about two hundred yards in front of Jared as he threaded his way through bushes and abandoned vehicles, following at what he thought was a safe distance.

Bart had told him the range on a handgun was not more than about twenty-five yards, and that was in the hands of a trained and experienced person. Jared didn't think that untrained drunk assholes would be good past ten yards, so his two-hundred-yard cushion felt right. The men were obviously intoxicated by now, their voices growing louder and louder with each gulp of the liquor.

The men went no more than three hundred yards up the street before turning into the yard of a small cottage-style house. Jared watched as the men moved onto the porch and sat down, talking, laughing and drinking. Jared watched from the cover of an abandoned SUV as the men sat on the porch. The cottage was well kept by its previous owners, making the thugs look starkly out of place on its front porch.

As Jared watched the hoodlums, his eye caught an ever so slight movement in the window of a neighboring house. He scanned the front and thought he saw a shadowy figure hunched in the front window as if watching the three men. There hadn't been many people on the streets, and Jared hadn't given it much thought till now, wondering if it was due to men like these. The kind of men who caused decent people to hole up in their homes, too frightened to venture out. He imagined a family with small children inside the house, held hostage by these animals. The thought angered him and then scared him equally as bad.

In the old world of just a few days ago, Jared could have been angered by some other human's driving, cutting in line or whatever, and he would have simply been angry, and that would have been the end of it. People could glare at each other and even raise their voice at one another, but the threat of physical violence was very low. Jared was quickly realizing a dirty look in this new and not so improved world would likely land you face down in a puddle of your own fluids. He wondered what the end result would be after the dust settled and people began living their lives again. Would it be a more polite society or a society in which people simply avoided contact with each other?

After some time, the men began to talk less, slump in their chairs, and generally look like a bunch of drunk and tired criminals. Jared moved around the block and climbed over a couple of fences until he positioned himself in the side yard of the house next to the little cottage. He was less than ten yards from the men and could clearly hear them conversing in their slurred slang. One of the men had actually passed out and was slumped over in the chair he occupied, while the other two talked about harassing him, but never did. Jared drew the Glock and slowly pointed it at the man he'd seen murder the two boys.

His breathing slowed as he held the weapon on the man's chest, simply enjoying the ability to point the gun at the man and have there be no consequences. He moved his finger to the trigger, thinking of the two young boys this animal had gunned down like dogs, his finger tightening ever so slightly on the weapon's trigger.

A calm had blanketed Jared, making him feel very comfortable pointing his weapon at these vermin. He thought as he took in the slack on the Glock's trigger how the man would be surprised and would never know why Jared had shot him. This animal would die with a huge question mark flooding his head. Another thought invaded Jared's mind: it was the other two men and how as soon as he shot their friend, he'd either have to flee or shoot the other two as well. This thought caused some anxiety, causing him to ease the pressure off the trigger.

Although the pressure was off the trigger, Jared held the sights on the man's chest as he sat with his friends, completely oblivious to how close the Reaper was to taking his putrid life. Something in the dark and far depths of Jared's brain told him to look up. He couldn't put his finger on it, but when he looked up, he went rigid.

In the window, not four feet from his head, was a man's face staring out at him. The man looked terrified. Jared had turned his head only slightly, keeping the Glock trained in the general direction of the three men, when the man in the window began slowly shaking his head as if warning Jared not to go through with his deadly intentions. Jared nodded ever so slightly, lowering the Glock to a low-ready position.

The man's head changed from a shaking motion to a nodding motion, his eyes darting back and forth between Jared and the men. Slowly, Jared lowered himself and began backing away from the men until he was in the backyard. Jared stood and was about to start for the fence when the back door creaked open and the man stood there assessing Jared.

"Thanks for not starting a war here in our neighborhood," the man whispered. Jared didn't respond as the man continued, "There are more inside the house. They would have come out and killed you and probably me and my family."

Jared nodded. "I saw 'em kill two kids a few days ago."

The man just blinked and stared back at Jared. The two men studied each other for a few seconds before Jared holstered the Glock and vaulted the rear fence, disappearing from the man's sight. Jared moved quickly as he made his way back to the Safeway. He grabbed his bike and trailer from behind the dumpster and wasted no time getting back to his mission at hand.

Jared entered the store without concern for who may be inside and was immediately greeted with the stench of rotten dairy. He covered his face with his shirt and tried his best not to vomit.

Once he secured all the nonperishable items he could carry from Bart's list, he pedaled in the direction of the gun store. As he pedaled, the realization of what he had done back at the cottage caved in on him like a broken dam. First, he felt cold and wet, then he began to overheat, and that was when the sweat began cascading from his pores.

He wasn't crying, but he felt like he was as he pedaled the bike with all his energy, his emotions roiling and bashing at his very sanity. He was hanging on by a thread, his vision slightly blurred with a complete absence of any sort of peripheral sight. As Jared spiraled towards an abyss of blackened uncertainty, he pulled the bike to the curb, retching the contents of his belly into the gutter. When he finished, he dry heaved a half dozen additional times, bent at the waist, streams of mixed bile and saliva hanging from his gaping mouth.

What the fuck had he been thinking getting that close to those guys in order to satisfy his want for revenge on behalf of the dead boys? He was so far out of his comfort zone, and now he was tossing his breakfast all over the ground, sweating and generally a ripe mess, for what? He hadn't even confronted the guys, he spied on them and this was how his body was reacting. He was having a goddamn nervous breakdown over nothing. What he had done equated closely to viewing a lion at the zoo, which he'd done in the past and never lost his lunch.

Jared's anger began creeping to the surface as he wiped his mouth and spat in a futile attempt to purge the horrific taste of puke from his mouth. Never before had he been so aware of his deficiencies as a man, and it angered him. He felt impotent in this new world, because he was unable to thrive like he had in the world of old. The anger boiled inside him, caused by the shame manufactured by his cognizant realization of where he lined up in this current and seemingly ever-evolving food chain. He previously stood at or near the top of the old food chain, and now he wasn't even sure he qualified as substantive nutrition on the scale of this new food chain.

After pulling himself together, Jared began pedaling back towards the gun store, slower than before simply because he didn't have the energy to push himself hard after his little episode. His stomach was empty and he felt dehydrated. A short time later he pulled to the rear of the gun store, dismounted, and knocked three times on the back door.

Bart cautiously opened the door, peering past Jared, scanning the rear parking lot as if expecting trouble. Jared sighed, pushing his way inside. He left the bike in the hall and went straight to the workshop, where he flopped into a chair and let out a long breath, trying to wrap his head around everything he'd just seen and done. Bart stood in the doorway, staring at him, not saying a word. Jared ran his hands over his face, feeling the beard that had begun to grow.

"I'll finish up tomorrow; I'm not going back out today," Jared rasped as Bart moved across the room and grabbed two plastic cups along with the bottle of bourbon. Both men drank in silence, Bart refilling their cups when they were dry. Jared drained his third cup and held it up, rotating it in front of his face.

"You know, Bart, I didn't drink before I met you. I think you're a bad influence." With that, he slid the cup across the table, and Bart refilled it without uttering a word. "Well, I mean, I had a beer every now and then, but I didn't keep booze in the house and never had more than one drink at a time. Didn't care for the taste and how it made me feel the next day."

Bart finished freshening up his own cup. "Well, my boy, if you're gonna run around town with a loaded gun in your waistband, getting shot at and pretty much living in a dying world, you should have a drink every now and again, ya fucking owe it to yourself."

Jared hoisted his cup towards Bart. "*Salute*, ole boy," he said, feeling kind of silly before drinking it down in one swallow.

Chapter 18

THE LATE AFTERNOON sun cast Jared's shadow long on the debris riddled sidewalk as he hoisted the last load of the day into the trailer, which was already burgeoning. He stood back with a prideful smile stretched across his face. He'd accomplished a lot and was about to head off when an idea came to mind.

He stowed the bike and trailer, ensuring they were well hidden, then set out on foot towards the house where he'd seen the man in the window. He carefully moved through the neighborhood, approaching the house from the rear, hoisting the bags over the fence. He wasn't going to knock or make any sound, he'd just leave the food on the back porch, where he prayed they would find it and hopefully make their lives just a little easier.

Jared had chosen two strong bags with plastic handles. Once he reached the fence leading into the rear yard of the house where he had seen the man, he secured a short length of rope to both bags' handles and scrambled over the fence. He pulled on the rope, hoisting both bags of food over the fence, turned towards the back door, and froze. The door stood hanging open, only connected to the doorjamb by a single hinge. The home was very dark inside, and it was apparent the door had been forced open.

When Jared was able to collect his thoughts, he found the groceries lying on the ground at his feet, the Glock clutched tightly in his hand. *When did that even happen?* he thought. Before another thought passed through his head, he was moving forward to the back door, offset to the left, making it easier for his right-handed shooting style to cover the dark entrance to the house and still stay out of any direct line of fire as he approached. Bart was changing him and doing it drastically in a very short period of time. One thing jumped out at him as he reached the door. The brass doorknob had what looked like bullet holes in it. Someone had fired rounds into the door and then kicked it off its moorings in order to enter the house.

Seeing the bullet holes gave Jared pause as he stood as still as a statue, looking into the inky darkness of the house's interior, the primal animal in him reared its head as he sniffed the air near the back door, searching for any evidence of what laid just inside the door frame. It all smelled of death and decay; hell, the whole fucking world was dying, why wouldn't it smell like that?

Jared was pretty much as scared as he had ever been and couldn't really imagine being any more scared. Had he reached his max in the scared department, like a car reaching its top speed? Well, if he had, he was still able to function, think and make decisions. This must have been what Bart had talked about, controlling your fear and falling back on your training.

He decided right then and there he was going in and helping these people. If they were all right, he'd leave them the food and, if they needed help, he would do what he could. He'd go back to the store and get bandages, medicine, or whatever they needed.

He braced himself for the unknown and squirmed through

the smashed doorway, entering the interior and making way more noise than he would have liked. Once inside, he stood and swept the Glock in a 180-degree scan of the room, keeping close to the wall.

Bart had showed him some simple ways to get into a less than friendly room with the least amount of exposure. Bart was adamant that Jared not over-penetrate a room he was entering for the first time. He explained to Jared that if he had a partner, that rule applied to them both, but if he was alone, that rule was golden. If you ran into the middle of a room, Bart had explained, now you had potential threats at 360 degrees on the compass.

If you entered, moved out of the doorway and to the left or right, and kept near the wall, you kept all the threats in front of you, 180 degrees, fucking half the headache. Bart had him practice this a hundred times and used as many different rooms and furniture configurations as he could come up with while confined to the gun store. He showed Jared how he could read a room from outside the doorway and enter it accordingly based on structural design and furniture placement

These lessons came flooding back as Jared scanned the small washroom. He waited for a solid thirty-seconds as his eyes began to adjust before moving through a doorway on his left and into the kitchen. From there he could see the living room and the body of a man lying face down near the front door, which was also slightly open. Like the back door, the front door was forced open and hung limply on its hinges. Jared could not be sure the man on the floor was the man he'd seen in the window, but he was sure the man was dead.

Jared moved to the man's side and inspected him closely. The man was shot in the body and possibly the legs and arms, but he'd also been shot several times in the back of the head. As Jared rolled him over, bullets actually fell out of his mouth, eyes and who knows what other holes, natural or manmade.

Jared dropped the man back to the carpet and stepped back, breathing heavily, a shiver running quickly through his tense body.

There was blood everywhere near the front door and, as Jared's eyes continued to adjust, he was able to make out in more detail the scene inside this little single-family dwelling. The tiled entranceway at the front door was soaked in bloody footprints. Jared studied the footprints like he knew what he was looking at. He almost smiled as he thought how utterly ridiculous this endeavor was, almost turning away, when the humor left him and he began to see a pattern, a story in the mess on the tile.

There were larger footprints, obviously belonging to a man or men, Jared checked the deceased man's shoe tread and determined the footprints in the blood were not his. There was a smaller set of footprints, then that changed, and Jared could see why. There was a woman's shoe, saturated in blood, off to the side of the entranceway, and then there was a small bare-foot print on the tile along with one small shoed footprint and the other larger footprints.

Jared found himself staring out the front door; they'd come over here from next door, killed this man, and taken his wife or daughter. Rage washed over Jared; he never felt this way before and hoped he would never feel this way again. A slight noise behind him nearly caused him heart failure as he spun, bringing the Glock's sights up in the direction of the sound. It was a cupboard in the kitchen ten feet behind him. He immediately moved off centerline to the left of the cupboard's door. Jared pointed the gun down at the small door and thought whatever was inside had to be a cat or some other pet; the cupboard was too small for a man.

He pulled the door open, careful to keep his finger off the trigger. He didn't want any frightened accidental discharges that would bring that horde from next door over. What Jared found in that cupboard changed the rest of his life, and it wasn't a cat. A small girl sat huddled inside the cupboard, feet pulled in, knees drawn to her chest, eyes wide with fright and wet with tears, but otherwise silent.

Did she witness her father's murder?, he wondered as they both stared at each other. After a few seconds, Jared lowered the Glock and then slid it into the holster, after which he leaned back, resting on his hands, then sinking the rest of the way onto the floor, where he sat looking at this tiny little human. She looked to be somewhere between five and seven years old; Jared couldn't be sure, as his experience with kids was right around zero.

Her small frail body was shaking, yet no sound came from her. She was crying, but doing it quietly. Had Bart trained this kid? Had the scene inside the house been a fraction less horrifying, Jared was sure he would have laughed out loud at the thought. Instead, he stared slack-jawed at the girl, chest tight, barely breathing, knowing full well the person taken by the gang next door had to be the little girl's mother.

As he sat there in a stranger's house, face-to-face with the family's recently orphaned child, a slight, but very powerful change began slowly seeping into Jared's very being.

"Wait here. I'll be right back." Jared hefted himself off the floor and moved to the backyard, where he left the groceries on the ground. He grabbed a bottle of water and some granola bars before returning to the house. He laid the items at the little girl's feet and stepped back.

"Stay here. I'll go get your mother."

The little girl just stared at him, crying silently. Jared stood, closed the cupboard door, checked that all four magazines he carried were in place, and then drew the Glock. He moved to the rear door and checked that the yard was clear. He listened and waited for five full minutes before exiting the small house and vaulting the fence the way he'd come. He moved to the yard directly behind the murdering horde's house and peeked through the fence boards, trying to discern any movement inside the house.

He wanted to walk up to the back door and just go on a shooting spree. Problem with that was he didn't know how many others were in the house, and he had to assume they were all armed. If he got himself killed, the little girl next door would die, hiding in a cupboard, starving, dehydrated, and probably covered in urine and feces. Worse than that, she'd die waiting for him to bring her mother back.

Jared shook the thought from his head as he caught sight of a lone man through a window in the back of the house. He saw the man for just a second before the recalcitrant human spilled out into the backyard through the back door. Jared ducked low and watched the man lower his zipper, relieving himself of the liquor he'd undoubtedly consumed earlier in the day. After he was done, the man returned to the house, slamming the back door closed.

To the right side of the rear door, Jared saw an access point to the crawl space, leading under the house. An idea began to take shape in his head, and he smiled in spite of the situation. Jared quickly returned to the small house the tiny waif was hiding in, and moved to the back porch, where several plants hung from hooks attached to the awning beams. Jared was able to remove the plants and unscrew five of the hooks, which he pocketed before returning to the rear of the horde's yard.

Jared took one last security check of his surroundings and then climbed the fence, entering the horde's yard. He wasted no time slithering across the yard to the access point. He pulled at the small piece of plywood, which succumbed to his actions with little effort. He rolled onto his back, grabbed the underside of the house's wall, and hauled himself feet first into the crawl space. Once he was inside, Jared reached back, drew the plywood back over the entrance and effectively blocking all outside light, leaving him in the semidarkness, but also leaving no indication of his presence.

Jared fished around inside his cargo pants pocket and withdrew a light stick, which he cracked and was immediately rewarded with the soft green glow of light. He could hear people's voices above him and could hear the floorboards creak when they moved throughout the house. Jared did not care a single bit about any of that right now, he had some work to do first, and then he would worry about where people were inside the house.

One hour later, Jared was finished with the first part of his plan. He crept around the entire crawl space, found every access point that led into the house, and marked it with a light stick. Based on his rudimentary understanding of plumbing and what he'd seen of the house next door, Jared guessed that the three access points were in two of the bedrooms and a coat closet near the front door. What Jared had also done was slowly screw a hook into the bottom of each access panel so that if the panel was removed and he wished to replace it, he'd have something to pull the panel back into place with.

He sat back, going over his plan. The access points were marked, the panels had the hooks securely in them, his weapon was ready, and he had more than enough ammunition. *Now what?* he thought. *Crawl out like a rat and start shooting?* He sat back and realized this plan was well thought out, just not completely thought out. He rested, drank some water, and even ate a power bar as he ran all the possible scenarios through his head over and over.

Something Bart always said came back to him. It had been when they were doing room-entry training and he was overthinking how to get into a room. Bart had stopped him and said, "At some point you're just going to have to do it. At one point you'll have to get off your ass, go through that door, and face the beast. You'll either make it or you won't, it's as simple as that, my friend."

Jared felt motivated by a myriad of emotions after seeing the girl, but now the adrenalin was beginning to fritter away, leaving him feeling gutted. Nothing in the tanks, the fatigue crashing into him so hard he nearly retched. Then fear bombarded his brain like a hailstorm, mixing with the fatigue and causing him to feel weak and ineffectual. *What was I thinking? Why did I even come back to the family's house? I'm going to get myself killed messing with these people.*

He looked out across the expansive crawl space, with all his hanging light sticks along with the hooks set in each hatch, and felt like he was looking at something someone else had done. Jared reached down and felt the smooth handle of the Glock, which further served to make the whole situation feel surreal and more like a Universal Studios experience than something born in reality. *Who the fuck have I become in the last several days?* he pondered. Less than two weeks ago, he would have never climbed under a house to even check for a plumbing issue let alone for...*For what?* he mused. *To rescue a mother?* Or was he there to exact revenge on the animals he'd seen butcher two young boys? He laid there on the cool hard ground for an hour, thoughts racing through his mind at speeds that would have made cable internet providers green with envy—two weeks ago, of course.

At the end of an hour, Jared had spent his entire emotional quota for the day and was left with his simple yet very effective analytical identity. He slowly moved his head, eyes tracking about the crawl space, assessing the placement of light sticks, hooks, thinking of his overall plan to engage these felons. Now there was an interesting word, *engage*. *What the fuck did it even mean? What did it mean now?* he wondered.

Two weeks ago, it had meant something different than today. Two weeks ago, if he planned on engaging someone, it would have been in a conversation not a gunfight. Now here he was about to engage a group of felons in a gunfight—why lie to himself? There would be no talking tonight; he planned on going up through those crawl space panels and shooting the ever-loving shit out of the men in that house.

He felt absolutely detached from who he had been two weeks prior, waiting for some part of his brain to take over and tell him to get the hell out from under that house and pedal his ass back to the gun store. No such part of his brain housing group came to his rescue. In fact, his heart quickened at the thought of his impending engagement, and not in the way it had in the past when he felt gripped by fear. This was a different feeling, one he felt he could control or even manipulate into something useful. Jared rationalized the whole thing to himself: if he was a beet farmer and woke up one morning to find his fields filled with corn by some unknown power other than God, well then, he'd be a motherfucking corn farmer, wouldn't he? *Adapt or die.*

Chapter 19

JARED COULD SEE through the vents in the foundation and knew it was late in the afternoon because the sun was disappearing behind the taller trees. He knew these men had stayed up drinking into the wee hours and hoped they would now be napping. He couldn't bank on it, but he could hope. He decided he would enter the house through an access panel in a rear bedroom, shoot whoever was in that room, peek into the hall and try to shoot more of the horde, then he would slide back into the crawl space and seal it up. Jared crawled to the panel and tested it.

The panel was snug, but he was able to work it loose with a little effort and hardly a sound. He pushed up on the panel, holding it up an inch or two so he could see into the room. There were no closet doors which offered Jared a clear view of two men lying asleep on two children's beds. The men's heavy breathing was the only audible sound he could hear.

Jared carefully slid the access panel to the side and rose to his feet. He stood in the access point, the floorboards near his waist, and the Glock trained on the two sleeping murderers. He felt like he should have some moral struggle right about now, but didn't. In fact, he felt no preemptive feelings of remorse in regard to what he was about to do to these men. He was glad for this and worried at the same time; he wasn't a violent person and had gone to great lengths to avoid all violence in his previous life.

He had not played contact sports; instead he competed in other ways, playing golf and tennis in high school. The last couple of weeks had changed him, and he realized these men would do far worse to him than he was about to do to them if they woke from their slumber.

Without further hesitation, Jared sighted on the closest man's head and just fucking pulled the trigger. The bullet passed through the man's brain, not causing so much as a flinch from the stricken soul. The second man sat bolt upright in the bed, staring blankly at the bedroom door. Jared shot him in the face, causing him to slump forward, and then like a slinky, he eased off the bed, sprawling out on the floor, blood flowing from his face like a garden hose. Without thinking, Jared picked up a child's boot from the closet floor and hurled it at the bedroom window as hard as he'd ever thrown anything in his life. His effort was rewarded with the shattering of glass as the boot exploded through the glass pane.

Shouts came from the front of the house as Jared slipped back into the crawl space, drawing the panel down behind himself. He immediately crawled to the front of the house and positioned himself under the coat closet access panel. He could distinctly feel his heart pumping blood—not thudding, but actually the contraction of the muscle as it forced massive amounts of blood through his veins and arteries. He was also pretty sure it was making noise, which alarmed him.

He kept the Glock trained in the direction of the ill-fated bedroom and its dead occupants. Jared hoped the animals would think someone had fired on their comrades from outside the window, but realized it wouldn't take a rocket scientist to figure out what had really happened when they found the boot outside the room and not inside. Then again, they were drunken, uneducated scumbags, who lacked any sort of forward-thinking skills, so Jared hoped for the best, but planned for the worst.

He could hear most of the shouting coming from the back area of the house and figured they'd found his handiwork and didn't much care for it. Jared's heart continued racing as he suddenly felt sick to his stomach. The adrenaline had come and come hard. Now he was suffering from its effects, and he looked down. His hands were shaking so badly, he holstered the Glock for fear of torching off a round accidentally. He knew what was happening, and he knew he had to hang on and ride it out.

He watched the access panel he had used to kill the two men in the bedroom, waiting for it to be removed and for scumbags to pour into the tiny crawlspace; it never happened.

After ten minutes, Jared had to smile, thinking how utterly fucked up all those pieces of shit were above him, and bizarrely, he liked it. They had no idea what happened other than there had been gunfire and two of their shithead friends were dead. Again, Jared was surprised by how little he felt in the way of guilt for having killed two human beings. He wondered what they were thinking and wished he could see or even hear them. If they thought someone had broken the window and executed the two in the bedroom, would they go next door looking for the culprit? This, in turn, could cause them to find and kill that little girl.

Jared moved around under the house, peering through the vents in the foundation, trying to catch a glimpse of the shit bags and what they were doing. He crawled to the side that flanked the house the little girl was hiding in, straining his ears in an attempt to ascertain whether they had gone next door. He heard nothing and was relieved.

After putting his knees and elbows through hell, he crawled back to the front area of the house and rolled to his back, the adrenalin beginning to wear off and fatigue beginning to envelope his body yet again. *How much more of this could his body and mind take?* he wondered. Then in the darkness, Jared shook his head, thinking how all of this stress was his own doing. He had chosen to crawl under this house and kill those two miscreants.

Every step of the way his mind and body begged him to stop, yet some part of him had not stopped. In fact, something inside of him charged forward with the ferocity of a Bengal tiger. Jared knew he could stop now but what would be the point? Maybe he should stop because the asshole he saw murder the two boys was not one of the two he'd gunned down in the bedroom.

Jared laid under the front area of the house for what seemed like hours, drifting in and out of a sleepy state, waiting for his next opportunity. The next opportunity finally presented itself; he heard voices accompanied by footsteps on the front porch. Several men entered the house and were talking about what happened or what they thought happened. Jared realized the men thought the attack came from a neighbor and overheard them discussing how they planned on going on a killing spree as soon as the sun went down. Jared heard them planning and realized, after listening to the voices, there were only three shitheads left alive.

Jared stretched and moved into a better position to hoist up the access panel, slowly pushing up on the panel, which rose up easily until he could see into the interior of a black room. Still hearing the men's voices and seeing a dim light seeping under the doorjamb, Jared knew he was in some sort of coat closet. He slid the access panel slowly to the side, felt around the small closet, familiarizing himself with its size, then stood up in the hole.

Again, the floorboards were near his waist like they'd been

in the bedroom. Jared knew the front wall of the house was directly to his right, so if he opened the closet door, he would be sweeping to the left, which, in theory, would be where the shitheads should be.

Jared weighed his options, trying to decide if he should try to open the door slowly or simply come out blasting. He analyzed these two choices, knowing both had pros and cons. If he tried to slowly open the door and by chance one of the shitheads saw a closet door opening after what had happened earlier, Jared was fairly sure they would simply pour a couple of hundred rounds through the closet door and that would be the end of him. He didn't care for that outcome---not even a little bit. If he were able to get the door opened slowly, he would have time to acquire his targets, but he was not comfortable with his fifty-fifty chance of getting ventilated in the process.

If he flung the door open, he would surprise the holy crap out of these three, but would have less time for target acquisition. Jared surmised a dynamic and fast operation was in order. Bart had always preached being fluid and keeping your opponent off-balance. Jared was pretty sure these guys' nerves were more than a little rattled after the mysterious killing of their fellow criminals. He further surmised they would experience an "oh shit" moment when he came blazing out of that coat closet, and that would be all the time he needed to kill at least one or two of 'em.

In the end he decided to fling the door open and shoot while standing in the access hole. Jared gave it not a second more thought, reaching forward, turning the doorknob and heaving outward on the door.

When the closet door flung open, Jose Martinez was sitting on a couch in the living room, talking with his two friends Geraldo and Matias. Jose saw the closet door swing open and saw a white boy standing in the access hole to the house's crawl space, which all seemed surreal. The man standing waist deep in a hole inside the closet did not fully register with Jose as a threat. When Matias pitched forward, smashing through a glass table, it registered—all of it. Jose tore at the pistol he kept shoved down the front of his pants as Geraldo also crumpled to the ground, clutching his throat. Jose's gun was out and he fired wildly at the devil in the closet.

Jared felt a tug at his right hip and then a burn at the side of his neck; he knew he got two of these guys and tried to focus on the third. As he aimed at the third man, he realized it was the same man who'd killed the two kids. Jared squeezed the trigger, the bullet catching the man in the left cheek, knocking him back onto the couch. Jared continued to fire as he rose from the access hole, exiting the closet. Jared was screaming at the top of his lungs as the smug look on Jose's face vanished, replaced with a look of panic.

Jared fired till the slide locked to the rear, indicating an empty magazine. Jose was shot and wounded badly, but not dead as Jared reloaded, crossing the room in two easy steps. Even as he walked in the open, he could hear Bart's voice. *"Cover will save your life; don't be a Rambo out there. Being in the open during an active gunfight is a sure way to die,"* Bart had said. *"Destroy your target; then and only then can you venture into the open."* Jared knew it was wrong, but he was so far off the reservation that neither fear nor training was controlling his actions at this point. Rage sat comfortably in the driver's seat, piloting Jared's every move.

"Where's the lady from next door?" Jared demanded in a slightly higher and more hysterical voice than he would have liked to use.

Jose didn't answer, as it would have been too difficult in his current state. He was pretty broken up, and he knew he would be dead soon, whether this crazy white boy finished him or not. He couldn't breathe, and from what he heard, that meant he had a collapsed lung. Jose stretched out on the couch, his eyes fixed on his gun which laid on the floor in the middle of the room. He couldn't remember how it had gotten there, yet there it was. Every gunfight he'd ever been in had involved him and several of his friends ambushing someone. He couldn't believe how absolutely violent this little encounter had felt. *What the fuck just happened?*

As Jose laid dying, he wished he could kill this white boy. *Where did he come from anyway?* He walked right out of a closet and killed them all and was undoubtedly the same person who'd killed Thomas and Manny a few hours before. He couldn't remember searching the closet after the gang had taken over this small home. Jose wondered if this guy had been in the closet the entire time. He tried to breathe, but ended up coughing and spraying blood everywhere. The man was standing over him, inspecting him now.

"You killed those two kids a few days ago, and now look at you," the man said.

Jose was confused now, dying and confused, not a state he much liked, but he didn't really have too much of a say in the matter.

"You killed the guy next door and now you're gonna die," Jared said as he stood towering over the dying man. "You could have helped those people; instead you've killed and turned this neighborhood into a lawless wasteland."

Jose stared back at Jared, wondering what the hell he was talking about.

"I was a computer engineer, man and now, in less than three weeks, I'm out here killing people in order to survive. You and your people did that to me, not this power outage; you did it to me," Jared shouted. "I should be drinking a mocha and checking my fucking email, not crawling around under your house, trying to figure out which room to pop up in so I could kill you."

It was then Jose realized what had happened. The bullet left the Glock, entering Jose's forehead, deflected slightly to the right, and exited through his left ear, where it lodged deep in a cushion of the couch.

Jared turned and swept through the house, searching for other members of Jose's group and the woman from next door. He found her in the bathroom, very dead and very naked. They had most likely defiled her in ways Jared didn't want to think of, and then cut her throat as she laid broken and helpless in the bathtub. The woman's body brought Jared back from the fog caused by the gunfight.

He quickly realized he wasn't shaking any longer, but that he was bleeding. He looked in the mirror and saw a nasty tear in the side of his neck. The bullet had grazed him, but it also caused a significant wound, which was oozing blood down the front of his shirt. His hip had also been grazed, but that had already stopped bleeding and was simply aching now.

Jared looked down at the woman lying in the tub before dropping to the floor and rummaging through the cabinet under the sink. He didn't find a first aid kit, but he did find a bag of feminine pads, which he ripped open, applying one to his neck. He pressed down, grabbed another pad, and did the same. He placed three of the pads against his wound and then searched for a way to secure them so he had the use of both of his hands.

He was about to take his own belt off when it occurred to him to use the belt from one of the dead bodies in the next room. They liked to sag their pants, yet they still wore belts; these people were essentially aliens to Jared. He had no understanding of their culture or any of their ways of life.

Jared moved back to the living room and chose Matias, who had the least amount of gore associated with his demise. Jared quickly stripped the man of his belt and returned to the tiny bathroom. The belt only wrapped around his neck once, leaving eight inches of length to flap around. Jared inspected his work in the mirror. He was a horrible sight with the blood-soaked pads secured to his neck with a length of red cloth belt. He looked like something out of a bad horror film.

Jared staggered out the front door and walked to the next-door neighbor's house. Inside, he found the little girl still holed up in the cupboard. He opened it, motioning for her to come out. She did the opposite, using her feet to push herself back farther into the recess.

He closed the door and sat against the wall, thinking about what had just happened, what he'd just done, and pretty much the state of his whole world. Jared was not a particularly religious man, but he raised his face to the ceiling and mentally sought some sort of divine guidance. Nothing happened, so after a few moments, he lowered his face into his hands and, again, cried. He did this quietly, but the tears flowed like rain down his face, dripping onto the filthy kitchen floor. This was beginning to be a regular thing, and Jared didn't even care, the recent cries somehow cleansing his mind, after which he felt refreshed, like he performed a reset of sorts.

Taking a deep breath, he wiped his face, opened his eyes, and stared directly into the wide and uncrying eyes of the little girl. She cracked the door of her sanctuary spot and was gaping wide-eyed at this man curled up on the floor of her parents' kitchen floor, crying like a baby. Jared could definitely see fear in her eyes, but not as much as he'd seen before. Much of the fear was replaced with bewilderment and curiosity.

The little girl slowly crawled out of the cupboard and slithered into Jared's lap, shocking him so thoroughly, that he didn't move. She made her way into his arms, glancing at her dead father for but a second before readjusting her head on his chest to face the opposite direction. Jared slowly drew his arms around the frail little frame of this tiny human and squeezed her to him, feeling her little body move with each breath.

Jared was an only child and had never had children, so this was all new to him in the sense that he had never had siblings or been around children as an adult. He knew one thing, he wanted out of this house and out of this godforsaken neighborhood. He carried the girl out the front door and looked up and down the street before walking back towards his bike.

He caught a couple of people staring through windows as he passed, and when he asked if they knew the little girl, they all quickly disappeared. People had more than enough to worry about with their own families and the lack of food, not to mention the violent nature of the streets in recent days. A man could leave his family to go forage for food and either get killed, or return to his home only to find his family dead or his wife gone. Jared didn't blame these people for ignoring him, but also realized it was an indication of how bad things were getting in the world. All these people knew was there had recently been a gunfight nearby and, now, a complete stranger was walking off with a little girl from their neighborhood, and no one was doing a damn thing to stop it.

As Jared walked, he thought back to his high school history teacher Mr. Lewis. The man was a veteran of some war and served in one of the armed forces; Jared couldn't remember which one. He did remember an entire day Mr. Lewis had spent talking about a letter written by Edmund Burke to Thomas Mercer in 1770. The letter became famous for a phrase Burke used: **"The only thing necessary for the triumph of evil is for good men to do nothing."**

Jared couldn't recall the whole class discussion, but it had made enough of an impression on him that he remembered the general message of Burke's letter. The man was trying to impress on Mercer the importance of banding together in order to fight evil. If evil guys like the ones he had killed could hold an entire neighborhood hostage, why couldn't the residents in that neighborhood get together and drive the assholes out of their neighborhood?

Jared thought about Bart, and how his own life had become remarkably better since joining forces with the old guy. Learn from the past, thought Jared; 1770 was not that different from now in that there were not too many support systems in place, and a man or woman had to take care of themselves and their family on their own.

Jared rode the bike full of supplies, the tiny girl perched atop all the canned food, winding his way through the streets. Jared decided he wanted to get back to Bart's place and would risk not moving slowly in order to get there. He had killed five guys not an hour ago and figured if anyone tried to stop him, he'd kill them as well.

The girl had not spoken a word and had not resisted when Jared took her from the house. She had made a decision in her tiny little mind, and it was to trust this stranger. He had no doubt she'd seen her father murdered; she'd seen him gunned down in the very room she watched cartoons in growing up. She had most likely seen her mother dragged from their home, and no doubt heard her cries of protest next door as the savages had their way with her. Jared shook the thoughts from his head and pedaled harder, feeling only dark warmth in his heart for what he'd done to those motherfucking animals.

Chapter 20

SWEAT SOAKED Jared's shirt and even dripped from his arm as he went to knock on the back door of Bart's gun store. Bart answered the door in his usual suspicious way, scanned the area, then stood clear as Jared forced his way in, pushing the bike, trailer, supplies and, lastly, the girl. Jared didn't say a word as he leaned the bike against a wall, scooped the little girl off the trailer, and carried her to the workshop, where he set her on a chair and busied himself getting her some water.

Bart stopped at the door, watching as Jared handed the little creature a plastic cup of water. The girl took the cup, tilted it to her lips, and didn't lower it until the cup was empty. Jared gave her another, and she did the same, handing it back expectantly. After she finished her third cup, Jared prepared a freeze-dried egg scramble and spooned some into a bowl, dropped a fork on the food, and slid it across the table to the girl.

She ate two bowls of the egg scramble before sitting back, her hunger temporarily at bay. Next Jared picked the girl up and carried her to the doorway where Bart was standing.

"Cover me," he said as he moved past the older man.

Bart grabbed a rifle from inside the workshop and followed Jared to the back door. Jared opened it and did a quick check of the lot before striding directly to the portable bathroom. He opened the door and set her inside, closing the door. The girl immediately opened the door and stood there, looking a little frightened.

"You want me to hold the door open while you go?" Jared asked.

She nodded and he held the door ajar, turning his head to look away, giving her some privacy. Bart mumbled something before taking a knee, facing away from the portable unit, and training the rifle out across the parking lot.

When the little girl was finished with her business, she stepped from the unit and looked up expectantly. Jared picked her up and headed back inside the building. He heard her use the portable unit and was relieved that she was fully sufficient in regard to toilet training. As he held her, Jared realized she smelled pretty ripe, and made a mental note to wash her the following day. He walked directly into his bedroom and placed the tiny form on his bed, drawing the covers over her.

"You can sleep here tonight. It's warm and safe," he said as he pulled the sleeping bag snug around her petite form. After tucking her into the bed, Jared stood and walked towards the door.

"Don't leave," came a barely audible voice.

Jared spun around, rushing to her side. "I'm not leaving you. I was going to go eat and then I'll come back."

She shook her head, tears welling up in her eyes. "Don't go," she pleaded again.

Jared sank to the floor next to the bed, leaning his head against the side of the mattress so she could see him. He watched as she relaxed a bit, wriggling deeper into the sleeping bag and, within five minutes, her breathing became rhythmic, letting Jared know she was asleep. Jared got to his feet, standing over her, thinking the last few weeks had probably been hard on the girl, but the last forty-eight hours had nearly killed her. She was half starved, dehydrated and probably hadn't slept in a couple of days. He looked at her closely, really for the first time, noticing her light brown hair, almond-shaped eyes and olive-colored skin. She was an angelic little girl under all that filth and grime.

Bart was patiently waiting in the workshop when Jared finally made his way through the door and fell into a chair in front of what remained of the egg scramble. Bart poured a healthy cup of whiskey for both men, sliding one across to Jared.

"What in the Sam hell are you gonna do with that kid?"

Jared chewed his food, swallowed, grabbed the whiskey, and took a long draw. After the whiskey, he set the cup down and leaned back. "Ah, I don't know, Bart. A better question would be what are we gonna do with her?"

"Now wait a goddamn minute," Bart blurted. "There is no we in this thing, whatever it is you've gone and done." Bart grabbed his cup and drained it, obviously upset. "Can't go grabbing kids and bringing 'em back here like this place is some sort of orphanage. Goddamn, boy, we ain't got enough for ourselves let alone the rest of the city."

Jared studied Bart for a long moment, then took another drink before speaking, choosing his words carefully. "Her father was murdered in front of her; her mother was dragged out of their house, taken next door and brutally raped and also murdered. I wasn't there, but I can almost guarantee she heard the whole affair with her mother."

Bart sat stone-faced, waiting for Jared to finish.

"I saw the family earlier, so I grabbed some extra food to leave on the back doorstep, when I saw the door was kicked in." Jared shook his head, remembering the scene. "I go inside and find her father shot to death in his own fucking living room. She's hiding ten feet away in a kitchen cupboard."

"So, you just snatched her up and brought her back here?" Bart asked.

Jared leaned back in his chair, eyes directed towards the ceiling for a moment before slowly replying, "No, not exactly."

Over the next thirty minutes, Jared relayed the day's events to Bart, who listened, never once interrupting. He sat stone-faced, listening to this computer geek tell him how he had gone out and, as an afterthought, decided to do a good deed, which resulted in five gang members being killed. Bart listened as Jared explained his plan and how he waited under the house, came up like a gopher, and laid waste to the vermin inside.

As Jared spoke, Bart noticed the blood on his pants and wondered what the neck wound looked like under all those bandages. As Jared explained how he used the feminine pads to stop the bleeding, Bart smiled inwardly. The kid was thinking on his feet, which was a very good thing if he wanted to survive in this new and very dangerous world. When Jared finished, he let out a long breath and finished his drink.

"Let's take a look at your wounds, clean 'em up so you don't get some godforsaken infection that ends up killing you." Bart got up and retrieved his first aid kit, dropping it on the table next to Jared. Bart laid out some bandages and antibacterial meds before removing the belt and ultimately peeling the maxi pads from Jared's bloodied neck.

"Ahhh, they got you good, kid. No real damage, but they tore a good chunk out of your fucking neck."

Jared winced as Bart worked on the wounds. In ten minutes, Bart had the wound on his neck cleaned and bandaged with gauze and real medical tape.

"Drop your drawers, kiddo," Bart commanded.

Jared gingerly got to his feet and removed his bloody pants, exposing the nice groove in his left hip, where the bullet had passed through the top layers of flesh and exited out the back of his trousers. This allowed Bart to clean and bandage the wound like a professional ER nurse. Considering his position, Jared bit his tongue and held back making any nurse jokes.

When Bart finished, he tossed a bottle of painkillers to Jared. "Take two tonight; it'll help you sleep. You can take more tomorrow if it's that bad. Just be careful, don't take 'em if you don't need 'em."

Jared opened the bottle and poured two of the little white pills into his hand.

"Last thing we need around here is a strung-out computer geek with a gun," Bart said, holding his hand out for the bottle.

Jared tossed the bottle back and popped the pills in his mouth. He washed them down with a swig from a bottle of water and stood. "You got another sleeping bag I can use?"

Bart nodded, getting to his feet before ambling off to retrieve Jared a sleeping bag. After getting the backup sleeping bag from Bart, Jared entered his bedroom. He could hear the girl's breathing the same as when he had left. In fact, she hadn't moved from the position he left her in. He quietly spread his sleeping bag on the floor next to the bed and climbed in. Jared could feel the day's events heavy on his soul as he drifted away into a very deep slumber.

Jared awoke to the sounds of Bart moving around inside the workshop. He rolled over and almost jumped out of the sleeping bag. The girl was sitting upright with her bag drawn about her shoulders, peering down at him. Her face was blank, not in a bad way, just staring, waiting for him to wake.

He smiled and sat up, rubbing the sleep from his eyes, then grimaced as the pain in his neck and hip struck like two simultaneous baseball bats dropping him back on the sleeping bag. The pain was so sudden and strong he just laid there a moment, mouth agape, quietly working through what was by far the most pain he'd ever felt. Slowly he started breathing again, grasping for his composure, trying to will the pain away. It did not work, but he was able to figure out some less painful positions.

Once he gained his feet, he reached out, taking the girl by the hand and leading her into the hallway, moving in the direction of the workshop.

Bart rose early that day, making sure breakfast and coffee were waiting when Jared led the hapless little damsel into the workshop. Bart glanced over, but stayed mute as Jared sat at the table, the girl crawling into his lap and resting her head against his chest. Bart looked over with a raised eyebrow. Jared shrugged, thinking he was along for the ride at this point.

Bart brought over two bowls heaped with sausage, eggs and whole wheat toast, the real deal, and it smelled wonderful. The girl ate slower this morning than she had the night before and drank much less. Jared and Bart ate their breakfast while watching the small child pick through her food, eating most of it before curling up back against Jared's chest.

Without warning, the little girl turned her head, looking up at Jared. "Can we go find my mom?" she quietly asked.

Bart and Jared glanced at each other before Jared responded, "Your mom's gone, and so is your dad."

The little girl sat up and squared her shoulders at Jared. "I know my daddy's gone, I saw it happen, but my mom was at the neighbor's house. I could hear her."

Both men sat speechless.

"She fought with those men. I think she was mad 'cause of what they did to my daddy."

All three sat in silence for a moment; then the girl returned to her nook in Jared's chest. "So, can we go get her?" the girl repeated.

"She's gone, those men hurt her real bad, and now she's gone," Jared said, the emotions welling up in him like an ocean swell.

Again no one in the room spoke until the little girl broke the silence. "Is that why you went over there and killed them all?"

This kid is something else, thought Bart. She kept amazing him with the stuff coming out of her mouth.

"I know what you did over there. You did the same thing they did to my daddy, and you said a lot of bad words when you were doing it."

Bart stifled a laugh and had to look away as Jared stared dumbfounded at this little creature in his lap. He now remembered he had indeed yelled some fairly horrible things at the men in the house when he burst out of the closet. It was like he lost control of his mouth in the throes of battle, and now he was being reminded of it by this little girl curled up in his lap.

Needing a change of subject and needing it quick, Jared asked, "What's your name?"

"Essie," replied the girl without raising her head from his chest. "I don't want to go back to my house, then," Essie said as Jared dipped his chin, nodding in hurried little gestures.

"Fair enough." Fair enough didn't even come close to how he felt about going anywhere near that neighborhood. He thought about his lack of remorse and how that bothered him more than the actual killings. Somehow Jared was thankful the little girl had entered his life. She took his mind off the fact he had slaughtered five human beings. Essie not only took his mind off it, but she was part of the validation process. Had he not found her hiding in that cupboard, he would never have had the drive to go next door and do what he'd done. He cupped her head in his hand and slowly rocked back and forth.

"Essie, I like that name. It's wholesome and has a nice ring to it," he said, still rocking the tiny form curled up in his lap. "How old are you Essie"? Jared prodded.

"Seven." She responded.

After breakfast, Jared occupied himself with setting up an

outdoor shower Bart had. It was a solar contraption and would produce warm water as long as it got direct sunlight. When Jared finished with the setup, Bart asked if he planned on putting her back in those clothes she was wearing. Bart had a way of letting Jared go down a road to nowhere and then calling him on it.

Jared held his arms in the air. "So, Master Jedi, where would one find clothes for a little girl?"

Essie sat in a chair, watching the men's exchange.

"How the hell should I know where to get clothes for a child?" Bart snapped.

Jared smirked. The old man usually had the answer, and here he was answerless. Jared enjoyed this briefly.

"I get clothes from Target," Essie murmured.

The men looked at Essie and nodded, like they knew that. Bart winked at Jared. "Looks like you're going to Target."

Back inside the workshop, Jared held a tape measure up, attempting to measure the length of Essie's arms and legs.

She made a face and backed away, saying, "The size is on the tag. I'm a size 7 pants and shirt."

Bart was loving every minute of this as he prepared a cup of coffee, glancing sideways at Jared while slowly shaking his head.

"Okay," Jared said, facing Essie, "I'm going out to get you some clothes, and Bart here is going to watch you. Is that okay with you?"

Essie glanced at Bart then nodded.

As Bart let Jared and the bike out the back door, he whispered in Jared's ear, "Get a size too big. Kids grow."

Jared mounted the bike, wincing at the pain in his hip as he pedaled out of the parking lot and onto the street. He hadn't taken any of Bart's pain meds until he knew he was going back out, and then he took two more of the little white pills. Bart changed the bandages again, giving Jared a chance to see both wounds in a mirror. When he saw the neck wound, it actually scared him.

It appeared much worse than the hip wound, but caused him significantly less pain than the jagged tear in his hip. He navigated from memory this time, no trailer, just a small day pack, racing through the deserted streets. Jared rode directly into the Target store, steering his way to the children's section. He stayed straddled on the bike and had the pack pulled around to his chest as he easily located the size 8s, grabbing several pairs of pants and several shirts, both long and short sleeve.

Jared was about to leave the store when the thought hit him: socks and underwear. Essie didn't wear diapers, so she probably wore underwear.

After he stuffed the pack with all the clothes, Jared pedaled out of the Target store and, instead of riding back to the gun store, he turned the bike deeper into the city, riding like a madman. His hip was throbbing and his neck had started to hurt more and more as he sped along a sidewalk and into a large parking lot. The REI store stood in front of him, dark and looted.

He wasn't overly concerned about striking out on this scavenging effort. After all, he was after a seven-year-old's all-weather jacket, a North Face or the like and, as he suspected, the children's section was literally untouched. Jared settled on a black waterproof North Face jacket for Essie.

People must have started to realize what was happening, and had looted most of the rest of the store. All the food was gone, along with nearly every piece of camping gear the store had carried. Jared remembered their sleeping arrangement and searched through the camping area until he found a small junior-size sleeping bag rated to 0 degrees Fahrenheit. He found a couple of light sticks and jammed them into his pack before leaving the store. He looked up and down the streets, saw no one, and began his journey back to the gun shop.

As Jared came around a corner, turning onto a street he intended to use to cut some time off his return trip, he locked the brakes on the bike and slid to a stop. Coming up the road was a large group of people pulling wagons and carrying children. Closer inspection of the group had Jared scrambling backwards, as several of the males in the group were armed with rifles. It was too late, they had seen him, and he could tell they were issuing orders to the women and children as the men moved to protect their group.

For a reason Jared could never identify, he stopped his retreat and slowly raised his hands, waiting as the group advanced. Everyone in the group was either grim faced or looked scared to death.

Jared was starting to second-guess his decision to stay and face this group as they drew abreast, but the armed men had their weapons hung at low ready. As much as this comforted him, Jared was also very aware of the fact that their low ready was in his direction, and Jared couldn't blame them. They were a haggard-looking group, desperate and frightened in appearance. Jared kept his hands up as they passed him one at a time. One of the men stepped away from the group and stopped in front of Jared, weapon low.

"I'm not one of the bad guys, man," Jared said to the man.

The man nodded and let the rifle hang by his side.

"Where you all headed?" Jared asked.

The man looked at the passing group. "Away from here, somewhere with no gangs."

Jared nodded his agreement with the man's statement. "Lots of that around here," Jared said flatly.

The man drew a deep breath, and Jared could tell he was not comfortable talking about where his little group was headed.

"I'm leaving too, just as soon as I get squared away with supplies," Jared blurted out, trying to gain the man's trust. He didn't know why he cared if the man trusted him or not. He was just so damn happy to be talking to another man other than the cantankerous Bart. "Headed to Florida to find my parents," Jared finished.

"Ah, hell," the man said, thrusting out his hand. "Name's Chad."

A huge smile spread across Jared's face as he grasped the man's hand, pumping it and smiling ear to ear. "Jared, I'm Jared."

Chad told Jared his group was headed to Monterey, where they were going to find work on a farm and earn their way, working for food and shelter. They had all come from the same neighborhood, which had recently fallen victim to looting and even murder. Gangs had begun looting the residential neighborhoods when the food ran out in the stores. They had even heard stories of women being kidnapped.

Chad told Jared the men had armed themselves and attempted to protect their neighborhood, and that was when three of his neighbors were killed. A gang had come in and began looting the homes and, when the men in the community stood up, trying to drive them out, a gun battle ensued, killing three of their men and two of the gang members. The attacks came more frequently after that until the people decided enough was enough.

As the last of the group's people passed the two men, Chad asked, "What are you doing riding around the streets? It's pretty dangerous out here for a group our size, not to mention someone alone."

It was Jared's turn to explain himself to Chad. Jared told him about the murder of the two kids and his finding the family dead and basically adopting their seven-year-old orphan. Jared left out the part where he single-handedly killed five of the gang members in a fit of rage, revenge and hatred. He didn't want to be judged and remembered something Bart always pushed, which was to make one's self seem less able so when the bell rang, your opponent would hopefully underestimate you.

As the last of the radio Flyer wagons was pulled past the two men, Chad gave Jared a friendly clap on the back. "I like you, Jared, and I hope you find your parents." With that, Chad rejoined his group and moved up the street.

For the first time in a very long time, Jared felt light of heart, maybe even a little happy. A simple conversation with a complete stranger had made his day, caused him to feel giddy, and painted a smile on his face. He turned and rode off towards the gun store.

Chapter 21

BART LET him in as usual, but cocked his head as Jared entered the store smiling and whistling a little tune. Bart closed the door and followed Jared into the workshop, where Essie was sitting, cleaning a pistol. Jared came to a screeching halt, took in the scene, and then stepped back out into the hall, where Bart was just catching up.

"Cleaning a gun, Bart? Really, you're having a little girl handle a firearm?"

Bart recoiled. "First off, did you get laid out there on your shopping trip?"

Jared shot him a warning look.

"She lives in a different world now, Jared. She will have to learn how to protect herself." Bart raised his hands, palms up. "No better time than the present."

The two of them re-entered the workshop and sat at the table with Essie. Jared grabbed a bottle of water, downed half of it, then set it on the table.

Bart gestured to Essie. "Smart kid there, she speaks two languages, Spanish and English."

Jared picked up a part of the gun Essie was cleaning, and started wiping it down, not saying a word.

"She's good in school, plays soccer, and takes dance lessons."

Jared placed the weapon part back in front of Essie and stood. "Wanna take a shower, Essie?"

"I don't care," she replied.

"Well, I'm going out back to set it up. Wanna cover me, Bart?"

Out in the back-parking lot, the two men set to hanging a tarp to give Essie some privacy during her shower, Bart doing more covering with his black rifle than actually helping with erecting the tarp barrier. As usual, he had a lot to say about how Jared should set the thing up and, as usual, Jared kept his mouth shut, following about ten percent of Bart's instructions. Jared finished with the tarp, having made a two-sided barrier at an angle like a V in order to minimize material and effort.

He stepped back to admire his work, with Bart standing next to him. They'd stacked pallets seven feet high, placed a black container of water on top, and had a short bit of hose draped down into the tarp shower area. The hose had a valve so the person showering could turn the water on and off as needed. The container of water was rectangular and only about six inches deep. It was more flat than deep and, when left in the direct sunlight, the water would actually get warm enough for a semi-comfortable shower.

"How'd you get her to talk to you about all that dance and soccer stuff?" Jared asked.

Bart smiled slightly. "Kids want to talk, girls especially and, if you give 'em the opportunity and you listen, they won't stop talking." Bart glanced around the parking lot before continuing, "She has seen what you can do and have done, and holds you in a different light than she sees me in."

Jared turned to Bart with an incredulous look plastered to

his face. "Are you trying to tell me she sees me as more of a threat than she sees you?"

Bart chuckled. "Well, yes and no, she sees you as her savior, a hero, but me...I'm just some old harmless grandpa-type guy, and I guess she views me more on her level."

"Ain't that a load of crap," Jared said in disgust. "An absolute load of crap."

"Hey, hey," Bart retorted, "that's a good thing, my man. She has a bond with you, man. Whether you like it or not, this kid's in your life for good."

Jared shot Bart a glare. "So now you're a psychologist?"

"You're her new father figure, buddy, embrace it."

"Father figure?" Jared asked.

"Yeah, father figure, you brought her here, gave her food and water, then gave her safe, warm shelter. Isn't that what fathers do?"

Jared turned and headed for the building. "I'm done talking about this with you. I'm gonna make sure the kid showers and gets into some clean clothes," Jared shot over his shoulder, causing Bart to laugh out loud.

"You just made my point. That's exactly what a father would do."

Jared stormed down the hall, thinking, *What does Bart know about kids and dads and, of all things, daughters and fathers? The bastard has something to say about everything. It's like having a full-size human version of Yoda around.*

He stopped before entering the workshop, not wanting Essie to see or sense any negative energy from him. He briefly composed himself before walking in. She was sitting at the table, with his pack open and all the clothes laid out in front of her. Essie looked up; fear quickly shrouded her innocent eyes, having been caught going through his pack.

Jared's wide smile immediately put her at ease. "You like any of them?"

Her voice was small and barely audible as she replied, "Uh huh, all of them."

"Pick a set you want to wear, and let's go get you cleaned up." Jared grabbed a Safeway bag and waited as the little waif of a girl carefully picked through the clothing, taking entirely too much time. Jared was about to urge her to hurry, but stopped himself. She was a little woman, and didn't they take forever to get ready? What was the rush anyway? Jared waited patiently as Essie chose an outfit, then traded the top for another top, looked them over, scrapped the whole outfit, and started over.

Who is she trying to impress here? he wondered. What Jared noticed was the socks and underwear she chose never changed; he made a mental note that it must be all about outer appearances.

Jared stepped forward and pointed to a top and bottom. "I like those," and that was the end of that. Out back, Jared set an old milk crate up inside the makeshift shower, with a bottle of shampoo and a bar of soap resting on top. Next he placed the new clothes on the Safeway bag, telling Essie to undress and place her old clothes in the bag.

Essie stood there staring at him for a moment before responding, "Who's going to wash me?"

Out of the corner of his eye, Jared saw Bart turn and stifle a laugh, training the rifle out across the rear parking lot in a false display of tactical poise.

"Ah, can't you wash yourself?" Jared asked, a slight quiver to his voice. Bart had his back completely turned now, and his shoulders heaved with suppressed laughter.

"You have to wash my hair. I can wash the rest," she said.

"I gotta work the water," Jared stammered.

"Bart can do that," she said, staring up at him.

Bart slung the rifle, moving to take control of the water

valve as Jared stood as still as a statue, watching Essie as she disappeared behind the tarp.

Bart had a shit-eating grin on his face as he raised his eyebrows and gestured towards Essie. "Go wash her hair."

"Why'd we even put this fucking thing up," hissed Jared as he followed Essie behind the tarp. Essie stepped into the tarped shower and wriggled out of her soiled clothes. Jared remained outside and watched as the little garments were tossed out and onto the ground at his feet.

"Start the water, Bart," Jared said. Jared grabbed the water nozzle and tested the water's temperature which was warmer than he would have expected. Without a word, he thrust the nozzle through the slat in the tard without invading the little girl's privacy and blindly sprayed her down with the warmish water. After he was sure she was rinsed and ready for soap, he instructed Bart to stop the flow of water. Jared fished about until he was able to grab the shampoo and haul it outside the shower.

"Okay, Essie, pop your head through the opening there so I can wash your hair." Jared ordered.

Essie's drenched face appeared through the slat in the tarp and Jared poured shampoo into her tangled locks and began scrubbing. After a few seconds, he stopped.

"You do it. Just do what I was doing with your hair. It's important you learn how to shower yourself." Jared said.

His sense of unease with the situation began to evaporate as the reality of their situation came into focus. He was the little girl's guardian and she was in need of a bath. He was ensuring her basic hygiene needs were being tended to and that was it.

Essie finished washing her own hair and, as she promised, she washed the rest, much to Jared's relief. Bart started and stopped the water as needed and never said a word. Jared stayed with Essie, helping her rinse from the safety of the outside of the tarped shower. When she was finished, Jared handed her a towel and then gathered her half-rotten clothes in the Safeway bag, leaving her to dress behind the privacy of the tarp. He took the bag and threw it as far as he could over the back fence down into the brush surrounding the creek.

When Jared emerged from behind the tarp, Bart was dead serious. He never smiled, nor did he laugh; he looked at Jared almost as if he were proud of the younger man. When Essie was dressed, the two men took the tarp down and hid it alongside the building, making it look like all the rest of the junk found behind a building in an industrial area. When this task was completed, the three went back inside. Jared and Essie sat down at the table in the workshop while Bart stowed the hosing from the shower in a locker against the wall.

Jared broke the awkward silence. "The clothes fit fine?"

Essie nodded in the affirmative, legs swinging off the chair, not quite touching the floor. Jared nodded as well, not knowing what else to do. How was it this seven-year-old kid could make him feel so uncomfortable? And to make matters worse, he knew Bart was loving every second of it.

The rest of the night was spent eating and drinking bourbon while Essie drank a soda and the men taught her how to play poker. Essie didn't talk much other than to ask a few questions about her hand, but she watched everything the men did. When Essie yawned, Jared put her to bed, stretching out next to her as she nestled into the kid's sleeping bag he looted from REI.

Essie turned in the bag to face Jared. "Can we get a brush and some hair bands tomorrow?" she asked. "We have to brush my hair after a shower."

Jared hadn't even thought of that. His hair was still fairly short and hadn't had the time to grow much since the event. "Sure, we can," he said. "In fact, you let me know all the things you need and I'll get them for you."

Essie just stared at him. "Can you scratch my head?"

Jared reached out and ran his fingers through her hair, realizing it was a tangled mess. He adjusted and scratched her head till she fell back against the small sleeping bag, her breath taking on that already familiar and rhythmic quality. She'd be asleep soon; he knew this about her and they'd been together for less than two days. What the hell was happening? First the old bastard had hijacked his life and, now, this miniature creature had him running around, washing her hair, shopping for her clothes, and tomorrow he would risk his life so she could have a brush and some hair bands.

Jared returned to the workshop, half hoping Bart had gone to bed. He hadn't. Jared dropped into a chair and grabbed the bourbon, swirling it like a fine glass of wine.

"What goes on in there that takes you twenty minutes?" Bart asked.

"We talk, she lets me know what she needs, and tonight I scratched her head till she fell asleep," Jared replied. "She also gave me a list for tomorrow, so can you babysit while I go out?"

Bart looked curious. "What does she need?"

"A brush and hairbands."

Bart nodded slowly, mulling this over as he brought the plastic cup to his lips and drank down the brown alcohol. As he swallowed the bourbon, he looked Jared right in the eyes and said, "I'd call that progress, Jared—I'd also grab her a toothbrush."

An image of the two dead boys and their toothpaste flashed into his mind, causing his heart to skip a beat. Jared quickly gulped down a generous amount of bourbon. It was easy here in the workshop to battle the fear. He just beat it back with the liquor, but out there on the streets he had to conquer it on his own.

The following night, Jared returned from Operation Get Hairbands with enough hair bands for an entire Girl Scout troop. He also retrieved two dozen hairbrushes and tooth-brushes because he decided to let Essie choose which brush she wanted so he didn't end up having to go back out.

This time out, he saw a lot more people, and not all appeared friendly. His gut told him to steer clear of them all. He hadn't taken the trailer, so he was fast and maneuverable, making it easier to keep a safe distance from the majority of people he saw. For the most part, the people he saw didn't appear to want to make contact with him either, so those encounters worked out nicely.

Jared had ridden up on a group of about ten people who immediately began firing their guns. He had pedaled in the opposite direction and never heard a bullet pass him, so he figured they just wanted to scare him off…they had succeeded mightily. Another more troubling encounter was with four men on a residential street. One man had stepped out as if to meet Jared, while the other three men took up positions behind abandoned vehicles and trees. The men were about one hundred yards from Jared when he turned and rode in the opposite direction, but before he had completed his turn, he saw the man in the street had dropped to a knee and was pointing his pistol at Jared. The man never fired as Jared rounded a corner and sped out of sight.

Jared watched Essie, seated in a chair toying with her food, and thought how he'd come to be responsible for a child, not only a child, but a little girl. How was he going to take care of a kid? He'd never even had a cat or dog. He had only been responsible for himself, and that had proven tough enough. He noticed her hair was still a tangled mess, and there were no hair bands holding her locks at bay.

"Why didn't you do your hair?" he asked.

She looked up with her almond-shaped eyes, feet swinging under the table. "You have to do it, I'm not old enough to do my own hair."

Jared shook his head. If he had to help her shower, then he'd surely have to do other things for her. He wished he had a list of things she could and could not do. If he knew the parameters of how he was expected to help her, he could mentally prepare himself for the ordeal, whatever it might be.

Jared rose from the table and went to his room to fetch the bag of brushes and hair bands. Upon his return, he dropped them all on the table next to Essie's dinner. "Pick a brush and hair band."

The little girl poked through the bag of brushes for a solid two minutes before settling on a simple black brush. She slid the brush over to him, turned in her chair to offer access to her tangles, and began going through the hair bands.

Jared picked the brush up, inspecting it and wondering why this one. When the answer didn't come to him, he reached out with the brush and attempted to drag it through Essie's hair. The maneuver jerked her head back, soliciting a yelp of pain from the tiny girl's lips.

Bart looked over the book he was reading. "Jesus Christ, boy, you're gonna break the poor kid's neck doing that. You either start at the bottom, or you grab her hair and hold it as you brush."

Essie never looked over her shoulder as she recovered and got back to sifting through the hair bands.

Even though he fumed inside, Jared carefully took the girl's hair in his hand and fought the brush through it over and over till the tangles submitted, leaving her golden hair to cascade over her small shoulders in beautiful flowing ringlets. When Essie finally felt the brush sliding smoothly through her locks, she quietly handed a hair band over her shoulder.

It took Jared three tries to get a ponytail secured to the back of her head. When he finished, she turned to face him, and he was taken aback by how lovely she looked. With her hair pulled out of her face, he was able to see just what a perfectly-shaped face she had, along with how large her almond-shaped brown eyes were. Essie's beauty and pure innocence was a stark contrast to the cruel and ugly world they were all trying to survive in.

"What?" Essie asked as Jared's stare lasted just a little too long.

He twitched his hands and shrugged his shoulders slightly. "You look like a different kid with your hair pulled up, that's all."

Essie turned and set about finishing her dinner while Jared collected all the brushes, stuffing them back in the bag.

Bart snorted with a raised eyebrow, pausing just a moment as if giving Jared a chance to fix something he'd messed up and, when he didn't, Bart spoke up. "What he meant to tell you, Essie, is you have a beautiful face, when we can see it."

Essie looked at Jared for confirmation, which he gave by quickly nodding his head before rushing out of the room.

After Essie ate and was in her sleeping bag, fast asleep, Jared and Bart sat in the workshop talking. Bart asked how Essie was going to affect Jared's plans of traveling across the country to reunite with his parents, and how he expected to take care of her along the way. Jared outright admitted he had no idea and told Bart he didn't even know if the trip was possible by himself, without the added burden of caring for a child. As gunfire could be heard in the distance, both men agreed he couldn't keep her in the city with it crumbling like pie crust. Now in the hushed aftermath that followed whatever conflict had triggered the rifle shots, both men sat quietly lost in their own thoughts.

Bart took a drink and broke the silence. "You know, tomorrow we need to work on the front of the store, make it appear to have been looted."

Jared frowned. "What do you mean?"

"I mean I intend to build a false wall, putting up shelves

and making it appear that there's nothing back here." Bart swept his hand in the direction of the hallway. "Build a real wall with a hidden entrance to the hallway."

Jared nodded. "You could come with us."

Bart sat back. "I've thought about that, but I'm not getting any younger, and I don't have the endurance you and Essie have. I'd slow you down and eat up precious resources. I would add nothing to your little travel group."

Jared sat a little straighter in the chair. "What are you talking about? You have all this experience with guns and have actually used them."

Bart just shook his head. "I'd be a burden, and no one knows that better than I—hell, I feel these old bones, and they are not in any condition for a trek across the good old US of A. Fact is, I don't think you'd make it, with or without the girl. Too much is wrong out there right now, and you don't come from a background that lends itself to surviving off the land."

Jared sat back in his chair, and again a cacophony of gunfire erupted a few blocks away, as if to corroborate Bart's prediction.

When the gunfire came to an end, Jared slumped back in his seat. "I have to get out of here and at least get into the country, where there are fewer people and, more importantly, fewer bad people."

Bart nodded. "I agree." More gunfire rattled off in the distance, and it was evident there were multiple weapons involved in the current disagreement.

"It's getting worse and we're barely two weeks into this. I have to leave, and I have to go soon."

Bart just dipped his chin in agreement.

"You just gonna stay here till the food's gone and then starve to death?" Jared asked.

Bart smiled tiredly. "Naw, I'm going to stay inside till the food's gone, and then I will go and get more. I'm not dying inside this shop; I can tell you that much. When I die, it'll be out there on the street, and it will be in the company of at least a few of whoever ends up getting me."

Jared wondered why the old bastard was talking like this, like he had his own death planned and was very okay with the whole idea of dying in the street like a dog. Jared could not put his finger on it, feeling he was missing something. He didn't know what he was missing and therefore hadn't the lightest idea what to ask Bart in order to better understand the old man's intentions.

The men discussed the future and talked about starting some rifle training, Bart showing Jared the rifle he intended to give him when he left the gun store. The weapon was made by Colt, and Bart called it an AR-15, semiautomatic, gas-operated, shoulder-fired rifle, whatever that meant. Jared handled the weapon briefly before locking it back in a safe.

They talked as the gunfire outside came and went. After a spell, both men were too tired to drink or talk. Jared literally fell into the sleeping bag and was asleep before his head had fully settled into the soft pillow.

Chapter 22

JARED SAT UP STRAIGHT; a feeling of dread trickled down his back like ice water. Bart had wakened him and was holding a hand over his mouth. Jared was so entirely unnerved by the manner in which Bart had dragged him from sleep, he didn't move a muscle. Although his body laid perfectly still and unmoving, his mind was racing, filled with questions and fear.

"Quiet. Someone's inside the shop," Bart whispered.

The trickle of ice water turned into a rushing river of icy adrenaline that sent Jared's mind racing even faster. Jared did two things he would later reflect on and wonder how he'd changed in such a short period of time. He reached for the Glock with one hand while softly placing his hand on Essie's bedding with the other. He felt the girl's small form and breathed a sigh of relief as he slowly rose to a kneeling position.

Jared could hear whoever was in their building moving stealthily through the front of the shop. Bart had dropped his hand from Jared's mouth and was resting it on his shoulder. Jared thought about all the lessons he learned about two-man operations inside a building, but all he could remember was

Bart's advice to be ready for the unexpected, and that every situation was different, and that everything he taught him would most likely not cover what would happen in real life when the time came.

He wasn't ready for this. *What the fuck am I going to do? Who the fuck is in the shop, and what are they after?* Jared's mind was racing to near light speed, his senses on high alert, smell and sight enhanced by nature's amphetamine coursing through his veins in the form of adrenalin.

Bart squeezed his shoulder and leaned in. "Wake her, let her know to be quiet, and have her hide under her cot. I'm moving to the hallway. Meet me there when you're done." Bart was so calm that it scared Jared even more, but somehow, through the absolute raw and unadulterated fear, Jared was able to access the very small piece of his mind that stored Bart's training.

Robotically, he reached out, squeezing Bart's arm twice, signaling he understood. After the two squeezes, Bart slid out of the room and into the hallway.

Jared leaned over the cot and gently placed his hand over Essie's mouth, careful not to apply too much pressure. "Essie, wake up," he whispered in her ear.

The girl's eyes flashed open; her body tensed.

"It's me, Essie; you have to be quiet. People are inside the shop."

She relaxed just slightly as Jared pulled his hand from her mouth.

"Please don't say a word. Just get under the cot and stay there till Bart and I get them out of here."

Without a word, she rolled from the bed onto the floor, slithering out of the sleeping bag and under the cot. *Jesus,* Jared thought for the second time, *was Bart training this little girl when I was out collecting supplies?*

Jared moved to the doorway, finding Bart kneeling and

peering into the inky blackness. The tarp at the end of the hallway moved, letting in a source of light. Jared couldn't tell if there was a full moon or whoever was out there had a light source. Bart recoiled, bumping into Jared as both men eased back into Jared's room, waiting like two coiled vipers. Jared saw the light flickering off the walls as whoever was out there passed through the tarp, making their way down the hallway.

Jared saw the man as he came even with the doorway; he was dirty and appeared to be in his thirties. He carried a large butcher knife held out in front of him. The storage room directly across from Jared's room proved the man's undoing. He came to the T intersection and chose the door on his right, the storage room. The two men on his left stood unseen, poised for action, while the hapless man turned his back and gently fumbled with the door handle.

Bart simply stepped across the hallway, placed the muzzle of his pistol to the man's head, and whispered, "Cry out or move wrong and I will pull this trigger."

The man froze, knife in his right hand, left hand still wrapped around the door handle. Jared was transfixed on what Bart was doing and never thought to look towards the front of the store.

In a loud voice the man proclaimed, "They got me. There are people back here."

Jared was amazed by a couple of things. The first was the calmness with which the man had warned his partner, apparently not caring about the consequences to himself. The second was how fast Bart pulled the gun away from the man's head and fired two shots into his right elbow, causing the man to scream and drop the knife all at the same time. Bart clamped the man around the throat with his left arm and dragged him back into Jared's room, bowling Jared over in the process.

The second they crashed to the floor in Jared's room, gunfire erupted from the direction of the tarp. The man had set the candle on the floor to test the door, and it continued to illuminate the hallway, but the muzzle flashes were very evident in the low-light environment. Jared was nearly deafened by the cacophony of gunfire directed their way at such close range.

"There's two of 'em, first room on the left," the man continued to the unknown assailant still in the front of the store.

Jared heard several sickening thuds and knew Bart was trying to cave the man's head in with his pistol.

From outside the room, Jared heard a man's voice. "I'm coming for you, buddy."

There was more gunfire, and Jared heard the tarp being moved. Jared looked down and saw the frightened face of Essie peeking out from under the cot. There was no thought process, he just acted, getting to his feet, kicking the wounded man in the head so hard he knew he would walk with a limp later as he moved to the doorway.

Jared ducked low, poking his head and weapon around the door frame. The man was standing lit by the light of the candle, reloading a revolver with the tarp partially draped over his shoulders. Jared held the man in his sights and fired several rapid shots. The man grunted then pitched forward into the hall, sprawling awkwardly with his limbs twisted in several unnatural directions. Jared stared wide-eyed at the felled man, nearly jumping out of his skin when the man shifted, grunted, and the last of his air was forced from his lungs in a long rasping wheeze.

"He down?" hissed Bart from where he was hunkered over the lifeless body of the first man.

Jared just nodded, transfixed on the downed man lying in the flickering light of the candle. This episode was different than when he shot the gang members. He didn't act out of anger in this instance and didn't have the luxury of time to think about what he was going do. These men forced both him and Bart to act instantly. No time to come up with a plan of action, just get out of bed and defend what was yours, and do it to the death if need be. There had definitely been a need and, consequently, there was a death.

Jared knew they held a tactical advantage, as Bart would have said. This was their home, they lived here, knew every square inch of the building and, more importantly, they spent countless hours training for just such an event. What rattled Jared to the core was that he did not automatically wake up; Bart had to wake him and, even though they seemed to have the upper hand at the moment, this could have gone the other way very easily.

Jared was brought back to the here and now as Bart shoved him roughly to the side as he dragged the unconscious body of the first man into the hallway.

"Hold that hallway and kill anything or anyone who comes through that tarp," Bart barked as he dropped the man halfway up the hallway. Bart turned and rushed past Jared, disappearing into the back of the store.

Jared stared at the two men who moments ago had been a dire threat to their existence. Now the men were piled up in a hallway somewhere in San Jose, one definitely dead and the other, well, Jared didn't know what Bart had done to him.

Bart returned and bound the man's hands behind his back with the flex cuffs. He finished the man off by binding his ankles and then securing his ankles to his wrists with a single cuff. This put the man in an arched-back position.

Jared remembered talking to Bart about prisoners and how to make sure they couldn't hurt you. They had not trained on the subject matter, but it had merely been a conversation over a few cups of bourbon one evening. Bart told Jared about using this tactic as a cop until some criminal son of a bitch had sued, and the police department had outlawed the use of hog-tying prisoners.

Bart returned, rifle in hand. "We're going to clear that front area and sweep the outside of the store. You ready to go?"

Jared nodded.

Bart stepped into the doorway, peering in at Essie. "Be right back, Ess," Bart reassured her.

She stared blankly back, obviously terrified.

Jared glanced back before Bart moved forward, closing on the two bodies.

"Cover your ears, boy," Bart exclaimed as he reached into his cargo pocket, producing several green light sticks, which he tossed past the two downed men, into the front of his store.

Before Jared could process the warning, Bart fired a rifle shot into the second man's head and tore through the tarp, turning left as he entered the green glow of the shop's showroom. Jared's ears rang, instantly feeling actual real pain as over 155 decibels slammed into his hearing canals sans ear protection.

He trained with Bart in this very room, knowing Bart expected Jared to follow him and cover whichever side Bart wasn't covering. In this case, that would be the right side of the room. Bart would be working the left side, clearing or ridding the place of any unwanted two-legged vermin. As Jared lurched forward, muzzle slightly turned inward, but not down, he almost laughed at the thought of being more scared of Bart's reaction to his not entering the room than meeting some desperate maniac inside the shadowy unknowns of the front room. He slid through the tarp before it could fall back in place, making a smooth entry to the right.

"I'm clear," Bart barked as Jared visually swept his side and came up with the same conclusion.

"Clear," Jared grunted as they moved forward, keeping abreast of the other as they transitioned through the small storefront, sweeping through the empty aisles. Bart had cleared everything out and lowered the shelves for just a situation like this one. They were able to easily clear the rest of the store-front within seconds, ending up at the shattered front glass door.

"Motherfuckers," was all Bart said, looking at the breach in his little kingdom's skin.

Silently they moved through the broken door, trying to step through the broken glass and onto quieter ground. Jared followed Bart as they moved in a 360-degree circle around the building, stopping at the rear door to inspect it for damage. The door did not appear to have been molested in any way.

The men moved on until they were back at the smashed front door. Bart looked the damage over again and shook his head before ducking back inside the store. He grabbed the dead man by the boots and dragged him out of the hallway.

"Check on Essie," he said as he continued struggling under the load, towards the broken front door. Bart was in opera-tional mode, and Jared had never seen him so focused and determined. He thought about asking what he planned on doing, but refrained from opening his mouth, instead going to where Essie was still curled up under the cot. She looked like a thousand pounds were lifted from her little shoulders when Jared darkened the doorway.

"You all good under there?" he asked.

She bobbed her head in the affirmative just as the trussed-up heap of humanity on their hallway floor stirred.

Jared pointed the Glock at the man and waited as the man strained mindlessly against his restraints, not fully conscious and apparently not realizing he was wrapped up like a broken and bloodied pretzel. Jared glanced back at Essie, seeing she had a direct line of sight to the trussed-up man in the hallway.

"I'll be right out here with that guy. Stay there. Everything's okay now. There were only two, and we got 'em both."

She withdrew like a turtle into the dark recess of her hiding spot, leaving him free to step into the hallway and approach the man, who was trying to roll over. As the man rolled onto his side, the look on his face showed he now understood his predicament.

"Shouldn't have come in this place," Jared quipped at the man on the floor.

"No shit," the man groaned.

The tarp rustled, and Jared nearly shit himself as Bart came back in, breathing heavily, sweat glistening off his forehead, and looking more than a little haggard. A small trickle of blood was visible in the corner of Bart's mouth as he approached Jared.

"You okay?" Jared touched his mouth. "You're bleeding."

Bart quickly wiped his mouth with a sleeve, continuing down the hallway, leaving Jared with the impression that now was not the time to ask personal questions about the old son of a bitch's health.

"Let's get this piece of shit into my room," Bart barked, reaching down and cutting the flex cuff that bound the man's hands to his feet. Bart also cut the man's feet free. Jared stepped forward, assisting in getting the man to his feet and into Bart's bedroom. Bart set the room up with three chairs, two facing the last one, and then roughly shoved the man down into the single chair.

He produced two more flex cuffs, cut the man's hands free, and used the new cuffs to secure the man's arms to the chair. If the man got up, he would bring the chair with him. Next, Bart used two more flex cuffs to bind the man's ankles to the two front legs of the chair. He removed the man's boots, throwing them out into the hallway, and dropped into one of the other two chairs, staring at the man and breathing hard from the effort.

Both men just sat staring at the other, Jared not daring to move in the doorway until Bart slapped the chair next to him.

"Sit, or go tend to Essie. You're making me nervous standing back there."

Jared retreated to his bedroom, where he got Essie out from under the cot and was about to tuck her back in bed, when she wrapped her arms around him and squeezed his neck so tight vertebrae popped and crackled, reminding him of trips he'd taken to a chiropractor. He squeezed back, holding Essie for several seconds until she loosened her grip, pulling her face back so they could see each other. Essie pushed her hair back from her eyes, blinking and smiling as Jared broke into his own wide smile.

He slowly shook his head, saying, "You're safe, and you always will be. I won't let anything happen to you."

Again, she wiped her hair back and nodded, never uttering a word. Jared hugged her tight again, then laid her in the cot, pulling the sleeping bag up to her chin.

After putting Essie back to bed, Jared re-entered Bart's room. The two men were still sitting in silence.

Jared's entrance must have jump-started something, causing the trussed-up man to shift in his chair, asking, "Is this really necessary?"

Bart lowered his chin, glaring down his nose at the man. "Necessary? I think it is very fucking necessary, especially after you and your dead friend come in here, break my front door down, and shoot the place up. We have a seven-year-old girl in here whom you two just happened to scare the holy fuck out of, for Christ's sake, so yeah, I think it's necessary." Bart leaned in menacingly. "And you fuckers broke the glass on my front door and fucked me out of a good night's sleep."

The man stopped moving and lowered his gaze. "We weren't trying to hurt anyone," he said weakly.

Another two-minute staring contest ensued, Jared trying to act tough by not breaking eye contact with the bound man. When Bart finally broke the silence, Jared was positive with absolute certainty that the last two minutes had been the most uncomfortable in his entire life.

"What's your name?" Bart asked the man, his voice softening, his shoulders relaxing just a hair.

"Adam," the man replied suspiciously, not sure of Bart's change in demeanor.

This was not Bart's first interrogation, and he knew time was on his side. He wanted to identify what this man knew about the outside world. He wasn't about to torture the man, the cop in him still controlling his moral compass to a certain degree; plus, Bart considered himself a decent man, one who sought to help people, not a person who took advantage of people, no matter how low society seemed to have stooped.

"Okay, Adam," Bart started, "what was tonight all about?"

Chapter 23

OVER THE NEXT TWO HOURS, Jared marveled as Bart prodded, manipulated and, at times, softly cajoled Adam into divulging almost more information than Jared could digest. Adam explained how the city had become so dangerous, not even children were safe. Women were fast becoming a common currency, making it dangerous to have women as part of your group. Most people were hiding in their homes, which wasn't proving to be very smart since it made it easier for those who sought to victimize them. Gangs were going from neighborhood to neighborhood, searching homes for food, weapons and women.

Adam told Bart he and his dead friend, Erik, were neighbors living across town in a fairly normal suburban neighborhood when the event happened. Both men worked together at a recycling center not far from their homes. He said they had been at work when it happened, and immediately made the walk home, getting in after nightfall. He and his family had treated it like every other power outage they'd been through. Adam said he knew something was different this time.

Adam was married to Mary, and they had a twelve-year-old

daughter, Maggie. The following day Erik and Adam got together and went for a walk around the neighborhood, looking for answers regarding what was happening. It seemed everyone they encountered was in the same boat as they were. No one knew a thing, and nothing having to do with electronics worked for anyone.

Adam told Bart not much changed for the first few days, but then they started hearing gunfire at night, along with the even more unnerving sounds of people screaming. In the span of four days, the neighborhood went from a safe place to a place where people huddled inside their homes, peeking fearfully from behind curtained windows, watching as bands of strangers moved through the streets, looking for food and much more. Adam said he and Erik decided to consolidate the families in Adam's house in order to set up a watch rotation. Erik was married to a woman named Betty, and they had three kids: two teen boys, Erik Jr. and Edward, and Erik's daughter, Tammy, was the same age as Maggie, and they were best friends.

The families moved all the food from Erik's house to Adam's house and set up a watch rotation using the two men, the wives, and the two teen boys. Erik Jr. and Edward stood watch together in order to keep each other awake and for peace of mind for both them and their parents. Erik had a small .38-caliber pistol, the same one he shot at Jared and Bart with, and the families were relying on Erik and the small handgun to keep them safe till the government could get going with some sort of relief.

Close to a week into the event, Erik's family's house was ransacked in the middle of the night. The two boys were on watch and woke their father to tell him people were in their house, breaking things.

Adam told Jared and Bart how hard it was for Erik to sit in silence and listen to all his worldly possessions being destroyed next door, not twenty yards from where he and his family sat hidden in their neighbor's home. His wife had cried all night, even after the people left the house. The following day both Erik and his wife refused to go to their house, saying the house was contaminated and was no longer the home they remembered.

Three days later, their group was without food and water. To make things worse, they were using the toilets and the house smelled like a sewer. Erik and Adam decided they would go out and find food, water, and see if they could contact any police or government personnel.

Adam said they left the pistol with Erik Jr, who was the older of the two boys, giving him explicit instructions to safeguard the women at all costs. The two men left, pulling a red wagon out into the neighboring area in search of supplies. They were not successful in finding a single scrap of food that trip and started their return home, taking a different route in order to scavenge along the way back to the house.

Passing through one of the neighborhoods, the men saw something that shook them to their very core. They had decided to pass through a very upscale neighborhood in order to check a shopping center and then continue home, when they found what appeared to be a half dozen surly men sitting on the porch of a nice house. The men were more than a little out of place, as they were hard men and heavily tattooed. Adam was no gang expert, but he'd seen enough news clips to know a gang member when he saw one, and these guys all fit the bill.

The troubling part about the whole thing was the thirty something-year-old mother, haggard and bruised, sitting on a chair in the midst of the horde. She looked pleadingly at the men as they passed by. It was glaringly apparent she was not there of her own volition.

Adam went on, saying he and Erik were not armed and continued on their way, seeing similar scenes five more times throughout the neighborhood. It was like these gangs had come in, killed the men, and taken over the households, keeping the women for heaven knew what. Adam seemed truly distressed when he described the scene in that neighborhood. Bart stopped the interview, cut the ankle bindings, and sat back down. Adam stretched his legs out in front of him for a long second and then thanked Bart before continuing his story.

When the men reached their neighborhood, they immediately knew something was not right. Smoke rose from several places throughout the vicinity, causing them to abandon the wagon and race to Adam's house, where they found the front door wide open. Erik found his daughter stabbed to death at the foot of the staircase, alongside Adam's daughter. Adam did not weep while he recounted the horrific details, but Jared could see it had been a life-altering experience, and the man who sat bound to this chair today was not the same man he'd been two weeks prior.

Adam described the house as he and Erik frantically searched for their remaining family members. They found all four of them in the kitchen near the back door leading out to the yard. From what they could tell, the boys had tried to hold someone off by blocking the back door. Whoever was on the other side of the door had beat on it so fiercely, the door had eventually fallen apart, allowing the assailant to hack the boys to pieces with some sort of heavy edged weapon.

The wives were killed next, obviously coming to the aid of the two boys, and had gone down in much the same manner, cut to ribbons and left lying atop the stricken teens. Their families' bodies were so badly damaged they couldn't imagine trying to move them all outside to bury each one, so the men had decided to burn the house along with the bodies in it.

Adam told them he found the revolver still in Erik Jr's waistband. The boy hadn't even drawn the weapon in defense of the house and its occupants. None of the adults were prepared for this kind of event, much less the children.

The men spent a few hours inside the house, mourning and holding belongings that had at one time been near and dear to each family member, before pouring gasoline on the carpets, drapes and stairway, trailing the accelerant to the front door, where they pooled it in the foyer. Neither man could bring himself to douse the bodies of their loved ones, so Adam grabbed two flares from the trunk of his wife's useless car, ignited them, and together both men tossed a flare into the petroleum-saturated home. The fire took off so fast, it blew out the windows, and within twenty seconds, the entire house was ablaze.

They both watched as the home burned everything they had known from their previous world. The fire consumed their mates, their offspring, and all their worldly possessions. No fire trucks came, no sirens sounded, no nothing, just the crackling fire and the occasional crash as part of the house caved in on itself.

Adam knew Erik was close by, but could not say what he'd done that night. Each man had focused on his own misery in his own way that night. He'd thrown the flare and retreated instinctively to Erik's front yard as the fire erupted. He had sunk to his knees, staying there until the sun came up the following day. By then the fire had burned itself out for the most part, and Adam's legs had fallen asleep, making it impossible to get up when he finally finished digesting what had happened and what he'd done in the aftermath.

He had flopped over, moaning in both mental and physical agony as the blood returned to his blood-starved limbs. When he was able to walk, he found Erik sitting on the steps of his home, shoulders slumped, cheeks stained from what was most assuredly a night of tears. When Adam got closer to Erik, he saw the blood-covered pistol in his hand and knew immediately what he'd been wrestling with all night. Erik never went through with it, but instead went back inside his house, the only time he ever did after it was ransacked and got a box of fifty .38-caliber cartridges.

The men set out with no particular place in mind to go. They trudged out of their neighborhood, shoulders slumped, two broken souls having lost everything, including their will to live, which felt reduced to a shadow of its previous state.

Funny thing, Adam explained, was how hunger and thirst work in the drive to live. The men were already hungry before their families were slaughtered, but the following day found them not only hungry, but thirsty as well. Thirst is by far worse than hunger and could kill a man in a matter of days. As they walked through their dying neighborhood, they knocked on doors, trying to contact anyone who might have seen who did this terrible thing, but no one would talk to them. It was like they had the plague.

As they scavenged over the next few days, they saw killings, dead and discarded bodies, and sometimes worse. They'd taken to searching cars for people's lunches or power bars. They were far less successful in this endeavor than they would ever have thought possible, but it had kept them alive.

A few days before they met Bart and Jared, the two went poking around an office building, hoping to get lucky and find snacks in abandoned desk drawers. They'd entered an office full of cubicles and were about to start tearing into the desk drawers when a man wearing full military camouflage stood up in the center of the cubicles. Erik and Adam were blocking the door, but this guy was so obviously part of the government, or what used to be the government, the two men were more curious than threatened. The man turned out to be as frightened as Erik and Adam were, which resulted in the men actually treating each other courteously.

The men spent the next hour talking and searching for

food together. Adam said it had felt good to be with a complete stranger who didn't pose a threat for a change. The guy relayed his story since the event, which was interesting, but far less tragic than Adam and Erik's story.

The guy's name was Brad and he'd actually been a Black Hawk helicopter pilot, stationed at Moffett Field, assigned to the Air National Guard's 129th Rescue Wing. He had been on approach to the base when the event hit, knocking the helicopter's entire flight system off-line. Brad had dumped the collective and began an autorotation landing, but his lack of forward airspeed combined with his low altitude gave him some problems, and he ended up landing much harder than he would have liked. The landing gear collapsed, the tail boom snapped, and the main rotors struck the ground, causing the aircraft to spin violently before coming to rest on its side.

Brad unstrapped himself, yelling to the other three men aboard, checking for injuries. No one was injured during the unscheduled landing, and Brad said he didn't think about it until he climbed from the sixteen-million-dollar paperweight, but not a single emergency vehicle had responded after the crash. At first, he thought maybe it was because the emergency happened so fast that he didn't have time to make a distress call, and the tower just hadn't seen him yet.

When, after five minutes, no one drove out to his crash site, he and his crew walked towards the hangars. As they crossed the airfield, they started seeing people running around as if something was going on. Looking back, Brad was even more perplexed, since the wreckage of his aircraft was smoking, which should have stood out on any airfield.

Jogging up to the hangar, they found some guys from their unit and were told all the power was out. One of the men asked them if they were aboard the bird on short and final when the power went out, and asked if everyone onboard was okay. When Brad assured him everyone was fine, the man ran off, and no one else inquired about the loss of a multimillion-dollar asset or the welfare of its crew. It was bewildering to him.

Slowly, things came into focus as more and more they realized not only the power, but everything that used power, was out. Rumors flew like bullets about a terrorist attack, although no one could say for sure what had happened.

Within an hour, the base commander had the base locked down, securing the gates and letting no one in or out. The 129th Rescue Wing had three Black Hawks out at the time of the event and had accounted for only one, and that was the smoldering heap of burning aircraft aluminum out on the tarmac. The other two had been on training missions miles away from the base, and with no way of communicating, no one knew if they had landed safely or not. The base had a large cache of MREs, which were the military's rations for training and wartime.

After the first week, things got a little crazy, with some of the guards being involved in the shooting of civilians trying to enter the base, demanding assistance from the base commander. He had refused, citing the need to remain ready for orders when Washington got back on their feet and re-established contact. The following morning was a watershed moment for many of the unit's people as the carnage from the night before was revealed by the rising sun. Fifty-three people were shot and killed at the main gate. Working parties had to be organized to remove the dead.

The following day a C-130 Hercules landed at the airfield and off-loaded several up-armored Humvees. The whole thing was very hush-hush, but rumors spread that the unit flown in was what the Army called the Unit, or Delta Force. They went out into the city and were gone for approximately six hours before returning with close to twenty civilians. This little Special Forces group took over an entire hangar, pulling their

C-130 inside along with their vehicles. They handled their own security and stayed the night before leaving the base the following morning on another ground mission.

The most viable rumor was they were sent from the government to gather people who were important to the survival of the nation. These were not mayors or governors; they were people in their twenties and thirties who built things the government would need to make it through the dark days ahead.

At the end of that day, the Special Forces operators returned, boarded the waiting C-130, and took off, disappearing along with the people they had come for. After the Special Forces boys rolled in and then left, the base commander appeared deflated and apparently was more than a little loose in keeping secrets from his staff. Brad and the rest of the base soon learned the government was paralyzed and had only the assets hardened against an EMP attack, which wasn't enough, as evidenced by the lack of governmental support.

After that, Brad volunteered to oversee the guard detail. After darkness fell, he walked to the fence, cut a hole in it, and walked off base, vowing to never be part of the killing of any American who was seeking food from their government, which had, over the years, created this culture of dependence. These times were fast becoming anything but normal, and people were becoming more and more desperate with each passing day.

After relaying the tale, Brad wished the two men good luck and they parted ways. Adam said he had the idea to get away from suburbia and get into the industrial areas to see if they could find a way to feed themselves there. They'd found a few granola bars and things of that nature in some of the shops and in the vehicles abandoned on the streets, but hadn't been as successful as they needed to be, when they'd happened on this place.

Adam explained that as soon as they broke the front door, they knew someone either lived here or had recently been here by the smell. It smelled lived in, with the aromas of food, coffee, and body odor lingering in the air.

Chapter 24

BART SAT BACK as Adam concluded his story, stretching his arms over his head then cracking his neck and rolling his shoulders.

"Watch him," Bart said as he got to his feet, leaving the room.

"That guy your dad or something?" Adam asked.

Jared chuckled. "Nope."

"You guys gonna kill me? You know, I don't care if you do, just make it fast."

Jared looked at the man and thought about how much he'd been through and all he'd lost, and was saddened that it amounted to enough that his life held so little value.

"I ain't killing anyone," Jared said flatly. "Too many people killing too many people lately," he finished.

Adam took a deep breath and looked down at his bloody arm. The bullets had passed through the meaty portion and never struck bone. Jared would never know if Bart did this on purpose or not, and he would surely never ask the man.

He nodded to the wound. "Hurt?"

"Yeah, it hurts a lot," Adam responded, the pain evident in his expression.

Jared didn't know what to say—or do, for that matter—and wished he hadn't asked the question.

Bart came back in the room with three cups of coffee and a bottle of painkillers Jared had scavenged for him days earlier. He set everything on the floor and turned to Adam. "I'm going to cut you loose. You do anything remotely stupid and I will kill you. You stay cool, and we can have a cup of coffee, and you can take some painkillers for that arm."

Adam nodded and Bart cut him from the chair, offering two white pills and one of the cups of steaming hot coffee. Adam didn't take the cup immediately, stretching his body and wincing at the pain from the gunshot wounds.

"Go grab the first aid bag," Bart said. Jared retrieved the bag and Bart set about cleaning the wounds and bandaging the arm. He made a sling securing Adam's arm to his chest in order to stop the limb from swinging and causing the man surplus pain.

"I really wish you all had waited till daylight and just knocked. Would have gone better for all parties involved."

Adam just nodded, staring down at the floor. "We didn't come in here looking for a fight. I called for Erik and he came shooting for two reasons, so I didn't die alone, and so he didn't have to be alone." He looked up, squaring his shoulders, and looked Bart straight in the eyes. "Our families died alone in the house we called home, maybe wondering why we weren't there to stop it, but they died alone." He drew a deep breath. "We talked a lot about that, and I guess neither of us wanted to die the same way. Back before all this, people wanted alone time, not so much anymore, I think."

He exhaled and dropped his head. It was obvious the arm was causing him a great deal of discomfort, and Jared found himself feeling sorry for the man.

After a long silence, Bart spoke up. "You did come in here and cause us to kill a man. You scared the living hell out of Essie and robbed us of a good night's sleep. Tomorrow, you gotta go. I'll give you that pistol your friend had and three days' food, hell, I'll even toss in a couple of bottles of water, but you gotta go."

Adam nodded, he looked like a broken shell of a human being and, again, Jared was nearly overcome with pity for the man who'd lost his family and now a close friend.

Bart stood. "You can sleep here for the night. I'm up and won't be able to get back to sleep anyway."

"Thank you," Adam murmured as Bart gave a wry smile.

"It's a goddamn weird world we live in now. A few minutes ago, we were exchanging gunfire, trying to kill each other, and now we're drinking coffee and you're about to sleep in my fucking bed."

Adam pursed his lips.

"Fucking weird," Bart reiterated.

Jared helped the one-armed man situate the sleeping bag, then closed the door and left him to sleep. Jared walked down to the workshop, where he could see the flickering light of a candle. He knew what he would see and he wasn't disappointed. Bart sat in a chair, mug of coffee in hand, staring at a wall in deep thought.

Jared pulled up a chair, also sitting in silence, gripping his own cup of coffee, but not drinking. He planned on trying to salvage a little sleep out of what was left of the night, and coffee would ensure he would stare at the ceiling, listening to Essie's soft breathing till the sun rose.

Bart's voice broke the silence. "Remember what happened here tonight, my friend, remember it and never forget it. Pass it on to everyone you come across, because it's what will bring this great nation back to her feet."

"Which part?"

Bart shot him an annoyed look. "You're a smart guy, Jared, but sometimes, I worry about you. Pay attention to life, not things, that was the problem with your generation and the world in general." Bart blew gently on the coffee before sipping the hot stimulant. "You lived in the material sense of things, computers, hardware, software, and whatever else you did. You let valuable lessons pass you by, missing golden opportunities to get better at being human and make this shithole world better."

Jared looked at this old man who, at times, was the biggest asshole he'd ever met and, other times, seemed like the most dangerous and uncaring man he'd ever known. Now, Jared was pretty sure the ole son of a bitch was talking about compassion and forgiveness. He almost laughed out loud, but thought Bart might knife him if he made light of the situation.

"You're talking about forgiving people and having compassion?"

"I'm fucking talking about being a better person, helping people get on their feet and make it in this place. Everyone seems to have a story, each one a little worse than the last," Bart snarled.

"Yeah, yeah, I get it. The world is what we make it. If it's full of shitheads, it will not be a good place to be. I get it, Bart."

"You can't just get it, kid, you got to live it, hell we all have to live it. Everyone out there has to be better to each other" Bart said.

"Then why are you...I mean we kicking him out tomorrow," Jared ventured almost timidly.

"'Cause justice shall be served. He made a huge mistake and got a man killed because of it."

"Well, I think if you help someone who is in a situation that could be the end of them, like him out there with that arm the way it is, they owe you and will be loyal to you on a level that's different from someone you've never done anything for," Jared argued.

"Ah, for crying out loud, I said pay attention to life, not overthink it." Bart snorted, taking a draw off the now cooler coffee.

Jared felt he gained the upper hand in this debate and pushed on. "We put him out on the street and he will die. We both know that." Jared shifted in his chair and continued, "So we don't actually kill him, we just cause him to be killed, like he caused his buddy to get killed."

Bart grimaced, pushed his chest out, and rolled his shoulders back. He wasn't happy with this discussion, and Jared wanted to be careful not to go too far, jeopardizing his own situation here at the gun store.

Bart relaxed his shoulders, releasing his breath through his nostrils. "Let me tell you something, Jared, I don't run a postapocalyptic foster home for fucked-up guys who weren't ready for this little hiccup. The fact that you are here is a mystery even to me. The only reason I can think of is our deal, and in hindsight, I probably could have done all that shopping if I'd got out there within the first couple of days."

"Then you bring home Essie, and I can't very well toss you two out on the street with her having gone through what she went through. Now you're telling me I should take in a third hungry and thirsty mouth, and not just a third, but a third who not more than an hour ago might have killed all three of us if we hadn't got to him and his friend first." Bart finished.

Jared sat silently, thinking about the whole thing and coming to the realization that this situation was not that much different than some messed up things he read about in his past life.

As if reading his mind, Bart continued. "Back when we had a judicial system, there were a ton of crimes that were pretty straightforward in the eyes of the law." He sipped the steaming beverage before continuing, "Murder wasn't one of them. Murder or homicide was a tricky crime, and we as humans realized that and, in doing so, our penal code, at least the California Penal Code, reflected our understanding that the act of taking another human life is quite possibly the most complicated crime or act we dealt with."

Bart sipped the coffee then swept his hand across his front. "Take the premeditated murder of a police officer, for example, which in turn carries a possible death sentence and was viewed by society as an exceptionally horrific crime, while the guy who walks in and kills his wife's lover after seeing the two engaged in a little one-on-one naked wrestling match is viewed nearly as an acceptable act, punishable by a couple of months in a county jail and three years' probation."

Bart set the cup of coffee down and laughed. "Hell, the conditions of probation were usually more lax than probation on someone with a DUI." He shook his head and stretched. "My point is, what homeboy back there did was egregious, but only in the sense of the act and not in a societal perception type way, if that makes any sense at all."

———

THE FOLLOWING MORNING, Jared woke Essie, fed her breakfast, and was combing her hair when Adam staggered through the door, looking pale, face slicked with sweat, and generally looking like hammered dog shit. Bart got to his feet, pulling a chair out and motioning the man to sit. Adam sank into the chair without a word. Bart grabbed the first aid bag and retrieved a pair of shears, which he used to cut away the blood-soaked bandages. Adam groaned low and guttural as his head fell back and his eyes rolled up in his head.

"I really wish you hadn't shot me," Adam croaked in a hoarse voice.

To Jared's surprise, Bart didn't say a word as he worked on the man's arm. The flesh around the entrance and exit wounds was bright red and already infected.

"Goddammit," Bart murmured as he poured hydrogen peroxide into the wounds.

Adam winced, but did not cry out. Essie watched intently as Bart worked on the man's arm. Jared was also watching, jaw clinched, hands balled into tight fists. He had to make an effort to relax his body as the medical procedure unfolded across the table from him.

After irrigating the wounds with hydrogen peroxide, Bart put on a pair of latex gloves and scrubbed Adam's wounds. This elicited more moans and gasps of pain from the wounded man. Bart stopped periodically, letting the man catch his breath. When he was done scrubbing the wounds, he injected them with an antibacterial ointment. Once this was done, Bart set about re-dressing the cleaned wounds and securing Adam's arm to his chest.

When he was finished, Bart smiled at Adam. "Guess we should have given you something for the pain before we went tearing into those holes in your arm."

Adam swallowed, unable to do much else.

Turning to Jared, Bart shook his head regretfully. "I need you to go back out and get more bandages. This is going to need to be changed a couple of times a day and we just don't have that many medical supplies."

Essie moved against Jared, nestling herself into a little nook, looking at Bart. "Why don't you go out and get it? He always has to go."

Both men looked surprised, their mouths hanging open, staring down at the usually quiet and withdrawn little girl.

"I'll be careful," Jared said as he squeezed her to him.

They all sat in silence for a solid five minutes before Bart got to his feet, breaking the silence. "Time to go, my friend."

Jared looked up, immediately realizing Bart was referring to the wounded man.

Adam nodded his head with a pained look as Bart reached under the table to produce a small day-style pack.

"There's water, bandages and some food like I promised," Bart said.

Adam staggered to his feet, taking the pack, and Bart showed him the way to the front of the store. Jared shifted Essie to the chair next to him, also getting to his feet, following the two men, who were slowly making their way down the hallway like condemned men. The three men ducked through the broken front door, Bart and Jared stopping short as Adam continued. He walked ten yards before he stopped and turned back to face the two men who were essentially sending him to his death.

"I really am sorry about what happened and, if I could turn back the hand of time, I would. We never meant to hurt anyone, and I just—fuck, I just guess I don't know what else to say other than I am so sorry."

Bart nodded slightly, but remained grim faced until Adam turned and headed up the street.

Adam had only gone another five yards when Bart called out to him, "Hold up, friend."

Bart disappeared into the shop as Adam stopped and looked questioningly at Jared, who shrugged, just as perplexed as Adam was.

A moment later Bart returned, carrying a small box of .38-caliber ammunition. He strode out to where Adam had stopped, handing the box to the half-crippled man. "There's fifty rounds there, not much, but more than you had."

Adam just stared at the gift.

"Far as I'm concerned, if we meet again, it's a fresh start, no hard feelings. Good luck to you. Hope you make it."

For a split second, Jared thought Adam was going to hug

the old bastard. For that brief moment in time, Jared stopped breathing in anticipation of a hug that never came. Jared was both disappointed and relieved and would always wonder if it had happened, how Bart would have reacted. He didn't think it would have been a positive reaction. In the end, Adam nodded his head, eyes glassy with emotion as he turned slowly, walking up the street before rounding a corner and disappearing from sight. Jared felt a flood of emotions course through him as the man rounded the corner. Guilt, sadness and an overwhelming sense of despair were just a few of them.

Bart's voice jolted him out of the dark recess of his pity party. "That was quite possibly the hardest thing I've ever had to do." With that, Bart turned and walked back into the shop, leaving Jared standing on the sidewalk in a world that had become so quiet his ears would ring if he stopped and just listened.

Chapter 25

JARED PEDALED the bike through the streets of San Jose, heading to a CVS Bart had mapped out for him. As he rounded a corner, Jared saw what looked like a woman ahead of him, pulling a child's wagon with a body splayed atop the carriage. The feet and hands dragged along the concrete while the woman struggled to pull the grisly mess along the sidewalk. Three weeks ago, the woman had probably walked her pure-bred poodle along this very sidewalk.

Jared slowed, looking for any sign of foul play, but didn't get the sense there was anything sinister about this scene, so he continued towards the woman. She was a woman probably in her early forties, with hair that seemed to have gone unwashed since this whole thing started. Her clothes were filthy, hanging on a frame that had obviously lost more than a few pounds since the event.

Everything about the woman was dirty, grimy, or otherwise distasteful as she trudged along with a grim look painted across her gaunt face. The body in the wagon was a man in his forties, dirty, thin and dead. His eyes were open, as was his mouth, and Jared could see where fluids were leaking from those orifices, both onto the ground and pooling in the wagon around his rotting body.

As Jared came abreast the grisly traveler, the woman turned, staring at him with absolutely no emotion.

"What do you want?" she said flatly.

"Nothing, just don't see too many folks out who aren't trying to kill me, and thought I'd say hi," Jared responded.

The woman just stared back, the tragedy of what was happening to the whole place written in the lines of her face like bold 72 font print. This woman was surely used to an easier life than she was living now, Jared could plainly see that. The folks who had it best were oftentimes the ones who suffered the most now. It appeared the criminals were taking the whole event in stride, seeming to thrive in the new environment. The closer you were to living like an animal before the event, the better off it seemed you were now. This woman had not lived like an animal, and she was suffering now, probably dragging the body of her husband in the wagon to who knows where.

"Who's he?" Jared asked, looking down at the body in the wagon.

The woman looked down at the body as if she'd forgotten it was there, then returned her gaze to Jared. "My husband, Frank," she answered matter-of-factly. "He died yesterday after his insulin ran out. We knew it would happen and, now, I'm taking him to the park."

Jared lowered his head respectfully. "I'm sorry for your loss."

The woman nodded her head before softening for a moment and replying, "Why, thank you very much," then turned and was about to continue when Jared spoke again.

"Why the park?"

The woman paused, looking back at Jared. "That's where

everyone is taking their dead." With that, she pivoted and continued her journey, leaving Jared behind.

Jared watched her for a few seconds before pedaling on past her without a word. He had only gone a few blocks when the odor struck his nostrils like a sledgehammer. A large park was ahead, and Jared could see the bodies littering the grassy open area. He pulled his shirt up over his face, slowly riding past the ghastly sight, where hundreds of bodies had simply been dumped on the grassy surfaces of the park. The woman was right when she said everyone was bringing their dead to the park.

As he rode past, he saw three more people dragging bodies into the park. He didn't stop, fearing he would retch if he stayed any longer. The bodies were simply strewn about the park, no one apparently having the inclination to bury their lost loved ones. America had become so soft they couldn't even dig a shallow hole to cover their family members. Half of them probably didn't even own a shovel, Jared thought. Hell, he hadn't owned a shovel.

As he passed the improvised graveyard, he couldn't stop wondering about the park's once pristine landscape. Jared shuddered as he thought of the families who had used this park for recreation and now were either lying dead there or dragging their dead family members to the very place they had sought out to enjoy a day of barbequing and relaxation.

Once at the CVS, he ran through his routine of watching the store before going in, then grabbing what he could find. When he didn't find many bandages for dressing larger wounds, he went to the aisle where the feminine items were kept, loading his pack with as many feminine pads as he could carry. Bart told him if he couldn't find bandages, then to look for feminine pads first, then paper towels and other absorbent materials. After all, the pads were specifically engineered to absorb blood; heck, he had proven their worth after being shot in the house next to where he found Essie.

After he had the medical supplies, he ran through the food aisles, looking for anything left behind by previous scavengers. The shelves were as bare as he had expected, but he had to check. Jared was about to leave when he saw a bag of Doritos wedged under a bottom shelf, barely visible. He grabbed the bag and gently placed it into the pack, careful not to crush the precious chips inside. This was a find. These days, with most of the food having been devoured for the most part within the first week, he and Bart had been living off rations. The chips would be a welcome treat and not for Bart or himself.

Once Jared had safely returned to the gun store, Bart rounded everyone up in the workshop. Once everyone was settled in, Bart sat back studying the group.

"We have to leave."

Every head in the room turned in unison. Jared raised an eyebrow.

"We?" Jared queried.

Bart's face remained placid as he slowly nodded his head in a grave and ominous manner. "I did the math, and I add about twenty percent to your and Essie's chance of survival."

"What does that even mean?" Jared blurted out.

Bart took a deep breath before answering, "It's a numbers game. You're already about forty-five percent in the red, 'cause frankly I think you detract from yourself a little due to lack of training and life experience."

Jared frowned at this.

"I felt that after all you detract from the group, my training and experience add enough to call it a twenty percent gain."

Jared shook his head, chuckling. "You'd be lonely if Essie and I left you, and that's why you want to come."

Bart waved the comment off. "With me you got a twenty percent chance of living; without me, you're both dead." Bart knew he'd spoken inappropriately even before Jared gave him the "what the fuck" look. He winced, looking at the little waif before saying, "Sorry, Ess, what I meant is everything is fine; we're all gonna live…as long as I come with you two."

Jared spent the next four days training and going over what he would need on the road. Bart continued Jared's training, also packing, unpacking, making lists, ripping them up, and making new lists.

Jared found himself sitting in the middle of a pile of gear, staring at it and understanding what each piece meant to his survival. He was slightly amazed by this since a mere three weeks before, he wouldn't have been able to name most of the equipment lying at his feet.

Jared found he was spending less and less time feeling sorry for himself and the situation he was in, and more and more time simply dealing with each day's obstacles. In the old world, people tended to dwell on their tragic lives. People before the event would lose a dog to old age, then hang on to the tragedy for years to come. They would post it all over social media so their friends could also dwell on their enormous loss.

Nowadays there was just so much bad in everyone's lives, one didn't have the energy to hang on to anything that had already happened and no longer had an adverse physical effect on their lives. Personally, Jared felt he had to use every ounce of his energy to survive in the here and now. Any reallocation of those energies could result in his and Essie's deaths.

Jared thought that if the world ever got back to normal, companies like Facebook, Twitter and a myriad of other social media companies simply wouldn't have the following they'd had before. Jared felt the people who survived these times would focus more on the actual faces of family and less on the screen of some electronic piece of engineering that streamed some insignificant celebrity's life struggle as they drove around

Rodeo Drive in a Range Rover, bitching about another insignificant matter.

People would get back to building actual relationships with other humans. In order to survive, Jared was forced to do just that. He would have never forged a relationship with anyone like Bart in the old days. Now...the old bastard was as close to a best friend as Jared had in the world.

By the end of the fourth day, Bart was satisfied with how they had packed everything into the bike trailer and packs. Jared was shocked at how heavy ammunition was, but Bart insisted on taking as much as they could possibly carry. Jared thought about how difficult it was going to be pedaling with all that ammo slowing him down, while Bart looked at the ammo as a way to eat and protect themselves. After Bart hefted the last case of .223 ammo into the trailer, he smiled at Jared.

"Each round could be a deer, and that's food for a week, maybe more." Bart patted the ammo case. "Or it could be a dead bad guy, one less we got to worry about killing us or taking all our stuff." Bart shook his head and continued, "Actually, come to think of it, taking our stuff would most likely kill us." He looked meaningfully at Jared, cocking his head. "Remember when the time comes, they won't just be trying to commit some petty theft, they will be doing something that will end up killing us all, including Essie."

Jared glanced at Essie, who sat on a crate nearby, quietly watching.

"Remember, your resolve has to run parallel with your convictions, Jared." Bart became even more serious. "Always, never wavering, you have to be like you were when you found her, lethal, and you have to remain that way for the rest of your life." Bart stood. "We leave tomorrow."

The following day found Essie perched atop the packed trailer while Jared pedaled in the lowest gear possible. Bart followed on a second bike, which was laden with saddlebags.

Bart had the bike in the back of the shop, and Jared hadn't even known the old guy had wheels till he brought it out the night before their departure.

Both men wore body armor, which Bart had insisted on until they were at least clear of the populated areas. Bart had both his and Jared's body armor set up the same. Rifle magazines were attached in front and on both sides along with a couple of pistol magazines and a pistol holstered up high on the chest. Bart told Jared it would be easier to ride the bike without a hip holster. Next to Essie were two day packs with enough supplies for a week.

These were in case something happened and they had to drop the bikes and move on foot. The packs were filled with food, water and ammo. Additionally, they had water-purification systems in both packs in case the two were separated. Each man carried a rifle and a pistol along with a few hundred rounds for the rifles and nearly a hundred rounds for each pistol.

It was slow moving, and Jared was not used to being so weighted down like this, since all his foraging was done with an empty pack on the way out and a single full pack on the way back, sans body armor, rifle and the trailer. He argued against the body armor and rifles, but Bart stood his ground, telling Jared that, when the time came to move and move fast, he'd be able to do it. Lastly, Bart had stuffed a medical kit into the pouch that held Jared's trauma plate, the hardened metal plate designed to stop high-velocity rifle rounds.

The kit was made by a group called Phokus and had several key pieces of trauma-related gear in it. Additionally, Bart added two Halo chest seals in the event one of them was shot in the chest and needed sealing. This was a double-edged sword, in Jared's opinion. Although Bart had shown him how each piece of first aid gear was to be applied, he had never actually done it on a live or dying person.

He hoped that if the equipment was needed, Bart would be the one applying it since he seemed to know what he was doing. On the other hand, if Bart were applying the first aid treatment, this would mean Jared had been shot, which wasn't at all appealing. Even less appealing was the thought of Essie being shot. Either way, if the trauma kits or IFAKs, short for individual first aid kits, had to be used, it was going to suck.

Bart explained that the IFAK and all the other goodies were not a be-all and end-all. They were simply one step in many that would have been taken to save a life back when the world was a much safer place. Bart told Jared the aid they got in the field was a way to give a hospital the best shot at saving someone's life. Now, they might apply a chest seal or wrap a shattered leg with a tourniquet, but they'd still be missing an essential piece of the survival puzzle. Minus the hospital component, Jared was fairly certain whoever got shot in the post-event world was a goner.

Their movement was made even slower by Bart's insistence that they recon every square inch of landscape prior to passing through it. He kept saying things like, "Patience will be the difference." Bart explained that while they sat wasting time, as Jared had put it, they were becoming accustomed to the sights, sounds and smells of the battlefield. This, he told Jared flatly, would place them at a distinct advantage over those acting in a rushed and desperate manner.

About twenty minutes into one of Bart's recon missions, Jared found himself getting fidgety. He just wanted to move on so they could clear the city before dark. Jared saw them just as Bart laid a hand on his leg, slowly gesturing down the street at the three figures. Jared's body doused him with an unhealthy measure of adrenalin as an icy blanket enveloped his heart.

Jared and Bart glanced back where Essie was huddled under some bushes, then back at the three men in the distance.

Bart slowly brought the binoculars to his eyes, scanning the area before leaning into Jared's ear. "Three guys, all armed."

Jared could see the men, one stood in a storefront alcove while the other two sat on the ground behind an abandoned car. It was apparent they were waiting for targets of opportunity and, if Jared's little group had simply rolled up the street without seeing these fellows first, it was pretty clear what would have happened. Jared shifted, feeling the heavy weight of the body armor, pack, and all the ammunition he was carrying. He thought about the discomfort he felt after being nearly beaten to death in that supermarket near his home, and came to the conclusion he would rather be loaded down than shot or beaten down.

Again, Bart leaned into Jared's ear. "Two options—we try to shoot all three, or we go around."

Jared cocked his head and just stared at Bart, who shrugged. "I figure we got about a seventy-five percent chance of success if we ambush these boys, and around a ninety-eight percent success rate if we go around."

"Just kill 'em?" Jared whispered.

Bart nodded. "I'm pretty sure we would get two. The third will most likely run, which makes for a hard shot. If he did get away, we'd have one very dangerous dude lurking around the area with a pretty good reason to want to do us harm."

"I vote for going around," Jared breathed.

Bart pursed his lips and nodded his agreement. "Although it sure would be nice to smoke those fuckers. They're gonna cause someone real trouble."

Both men crawled back to Essie and began moving away from the three men waiting in the distance.

Jared and his group picked their way through the city to the outskirts, where they actually saw a few people, none of whom spoke a word to the group, and none of whom were armed.

Bart stopped just as the sun's rays were beginning to wane, wiped his sweaty brow, and surveyed the surrounding area. There was a golf course to his left and Mt. Hamilton Road to the right. Bart looked up Mt. Hamilton Road and then back over at the golf course and then around at the surrounding houses. Without a word, Bart pushed his bicycle off to the left, down a small embankment and, through some trees before stopping at a chainlink fence, where he rummaged through his gear, produced a small pair of bolt cutters, sliced through the fence, and then motioned for Jared to follow him onto the golf course.

Jared gingerly made his way down the embankment and through the freshly cut fence, being careful not to dislodge Essie in the process. Bart pushed the heavily laden bike about three hundred yards into the property before pulling up under a grove of trees. As Jared caught up, Bart dropped his pack and began pulling items from the saddlebags.

"We'll camp here for the night."

Jared looked around questioningly. "Here in the middle of a golf course?"

"Yep, look at all that open real estate someone would have to pass over to get to us. Come nightfall the moon is up, and those greens will look like the sun's out." Bart stopped unpacking for a second and gestured back towards the road. "We head up Mt. Hamilton and we're going to run into country folks. They have two things I don't think we should deal with at night—dogs and guns. This is the safest place within miles."

Bart went back to setting up camp, pulling out a small stove he used to heat water, which he added to a large packet of food. He mixed the water and food before sealing the packet and setting it aside. Next, he and Jared set up a small two-man tent under some of the heavier brush. Bart stacked more foliage around and over the top of the tiny tent. Once this was done, Bart walked out into the open and inspected their encampment, satisfied they would not easily be seen from outside the trees. Bart returned to the food packet and promptly devoured a quarter of it before it seemed he took a breath.

Jared had unpacked his trailer and was about to start hauling items to the tent when Bart stopped him.

"Sleeping bags and weapons, everything else needs to stay packed and ready to move. If we have problems tonight and have to run, the only things we'll lose are the tent, one sleeping bag, and Essie's bag."

Jared didn't say a word, instead opting to just repack all the gear he intended to take into the tent. After finishing up, he grabbed his sleeping bag and started towards the tent.

Bart interjected, "We can share my bag. One of us has to be awake at all times." Bart reached in a jacket pocket and pulled out a watch. Days before, Bart had asked that Jared pick up several wind-up watches. He then built a small sundial, simply proclaiming the time was high noon. Having an accurate timepiece was not really that important to Jared, but what seemed more important was having two watches in the event they had to separate and wanted to meet at a certain time.

Bart held the watch up, inspecting the timepiece, then began winding the thing. "Gotta wind these things every day or they stop working." Bart finished winding the watch and tossed it to Jared.

Jared decided he'd take the first watch and reset the old timepiece to 10:00.

After the trio had eaten and Essie was safely tucked in her sleeping bag, Bart started for the tent as well, but stopped short, turning to Jared.

"Don't fucking fall asleep," Bart croaked.

Jared nodded ever so slightly.

"I'm serious about this. Sleeping sentries have no goddamn

friends, boy. If one of the crazies out there don't kill you, I will, so don't get lazy. All our lives depend on you being awake and alert." Bart gestured to the tent, where Essie was sleeping, as if to drive his point home.

Jared just stared back till the ornery old cuss turned and entered the tent. Jared had learned whether he responded or not, Bart was going to rant about certain things. Jared also had little doubt in his mind that if Bart found him asleep on watch, Jared would have lived his last day on this earth.

After Bart and Essie were fast asleep, Jared sat in quiet contemplation of the new world, listening to the sounds of the surrounding neighborhood. Once in a while he would hear voices, but they never came near the encampment. In the distance, Jared heard gunshots on more than a few occasions and, when gravity began dragging his chin to his chest, he got to his feet, creeping along the tree line in order to keep himself awake and alert.

He scanned the open and surprisingly well-lit greens for any signs of humanity. Thankfully he found none under the nearly full moon. Bart had been right; the greens were like a moat, a highly visible moat that would afford an advancing party zero cover from sight or bullets. Jared was sure if someone tried to walk into their camp, he would have no problem seeing them long before they got anywhere near them.

As Jared sat listening to the gunfire and occasional cry from what he could only think had to be a doomed human, he had to wonder at the schedule humans kept before and after the event. The gunfire and screaming ramped up at around ten o'clock and was going strong by midnight.

No matter the event, humans didn't really change that much. Yeah, sure, they adapted and, to the untrained eye, it could seem like everything was different, but Jared knew better. People had to eat and provide for their families no matter the state of the world. People had stabbed each other in the back in the workplace before the event, albeit not in the literal sense, but they had worked within the rules of the game at the time. Now that the rules had been significantly altered, people were quite literally stabbing each other in the back in order to survive and provide for their families.

The event had served to exacerbate everything from the old world. Society of old tended to follow a socialist path in creating an equal playing field for all life's players. After the event stripped the protective cloak of law and order, people were exposed for who they really were. No more hiding behind the threat of calling the cops over a matter that nowadays would be laughable.

Nowadays if some snot-nosed millennial puke lambasted his or her barista for not making their favorite coffee drink to their liking, they'd likely be killed on the spot. Alas, the baristas were all gone, and Jared was pretty sure he and others like him were being more polite to each other these days. Jared was also fairly sure those who weren't being polite had better be ready for whatever came their way.

After he had taken a short tour around the camp, he sat back down, the chill of the night causing his legs to stiffen and his back to ache. He stared down at the watch on his wrist, which read five minutes to two. Jared slowly made his way to the tent, crawling to the entrance, where Bart was already up, fully dressed, wearing his body armor. The older man pulled himself from the tent, stood and stretched, letting out a low guttural moan.

"Anything going on out there?" he asked.

Jared shook his head, glancing out across the golf course. "Some gunshots, but nothing close."

Bart wrestled with his pack, pulling out a small stove, which he positioned between one of his bicycle's saddlebags and some boxes, effectively blocking the small flame from the view of anyone who might be looking in their direction. Jared found himself suddenly very wide awake as he watched Bart make a single cup of coffee.

Bart looked up and shook his head. "None for you, lad, you need to sleep. Can't have you up for twenty-four hours and then hope you stay awake tomorrow night on watch." Bart shook his head again and went back to setting up the tiny stove.

Jared got to his feet, making his way through the darkness to the tent, where he found Essie curled up in her small sleeping bag, sleeping soundly. He climbed into Bart's bag and could still feel the older man's heat. This assisted him greatly in drifting off to sleep, the rhythmic sound of the small girl's breathing helping the much-needed sleep come. His mind began to dream of the three men earlier in the day.

With lucid clarity he played out a scene of him behind his rifle, sights on the men with Bart to his side murmuring a slow countdown. Jared calmed his breathing as Bart murmured, "Two, one." Jared held his breath and gently, ever so gently squeezed the rifle's trigger towards the rear. He could see the man in the sights as the rifle bucked in his shoulder. He heard the dual pop of both his and Bart's rifles as they barked in unison. He stared over the front sight and saw two men dropping to the ground while the third man dropped to a crouch in the half second or so before he would run and become a nearly impossible target. Before the two men had stopped moving, a third shot rang out and the third man dropped. Essie's voice rang out. "I got him!"

Jared sat upright, sweat covered his face and neck.

Essie sat wrapped in her bag from the waist down, hands held up in a clapping position. "I got him," she said again, opening her hands, showing Jared a dead mosquito.

Jared found his breath coming in ragged gasps as he tried to drag his soul from the dream world and deposit it back in the real world. He reached out, hugging Essie to his chest.

"Yes, you did," was all he could say as he sat in a tent on an abandoned golf course, holding a dead family's small daughter like she was his own.

Then as tragedy often does to men, Jared almost laughed out loud. He had never dreamed of killing another human being. Now not only had he taken a life, but had done it before ever dreaming of doing it. The sequence of events was absurd to him. A month ago, he would have been troubled by the dream he just had; now---it just seemed weird the actual killings had happened before the dream. Weren't people supposed to dream of something, then do it? Jared knew if Bart could read his mind, he'd accuse the younger man of overthinking the whole thing.

He shook his head, trying to clear it so he could focus on the here and now, gave Essie a tight squeeze, and unraveled himself from the sleeping bag.

Chapter 26

OUTSIDE, Bart had breakfast waiting as Essie and Jared crawled out of the tent. Only the second day and Jared did not look forward to another day of hard work moving through the countryside astride an overloaded bicycle. He suggested they use highway 152 to cross over to highway 5, but Bart had insisted that would be a great way to get killed, since everyone would be using that road.

Bart's theory was that once people got out into the countryside, they would quickly run out of things like food and water and would not hesitate to do whatever they had to in order to obtain life's essential items. Bart had instead chosen Mt. Hamilton Road, which would be much harder on the group, but would be safer, in Bart's estimation.

"It's deer season year-round, and we have ourselves an endless stack of tags, both doe and buck," Bart said. He explained they didn't have enough food to make it to the next state and would have to shoot meat when they came across it. The food they carried was like a reserve cache that they would eat until they found wild game.

Once they were deep into the Californian countryside, they

would try to make wild game their primary source of food while using their current food stash as side dishes from time to time just to spice up their diet. Bart also hoped to stumble across gardens they could forage from for the much-needed nutrients vegetables provided.

"One more thing," Bart said. "I took a little stroll and found the clubhouse and the pool and filled all my water bottles. You should do the same."

An hour later, the two men and the little lady stood at a three-way intersection on a country road across the street from the golf course they'd slept in. The street sign read "Mt. Hamilton Road." Jared was eager to get moving, Bart not so much.

"This is where everything changes. People will be less apt to take what's not theirs, but they will all be armed out here." Jared squinted, staring up the road as Bart continued, "Armed and very capable in the use of said arms. Remember, out here manners are everything. Be polite no matter what. If we end up killing someone, we call him "sir" right up to the point he draws his last breath."

Jared nodded as he glanced about at the surrounding houses, focusing on one house nestled on the corner with a small white wall around its front yard. The wall was only a couple of feet tall, and the only thing it would have served to deny access to the property was a toddler. *Well, there's something you won't be seeing in the future, a wall that serves no fucking purpose whatsoever.* Sure, a month ago the wall had served a purpose, it looked quaint, *but now it looks pretty goddamn lame,* he thought.

He let out a long breath, mounted the bike, checked that Essie was hanging on, and pumped hard on the pedals, pushing the bike forward and across the street. Jared stole one last look at the little wall, shaking his head in disgust. *Quaint is dead.*

The trio moved up the country road at a snail's pace in

complete silence, with Bart in the lead. Every few hundred yards, Bart would make one of his annoying stops and glass the area they were heading into. Jared knew these stops could and had saved lives, but they were really slowing them down.

When the sun hung low on the horizon, Bart began looking for a suitable camping site. Jared was so exhausted from pedaling all day, he would have been happy dropping to the ground on the side of the road and drifting off to sleep, wrapped only in the clothes he was wearing. Bart wasn't having any of that nonsense, and Jared knew better than to even suggest a campsite close to the road.

Jared thought of all his excuses, like they were using a small stove that emitted no smoke, so why would they have to worry about being spotted, or the fact that they kept a lookout up twenty-four hours a day, or the fact that their footprint on the local terrain was less than that of a rat with the way Bart ran this little outfit. In the end he remained quiet, knowing Bart would make the right and safest decision for their group and, quite frankly, Jared wasn't up for an argument with the most stubborn man he'd ever met.

The road they were traveling on cut through the country-side, with a drop on one side and steep embankments on the other. After a bit of scanning on Bart's part, he dismounted, grabbed the tent and sleeping bags, and tossed them to the ground.

"Let's drop these bikes on the downward side, hide 'em in some bushes."

Jared nodded and pushed his bike behind Bart's to the edge of the road. The drop-off was not severe, and the two men easily secreted the equipment in the undergrowth a good twenty meters from the roadway. Once back on the road, Bart gestured to the opposite side and began making his way up to higher ground. Both men had their day packs on and had split the extra gear, with Jared carrying both sleeping bags while

Bart carried the tent. Essie scrambled along between the two men, the three fighting their way up the soft and shifting embankment.

Like most hills, this one seemed to go on forever. After what seemed like an hour, the tiny group crested what might be called the top. There was a very good view of the road below, and Jared could see bits of the road for miles in both directions as it snaked its way through the hilly countryside. For a moment the two men just stood panting, taking in the expansive view until Essie broke the silence.

"What if someone takes your bikes?"

Bart lifted the binoculars to his eyes and peered back in the direction they'd come. "I can see right where we left them. They'll be fine." He turned, glancing at Jared, eyebrows raised ever so slightly before stealing a glance at the little girl.

Jared gently patted her windswept hair. "Don't worry about those bikes. No one will find them way down in all those bushes."

Essie didn't even look at Jared, but instead looked directly at Bart for assurance.

He smiled and nodded his head. "He's right, they'd have had to see us put them in there and, from where I'm standing, it don't seem like there's another living soul round these parts for a hundred miles."

With that, Bart turned and shuffled off, looking for a suitable campsite. Jared watched him go and was troubled by the labor in Bart's gait, not to mention it seemed like the old guy was wiping his mouth again, and Jared remembered seeing blood on the man's kerchief more than a few times in the last few days. Originally, Bart had intended to stay put in the city because he was getting up in years and hadn't felt he would be able to survive a long trip on foot or bicycle. Somehow, Jared and Essie had changed all that, and now Bart was leading this little expedition across the Californian countryside.

Maybe he knew he would die no matter where he was or what he did, and Jared thought maybe, just maybe, Bart didn't want to die alone. Maybe dying on the road with other people was better than dying alone in the comfort of his shop. Jared shook the thoughts from his head. Bart was not the type of man to lie down on the side of the road and just pass on. He was pretty sure the cranky old man would either die in some sort of fight, accident, or in his sleep.

Essie stepped away from Jared, walking maybe three paces out towards the edge of the hill they had all just climbed.

"My mom would have liked this." She swept her hand across the front of her little body, indicating the view.

Bart interrupted the silence that followed Essie's statement when he limped back to the group. "Let's get off the crest here so someone doesn't see us standing up here on top of the world." Bart motioned for the duo to follow and started off into a small grove of scrub oak.

Once under the cover of the oaks, Bart and Jared set about getting their camp set up while they still had the sun's light. The tent went up, after which dinner was quickly prepared. The trio sat on the hard ground, eating in absolute silence, each person lost in their own thoughts or nightmares.

Jared glanced at Essie, catching her staring blankly at the ground. He studied the little girl for a long while, wondering what a therapist would do with her. Essie's mouth slowly moved as if she were speaking softly to someone or something, though no audible words came from her. Jared had few social skills, and those he did have were about as sharp as a bowling ball, so when it came to Essie, he was at a loss.

Not only was she female, she was a little kid, and he hadn't had much experience with either. *Fuck it*. He reached out and laid a hand on her shoulder in an effort to…well, he didn't really know what, comfort her, break the staring contest she was having with the ground, or maybe just interrupt the dreadful memories she was most assuredly pouring over in her tiny head.

Essie spun on him like a miniature cougar, fire in her eyes and a snarl on her lips. In spite of being three or four times her size, Jared recoiled, sliding backwards on his butt.

"Why didn't you come sooner?" she snarled. "You could have saved them."

Jared knew exactly what she was talking about, but had never been more at a loss for words. He started to say something, but the words stuck in his throat. What could you say to anyone who'd lost their parents in the manner Essie had? The few times Jared's co-workers had lost loved ones, he felt so entirely awkward and uncomfortable that he chose to avoid them until enough time had passed and the subject didn't need to be addressed. Now this small girl was holding his feet to the fire for something he didn't have a bit of control over. Suddenly she flew at him, beating against his torso with her small clinched fists.

"You didn't come fast enough," she screamed as Jared tried to control her flailing arms. "You didn't save them 'cause you were late." The last statement came in sobs as her rage was quickly replaced by the anguish of losing her parents.

"That's about enough of that," came Bart's gentle, but authoritative voice from behind the squabbling two. Bart's face was a mask of seriousness as he approached the pair. "You, young one, should mind your manners."

Both Essie and Jared directed their attention to Bart. Jared temporarily forgot how shocked he was, while Essie's emotions ebbed ever so slightly.

Bart stopped short of the two, surveying them with fatherly firmness. "If he hadn't come at all, you'd have starved to death in that cabinet back at your parents' house."

Jared shifted uncomfortably, glancing at Essie who, until a

few seconds before, had never shown she'd been adversely affected by the slaughter of her parents.

"I get you miss your mom and dad, but the bottom line is neither of them were able to take care of you, and Jared here not only has taken care of you, but he most assuredly saved your life, and for that you should be grateful."

Little Essie's shoulders slumped with this last remark, her head hung low, and she was back to staring at the ground, looking quite possibly like the most vulnerable thing Jared had ever seen. Emotion roiled inside him as he watched this tiny, fragile female human being in such a pitiful state. He felt his cheeks begin to heat up and knew the tears would come if he didn't do something and do it quickly.

He dropped to his knees in front of the waif, gathering her in close. She did not resist, instead burying her face in his chest, sobbing quietly, her tears wetting his shirt. He in turn buried his face in her hair, where he could smell her scent, which was strong since bathing had become a luxury and not a chore.

They held each other this way, rocking slowly back and forth, each quietly dealing with their own overtaxed human emotions, which seemed to be manufacturing demons like Ford did cars. Jared could not begin to imagine what was going on in this little girl's head after all she had been through. He felt like a real heel for not being more aware that she might not be okay after her ordeal. More angering was his feeling of absolute helplessness when it came to Essie's mental health. He was convinced that, given the opportunity, he'd cut off his thumb in exchange for an hour session with a child psychologist for Essie.

Jared vowed to be more aware and in touch with how Essie was acting and feeling, swearing to himself he would be there for her in more ways than just protecting her from harm. As he felt her small frame engulfed in his embrace, he realized he felt for her in a way he had never felt for a child before. Kids were cute and even funny sometimes, but he'd never thought about really caring about one in a fatherly way.

There had never been any kids in his life other than his co-workers' children. Those kids seemed to run their parents ragged, making a lot of unnecessary noise when Jared was around them. He hadn't much cared for any of them and, upon further reflection, he'd gone to great lengths to avoid these co-workers and their grimy, screaming, ill-mannered offspring. Now here he was with Essie, feeling like, well, like a parent, he guessed.

THE FOLLOWING day was sunny yet cool with little to no breeze. Cirrus clouds hung high in the sky and were the only things breaking up the solid blue ceiling. Jared worked the pedals of the bike as the trio moved along the road. Bart was constantly grumbling about ambush points and the lack of visibility as the tiny group moved up the road. They didn't have much of a choice with all the gear they were dragging along.

If they'd tried to move through the open countryside, they would have had to lose the bikes, the trailer and whatever gear they couldn't fit in a pack. Essie would have had to either walk or be carried, and Jared didn't think carrying the girl would have been a viable option. He also didn't think she would have been able to keep up if the group was on foot. Come to think of it, Bart probably wouldn't have been much better. This was most certainly the reason he was so bent about having to stay on the road. He was a liability, and Jared knew that irked the holy hell out of him.

Jared was also sure Bart had one of those math formulas worked out in his head, where he had calculated his worth into a percentage or, more accurately, his liability. By the sound of all Bart's grumbling, Jared was about as sure as he could be that the numbers or percentages or whatever the old bastard came up with were not in the green.

The group came to a bend in the roadway and stopped. Jared knew now to stop, letting Bart haul out the binoculars so he could scan the straight portion of the road ahead. Jared was glad to take time to rest his tortured legs, get some water, and check on Essie. While Bart grumbled and scanned, Jared plucked a water bottle out of a pouch on his pack, offering Essie the first drink, which she declined. He drank long from the bottle, letting the fresh water run down his throat, cooling his insides.

Bart finished and stepped back to Jared. "Problem is, if someone is hiding or lying in wait up there, we probably wouldn't even see 'em." Bart shook his head, gesturing to the water and holding out the binoculars in exchange.

Jared completed the exchange, then peered through the lenses, searching the road along with the surrounding countryside. There was a drop on one side and the usual embankment on the opposite side. Jared stopped scanning, focusing on something up the embankment from the road. He adjusted the focus, but that only made it worse, so he refocused, trying to locate the oddity again. He wasn't sure what he'd seen, a branch or maybe just an irregularity in the ground.

Bart finished with the water, nudging Jared while holding out his hand for the optics. Jared turned, still holding the binoculars halfway to his face.

Chapter 27

"WHAT?" Bart asked.

Jared slowly shook his head. "Don't know. I thought I saw something that didn't belong, but it could have been a branch or, really, anything."

Bart looked serious now. "Did it move?"

Jared lowered the glasses, shaking his head, relaxing a bit. Nothing had, and, the more he thought on it, there was nothing to indicate he'd seen a threat. Hell, the first night on the golf course, he'd seen all kinds of things that were not real. The inky blackness of night coupled with the stress of the world coming apart at the seams could make a person see all manner of imagined beasts.

Bart took the glasses and scanned the road ahead. "Describe what you saw and where it was," Bart hissed, keeping his voice low.

Jared pointed up the road. "Right side about halfway to the next turn, up in the bushes. Looked like a pipe or a darker branch or something; then I couldn't find it again—probably nothing."

During the entire exchange, Essie sat atop the trailer,

watching the men occasionally glancing up the road, but she never climbed down and never made a sound. Jared turned back to her and gave her a reassuring smile as he stowed the water bottle.

"Have her vest up," Bart barked.

Jared reached into the trailer, pulling out a ballistic vest, which he lowered over Essie's head and shoulders till she was effectively mummified in Kevlar. The vest was so big she looked like a scrawny turtle in an oversized shell.

Bart took one last long look through the optics before letting them hang loosely around his neck. Bart climbed back on his bike and pointed it back up the road. He glanced back at Jared, who shrugged, and then they were off. Jared thought this was what Bart had meant when he said sometimes you just gotta fucking go and get it done, even if it feels wrong.

As they moved forward, Jared lost track of where he thought he'd seen the oddity, until a voice boomed out from above them like a cannon blast.

"That's far enough, and don't think about laying a hand on those rifles."

Bart swore under his breath as both he and Jared turned their heads up the embankment, where a grizzled old man, about Bart's age, was getting to his feet. The man was pointing the business end of a shotgun at the small group, and he had the high ground.

"Shannon, come on out. I got 'em covered." From the slope behind them, a woman in her late twenties emerged, carrying a large silver revolver, which was also pointing at the group. "You all drop those rifles and pistols on the road and step back," the old man shouted from on top of the embankment.

Bart had looked over his shoulder, but he never turned from the old man holding the high ground. "Not going to happen," Bart said as he let the rifle slowly swing around to his front without ever using his hands.

The man tensed, shaking the shotgun at the group. "Don't you touch that rifle, mister."

Bart held his hands loosely at his sides, the rifle hanging from the sling well within easy reach should he feel the urge to use it. Jared watched; he'd seen Bart start from this position during training, and knew full well Bart could have the rifle up and in working order in less than a second.

Jared's breath began coming in quick shallow gasps as his mind tried to keep up with their evolving situation. He knew he had to calm his breathing, Bart had talked to him about this, and he knew Bart would be counting on him for help when the shooting started. He fought the panic back and, in an effort that could have moved a house, he began to think rationally regarding his situation.

Bart was engaged with the old man who, in Jared's opinion, was their greatest threat. Jared surmised Bart would shoot the older guy first and, if Jared didn't get rounds on or at least at the woman, she'd shoot Bart in the back. If he remained frozen in place, he was fairly certain Bart would shoot him if this woman didn't finish the old-timer first. He had to shoot the woman if Bart and the other cranky old fucker started slinging lead.

The thought of shooting a woman almost sent Jared into another of his supercharged overthinking sessions, but he spied Essie in his peripheral vision. Although the sight of Essie didn't fully quash his qualms about killing a woman, it helped enough for him to focus on the dangerous situation they were facing.

Jared took a deep breath, exhaling so loudly everyone turned and looked at him. Shannon was an attractive gal in her late twenties, and she looked terrified as she clutched the revolver.

"Take it easy," Bart soothed to no one in particular. "Ain't no one gonna do anything crazy here."

"Drop the guns," insisted the old man, his voice cracking ever so slightly.

Bart looked down, shaking his head slowly. "Yeah, you got the high ground, but you have a shotgun, and, yeah, you may put some lead in one of us, but we're gonna kill one of you, that's for sure."

Jared was still breathing like he had run up a couple of flights of stairs, but now he was seeing things a little more in a tactical sense. He turned slightly towards the woman, relaxing his shoulders, allowing the rifle to slip around to his right side, where he could access it quite easily. The slight change was not lost on the old man, and he tightened his grip on the old shotgun.

"This is your last warning, drop the guns," he almost begged.

Bart saw Jared let the rifle move to his front, saw the fear on the woman's face, and heard the shake in the old man's voice. He knew they were about to get into a gunfight. Bart wished to avoid this at all costs. A gunshot wound in the present world, however minor, could very well be a death sentence. Bart didn't think they were being robbed, so the only thing left was these people were protecting their home. *Probably a father and his daughter*, Bart thought, wondering where the mother was. He hoped she wasn't somewhere off in the distance with a scoped rifle, just waiting for them to make a false move so she could put a high-velocity bullet through one of them.

"I don't take kindly to folks pointing guns at me, but I'm willing to give you all a pass, seeing as the world recently fell apart and you're probably worried about someone coming out here and taking what you got."

The old man stood silent, studying Bart as he spoke.

"We are not putting our guns down; we are also not here to take anything from anyone, so please point those weapons somewhere else before one of us gets shot."

Bart turned his head and looked at where Essie was perched inside the vest. "Hell, we got a little girl, for crying out loud, and you all are scaring the goddamn hell out of her."

The woman looked up at the old man, obviously taking her lead from him. There was a long pause; then the old man lowered the shotgun.

"What do you all want way out here?" With this, both groups visibly relaxed, the woman lowering the revolver while both Bart and Jared returned the rifles to their backs.

"We don't want a damn thing," Bart said with a half-smile. "We got everything we need right here, and we ain't in the business of takin' what's not ours unless the owner isn't around and wouldn't miss it anyway."

"We don't rob people," Jared blurted out.

The old man slowly made his way down the embankment, coming even with the group, giving the woman a reassuring nod before extending his hand to Bart first and then Jared.

"Name's Calvin, and this is Shannon, and we were not robbing you folks."

Bart shook the man's hand, gesturing towards Essie. "That's Essie; she's Jared's charge. He picked her up back in the city; both her parents are—well, not around."

Calvin and Shannon exchanged concerned looks then stared at Essie.

Bart cleared his throat. "I'll explain later. This is not the time nor place to be speaking about her—experiences." He finished by giving Essie a reassuring nod before breaking into a broad and almost warm smile as he turned back to face the two standing in the road before him. "So, what's with the ambush and the 'lay down your guns or else' routine?"

Shannon straightened, but remained quiet.

Calvin's nostrils flared ever so slightly as he spoke. "Been a lot of bad things happening in the world over the past month or so."

"Fair enough," was Bart's only response.

Feeling he needed to explain more, Calvin continued, "Not much happened up here at first; most folks are pretty self-sufficient and keep to themselves." Calvin shifted, gazing back down the road in the direction Jared and Bart had come. "Couple of weeks back, we kinda figured something bad had happened, so I saddled up one of our horses and headed down the hill. Once I could see the city, I knew something terrible had happened." He waved a hand across the sky. "Lots of smoke and fires down there."

Calvin told them how he left the horse tethered, keeping out of sight when he realized there were a lot of fires and no firefighters doing a thing to extinguish them. He'd been around long enough and had a lively enough imagination to come to the conclusion that if there were no firefighters, there probably weren't many cops either, and that meant danger.

Bart stopped him, asking if the group could move off the road into some cover so they didn't get walked up on standing there in the middle of the street talking about old times. Calvin showed them to the top of a knoll close to where he'd been when the two groups came in contact. From their position atop the knoll, they could see the road in both directions. Bart gestured to Jared in the direction they'd been heading, while he turned, searching the road in the opposite direction. This wordless communication did not go unnoticed by Calvin.

"You two related?" Calvin queried.

Bart shook his head. "Never met the kid until after the party got started."

"You a cop?" Calvin grunted.

Jared looked up for Bart's reaction, which, not surprisingly, was nothing.

Calvin slowly nodded his head knowingly before turning to Jared. "You ain't no cop though," he said with just a little too much conviction for Jared's liking.

Jared didn't know why this bothered him, but it did. He'd never been worried about appearing tough before the event and wondered why he felt slighted now, when he was sure Calvin was not going to follow up his "you're not a cop" proclamation up with "you in Special Forces?"

Calvin did not disappoint. "You a dispatcher or something?"

Bart chuckled at this as he gazed off into the distance.

"No, I worked for a tech company," Jared said flatly.

Calvin let it go, turning back to Bart. "Where you work?"

"I haven't worked as a cop for years." Bart said, shaking his head. "I worked for San Jose PD when I did work, but that was a long time ago, and I ain't no cop now."

Calvin seemed to accept this. "Can always tell you cops, something about how comfortable you are around folks. There's a little country in every cop, they'll talk to anyone, and they always get twice as much information as they give."

Bart smiled at this. "Yeah, I guess so."

Jared moved to the trailer, plucking Essie from atop the gear, setting her gently on the ground. Next he offered her a small bottle of water, which she drank from before handing it back and taking the small packet of fruit snacks Jared held out. Shannon watched the interaction between the two with intent interest. Jared rifled through the trailer, pulling out a small stove along with some coffee. He prepped the water, making two cups, offering them to Calvin and Shannon. "Coffee?"

Both Calvin and the woman bobbed their heads eagerly, so Jared prepared two more cups before joining the group sitting in a small circle, hugging their mugs whilst sipping the steaming hot beverage. Jared wasn't sure of the date, but it had to be early to mid-October, and the temperatures were starting to drop as the afternoons crept towards evenings.

Calvin continued his story, telling the group how he ventured on foot into the city, trying to find out what happened. He'd seen some folks, but no one spoke to him. Everyone looked scared, and the only folks he'd seen on the streets were the type he felt should be avoided.

Calvin made his way maybe a mile into the city limits when he ran into four men who were less than well mannered. Calvin was not armed and hadn't even thought of arming himself before coming down to the city. To him, this thing felt like a large-scale power outage that would be remedied within a few days. He was looking for answers, not trouble.

The end result was a large cut over his left eye and a gunshot wound to his left forearm, which he received during his resistance to them taking everything he had on his person. He hadn't brought much, except for the clothes on his back, and was glad he had the wherewithal to tether the horse before he walked into the city. Beaten and shot was no way to make a twenty-mile hike back home.

Calvin had been left bleeding on the ground, confused, no cell phone, no police, no medics, no nothing. After a bit, he hauled himself to his feet and started back to where he left the horse. His arm pained him greatly and continued to bleed till he stopped and wrapped it with his shirt. He still had the use of his fingers and hand, so he figured the bullet hadn't broken any bones as it passed straight through, exiting the arm on the opposite side.

The horse was right where he'd left it, and he wasted no time in getting the animal turned away from the city, heading back to his home in the hills. The ride home was miserable, but uneventful compared to when the ill-mannered folks bonked him on the head, shot him in the arm, and took his boots and wallet. What the hell were they going to do with his wallet anyway?

Once Calvin got home, he boiled water and flushed the wound on his arm, which nearly caused him to lose consciousness. Next, he cleaned both his arm and head wound, packing them with antibiotic ointment before wrapping his arm and covering his head wound. Jared could see the scar over Calvin's eye, which had healed nicely, but would remain a fairly noticeable scar for years to come. Calvin pulled up the sleeve on his jacket, revealing a small scar on one side and a somewhat larger scar on the opposite side where the projectile had fought its way out of his flesh, taking a little with it.

Jared thought about bringing up the beating he'd taken in the grocery store, but decided it would only give Calvin an opening he didn't feel like listening to. Maybe if he'd been shot or stabbed, he would have brought it up, but he hadn't, so he kept his mouth shut.

During Calvin's storytelling hour, Shannon had moved closer to Essie and was now sitting next to her, quietly whispering back and forth with the little girl. Jared pretended not to watch as Essie actually smiled as she conversed with Shannon. The two other men also noticed the newly formed alliance going on, which included females only. Suddenly aware, both girls stopped, locking eyes with the three men staring at them.

Essie looked shyly at Jared. "What?"

Jared shook his head, pursing his lips in a tight smile. It pleased him to see her interact with another female. He couldn't put his finger on it, but it felt good to see Essie happy and in the company of the softer gender. His father had always told him kids needed a mom and a dad. He told Jared a mother infused a humanitarian element in a person, and a father infused a survival element. When the two were properly blended, you'd have a fine human version of thirty-year-old blended Scotch. Now sitting there watching Essie and Shannon whisper back and forth, he understood what his father meant.

As Calvin finished telling as much of his story as he planned on telling without getting a little in return, he nodded at Bart. "What's your story?"

Bart took a deep breath. "Not much to tell. Lights went out, Jared there showed up, and we decided to get out of the city before the whole place came crashing down."

Calvin crossed his arms and cocked his head to the side. "You really gonna feed me that line after telling me you're not a cop anymore and hearing my story?"

Bart exhaled the breath he'd drawn and was about to speak when Jared leaped to his feet and froze, facing the direction of the city. A second later, the entire group heard the same sound, a sound none of them had heard in more than a month.

Bart leaped to his feet. "Everyone down," he hissed, bringing the binoculars to his eyes and scanning the road as Jared moved to Essie, scooping her up and planting her firmly in the trailer. He deftly dropped the ballistic vest over her and softly patted her head till she lowered herself into the vest like a turtle.

Jared crouched as he moved to Bart's side, peering off into the vast countryside. The sound was an older Volkswagen Beetle puttering its way up the road not more than half a mile off and closing.

"Just don't move and they'll pass right by," Bart said, his eyes still fixed to the binoculars.

Calvin scrambled to his feet, but Bart grabbed him. "Stay down, man."

Calvin tugged out of Bart's grasp. "They're headed straight towards our place and, if they take everything, we won't survive," Calvin snarled.

Jared watched Bart purse his lips for a split second before shaking his head.

"Where's your place?" Bart asked.

Both Calvin and Shannon gave each other a look as the sound of the approaching Beetle became louder and louder.

Bart put the glasses back to his eyes, taking in the approaching vehicle. "Got four bad-looking dudes in this car," he said, dropping the binoculars from his face. "You got stuff at your place worth fighting for?"

Neither Calvin nor Shannon answered.

"How far is it?" Bart snapped.

Both remained silent, but Shannon looked terrified. Bart unslung his rifle, placing the butt end in the dirt. "Listen, there are four guys, and all of them are armed." He pointed Calvin's shotgun then the pistol Shannon had. "And they're armed a hell of a lot better than the two of you are." Bart looked at Jared as if he was going to seek approval for what he was about to do, then turned back to Calvin. "You and missy go up there and get in a gunfight and I bet you either lose or get hurt so bad you might as well have lost."

Calvin hefted the shotgun. "I can't just let someone come onto our property and clean us out."

Bart stood, straightening his old and very stiff back. "Leave Shannon here with Essie. Jared and I will come with you. Three on four is a lot better odds than two on four." Bart nodded at Shannon. "She can look out for the girl, and we can go to wherever your place is and make sure they don't clean you out."

The sound of the Beetle was close now, and Jared was beginning to get that borderline panicky feeling he seemed to have to wrestle with almost every day lately. He hated the feeling, mostly because when something happened, he felt Bart became calmer. He so wanted to have a calm wash over him when things fell apart, but he hadn't spent a lifetime preparing his mind to act that way, so he suffered. Maybe it was because it made him feel less of a man when he was coming apart at the seams and the man next to him was talking nonchalantly about taking a little walk and getting in a gunfight. He took a deep breath, trying to steel himself, fighting for control of his body as adrenaline gushed through his veins, threatening to wrest all control away from him.

"You good?" Bart barked.

Jared snapped his head up, eyes wide, giving a terse nod.

Bart raised his eyebrows, turning ever so slightly towards Shannon. "Want me to take her instead?"

Jared's face flushed as he shook his head. "I'm fucking good," he blurted, causing Bart to frown disapprovingly at Jared's vulgarity in front of Essie.

The Beetle was nearly even with them as Bart stood, moving to Calvin's side. "Which way and how far?"

Calvin took one last look at Shannon, who moved to Essie's side and began moving her along with the gear towards a thick clump of bushes. "Just over that hill, maybe a quarter mile or so. It's a bit farther using the road, so we should be able to get to the house about the same time they do."

The Beetle passed their position, continuing up the road, the engine noise slowly dissipating as the three men moved through the knee-high grass in the direction Calvin had indicated. No one spoke as they huffed and puffed their way up the gradually inclining slope, listening to the faint sound of the Beetle. As the three neared the top of the slope, the sound of the Beetle stopped.

Calvin spoke back over his shoulder without stopping. "They're at the front gate. It's locked, so they'll have to either walk in or cut the lock."

As if to answer him and prove him wrong all at the same time, the engine could be heard as it revved, engaged and powered the Beetle into motion. The noise that followed was a scraping metallic sound. It was obvious to all three that the Beetle had simply run through the gate.

Once at the top of the hill, a small house could be seen nestled next to a small creek near some old oak trees. The Beetle still had not made it up the driveway, which looked to be several hundred yards in length. Bart halted the group, surveying the scene below, his eyes narrowed to mere slits, rifle clutched in old but still strong hands.

"Jared, stay up here and hold the high ground. If we go loud down there, do what you can to cover us. The minute you start taking fire, get the hell out of here and back to Essie. We're going down and, if we get ourselves killed, you will have to be there for those gals." Bart looked back at Calvin. "You and I are going down and seeing what these boys are up to. Jared, show no mercy; put 'em down if it goes that way. We get into it with them boys and they'll most likely try to get back to the car; that's when you clobber 'em. They won't expect it." Bart winked at Jared. "We're outnumbered, but we got the element of surprise on our side and, by God, that adds five or six guys' worth."

Without another word, Bart turned, moving off around the hill in the direction of the small house, with Calvin in tow. Jared settled in and watched the two older men make their way through the scrub brush to the rear of the house just as the Beetle came into view.

As seemed usual lately, his heart began to race. He breathed in deeply, trying desperately to calm his shaking hands. He had so much adrenaline coursing through his body that his senses were queued to levels he'd never felt before. Lying on his stomach, he could literally smell the decomposing leaves beneath him as if he'd buried his face in the earth and drawn a long deep breath solely through his nostrils. Just knowing he was on the edge, coupled with some deep breaths in through his nose and out through his dry mouth, helped calm his shaking nerves ever so slightly.

Chapter 28

THE DRIVER STOPPED the Beetle in front of the small house, and four men spilled out onto the gravel drive, surveying the property. Jared watched as they glanced this way and that, moving towards the front porch, in what appeared to be a very disorganized and disjointed group. He watched everyone in the group sweep another team member's back with their weapon no less than three times before they reached the front porch, and Jared had to smile, thinking if Bart were in charge of these lunatics, he likely would have shot all four simply for the weapons-safety violations Jared had witnessed in the last thirty-seconds alone.

All four men appeared to be some Hispanic race, and all were heavily tattooed, some even showing ink as far up their necks as the jawline. Jared wasn't up on gang tattoos before the event, and he hadn't studied up after, but he was pretty sure these guys were gang members before the event and hadn't converted after the power went out.

▭

SALVADOR STOOD ON THE PORCH, peering through one of the front windows. His brother, Jose, and their two closest friends, Raymond and Steve, peered through windows on the other side of the front door. Salvador was born in San Jose to parents who'd illegally crossed the border somewhere near San Diego and had moved north through California before settling in the Bay Area, where they both found work. Salvador's brother was born a couple of years later, and both boys had pretty much raised each other while their parents scratched out a living, working two and sometimes three jobs each.

The streets were where the boys grew up, meeting the older brothers of friends, and eventually getting mixed up in running errands for these older brothers, and finally being accepted into a gang. Gang initiation had come in the form of a beating by other gang members.

Salvador remembered being beaten to the ground, where he was beaten and kicked some more. He tried to cover his head while lashing out at his assailants when the opportunity presented itself. Salvador remembered wondering when or if the beating would ever end. Then as quickly as it all started, the assault ended, and he was helped to his feet, hugged and even kissed by the very boys who had seconds before been beating him nearly unconscious.

When Jose's time came to be jumped into the gang, Salvador was first in line and had beat his brother harder than any two of the other gang members. He had also been the proudest when Jose had fought back, but eventually gone down without a sound, taking the beating with silent honor. Salvador was crying after the beating, holding his brother and welcoming him into the gang.

From that time on, they had not depended on their parents, but instead looked to the gang for everything. The gang had provided food, entertainment, women, counsel, and anything else one of its members needed or wanted. Salvador couldn't remember ever having another meaningful conversation with his parents after he'd been accepted into the gang.

If both boys hadn't been so hardened by the streets, they would have seen what good people their parents were. They would have seen how hard their parents had worked so the two brothers could grow up in a safer country. Instead they unwittingly worked to make their new home as dangerous as the home their parents had left behind.

When Salvador was sixteen and Jose was only fourteen, they were tasked with a drive-by shooting on a rival gang's stronghold. The then gang leader, a man of twenty-four years, had assigned two other gang members to assist, but Salvador had refused their help. Instead he and Jose had gone to the house, but as an alternative to driving by and spraying the structure with indiscriminate gunfire, they knocked on the door and fought their way through the house, killing every male they came across.

They wore masks and were never identified in the murders of seven rival gang members. Looking back, the cops were so stupid; they'd talked to everyone in Salvador's gang except him and Jose. Everyone else had kept their mouths shut out of loyalty to the gang and probably a little fear of these two maniacs who'd single-handedly wiped out nearly an entire rival gang in one incident.

This act alone drove the two brothers up the chain of command within the gang in no time. Members from other allied gangs stopped to pay respect after the killings, while both brothers reveled in their newfound stardom. When Salvador was eighteen, a shootout left a void in his gang's leadership. There was no argument from a single member as Salvador took the reins of the gang and went to work. Within three years, his gang was a force to be reckoned with in the South Bay. Salvador controlled nearly seventy-five percent of the San Jose drug and prostitution scene; then the power went out.

At first it seemed like a godsend, no cops, no law, no one to stop them from doing whatever they wanted, but within the first week Salvador realized this was a whole new world where he would have to reprioritize what he thought was important. Drugs were still important to those junkies so hooked on them they had only a vague realization of what was happening, but they made up the minority of his customers. They were sketchy at best, rarely had enough money for what they needed, and were generally more hassle than they were worth. The working class, on the other hand, were by far his preferred customers; they had money and weren't as desperate and unpredictable as the junkies.

Within that first week, those predictable customers had other things on their minds, like family and food, so Salvador began holding grocery stores hostage. Salvador lost six men in the first two days he started controlling stores. He realized quickly that if he made his men visible, there was far less likelihood of a gunfight, or any fight for that matter. People actually would walk up and ask questions about the store, along with the availability of goods. When the situation was explained to them, they would leave, either returning with something to trade, or they'd never be seen again.

One problem Salvador faced was he needed ammunition, meaning rifle ammo, 9 mm and .45-caliber ammo. Surprisingly enough, even in California, there were quite a few people who owned firearms. Unfortunately, most of them were .38 Specials or .380-caliber jobs. Some brought shotgun ammo, which he took, but he needed ammunition for his gang's rifles and most of these Californians didn't have what he needed.

What Salvador didn't know was that people who had rifles and stockpiled their own ammunition would likely never trade it and most assuredly would not trade it with the likes of Salvador and his gang. Four of the gang members killed in those first two days were shot by someone from a long way out. None of the gang members saw or heard anything other than the shot. Two had been head shots, and the other two were center mass body shots. Although Salvador had experienced being shot three times himself, he was no ballistics expert, but by the size of the wounds in his fallen brothers' heads and chests, he was sure they'd been killed with a rifle round.

After the sixth man was killed, Salvador led his remaining men through the surrounding neighborhoods and did things he would never have been able to do before the power went out. When they were done, smoke rose from fifty homes and bodies littered the streets. He left someone from every home alive, making sure he let them know why he was killing.

The second week brought more desperation to the streets, and his stores were actually attacked on a regular basis. He lost more men struggling to adapt to the ever-changing world. By the third week, the stores were empty, and now he was in jeopardy of starving, so he rallied his gang, setting out across the city in search of food and supplies. He'd seen Jose kill a man over a four-pack of toilet paper and remembered feeling relieved, since the stuff was becoming harder and harder to find.

On one occasion, a man claimed to have a working motor vehicle and offered to trade it for food. Salvador talked a little turkey with the man before agreeing to a deal. When the man left and returned with an old VW Beetle, Salvador almost called off the deal, but his better judgment told him cars were not a thing to pass on in the new age.

After the end of the fourth week, the city seemed nearly dead, both in the people sense and food-supply sense, so he adapted yet again, setting out into the countryside in search of food. The first little ranch house they set upon was occupied by an old woman with a shotgun. Three of his men had killed the old woman before she got a shot off. They'd searched the house and a barn, leaving with an assortment of canned veggies, fruits and probably fifty pounds of beef jerky.

They were about to leave when one of Salvador's men located a cellar off to the side of the house, where they hit pay dirt. They weren't more than fifteen miles up into the hills, but these folks seemed to be preparing for the end of the world. Salvador vowed to keep plundering these country folks, and they loaded the bounty into the Beetle before returning to their neighborhood.

This was Salvador's second trip into the hills, and he hoped they would be half as successful as he had been on the first trip. The place looked lived in, but he didn't get the sense anyone was home. *All the better*, he thought. Salvador tried the door, but it was locked. No problem, he stepped back and kicked the thin door right off one hinge, leaving it dangling by the remaining hinge. The four men moved into the structure, guns raised, looking through each room before reconvening in the kitchen. The recalcitrant four began tearing through the cupboards, searching for food or anything of value.

IN THE BUSHES to the rear of the small house, Bart and Calvin could hear the muffled voices combined with the banging of pots, pans and cupboard doors.

Calvin struggled to get up. "Sons of bitches," he snarled.

Bart hauled him back down. "Easy, killer, let 'em do their thing. They aren't leaving with a thing."

Calvin sank back to the ground, nostrils flaring, shotgun gripped tightly in his hands, angry rage roiling through his old boney body.

Bart patted his arm and smiled. "We got this, my friend. Look at 'em—no one even watching the car," Bart whispered, thinking a car was one of the earth's most prized positions now, and these nitwits hadn't even put a guard on theirs. Bart shook his head as he pulled the old handkerchief out of his pocket, muffling a couple of coughs with it. As he pulled the rag away from his mouth, he could see the bright red splatters his ailing body had expelled. He quickly stowed the bloody evidence, bringing his rifle back up and sighting on the house.

⸻

BACK ON THE HILL, Jared felt like he was being electrocuted as he tried in vain to calm his nerves. He lost track of Calvin and Bart when they went to the rear of the small house, and now he couldn't see any of the gang members, but he could hear them inside the house as they ransacked the place. Not knowing where the two older men were was more than a little unnerving. Jared wished he had a walkie-talkie so he could find out what was happening.

Had he thought about it in a tactical sense, he would have realized he probably had the best view of what was going on down below even though he was the furthest from the house. He had the high ground, and Bart hadn't left him there by accident. He felt like he should do something, move, shoot, call out to the older men, something. Instead he stayed put, nerves twitching, mind racing, adrenaline pumping.

⸻

BART SAT HUNCHED over in the bushes, running scenario after scenario over in his head. He could go in shooting, probably getting one or both of them shot or killed. He was pretty sure he wouldn't have an issue convincing Calvin to follow him into the house no matter the plan, but that scenario was beyond terrible.

He moved on to the next plan, wishing he had some way of

talking to Jared so he could be fed information helpful to his decision-making. They could wait till the guys came out, got in the vehicle, and then simply ambush them. Shoot the holy hell out of the car and all four occupants, but Bart didn't like that plan either. Yeah, he'd probably kill or incapacitate all the gang members, but they'd also destroy the only working vehicle Bart had seen in more than a month, and he wasn't sure he wanted to do that.

As fate would have it, Salvador forced the issue by coming out the back door and heading straight for the bushes Bart and Calvin were hunkered down in. As he approached the two older men, he unzipped his pants, hollering something over his shoulder in Spanish.

The whole thing evolved so quick, Bart knew Calvin would be on full overload, so he didn't count on any help from the man. Bart saw Salvador moving directly toward him and knew what was coming. The man would see them and, though Bart was sure he would be surprised, he knew he'd be more surprised if Bart simply stood up and shot him dead. Bart also knew that, with the guy dead, he couldn't warn any of the other ass bags in the house, and they would be confused after hearing a single shot. Bart hoped they would think this dumbass had had an accidental discharge, and simply saunter out the back to mock him, and that was when the real shooting would start.

When Salvador was twenty feet from the two, Bart stood up straight and shot the man in the face with his rifle. As Salvador's body dropped straight to the ground in a heap of bloody gang-member mush, the racket inside the house stopped. Bart immediately moved laterally and towards the residence, getting off the center line of the back door.

His plan was to spread out and create distance between him and Calvin, making it impossible for the gang members to fire on both of them at the same time. Shouts in Spanish erupted from inside the house as the back door blasted open, the three remaining gang members spilling out into the rear yard. Bart ducked as Calvin's shotgun roared from behind him. *Ah, the old fucker wasn't mummified by my sudden violent and deadly act.*

The three gang members were so close, they all caught pellets from Calvin's blast. Yelping and bleeding, they searched for a target while climbing over each other in an attempt to return to the safety of the small house. Without thinking, Bart brought the rifle to his shoulder and fired nearly a dozen rounds at the retreating mass of worthless humanity.

Two of the men went down while the third made the back door, disappearing inside the house. Another blast rocked the quiet mountain air, causing Bart to wince as more double-aught buck slammed into the already downed bodies of the two stricken gang members. Bart heard a single shot from inside the house, most likely an accidental discharge from the panicked gang member who had just been witness to fifty percent of his group being gunned down right before his eyes.

Bart smiled inwardly, knowing he had the upper hand for the time being. Calvin rushed towards him, intent on entering the house, but Bart grabbed him by the shoulder, directing him along the side of the small house.

From the front of the house, Bart heard several shots, a pause, then a few more shots before all went quiet. He took a knee, making damn sure Calvin did the same, directing him to watch their six. Bart inched his way towards the front of the house, stopping short and scanning as much of the yard as he could see. The Beetle was still there, as was the last gang member.

The guy was sprawled out in a less than natural position, rifle still slung and underneath his body. Bart could see both the unmoving man's hands, and they were nowhere near the rifle and its trigger mechanism. Bart stared at the man, looking for any signs of movement, but saw none. He raised his rifle and fired three rounds into the downed gang member, then stood and called out to Jared, "You good up there?"

———

JARED HEARD gunfire erupt from the rear of the house, but couldn't see anything from his position. The front door burst open, and one of the gang members came staggering out, bleeding and clutching a rifle. Before Jared realized what he was doing, he had the man in his sights and was pulling the trigger. The first round struck the man in the shoulder, and the next two rounds went wide. Jared had adjusted, firing two more rounds as the man plunged headfirst onto the dirt drive.

The next few seconds seemed like an eternity as Jared searched desperately for any sign of life below him. The gang member was not moving, and he had no idea where Bart and Calvin were until several shots rang out from the side of the house, causing Jared to nearly piss himself. When Bart called out to him, Jared was overcome with relief. He leaped to his feet, coming out of his hiding place on the hill, and made his way down to the house, where Bart and Calvin were inspecting the downed man, who was currently providing nourishment to the yard's vegetation in the form of blood loss.

Jared had never been so happy to be with other people in his life. Waiting on that hill had nearly seen him come apart at the seams. He felt so alone he'd nearly lost it and just called out or, worse yet, come down to the house, where he likely would have either been purposely shot by the gang or accidentally shot by Calvin or Bart. Well, on second thought, if he had melted down on that level and Bart had shot him, it probably wouldn't have been accidental.

"We nabbed the other three in the back there," Bart said, gesturing down the side of the small house.

Jared stared at the fallen man, then blankly down the side

of the house as Bart placed a hand on his shoulder. "You did good, kid. You did good."

Calvin spat at the man on the ground. "Sons of bitches tore up the house." He turned and stalked off towards the front door, disappearing inside.

Bart scanned the area, then nodded back up the hill. "Why don't you go get the girls. They're probably scared half to death after all the shooting."

Jared gave a slow nod, turned and walked slowly up the hill.

"Hey," Bart called after him.

Jared stopped, turning to stare numbly at the old man.

"Remember a couple of things, boy, death is just that, death. Don't make more of it than what it merits." The older man stepped closer to Jared, lowering his voice. "Examine it and how it affects you; then you can apply the appropriate emotions to it."

Jared tilted his head ever so slightly. He had no idea what the old bastard was talking about now. Hell, he wasn't really in the mood or the state of mind to absorb any of Bart's veiled lessons at the moment.

"C'mon, man, think about hitting a squirrel with a car, no big deal, right? Now think about hitting a dog and, well, quite frankly, it will be a little worse on your conscience." Bart turned, gesturing to the downed gang member. "This turd isn't even a squirrel, and we are far better off without him. Fuck, let me rephrase that, we all are a shit ton better off without him lurking around trying to kill, steal or whatever." Bart held his hands out, palms up. "You should be celebrating. Save the morose shit for a time when one of these motherfuckers hurts one of us."

Jared nodded more in understanding than in agreement, turned, and resumed his trek to retrieve the womenfolk.

Chapter 29

AFTER JARED LEFT, Bart searched for and found the keys still in the Beetle's ignition. He opened the door and dropped into the driver's seat before turning the key. Despite the appearance of the vehicle, the rattle trap sputtered twice, then sprang to life in that loping VW way.

"Holy fucking shit," Bart exclaimed, marveling at the first car he'd seen in weeks. Although he'd grown up in the age of automobiles, this truly seemed like a miracle.

Calvin burst out the front door with the same look on his face as Bart wore on his own. Bart stepped out of the chugging Beetle, smiling broadly as a slow grin stretched across Calvin's face while he shook his head.

"What a beautiful piece of shit," Calvin yelled over the hum of the vehicle's motor.

Bart nodded in agreement. "And it's all ours."

Calvin lost the grin, regarding Bart more than a little suspiciously. "Ours, or yours?"

Bart leaned his head back, exhaling long and loud. "Jesus Christ, my man, can't we just fucking enjoy the moment without worrying about who gets what and who's gonna fuck over who?"

"It's a legitimate question, Bart," Calvin countered as Bart reached inside the vehicle, shutting the sputtering Beetle's motor off.

In the silence that followed, Bart closed the door and slung his rifle purposefully to his back. "Listen, man, it's ours, as in your group's and my group's. We both need it—we both need it now more than ever." Calvin was silent, so Bart continued, "These boys lying in your yard got friends and lots of 'em, and they're gonna come looking for these guys when they don't come back. Now do their friends know where they went? I don't know the answer to that, but if they do, then those other boys will be headed to your house soon enough.

"Secondly, these kinds are not known for their turn-the-other-cheek ways, if you know what I mean." Calvin remained silent as Bart kept talking. "They are a…how would you say it? A vengeful group of assholes." Bart gestured back to the Beetle. "Plus, we got their car." And with that Bart smiled an evil grin.

Calvin let the shotgun hang, holding his arms out. "So, what are you saying?"

"What I'm saying is we all have to get the hell out of here and sooner than later. You and your daughter can ride with us to a safer place, and then we can all decide what happens to the car."

Calvin looked puzzled. "Daughter? Shannon? She's not my daughter, she's a schoolteacher who lives up the road. Hell, she came down about two weeks ago 'cause she ran through all her food and water and didn't know what else to do. She was headed down to the city, but I talked her out of that. Couldn't imagine a female going down there would have a very good experience."

Bart regarded the other man for a moment. "Okay, she's not your daughter."

"She's not my anything," Calvin quickly added.

Bart backed up a step, holding his hands up in surrender. "I didn't say she was your anything, friend." Bart thought briefly about irritating the little nerve he had unwittingly struck, but thought better of it. "We gotta go more 'cause we got their car than anything else," Bart said, changing the subject. "Car thieving wasn't a big deal a month ago, but a hundred and fifty years ago if you stole a man's horse, they'd hang you for it. I think we just got knocked back a hundred and fifty years. The difference in having a horse or a car now can very well mean the difference between living and dying."

Jared and the two girls interrupted the conversation as they crested the hill, scrambling down towards the two men and the gruesome mess that had once been Salvador and his crew.

Bart threw up a hand to Jared. "Hold tight a minute while we clean up," he shouted.

Jared didn't miss a beat, grabbing both girls by the arms and turning them back up the hill. After they vanished over the top and out of sight, Calvin and Bart set to dragging the dead bastard back to the rear of the little house, where his dead bastard friends were patiently waiting.

It took about five minutes to drag the Beetle's prior owner and his three friends into some bushes to the rear of the house, where they were summarily tossed down an embankment, coming to rest in the bottom of a small dry seasonal creek bed. Bart returned to the front of the house, trying to kick some dirt over the blood-soaked drive, but finally gave up, calling for Jared and the womenfolk.

AFTER THE SHOOTING, Jared had trudged up the hill, finding the girls huddled in some bushes. Shannon was visibly ecstatic to see him coming instead of some Hispanic gang member. She was obviously shaken, but holding it together for the sake of Essie. Jared let them know the house was safe and all the bad guys were gone, which was how he put it.

Neither woman nor girl questioned the meaning of the word *gone* as they walked back towards the house, but Jared couldn't help noticing Essie was hanging closer to Shannon than to him. He wasn't hurt by this; instead he was curious about it, like some experiment he was able to watch unfold as a third party.

After Bart sent them back up the hill, Shannon told Jared she was a schoolteacher in Fremont, lived by herself in a house on forty acres just about two miles up the road, and had bought the place five years ago. Shannon said although the commute could be a bear, she liked the peace and quiet after dealing with middle-school heathens five days a week.

Her summers were what she lived for; she told Jared she would sometimes go an entire month without leaving her property. She read books, drank coffee and enjoyed the beautiful countryside for weeks at a time, saying it was always a shock to go into town for food and other life necessities.

As Shannon spoke, Jared realized for the first time how naturally pretty this woman was. She had long dark brown hair, emerald green eyes, and smooth olive skin. From what Jared could tell, she appeared to either run or participate in some other form of exercise. Bart's loud voice boomed from below, bringing Jared back to reality, causing him to shake his head ever so slightly.

He wasn't one to ogle a female or even talk to one, for that matter; now here he was admiring her every feature. All this run-and-gun stuff might be adding testosterone to his body and in turn causing him to think with his little head instead of his big head. He'd been able to avoid that fairly well most of his life, and now when distractions like that could mean death, he was acting like a sixteen-year-old.

Down in the front yard, Bart laid out a plan to load everything they could load into and onto the Beetle, then move east, away from the city. Shannon protested, saying her place was two miles up the road and they could stay there for now, but Bart wasn't having any of that. "We can't be anywhere near this mess when their friends come looking for them."

Calvin, who had been quiet till now, stepped forward. "We should load up and move farther into the mountains." The beleaguered group listened as he continued, "I saw people come out of the mountains on horseback after the first week or two, heading to the city for food, water, maybe answers, I don't know. I didn't see a one of 'em come back."

They talked amongst themselves, and it was decided that the people who'd left their homes in the relative safety of the mountains had probably died with most of the rest of the people in the city areas. They were probably either robbed or met with some other equally tragic ending. This meant there would be many homes ahead that would likely be vacant or inhabited only by women, children or corpses. No one said it, but they all hoped to find a vacant home and not one inhabited with the dead or dying.

Under the direction of Bart and Calvin, the group salvaged the supplies from the house, rigged a hitch for the bike trailer so they could tow it behind the Beetle, and prepared to leave. Before they finished packing, Jared opened the front of the Beetle and found food, water, ammunition, a tent, and four sleeping bags. He felt immediate elation, which helped with that wrung-out feeling he had after killing another human. Sure, he killed the day he found Essie but that was somehow different. He'd been nearly blinded with anger and hadn't really thought about his own safety.

Today was different. He was alone, calm, and then scared with nothing happening. Then, bang, he was in a gunfight, and, as fast as it all started, it was over. Those few seconds were able to ruin his entire day, leaving him feeling exposed in this new world. Although he had won a gunfight, Jared couldn't help thinking that a man could only get in so many of these things before he got shot or killed. It was a simple game of odds. You either won or lost and, the more you won, the more likely you'd soon incur a loss. He shuddered at the thought of lying face down in the dirt, dying, and leaving Essie to fend for herself.

The discovery of the tent and sleeping bags seemed to calm Bart's nerves by about five percent. He reasoned if the gang had a tent and sleeping bags, maybe they wouldn't be expected back today, which gave his group more of a head start. He still urged the group to pack quickly.

Once they had everything they could stuff, strap down, or pack, they loaded into the Beetle, and Bart instructed Jared to drive. The two bikes were strapped to the roof, the front trunk was stuffed to overflowing, and the trailer was repacked with more gear than Jared would have been able to tow with the bicycle. They had even packed all the gang's weapons and ammunition. Even though the weapons were different than any Bart's group were carrying, he felt they might be able to use them for trading purposes in the future.

They slowly rumbled out to the road, where Bart had Jared pull to a stop while he climbed out, tore some branches off a nearby tree, and used them to sweep away any sign of the vehicle's tire tracks in the loose dirt drive.

"Better the whole disappearing-gang-member trick be a complete mystery," he said after re-entering the Beetle. Jared put the tiny vehicle in gear, and they lurched forward as he snuck a peek in the rearview mirror, seeing Essie perched on Shannon's lap, staring out the window at the passing landscape.

The little girl seemed to find some sort of comfort in Shannon that Jared was unable to give her. He didn't understand it, but it seemed to make Essie happier having Shannon around, which was fine with him.

He drove slowly, stopping before a bend in the road so Bart could get out of the little German car, glassing the real estate ahead before stepping back into the vehicle and directing Jared to drive like the old man was an Army general or something. Jared thought about pointing out the fact that the recon routine had not stopped Calvin and Shannon hours before from getting the drop on them. Ignoring his better judgment, Jared mentioned this little tidbit and was told flatly by Bart, "It's to avoid any roadblocks more than anything else. Can't give no one a ground ball," leaving Jared unsure of the man's exact meaning, but imagining it implied something like he didn't want to make it easy for anyone trying to grab an easy meal.

Then again, Jared thought back to the year his father talked him into going out for Little League baseball, remembering the ground ball that had come rolling out to him; then at the last moment the ball took a bad hop and struck Jared full in the mouth, giving him a bloody lip and effectively ending his baseball career. So maybe Bart meant something else, he couldn't be certain. The fucking old man was the strangest person Jared had ever encountered. Half the time he talked so straight to you, it was insulting, while the other half of the time he spoke in riddles, leaving Jared befuddled.

They drove about ten miles into the mountains before Calvin broke the silence. "Don't want to go too far. You hit highway 5 and, well, who knows what's going on over there."

Jared glanced at Bart, who just nodded, staring out the window, leaving Jared wondering what he should do. They drove on for another three or four minutes before Bart motioned to the side of the road, where Jared obediently pulled the overloaded Beetle to the dirt shoulder near a gated drive.

Without a word, Bart got out and inspected the entrance, walking back and forth, studying the gate and attached fencing. After his barrier inspection, Bart came back and dug through the trailer, coming out with a pair of bolt cutters. Calvin climbed out, joining him as Jared sat in the Beetle, watching the two men discuss their next move.

Sitting in the Beetle, Jared, Essie and Shannon watched the two older men as they paced about, tugging on the gate and inspecting the fencing.

"How old is Bart?" Shannon asked.

"Dunno."

"I think he's pretty old," Essie chimed in.

"I think he's old enough to have seen black-and-white rainbows—and not in pictures," Jared said, causing Shannon to laugh out loud. Both quickly covered their mouths, stifling the sound of their laughter for fear the two old bastards would want to know what was so goddamn hilarious. Both knew they'd have to come clean with Essie there, and neither liked that thought.

The older men returned to the vehicle, eyeing the two adults sitting inside, looking like they'd been up to something, but holding it together, or so they thought.

"What the hell is going on?" Bart asked, bending over so he was on the troublemakers' level and staring straight at the older two with a suspicious look etched in his craggy face.

Jared shook his head, stealing a glance at Shannon, who didn't respond.

"Did you really get to see black-and-white rainbows?" Essie asked, causing both Jared and Shannon to cringe.

Bart scowled for a brief second before responding, "Ess, grown-ups see and do a lot of magical things and, yes, I'm sure I've seen a couple of black-and-white rainbows. Hell, Jared there is gonna be able to show you how to push up daisies if he isn't careful." Bart started to back away from the vehicle, then ducked his head back inside the window, locking eyes with Shannon. "Watch it, missy."

Once he finished straightening the younger adults out, Bart cut a length of the lower strand of barbed wire, bringing it back to the gate. Next, he and Calvin cut the fence away from its moorings on one side of the gate, then peeled back the barbed wire fence, motioning for Jared to pull the vehicle through. He obliged, after which the older men set to mending the fence using the lower strand they'd scrounged.

When they were done, the fence and gate appeared to never have been tampered with. Next Bart again set about sweeping away the tire tracks with a leafy branch, motioning Jared up the dirt road as he slowly followed behind like a Merry Maid, sweeping and scanning the road behind them. This went on till the paved road was no longer in view, then went on for a while longer. *Jesus, this guy is paranoid,* thought Jared.

Once Bart was back in the Beetle, he kept Jared driving at a snail's pace, scanning, stopping, then scanning some more.

"We need to make sure we don't walk into a gunfight out here," Bart said. "People out here are more than a little protective of their land, and that was before any monkey business went on with the electricity."

Jared stared silently ahead as they crept along.

"I think we should find a place to camp for the night," Bart continued.

Shannon leaned forward in her seat, still clutching Essie. "Why don't we just find an empty place out here and sleep there?"

Bart slowly shook his head while rubbing his stubbly chin with a dirty thumb and finger. "Don't think that's the safest thing to do. Someone comes home and finds a bunch of armed people in their house, they're likely to shoot first and ask questions later." Bart shifted, scratching his stubble-laden jawline. "If we set up a camp out of sight and send out scouting parties, we can learn a little about this area. If it takes a couple of days and none of us gets shot in the meantime, well, I think that's worth it."

Shannon didn't look too keen on sleeping outside, but held her tongue, especially after the "watch it, missy" instruction from earlier.

Chapter 30

AN HOUR later the group found a spot to set up camp in a natural depression not visible from any part of the dirt road they'd come in on. Bart's plan was simple: he and Calvin would go out the following morning and scout the area for an uninhabited and suitable place to lie their heads for a while.

Although he hadn't said it, Jared felt pretty sure Bart wasn't fully comfortable throwing all his trust in these people. Jared wondered what it was Bart thought they would do. If Bart and Jared scouted together, did Bart think Shannon and Calvin would make off with Essie? That didn't make sense, since people were having a difficult time just trying to feed and hydrate themselves in this new cruel world.

Taking on another mouth didn't make any sense to Jared. He wasn't so naive that he couldn't imagine the two taking off with all their food and ammo. Now there was something that made sense, but he still couldn't see Shannon going for that. She hadn't said too much, but Jared had a feeling she was a good woman in a really shitty situation. One telling thing the woman had done was taking Essie under her wing, and this act had not been lost on Jared.

As night fell and the wind picked up, the group set up watches, retiring to either their post or bed. A roar in Jared's ears woke him with a start, causing him to sit straight up in his sleeping bag, staring into the absolute blackness of his tent. As his head began to clear, he realized he wasn't breathing. He took a long, controlled breath as the roar reached a crescendo and then began to fade. When Jared's brain had completely engaged and escaped its state of hibernation, he realized the roar was a helicopter. The thing had been low and moving west towards the city, causing the camp to stir for a bit, but eventually everyone went back to their tents when the aircraft didn't return.

The following morning was crisp. Steam rose off the grassy hillside as the sun began to cast its rays into the shadows. Jared could see his breath as he drew his jacket up around his neck, watching Bart hover over a small stove, boiling water for breakfast. Essie and Shannon emerged from another tent. Both females were bundled in warm clothes, trying to stave off the cool morning air.

Bart turned as Jared approached. "Haven't heard that bird again. Must have set down at one of the airports."

Jared nodded. "Wonder if they were here bringing aid."

Bart shook his head. "One helo is not a humanitarian mission. Remember what Adam said about them grabbing people valuable to the government?"

Jared looked in the direction the helicopter had gone. "Didn't he say a whole bunch of dudes rolled in with helicopters?"

Bart scratched his stubbly face. "Maybe it's so damn bad, they can't send as many, or maybe they don't have that many anymore." He shook his head. "I don't know why they would fly down there with only one aircraft; the city is a mess. Seems like more would be better...safer, unless they're stretched so thin one helicopter is all they can afford to send."

OVER THE NEXT WEEK, Jared, with Shannon's help, tended to the camp while the two older men reconnoitered the area for a suitable place to call home for the time being. Bart found the dirt road was maintained fairly well, running for about five miles back into the hills, with three houses along the way. Two of the houses appeared to be small summer hunting lodges, while the third one showed signs of recently having been occupied as someone's permanent residence.

Bart searched the first two structures, finding they had little to offer in the way of supplies. Both were vacant, and showed signs they had been for some time, complete with a musty smell and cobwebs.

When the two older men found the last place, they watched it for most of a day before returning to their encampment. The two returned to the third house early the following day and stayed overnight, watching to see if any humans came or went. The two men returned after their overnight trip proclaiming they had found a new temporary home. Bart ordered their current home be broken down and packed so they could move.

Once they were packed, they drove the Beetle towards the place Bart had described. Bart directed Jared to an area surrounded on three sides by the low rolling scrub-oak-covered hills of the area. The group set up camp, prepared dinner, and ate, after which Bart cleared his throat.

"I'd like to go down to that ranch house with the men if that's okay with you," he glanced at Shannon, who looked apprehensively at Calvin. "We'll take the car so all you have to do is fire off three rounds and we'll come a-running. It's a bit of a walk, but only a few minutes in the car."

Shannon wrapped her arms around Essie as a look of unease stretched across her already stressed features. Jared looked at Bart, thinking how the man was always scheming, always working on ways to better his odds. Jared would never have thought about this situation like Bart had. The car would do Shannon no good if someone threatened her and Essie, and it would take the men quite a while to get back, but with the car they could come back in a matter of minutes.

"I guess we'll be all right," she said.

Bart nodded his head before turning to Jared. "I want you down in that house with me when we clear it. The three of us can clear the place nice and slow. Don't want to walk into anything we can't back out of. If the place is booby-trapped, we back out and move on, find another place to stay."

Calvin cocked his head. "What if we can remove whatever trap we find down there?"

Bart shook his head. "Nope, if someone took the time to set up some sort of booby trap, that tells me they plan on coming back at some point."

No one in the little group could argue with Bart's logic, so it was agreed the three men would go and secure the ranch house while the two females remained hidden in the hills until such time as the men deemed the ranch house safe and returned for the women and gear.

"Tell ya what," Bart said. "We wait and watch for two days, make absolutely sure no one is living in that place, and then we can go down, clear the structure, and get inside the house and out of this cold."

After settling into their new campsite, Bart went out and did some light surveillance on the ranch house before returning to the group.

"Screw it. Let's go secure that place tomorrow morning," he said, slumping to the ground, back against an old oak tree.

Jared looked at his old friend, and the man looked tired, not just tired, but physically fatigued, run-down, and more than a little haggard. Hell, the guy hadn't even planned on coming out of the city due to his age and general poor physical condition. Jared was glad he had, but for the first time he wondered how long Bart would last out here.

They needed to get off the road and into a place of shelter sooner than later and not just for Bart. Essie and Calvin weren't built for sleeping outside in what was quickly turning into some rather cold weather. Jared didn't know the exact date, but he made an educated guess, figuring it to be mid to late October with the temperature in a daily nosedive.

———

THE MORNING CAME and Jared was up, fed, and ready to go before Bart or Calvin had cleared their sleeping bags. When the two older men were finished eating and drinking hot cups of coffee, they moved the womenfolk into a secluded area, made sure Shannon's pistol was loaded, then set out towards the ranch house. Jared drove while the three men sat in silence till Bart directed him to pull the small German car to the shoulder.

The men spent a couple of minutes backing the Beetle into a thicket, then covered it with vegetation. When they were finished camouflaging the Beetle, they moved off through the brush. Bart led the way, rifle at low ready, head turning from side to side, eyes darting, always on the lookout. Jared followed, trying to emulate Bart's movements, like this would make him more effective.

The three men low crawled the last bit to a rise, where they could peer down onto the medium-sized ranch house.

Without turning his head, Bart whispered, "See anything that looks moved, changed or disrupted?"

Calvin slowly shook his head. "Nope."

Without warning, Bart dragged himself to his feet and slowly began walking towards the ranch house. "Keep your weapons slung low, but ready. Let's not appear to be too threatening here," Bart said without so much as a glance back.

The two others scrambled to their feet, spreading out on either side of Bart as they approached the deserted domicile. Bart moved expertly to the side of the house then slithered up to the front porch without ever once exposing himself or the others to anyone who might be waiting in the front of the residence. He slowly moved onto the porch, taking a quick glance through a dirty front window.

The front door was unlocked, opening easily if not a little noisily, the old hinges screeching in protest as the door swung inwards. Bart stepped out from beside the door, using his angles to clear as much of the interior as possible without entering the structure. He moved from one side of the open door to the opposite side, rifle up, pulled tight in his shoulder.

"Clear," Bart hissed, gliding through the open doorway and moving left. Jared bolted forward, not wanting to leave Bart alone inside an unknown. As the two men entered the house, Calvin quickly followed. Once inside, the place smelled old and musty, devoid of human life or that lived-in smell most occupied residences had.

The men quietly moved from room to room, Jared and Bart working together while Calvin mostly just followed. Jared realized it was the training and time he'd spent with Bart at the gun store. It was paying off right now, and secretly he was proud as he stole glances at Calvin, who seemed impressed at the deadly ballet moving gracefully through the house just ahead of him.

When Bart and Jared entered the kitchen, a small furry body bolted from a corner. Bart's weapon was a blur as he brought it to bear on the fast-moving form. Jared felt a stab of panic as it pummeled his heart and nervous system. Calvin staggered backward a step, not being able to see past the two men blocking the kitchen doorway. Whatever it was raced through the kitchen, then as fast as the situation seemed to spiral towards chaos, it stabilized as the trio realized it was a raccoon. The poor creature was trying like hell to evacuate the residence.

As soon as the raccoon was able to dart past the three men and scramble out the front door, Bart seemed to forget the whole encounter. He moved deeper into the structure, weapon up, clearing corners and patiently waiting as his slower partners tried to keep up. Jared's heart actually felt like someone had administered an electrical shock to it along with his entire nervous system. The ranch house had a staircase leading to the second floor, but before Bart started up, he looked at Jared and frowned.

"Breathe, my man, breathe."

Jared took three deep controlled breaths and instantly felt better.

He'd been going along clearing rooms, feeling so adequate working alongside Bart until that raccoon spoiled everything. He took another long deep breath, blowing out through his mouth, thinking he had been a much better dot-com guy than a post-event survivalist guy. By the time they finished clearing the ranch house, Jared had his adrenaline under control. Now he was feeling spent instead of panic stricken, and at a complete loss as to which was worse.

The top floor was host to a bathroom along with three bedrooms, which the men quickly searched and found were as deserted as the rest of the house. From what Jared could tell, it didn't appear anyone had occupied the house for weeks, maybe longer, he wasn't sure. The men exited the house, searching the barn and a small outbuilding, but found no indication of the ranch's occupants.

After searching the yard along with the outbuildings, the three men stood in the drive, contemplating their next move.

Calvin nodded to the side of the residence, where a storm-shelter-type door could be seen protruding from atop the ground. "What do you think that is?"

Bart studied it for about one-one-hundredth of a second before bringing his weapon to the ready. "We missed something. There's a basement." He was already running towards the front door of the house, yelling at Calvin, "Cover that outside door. Jared, follow me."

Jared followed Bart into the house for the second time in less than ten minutes. Bart was inside, scanning back and forth, looking for the thing he'd missed. He turned, squatting down so he could look through one of the windows in order to orient himself with where Calvin was standing outside the residence. Bart slowly returned his attention to the inside of the house, searching the walls, floor and even the doorjambs.

He moved deliberately into the dining room, getting down on his hands and knees. Jared watched as the old man pulled the carpet back, exposing a thin crack in the floor that could only be part of a trapdoor. The carpet had been laid over the top, hiding the door from view, while the heavy table was placed on top of the carpet, further discouraging anyone from the effort it would take to expose the bare floor. Bart moved to the window nearest Calvin, forcing it open.

"Hey, we got a trapdoor in here, and it doesn't look like they could have accessed it from inside unless someone covered it for them, so heads-up out there. We're gonna open it up in here."

Together, Jared and Bart moved the table before throwing back the carpet to reveal a rather large trapdoor. There was a place for a lock; however, no lock was attached. Bart attached a piece of cord to the handle and gave the other end to Jared, motioning for him to pull the door up and open. Bart quickly moved to the top of the door, training his weapon on the opening as Jared began to draw the door open.

Before Jared could stop it, the door flopped open with a

loud bang. Bart simultaneously swept the muzzle of his rifle down and across the hole in the dining room floor. There was a set of steps leading down into the basement area, where shelves could be seen on both sides of the bottom.

"Toss me a light stick," Bart barked.

Jared grabbed a light stick from a pocket and tossed it to the older man, who snapped the stick before dropping it into the darkness below. He slung the rifle to his back, feeling it a bit cumbersome for the dark and likely confined space he was about to enter. Bart drew his pistol and started for the opening.

"Fucking be nice to have a weapon's light right about now," he grumbled before slowly lowering himself down the staircase, pistol up and at the ready.

Jared stood at the top of the stairs; the whole staircase was just too small for two men to be on in case there was gunplay, so he waited till Bart was clear of the last step. Once Bart reached the basement floor, Jared scrambled down the narrow wooden steps, sweeping his pistol left and right across the dirty shelves of the basement.

The two cleared the rather smallish basement in a few seconds. Jared dropped additional light sticks as they moved about the basement, effectively bringing its interior to a dull green glow. Bart walked to a far corner, banging on the door Calvin was covering. There was a latch on the inside of the door, which kept anyone on the outside from opening it.

Bart pulled the latch back, locking it into the open position. "Hey, Calvin, don't shoot, but open this door so we can get some more light down here."

The door rattled in protest as Calvin heaved it up and into the open position, allowing light to cascade into the dank basement. Both Jared and Bart caught their breath at the same time; Bart was the first to react, letting out a low whistle. Calvin squinted down into the dark hole, backlit by the bright afternoon sky, completely unable to see what had evoked the whistle from Bart's old weathered lips. Jared stared at the surrounding shelves, which were laden with canned and jarred goods from the floor to the ceiling. They were labeled and organized in a manner that screamed obsessive-compulsive disorder.

Jared was no clinician, but he knew enough to thank God that whoever had lived on this little piece of property had suffered from both the obsessive and compulsive behavior. He wasn't sure if a person could suffer from just one, but was glad for this poor tortured soul's dual disorder. He or she had obsessed over some sort of impending fate where food would be gold, and had then compulsively stockpiled food in this basement. *Why would they leave it?* he wondered.

Bart must have been wondering the same thing, because he flew past Jared. "Coming to you, Calvin," he barked, clambering out of the basement, directing Calvin to take to the high ground in order to watch all conceivable routes of ingress to the ranch house.

Jared stood in the food cache, mind racing, wondering who had done this and where they had gone and why? When Bart didn't immediately return, Jared began poking around the basement, doing a visual and mental inventory of the food stores covering the shelving.

As he made his way towards the entrance leading to the interior of the house, he cracked another light stick, bathing the shelves in the dullish green light. On the floor, he noticed a couple of broken jars of some unidentifiable matter. He moved closer, directing the light towards the mess on the floor. Jared looked at the nearby shelves, noticing they were the only bare shelves in the entire basement.

He began to piece together a picture of what had gone on with the owner of the house. They had hurriedly taken what appeared to be a decent amount of the food stores and, in their hurry, dropped a jar or two, leaving the mess he was now standing over. The spoiled food on the floor was dried, giving the mess the appearance of having been spilled at least two weeks prior. Jared moved back to the opening leading to the yard and pulled himself out just as Bart returned from the barn, meeting Jared in the middle of the yard.

"Someone left in a hurry. Broke a couple of the jars trying to get them up into the house," Jared said. "Don't know why they left in a hurry, just seems like they did 'cause of the broken jars."

Bart scratched his unshaven beard, turning to look at the barn. "They might have had a running tractor—there are tracks leading from the barn, but I haven't seen a tractor on the property." He shrugged. "Who knows, man."

His shoulders seemed to droop ever so slightly as he scanned the yard. For the first time since they left the gun store, Jared realized just how old Bart was. He seemed so stalwart in his preparation efforts before and as they'd moved out of the city and into the mountains, but now Jared looked upon the aging man, seeing a very old and very weary human being who seemed to be barely hanging on at the moment. Jared had a brief moment of sorrow and empathy for the old man, but this was instantly replaced with near panic.

The thought of being out here with Calvin, Shannon and Essie alone nearly caused him to release his bowels on the spot. He clinched his stomach, fighting the actual feeling of pissing himself. He paused, taking stock of his body, and realized his breath was coming in short choppy gasps, and he felt chilled. Jared was suddenly cold down to his bones, the way only a cold fall California day can do with its wet chill.

He had traveled some before the event and spent time on the eastcoast during the winter months, experiencing some fairly low temperatures, but he always felt colder in California. Wet cold versus a dryer cold, he thought, and the wet cold was just damn miserable. While Jared wrestled with his fear beast,

Bart turned away, pulled the bloody handkerchief from his pocket, and muffled several coughs before replacing the handkerchief without his usual blood inspection.

BART COULD FEEL IT, and it was starting to win, taking hold of his life with its icy claws. He didn't know how much longer he could keep up the charade and didn't look forward to Jared's reaction when the truth was finally out in the open. He felt sick all the time, the smallest amount of physical exertion left him spent and, since every day took the effort of ten days in his old life, well, he was pretty fucking beat most of the time now. The blood, well, the blood meant the end was coming, and coming quicker than he thought a few weeks ago.

Once Bart set up a watch, he got to inventorying all the food stores in the basement. He lamented on how to secure the basement from an intruder forcibly entering from the outside. Bart didn't want to permanently block the entrance off in case they needed to escape through the basement. Jared came up with the idea of lining the inside of the staircase leading to the outside with two-by-fours just under the ground's surface level.

They could then tear out all the wood aboveground, placing the door a couple of inches below the ground's surface onto the newly fashioned wooden frame. After the door was in place, Jared suggested they shovel dirt on top until the surface was level with the rest of the yard. They could then use branches to wipe away all signs of their excavation. The basement would not be any more physically secure than it had been before, but if someone didn't know it was there, it was actually better than the biggest lock in the world.

Bart listened to Jared's plan then nodded his approval. "Let's get to work, but we need to dump the dirt in another part of the yard so there's no way to tell we've been digging around here."

Calvin scavenged the wood, hammer and some nails while Shannon sat on a small knoll near the house, keeping watch on the road in both directions. Essie nestled close to Shannon, clutching her small jacket around her neck as the wind kicked up a little, seeming to drop the temperature by twenty degrees. Within an hour, they were shoveling dirt onto the door, careful not to put so much that they wouldn't be able to push their way out from inside should the need rear its ugly head. Jared was pretty sure that, with the adrenaline dumps he'd been getting lately, he could have lifted a car off the trapdoor if needed.

Chapter 31

JOHN WAS thirty-six years old and had been in the military the same amount of time he hadn't been in the military. He joined when he was eighteen, going straight to Marine Corps boot camp to suffer for the thirteen weeks it took to earn the title of United States Marine.

After he finished boot camp and while he was at the Marine infantry training school, he heard about a specialized unit called Recon. The unit was rumored to be home to the best of the best and, since John thought the Marines were the best already, he felt driven to be part of this Recon community. It sounded like what he was looking for based on the newbie rumor mill, which never stopped swirling with tales as tall as the Sears Tower.

So, when a hardened Recon Marine came around looking for volunteers, John and eight others raised their hands; the rest of the pussies had just stared down at the ground, too ashamed to look the Recon Marine in the eye. John was embarrassed to be part of this group who stared at their boots when asked to volunteer for a man's job. John didn't realize till years later the guy had walked into the barracks and essentially washed out fifty guys without wasting a single tax payer dollar or man-hour, using only his hard-ass demeanor. John and the eight other unfortunate souls would find out just how hard this guy really was in the coming weeks.

The next four weeks nearly killed him, but as they kept saying to him, what doesn't kill you makes you stronger. John felt the jury was out on that load of shit. The twin towers came down the following year, and John found himself first in Recon, then Force Recon. He was deployed constantly. He fought, came home, rested, started training, then would go back to fight. Once while back from deployment, two men from the Army came by his unit, asking about him. He was called off one of the ranges and met with these men in his Sergeant Major's office.

The men were professional and to the point. They were from the Army's most elite tier one unit, known by some as Delta. John knew it by its latest name, CAG, or Combat Application Group and, although the Unit had many names, this was the current name in fashion at the time. They asked if John was interested in applying to "the Special Missions Unit." Now there was a new name John hadn't heard. They quickly explained the selection process would take place in six months, and they would provide a workout regimen for John to use to ready himself for the selection's grueling demands.

In the end, John applied for the selection process, working hard for the six months leading up to the date. When the day came, he simply packed, hopped on a flight for Virginia, and left his Recon community behind…forever. He was picked up at the airport by a man who looked more like a truck driver than a military man. During the ride, John didn't say much and the man said less. The man never offered his name, and John never asked. He would later come to know the man as Vince, and they would be lifelong friends, fighting side by side on many missions.

The selection process started the following day, demanding more from John than the Recon community ever had. He had considered his old unit a very professional unit and, by most standards, it was, but this group was by far the most closed-off and professional bunch he'd ever worked around. It was downright fucking spooky how quiet they could all be. Nothing excited this group; he'd never seen a unit so close with so few words.

John also considered himself a very physically fit Marine, but these quiet professional warriors weren't impressed, always talking about the importance of being mentally fit over being physically fit, not that they weren't physically fit—they all were. It was a common belief that one of these elite soldiers could requisition the body of a lesser human, like a civilian, and still operate at tier one levels based on their mental toughness. The deeper John made it into the selection process, the less he doubted this little proclamation.

John's final test was a thirty-mile movement called black time. No one told him how much time he had, nor did they give him any updates on how he was doing. For all he knew, he was way behind schedule the entire thirty miles. He had a full load out and knew it would be hard, but he pushed hard in the beginning when his body was fresh.

He knew there would come a time when he would be forced to push hard using his mind more than his body, so he decided to use his body while he could. He basically treated it like a sprint. He ran when he could and he always walked fast. He stopped every hour for two to five minutes to change his socks and check his feet. He knew if his feet went, so went his chances at finishing this nightmare of a selection process.

Just about the time John thought he was at his limit, he rounded a bend in the dirt road and saw a single man standing next to a Polaris off-road vehicle. The man saw John and glanced nonchalantly at a stopwatch, then just waited.

John ran the last bit, reaching the man, but not dropping his pack.

The man held out his hand. "Welcome to the Unit."

John had made it. The next few months were no easier for John as he was pushed through all the in-house training the Unit put its new operators through. In the first few weeks he started to think he would never reach the level these guys operated at. They would take down a building, moving and shooting at speeds that made John's head swim. For the first time in his life he was not able to keep up and this aggravated him. At one point one of the instructors must have sensed John's frustration and came by after they'd finished up on the kill house.

"Hey, man, we all went through this. You will get better, believe me." That was all anyone said to him.

Sure enough, John did get better, a lot better. He became one of the Unit's better shooters with both the H&K 416 and the Glock 21 he carried. By the end of his training cycle, he felt more at home in the kill house than in his own home. He went to every conceivable school and training one could think of and then a few more he'd never even thought of. If the training wasn't already offered and someone came up with the idea and could justify its usefulness to the Unit's operators, they went. They learned to ride horses, canoe, kayak, ski, skydive, dive, swim—you name it, they learned to do it.

Then John deployed with the Unit and, wow, they worked day and night and did some of the most dangerous missions in some of the most hostile areas of the world. The Unit did not baby its members, but it did take care of them. They got the best gear and even had a branch of the Unit whose sole job it was to seek out new equipment and put it to the test. If an operator got hurt, they were sent to some of the best medical facilities in the country and then rehabbed alongside professional athletes: "Hey, my name is Adrien Peterson. I play for the Minnesota Vikings, and I'm here rehabbing a bad knee. What's your name?"

"Oh, my name is John," end of conversation. Not, "Hi, my name is John and I'm part of an elite unit and, well, I was out killing the holy-loving dog shit out of some bad motherfuckers and you know how dangerous that can be and, well, one fucker took a rifle and shot a hole in my leg, so here I am. Oh, I almost forgot to tell you the best part, we were in North Korea when all this happened, how fucking insane is that?"

Today John was on another mission, riding in a Black Hawk like all the other times, except this time things were different, very different, and in a bad way. John was stateside when the event occurred. Many of his comrades were in other parts of the world and hadn't been heard from since.

The Unit had far more men deployed to the far reaches of the earth than it ever had back at Fort Bragg, North Carolina. John and a dozen operators huddled in the war room, with the dim backup lights making their faces look greasy. No one knew what had happened, and their tech people worked to find answers. Questions flew like confetti in the room. In the end they were briefed on what had happened and what the US had done to its enemies and allies alike.

There were exactly thirty-two Unit operators accounted for in the country, and they were all being tasked with gathering national assets. Those assets turned out to be people. The thirty-two operators were split into thirty-two different groups, acting as advisors for the gathering teams. The gathering teams were a hodgepodge of Navy, Marines, Army, Air Force, Reservists and even a few police officers with prior military backgrounds. It hadn't all gone smoothly, and some of the teams had even lost people during their missions.

John leaned back against the helicopter's inner skin, eyeing the six-man team he was tasked with keeping alive during these gathering missions. Two of them were airmen, while the other four were soldiers from noncombat units. Two cooks, a mechanic and a clerk—a fucking clerk for fucking fuck's sake. They weren't bad people; it was just that John was fairly sure not one of them could have found his own ass with both hands a lot of the time.

The bird shuddered slightly, beginning a slow turn to the right as the pilot's voice came across the radio. "Five out, boys and girls."

John looked out the window and could see the city sprawled out under the aircraft. John glanced at the crew chief, who was readying the fast ropes in preparation for the team's speedy departure from the aircraft. Aerial recon indicated the target area was too confined to set a Black Hawk down, and flying farther away to a parking lot would void the element of surprise. This particular target was apparently very important to the rebuilding of America, and the higher-ups wanted no chance of him getting spooked and taking off.

With all electronic gear down for the most part, he would be impossible to track or locate. The only electronic gear working these days were inside structures that were structurally hardened to withstand an EMP attack. This very helicopter had been parked inside a hardened hangar and, after the flares subsided, the old bird fired right up and flew like a charm. Problem was, there were only about twenty in the entire country.

The plan was to drop half the team in the rear yard, and then the bird would shift, dropping the rest of the team in the front yard. The helo would leave, and the team would follow a surround and call out type operation. There would be no bursting through the front door and getting shot, at least not today.

The big bird flared nose up, the pilot bleeding off airspeed and altitude at the same time. The team stood and moved to the door as the crew chief pushed the fast ropes up to the opening. John stole a glance at the pilot as he eased back on the cyclic, lowering the collective in unison. John could see the man's feet fairly dancing on the pedals, keeping the big bird straight and in trim. This pilot wasn't the best John had flown with, but he wasn't bad.

As the target house slid under the big helicopter, the pilot eased the cyclic forward and pulled up on the collective, bringing the craft into a hover over the backyard. The ropes went out, and four of the team members disappeared out the side doors, clinging to the ropes as they rocketed to the ground. The entire operation took less than five seconds.

The pilot had positioned his steed so that the front yard was directly to his nine o'clock, and he easily slid the big bird to the left, stopping over the front yard. John and the other two went next, leaving the big bird empty except for its crew. Once the last operator was on the ground, the pilot pulled power, driving the giant machine back into the air.

The pilots John was used to working with would have been climbing before the last man had cleared the fast rope. Hell, when they were inserted riding in on the outboards of the Little Birds, those pilots could be downright scary. The little birds were a small aircraft made by McDonnell Douglas Helicopter Systems, and were designated MH-6 Little Bird. The aircraft was small, nimble and could get guys into places a Black Hawk just wouldn't fit. The little birds had a crew of two and came in various configurations ranging from an armed version to the transport version John and his folks rode on from time to time.

The pilots would come in so fast; John was sure they'd splatter on a rooftop like flies. Then came the g-forces and somehow the little bird's skids would kiss the rooftop and, as eight hundred pounds worth of gunfighting operators left the aircraft, the tiny helicopter would simply spring back into the air with little to no input on the controls by the pilot. The pilots told John and his boys that, if they didn't get off with the group, the bird was leaving regardless.

It never happened, but John would have felt pretty fucking stupid if he hadn't gotten off in time and ended up, in the air, watching his unit take down a building. If that happened, he knew he would be eating shit for it when the op was done.

John was last out of the thundering bird and hit the ground running for the cover of a large truck. John's old pilots also would have put him closer to the target house and not out in the street. The rotor wash from the Black Hawk pounded the men on the ground as the bird climbed out and away leaving the team in a growing quietness.

John always felt a peacefulness envelope his spirit after an insertion; his body would go through an adrenaline dump that accompanied the chaos of experiencing a multitude of sights and sounds as he sat in whatever aircraft was doing the ferrying. He would try not to go deaf from the roar of the aircraft's engines. The transition from yelling over a headset inside a thundering helicopter to whispering to his team after the aircraft left was a welcome and tranquil relief. There were a few times when the noise of the rotors had immediately been replaced with gunfire; those times were few and far between. He and his running dogs tried not to get dropped into firefights since they tended to result in crashed helicopters, injured men, and sometimes the outright death of all involved.

Most of the time, they made several false insertions on their way to the actual insertion point, unless it was a hard target in a built-up area like a town or city, in which case, they got on board, flew straight to the target site, fucked a bunch of shit up, and left.

John remembered being dropped off in Afghanistan on top of a mountain and how quiet and peaceful it would feel after the insert bird was gone. Those twenty or thirty minutes while they got comms up and acclimated to their surroundings were some of the most peaceful times of his life. Ironically, they were oftentimes followed by some of the most asshole-clinching, ball-sack-shrinking times of his life as well.

When he died, if they ever were able to do a forensics study of his brain, it would show so many highs and lows he was sure it would look like a chart of America's economy over the past thirty years. He was okay with that; he didn't like the in-between. He craved the highs and needed the lows to recover. John had no use for the in-between stuff.

John clicked the radio twice and received the same from the team in the backyard. They were all in place, and it was time to start calling this guy out so they could move to the pickup landing zone (LZ) a mile away in a Target parking lot. John took a deep breath.

"Barry, it's John. I'm with the government and we've been sent here to pick you up." John was careful not to use the word take when addressing these folks. No one wanted to be taken anywhere. People were already scared, and more than a couple of gunfights were caused by the thought of a government that had already failed them coming in and taking them away from their home.

Here in San Jose, California, the chances of a gunfight were less than, let's say, somewhere in Texas or, worse yet, Idaho, but John had been surprised before, and he didn't intend to get shot by some computer nerd who had played just a little too much Call of Duty and owned half a dozen guns he knew nothing about.

John waited a full thirty-seconds before repeating his announcement and, still nothing. After the third attempt, John keyed his mic. "Hold on the back and lock down the sides. We are moving on the front."

All he got back were two clicks. He smiled to himself, he taught them well, and they were starting to come along in their tactics.

As John left the cover of the truck, a voice boomed out from the dark house. "What do you want?"

John didn't know why, but he nearly shit himself. "We're here on behalf of the president himself. He is asking you to come with us, and you will be briefed on what they need from you."

Silence followed and John wondered if he imagined the voice. Then it came again. "How do I know you won't just shoot me when I open this door?"

John shook his head. Jesus Christ, why did these intellects always have to be so damn paranoid? "'Cause if I intended to shoot you, you'd be shot already, and I wouldn't be standing out here talking to you."

"I choose not to go with you," came the voice.

John moved back to cover and took a knee. "Listen, we are who we say we are. Who else is flying around in a fucking Black Hawk these days?" *Jesus*, John thought, *who would have been flying around this neighborhood in a Black Hawk even before the lights went out?*

The man's refusal took John by surprise. All the others were suspicious, but when they came to believe John and his little crew were really with the government, they nearly ran into their arms and the safety, or ill-perceived safety, of government protection.

"I demand you leave and do not return," the voice boomed back.

John had been briefed in regard to a refusal and, although they were briefed, no one thought it would really happen. It hadn't happened to date, to any of the teams.

"Well, there's the problem, my friend. The president told us to ask first and, if you didn't willingly come, to force you to come."

More silence.

"I'd really rather not force anyone to do anything, if you get my drift."

The silence continued.

"So please come on out, and let's go see what they need from you."

John had been briefed on Barry, and he knew there was a grading system in regard to how valuable a target was to the government. The grading system was a 1 to 10 system, with 1 being the lowest priority, and Barry had graded out at a 10. He was the first 10 John had gone after, not that he cared what number was assigned to his targets.

He couldn't care less what some computer geek graded his target at; what he cared more about was the guy's background and his experience with violence and firearms. Just because the guy could figure out how to get the Hoover dam operating on vegetable oil or some other infrastructure bullshit, John didn't care. His concerns were about staying alive and keeping his troops alive.

This Barry guy hadn't raised a single red flag during the intel briefings John attended. The intel guys weren't even sure if he'd still be alive, with all the violence in the cities these days, not to mention water and food shortages...check that, shortage wasn't the correct term for something that simply no longer existed. The folks in these built-up areas were experiencing a food and water absence.

John sat behind the truck, wishing the guy would just come out so they could move to the evac LZ, when a long string of automatic gunfire erupted from the rear of the target structure. Before the rattle of gunfire subsided, the garage door opened, exposing a man sitting astride a motorcycle. The man had a pulley system linked to the overhead garage door and had opened the door by hand. The bike's engine leaped to life, which shocked everyone on the mission, and then it simply rocketed across the front yard, turning easily onto the street before disappearing into the night.

John was already up and running in the direction of the bike, calling for the bird to get eyes on and track the guy. After a terse reply from the pilot, John switched his radio back to team comms, getting a situational report from the team members on the back side of the building. The rear team reported no one was injured, and were oblivious to the fact that a motorcycle had literally jumped out of the garage and sped off into the night. This target undoubtedly had no wish to be part of the gentrification of the country.

Chapter 32

JOHN SLOWED his run to a walk, his mind racing, trying to assemble a plan of action for a situation that was evolving at breakneck speeds.

"Hold the structure," John barked into his lip mic. John figured there were at least two guys in the building, and he was absolutely sure he'd only seen one person on the motorcycle. He was also pretty sure it had been a man even though he was wearing a helmet. John was not a motorcycle enthusiast, but he'd been to motorcycle schools and had actually used motorcycles overseas a few times.

He had a rudimentary working knowledge of the different gear and motorcycle models. This guy rode some sort of dual sport-style motorcycle, which appeared loaded down pretty heavily. The rider was wearing a helmet, so John could not say if it had or had not been their target, Barry.

Finally, he stopped in the middle of the street, turned, and ran back to the house. Once at the house, he switched channels, calling the air crew and asking for their status. They were still circling and had not located the bike at that time. John switched back to the team channel.

"Move to breach point," he whispered into the mic. He knew the team members at the rear of the structure would already be staging to the side of the rear sliding glass door. He and the rest of the team moved to the garage, cleared the empty room, and staged on the door leading to the interior of the house. Again, he keyed the mic. "Three, two, one," he hissed into the mic.

On one, the team deployed flash bangs into the structure. The noise was deafening as the devices momentarily brought the interior of the house to life. Before the deafening sound of the flash bangs subsided, the two teams swept into the house. John was as careful as he could be, watching for booby traps while clearing the interior of the residence. The team used night-vision goggles and infrared lasers, or PEQs, to scan each room. This allowed the team to work in complete darkness, leaving an enemy without goggles at a distinct disadvantage.

Within thirty seconds the house was cleared, leaving John standing in the middle of the family room near the back of the house, staring at something that gave him a bad feeling. Mounted on a table, slightly back from a window, was an AK-47 assault rifle. The trigger had a small line attached to it that led out to the garage. There had only been one person, and he pulled the line activating the weapon as a diversion before he rode straight through his perimeter and off into the night.

"Well, goddamn," John said to himself. "Bastard got us."

John's earpiece crackled.

"Boss, we got company out front, 'bout twenty or thirty not-so-friendly-looking dudes."

John crouched, moving through the house towards the front room. "Are they armed?"

"Hell yeah, they are. Every single one has a rifle," came the response.

John stood back in the shadows of the front room and brought his rifle's scope to his eye, and he could see at least fifteen heavily armed men moving towards the front of the house.

"Boss, they're trying to surround the house. Guys are moving towards the side yard."

John leaned into the earpiece as if he might miss some crucial piece of information. He knew he couldn't allow the team to be flanked, but wasn't quite sure how he could stop this from happening in the short amount of time it was going to take the group out front to achieve this tactical maneuver. John had endured as many bad situations as he had good ones and, this, he thought, wasn't a good one. Sooner or later he was going to pay one way or another with either a limb or his life.

He thought briefly about speaking out and attempting to negotiate with these people, but as quickly as the thought entered his mind, he swept it aside as not effective and only offering an advantage to his opponent. The armed group outside hadn't actually fired a shot or physically threatened John and his small team, but the fact that they were tactically maneuvering on them left little doubt in his mind as to their intentions.

Food was most likely their first priority, and what little rations the team carried would be seen as a gold mine once the group pulled it from John's and his team's dead bodies. He wasn't going to let that happen.

He keyed his mic. "We are about to be contacted, people. Make ready for a fight. Rear team, hold the flanks and rear. We will come to you—through the house." He quickly switched channels, hailing the helicopter crew. "We are about to have heavy contact back at the target building, need immediate gunship support. Be advised bad guys are armed with rifles. Break." John looked back out at the group, who were now nearing the front yard. "Watch your altitude and monitor our progress to LZ Kilo Mike Mike." John instructed the flight crew, referring to an alternate pre-planned extraction site.

Before the helicopter crew could answer, John switched back to his team channel.

John set the stage, and now all there was to do was fight. He learned long ago that the man who threw the first punch always started the fight with a one-punch lead. He raised the rifle to his shoulder and, with lightning speed, sent seven rounds downrange. Seven armed men in the front yard went down, four for good and three screaming with horrific wounds, out of the fight and most likely headed to their graves within the next few hours.

As John turned to move, the two team members in the front room with him began firing into the advancing body. In unison, every member of the hostile group opened up on the front of the house, shattering windows and splintering wood frames around doors and windows. John had never been faced with such dismal odds in all his life. All the shooting drills he ever ran never addressed how to wipe out twenty-five bad guys before they wiped you out. This was going to be a running gun battle.

John had practiced shooting drills firing at up to five targets for speed, but any more than that, a man needed to become fluid, harder to track. He needed to move in order to keep the enemy shifting and off-balance. If they were moving, John knew the enemy would have a much tougher time putting accurate fire on him and his team. A moving target was extremely hard to hit, and a moving target who was returning accurate fire was even more of a handful.

As John turned and took his first step, two things happened that sickened him. He felt a round slam into the rear plate of his body armor, and he heard a softer slap as a second round found someone else's softer armor. He didn't fall, but he sure as hell wanted to as the round pounded into his back. He heard a cry from behind him and saw one of the two team members down while the other stood over his downed partner, pouring rounds through the shattered front windows of the little house.

John reached back, grabbed the downed man's web gear, and pulled him into the next room. The windows and walls of that room were already leaking bullets like salt out of a shaker. John pulled his wounded comrade into the room and dropped to the ground just as he heard a loud thwack come from the front room.

No scream or cry followed the sound as John slid facedown towards the door, trying to assess the situation in the front room as bullets continued piercing the tiny house's walls. John realized his team was not engaging the enemy, leaving him with a sinking feeling in the pit of his stomach.

The second man in his team laid crumpled up on the carpet, ass in the air, face down on the carpet, blood flowing freely from his face and head.

John turned back to the man he pulled to safety and began pulling away gear, trying to find the wound. He'd seen men die in battle, and the man in the front room was as dead as any person he'd ever seen. There was nothing he could do for the man, and the situation was deteriorating so quickly, they would likely all die if he took ten-seconds to pull the dead man into the room with his buddy.

From what John could tell, his wounded companion had been shot through the chest and was having more than a little trouble breathing. He needed to get the man out of the house and to a medical facility or he would surely die. Deep down, John knew the man was dead already, considering the situation and how moving him and fighting to the level that was going to be needed was simply not possible.

This was a dick sandwich if ever there was a dick sandwich, and John was starting to feel the frustration roil up in him, turning to anger. He reached under the dying man, scooping him into a shitty version of a fireman's carry. He staggered to his feet, wondering how two hundred pounds on a bar was ten times easier to lift than two hundred pounds of man. Once he was upright, he smashed the push-to-talk button on his vest, calling out to the other team members.

"Coming to you, and I have one WIA." As soon as he began moving through the house, shots crashed through the walls as the people on the outside caught glimpses of him passing the windows.

John bounced off the doorjamb, stopping in the family room located at the very rear of the small residence. The remaining four members of his team were there, weapons pointed outward, scanning for threats. They weren't really covering the flanking maneuver sitting inside the structure, but John bit his tongue.

As the team members glanced in his direction, John caught looks of shock on their already strained faces. That was when he felt the warm wet flow down the backs of his legs. John knew he wasn't bleeding and almost just dropped the man he had over his shoulder. Instead he gently lowered the now motionless man to the floor, and placed him in the center of a pool of his own blood. John saw then what happened. The man had taken a round to the head while John carried him through the house. Most of the right side of his face was gone, the gaping hole emitting an obscene amount of blood.

John took the scene in and was both angered at the loss and relieved, as this would be one less thing to deal with as the team fought its way out of this mess.

"Get ready, people," John called out. "We are going to move across that backyard, and I don't want to spend more than five to seven-seconds in the open." He made eye contact with every operator in the room before going on. "Follow me, and do as I do. Cover each other, and stick close. I don't want to have anyone separated from the group."

John quickly raised his rifle and scoped several windows

from back in the shadows of the dark room before moving toward a large window that faced the side yard. John felt that if they ran out into the rear yard, they were likely to be set upon from at least two sides and possibly three. It was the move the group outside was set up to deal with and would put John and his people at a disadvantage. He was going to go out the window, fight his way to the rear of the residence, and then move laterally over some fences before moving to the south, which was the direction the rear of the residence faced and the direction their LZ was in.

This was tactics on the fly at its very best, and John was keenly aware that he was in dangerous waters at this point. He was forming and initiating plans all in a matter of a few seconds, with no research or much thought. Basic tactical instincts were at work—no time for elaborate plans at this point in the fight.

In ten seconds, he laid out the plan to his team. One would create a diversion at the rear sliding glass door, John and a second team member would breach the window and engage any hostiles at the side of the house, then they would move through the window and over the neighboring fence.

Within fifteen seconds, the rear sliding glass door was breached along with the window, and John found himself firing on three men between him and the front of the house. John snapped off half a magazine leaving all three men on the ground, dead or dying. His counterpart found no targets between the window and the rear of the small house.

John moved swiftly out the window, covering towards the front of the house, jumped the fence, and covered his mates' progress as they followed him over the fence. They could hear shouts from the front yard, but didn't wait around; instead they turned and ran south. John and the team cleared two more fences then stopped briefly before crossing a street.

In the distance to their rear, they could hear sporadic

shooting and a whole lot of yelling and cursing. John had no doubt that after he and his team had killed possibly ten or more of these guys, they were no longer just after food. Revenge had undoubtedly been moved to or near the top of their "shit that had to get done tonight" list, and John had no plans of allowing them to check that box off.

John led the team for half a mile as fast as their burning lungs would allow, leaping fences, sprinting across roads and crashing through dark cluttered backyards before he stopped and set up a hasty security position. He switched channels, only catching the last of the pilot's transmission.

"Hope you all aren't in that mess." The sound of the helicopter was in the distance, and the sound of rifle fire could still be heard. John supposed the group had tired of losing guys and simply done a surround and shoot or burn operation.

Breathlessly John spoke into the headset. "We are out of the target structure, I say again, we are out and had to leave two KIA. Do not engage hostiles unless they are following my team, I say again, do not engage hostiles unless they are following us to the LZ."

In the fog of war, John had almost ordered the helicopter crew to fire on the unfriendlies before it occurred to him, he would be ordering the air crew to fire on Americans out looking for food and answers. Sure, they had killed two of his people, but he had most likely killed four times that many of them. He ran his tongue around the inside of his mouth as if trying to irradiate a bad taste. Fighting with fellow Americans left John feeling sick to his stomach.

Hoping the aggressors would be tied up figuring out where he and his mates went, John decided it was a good time to get moving towards the LZ. He took one last look at his map before moving off in a southerly direction, his pace significantly slower than it had been a minute before.

The team made it to the Target parking lot without further

incident, setting up a security perimeter in order to make a safer LZ for their ride home. A short time later, the helicopter made its approach to the parking lot. The large aircraft barely settled on the pavement before John and what was left of his team scrambled aboard. The pilot pulled power, guiding the large aircraft into the night sky before nosing over and turning to the east.

John sank back into the seat, leaning against the bulkhead, wondering what in the hell had just happened and how the hell it had happened so fast. He had participated in plenty of fights during his military career, but they had all been with experienced and hardened warriors, not a bunch of kids thrown together, trained over a weekend, and then dropped on a target that would have put him and some of his most trusted mates to the test.

What ate at him the most was leaving the two KIAs behind. It may not have seemed like something that bothered him based on the speed with which he made the decision to leave them, but that could not have been further from the truth. He'd never left a mate behind, and tonight he'd left two.

The helicopter was traveling at just under 140 knots and holding steady at 1500 feet AGL or "above ground level." Both pilots were wearing night-vision goggles and both were starting to relax a little when the twenty-eight-pound goose crashed through the right-side windshield. The goose impacted the pilot's helmet, slightly off center to the right, breaking his neck and killing him instantly. In death, the pilot doomed the aircraft as he stiffened his legs, applying pressure to the left pedal, causing the aircraft to turn violently, the tail swinging around as the craft shuddered and groaned in this unnatural state of flight.

In the back of the Black Hawk, the crew chief had a ruck containing a can of ammunition, food, water, and an M4 strapped to the outside in case he had to leave the aircraft during one of their missions. The ruck was stuffed under a seat, but not secured or tethered. When the dead pilot kicked the left pedal, the ruck came free of the seat before being jettisoned out the open door.

Not a big deal except that the tail rotor was coming around and literally tried to eat the ruck along with its contents. If not for the rifle and ammo can full of ammunition, the tail rotor might have survived; instead, the leading edge of one blade was destroyed, causing an unbalanced state and, from there, the aircraft began to shake itself apart.

John knew immediately they were in big trouble and reacted by trying not to shit himself. Whatever had happened couldn't be reversed now, and he was in this damn thing to the end. The copilot, although dazed, was fighting for control of the aircraft like a pro, reacting more than flying at this point.

As soon as the tail rotor came apart and the bird began to spin, he dropped the collective, struggling to achieve something close to straight and level flight as they dropped like a stone. John saw what he thought were feathers streaming from the cockpit like some scene from a Playboy Bunny pillow fight. The scene was surreal and provided John with a brief moment of escape from his current predicament.

The copilot's voice brought John back to the here and now as he called out to his passengers, "Hang on, we're going down hard."

It was then that John realized he was alone in the back of the aircraft. He realized quickly the remaining team members had been sitting on the floor, not tethered to the craft. They all must have been ejected through the craft's two doors, which the crew chief removed prior to the mission.

The crew chief was another story. Where had he gone? He was always strapped to his workstation. John knew he'd seen the strap as they came aboard. It was then John saw the strap tautly draped out the doorway. The crew chief was hanging outside a crashing helicopter, not good...for him.

Before John could move to help the stricken crew chief, he was pushed into his seat as the remaining pilot pulled the collective into his armpit, trying desperately to slow the helicopter's descent before impact. John had been on two helicopters when they crashed or, as the pilots liked to say, made unscheduled landings.

John knew the man hanging outside the aircraft was likely a dead man if he remained outside the helicopter when it struck the ground. John also knew if he unbuckled in an effort to help the man, he'd likely die as well. The ground reached up and smashed the aircraft, mercifully making John's dilemma a moot point. All John could do was tuck his chin and hold his arms into his body armor as the disaster unfolded around him.

The copilot did an admiral job of landing the broken craft in an open clearing; the problem was he came in fairly straight and struck a large rock, which ended his life on the spot. The aircraft spun after impacting the rock, then rolled onto its side, crushing the already doomed crew chief.

John closed his eyes and only opened them after the deafening noise of the crash had subsided. John's mind was already working ten steps ahead of everything else happening around him as what was left of the main rotor ground to a stop after chewing up some turf and shearing most of its blades completely down to the rotor hub. John could hear the high-pitched whine of a much fucked-up turbine engine and smelled jet fuel. He had to get out, but he also had to make sure he left with items he would need to survive.

He switched on his headlamp, located his ruck, rifle, and two ammo cans full of rifle ammunition. The aircraft was on its side, so John hoisted the gear up and out the side door, which was more of a sunroof at this point.

Again, John saw the feathers swirling around the shattered

windscreen and then it hit him; they'd suffered a bird strike. A fucking bird had likely killed seven people and destroyed a multimillion-dollar aircraft. Holy shit, John thought, multimillion wasn't even close anymore, that Black Hawk was a nearly extinct species. Hell, it was priceless, and some flying rat had deprived mankind of this prized possession. John almost laughed at the absurdity of it all.

Fire began to burn somewhere near the cockpit as John pulled himself up and out of the carnage. Strangely John wondered how flammable feathers were. He dropped himself to the ground with his ruck and ammo cans before dragging everything a safe distance away. John had stowed his night-vision goggles after the pickup, and now he fished them out of his ruck. John attached them to his helmet, switching them to the on position. He scanned the area, weapon held at the ready, having no idea where he was and not wanting to get jumped a second time in the same night.

The wreckage had quieted down a little, only emitting a hissing sound as the fire burned the wrecked hull of the flying machine. He shook his head as he thought that, not more than a minute ago, the machine had been flying and flying well. Now it laid in a heap of burning metal, wires and other toxic materials.

As John scanned the area, he took inventory of his personal well-being and found he was a little sore, but didn't seem to have sustained any significant injuries.

John loaded the ammo cans into the ruck and then scanned the area again, looking for some higher ground he could get to in order to watch the wreckage for a day or two. John felt if there were people around, they would be attracted to the crash site. If no one came, he'd know he was pretty much alone out here...wherever here was.

John was sure that when he got to higher ground, he'd be able to use his map and compass to pinpoint his exact location.

Once the sun came up, John had to only identify a few prominent terrain features, which would allow him to triangulate his position to within a few yards.

After an hour of walking, John was perched a thousand feet higher in altitude than the crash site and nearly three-quarters of a mile away. He had a perfect line of sight to the site and the surrounding area. He set up a hasty OP (observation point) and scanned the entire area, looking for movement. The small fire in the cockpit had taken off and engulfed the entire aircraft as John was leaving, and the wreckage was still burning in the distance although there was more smoke than flames now.

John turned the night-vision goggles away from the wreckage, scanning the rolling California hills, looking for his teammates who had been thrown from the helicopter as it began its unscheduled landing. He stared at the crash site, trying to estimate how far the helicopter had traveled after it started coming apart. He could only make an educated, or uneducated, guess on how high they were upon impacting the bird and what their descent rate consisted of on their way to the ground.

He worked the two factors around in his head and came up with his search area. It was far too large an area to search on foot, coupled with the fact that falling from a helicopter traveling at over one hundred knots at over a thousand-foot altitude was one of those things that usually ended one's time on earth. In fact, John couldn't remember a situation in his past with similar elements that hadn't resulted in an operator's death.

John spent the next hour watching the crash site along with the neighboring fingers, draws and other terrain features within his field of view. He never found so much as a trace of his fallen comrades.

Chapter 33

BARRY ROCKETED OUT of the garage on the motorcycle, laden with all he could carry and then a little more. Yeah, he knew it would make his chances of crashing significantly higher with his balance thrown completely off, but what choice did he have? He had a large pack strapped tightly to his back along with more gear strapped to the front, back, and sides of the motorcycle.

As he blasted out of the garage, he saw a couple of soldiers scrambling to block his path, but they either weren't fast enough or had taken bad angles and were unable to intercept him. He also saw a larger group of civilian-clad people approaching from down the street. These folks were so shocked to see a functioning motorcycle they simply stopped and gawked at him as he rode straight through the middle of their horde.

It was one of those moments where Barry willed the folks not to open fire, grab, or otherwise molest or interfere with his getaway, and it worked. *I am Yoda, Jedi Master. You will let me pass.* He smiled inside the helmet. Before anyone could react, Barry was past them and racing out of sight and range.

The gun Barry had set up was making a racket, helping divert the civilians' attention back to their original objective. Barry hit a straightaway and rolled the throttle back, feeling the bike respond. In less than a minute, Barry was out of his residential neighborhood and onto a freeway. Feeling a little safer, Barry slowed his speed, glancing back over his shoulder. His heart sank as he saw the road was clear to his rear, but the sky was not. The UH-60 Black Hawk loomed to his rear at about five hundred feet altitude. *Fuck, fuck, fuck*, Barry thought. *Goddamn helicopters were not planned for.*

Prior to the event, Barry worked for a company that did a ton of contract work for the federal government on many different projects. They made some things, but they did a tremendous amount of research and initial development for other companies, who would take their ideas, pay for patent rights, and manufacture whatever it was Barry's group had developed. Mostly all of his work was classified and was geared towards weaponizing any and everything the government could get its hands on. His company led the industry in researching and developing nanotechnologies for future weapons.

Barry worked on dozens of projects the government gave his company, and was very familiar with the way in which the feds operated. One project had been to develop a weapon to disable an entire country, but only in a temporary manner without killing its people. That was easy since the technology already existed. After his team pitched an EMP or electromagnetic pulse weapon, augmented with some other technologies, tactics and methodology, the feds asked that they take their plan and plan against that plan.

This got Barry thinking about how vulnerable the US was against such an attack. His team came up with ways to harden the country against such an event and presented it to the stiffs in Washington. The federal government balked at the price of hardening all of the US and its infrastructure. The cost was simply too much, and the people would never agree to spend that kind of money to protect themselves against a threat that might or might not be a real danger. That was fine with Barry; he didn't have time for folks who refused to help themselves.

He hardened almost everything he owned, put himself through more classes on shooting, stockpiled nonperishable foods and ammunition, but he never changed a thing about himself as far as any co-workers were concerned, and would often chuckle at the thought of his Silicon Valley friends finding out about his little secret.

Although Barry felt competent with every firearm he owned, he also knew he had absolutely zero experience actually using the weapons in a real-life situation with adrenaline pumping and bullets flying. He was smart enough to know when this time came, it would be nothing like standing on a square range with some retired cop yelling "threat" before he engaged stationary paper targets that, to date, had never fired back.

Barry knew his best chance for surviving in the new world was to run, hide and avoid conflict at all costs. He also knew he wasn't climbing into bed with the government that had knowledge of the very threat that had recently unraveled almost a hundred and fifty years of technology and done nothing to prevent it. He would run, and he would survive on his own, and they could kiss his lily-white ass, as far as he was concerned.

Barry guided the bike east towards the foothills, tense and fearful at every turn. The last thing he wanted was to encounter some of the people he knew were roaming the streets. The bounty he had strapped to his bike would trigger an immediate conflict with anyone still alive and half starved. The moment he could, Barry pulled the bike off the street and rode cross-country, where the going was much slower.

Barry's plan was quite simple: he was heading into the center of the country, where he would find folks like himself, who were good folks, knew how to survive, and where he would offer his expertise as long as they let him join their group or town or whatever they had. If the fucking federal government felt he could help get the country back on its feet, he had little doubt he could almost single-handedly get a small town on its feet and self-sufficient.

As the sun began to rise, Barry crested a hilltop, stopped the bike, and withdrew his binoculars, scanning the sprawling landscape. In the distance, he saw a small farmhouse with several cars parked on the surrounding grounds. He opened the gas cap and, using his legs, shook the bike back and forth, assessing the amount of fuel on board. The sloshing seemed to match what the gas gauge read.

Barry dismounted, securing the bike in a thicket along with his pack before finding a spot on the hilltop to watch the farmhouse. He watched the tiny homestead for three hours, seeing nothing more than a bird or squirrel moving on the property.

He moved off the hilltop to his bike, stripping the machine of all the gear. He squatted next to the pile of gear and opened a small saddlebag, pulling out a small hand pump, which he intended to use to siphon gas from the cars on the farm. He stuffed the pump in his cargo pocket and slung his short-barreled AR-15 across his shoulders. Barry turned and dug through another bag, pulling out a plate carrier, which he pulled on, tightening the straps.

During his time on the range, he was introduced to a whole different culture that, before he started shooting, he didn't know existed. He heard guys talking about the plate carriers and how they housed ballistic plates that would defeat a rifle round. He listened to all the bravado talk by guys on the range who postured and bragged. It seemed many of them preferred to wear only the front plate and leave the rear plate at home in the spirit of reducing weight.

These gun-range commandos liked to do their training in comfort. Barry thought this sounded like a surefire way to get shot in the back. Murphy's Law seemed to always rear its ugly head when he tried cutting corners. In the end, Barry kept both plates and dumped all his other gear so he would be lighter in case he had to make a quick exit from the farmhouse property.

He learned a valuable lesson when he left his house the night before. A fully loaded motorcycle was an absolute pain in the ass to ride at anything more than a snail's pace. Lighter and faster now, Barry started down the hill towards the farmhouse, wearing the plate carrier and carrying only a rifle, pistol and his fuel pump.

Once he arrived outside the house, he slowly rode in a circle around the perimeter in order to see if anyone came out to see who had arrived. Barry was sure that after all these weeks with no vehicles, the sound of his motorcycle would bring any occupants out in a hurry. No one came outside, so he stopped next to an old Ford F-150.

Without dismounting or shutting the bike down, Barry fed the longer end of the pump's hose into the Ford's gas tank, then fed the shorter bit of hose into the bike's open tank and began to slowly work the pump's lever. Five pumps later, he was rewarded by the sound of gas splashing into his bike's fuel tank. He pumped until his bike's fuel tank was full, withdrew all his hoses, and emptied the excess fuel into the dirt before stowing the pump in his cargo pocket.

Barry gunned the bike, riding quickly back up into the hills. Barry knew he had about a six-hundred-mile range with what he had in the tank right now. He would top the fuel whenever he could, no matter how much or how little he had on board. The bike was a beauty and he had done some research before buying it. BMW made great overland-type bikes and, with very few changes, the bike was ready for just about anything.

The best thing he had done was add an aftermarket fuel tank that added more than four gallons, making the total fuel capacity twelve gallons. Depending on how he rode, the bike was rated at fifty-five miles per gallon. Barry rounded it to six hundred and felt pretty good about his chances of finding fuel before he ran out. He returned to the spot where he hid his gear and dismounted, shutting the bike off. He was starving and set to making something to eat.

As Barry sat eating his meager breakfast, a small tendril of smoke in the distance caught his eye. Smoke out in the hills made him wonder what was burning. He half wanted to go investigate, but knew it would not be a wise decision and could end in disaster for him. The bike made noise and would alert anyone in the area of his approach, so he figured he would stick to trying to skirt the smoke and get out into the central valley. Barry felt if he could reach the central valley, he would be able to make much better time since it was so flat. He might even use some of the roads.

When he finished slurping down the paste that was supposed to be some sort of egg breakfast, he loaded the bike and climbed back on, facing the direction he intended to go. Suddenly he felt the weight of last night's events hit him hard, causing him to feel weak and nearly topple off the bike. He was exhausted beyond words and knew he had to rest soon before he made a mistake.

He shouldn't be in a rush. After all, it wasn't like he was on any sort of timetable. There were no deadlines, no meetings to keep, no appointments he had to attend. He could go at his own pace, a pace that was the safest for him and afforded him the greatest chance of survival.

Just making and eating breakfast had taught him a valuable lesson. He did a ton of research and felt fairly certain he purchased and brought most of the gear he needed to survive; however, he hadn't really practiced with any of it, which was evidenced when he burned the shit out of himself while boiling water. He added too much water to the dehydrated breakfast and had to suffer through eating the runny paste. Not a huge deal and definitely a first-world problem, but a very telling experience in his opinion.

Barry found a nice deep draw covered in vegetation, not visible from any structures or roads. He made his way to the bottom and began riding up the draw, finding it was a dried creek bed. He rode a distance up the creek bed until it was blocked with a pile of tree branches and other debris.

He covered the bike in branches, pulled out his sleeping mat along with his sleeping bag, crawled in, and almost immediately fell asleep. He dreamed bandits took his bike and all his gear, while still he slept a long, deep sleep.

JARED SAT INSIDE THE HOUSE, a small candle providing a pitiful amount of light in comparison to nights gone by. Shannon sat on the couch, reading to Essie under another candle's doleful light. Calvin was outside on watch, and Bart was asleep in one of the bedrooms. It was early evening, and the house was dead quiet except for the low murmur of Shannon's voice.

It started faintly, causing everyone in the little house to stop what they were doing and listen intently. Jared leapt to his feet and raced outside just in time to hear what sounded like a fairly large helicopter pass overhead, heading towards the city. Jared raced around the side of the house, hoping to catch a glimpse of the helicopter, but the aircraft was operating without lights, leaving Jared staring up at what appeared to be a blackhole in his opinion.

Seconds after the aircraft thundered over the house, Bart staggered out, pulling on a jacket and dragging his rifle by the sling. Jared turned as the noise faded in the distance.

"Hey, we don't know anything about that bird. I wouldn't recommend running out in the open like that in the future," Bart said as he came up to Jared. He looked back at the doorway to where Shannon and Essie stood, and nodded his head as if to make sure they knew his advice extended to them as well. Shannon pumped her head in the affirmative.

"It's obviously the government," Jared said.

"That's what worries me," Bart responded before turning on his heel and walking back into the house.

Jared walked out to where Calvin was and made sure he was good, before returning to the house. Bart had not gone back to bed, but instead sat in a chair sipping water, a look of concern on his weathered old face. He also had a blanket wrapped around his shoulders, looking older than ever.

Jared pushed the thoughts of Bart's health struggles in the current environment out of his head as he sat down next to the older man. "What's wrong with the government knowing we're out here?"

Bart looked up with bloodshot eyes, his shoulders drooped, his brow creased with furrows caused by concern. Bart breathed in deeply before replying, "The goddamn government either caused this or allowed this to happen. By caused it, I mean they either actually did something to cause this or their naive foreign and domestic policies caused some other government to bring this on us."

Jared shifted in his seat. "Yeah, but FEMA, the National Guard, aren't they all in place to get folks back on their feet after something like this?"

Bart looked at Jared like a father whose son had just made a poorly thought out and naïve statement about life. "The government is simply a tool for the people who run the world, enabling them to harvest money from the country's population for their coffers." Bart swept his hand across his front. "Everything the government does is controlled by plaintiff's attorneys and people who run corporations. They spend hundreds of millions of dollars getting politicians elected and they don't do it out of the goodness of their hearts. People always blame corporations—as if it's just corporate greed. It's human greed."

Jared cocked his head slightly and Bart continued, "Take all the humanitarian aid the US government sends to Israel, billions of taxpayers' dollars going to help Israel, right?" Without waiting for a response, he forged on, "What do you think Israel spends those billions on? Weapons, and who sells them those weapons? Fucking corporations that are mostly based in the US of A, my friend. It's how the rich launder our tax dollars right into their bank accounts."

Bart drew a deep breath. "So, excuse me if I'm a little suspicious of the organization that a month ago had access to roughly forty percent of every American's yearly income and suddenly has been cut off. I imagine that right about now they are doing everything in their power to regain the death grip they once had on the US population."

The old man took a sip of water.

"Past practice tells me they are looking out for themselves and could give two fucks about you and me, unless, of course, we have something to offer them." Bart shook his head in disgust. "They took what they wanted before, using social media along with the news media to blind everyone to what they were really doing. Now it's my guess they're just fucking taking what they want by force. They have no way to manipulate the masses and, quite frankly, no need to since they're pretty much the only people with aircraft, and armored vehicles."

Jared thought about the world before and how the old

bastard was on the mark about taxation and how people had given nearly half their yearly earnings to the government without so much as blinking. *Where had all that money gone?* he wondered. The two men sat in silence as Jared mulled over this thought. A month ago, he would have dismissed this old man's ramblings as those of a conspiracy theorist. Now after the electricity was shut off, he had to give this theory, opinion, or whatever it was, some serious thought.

"Think about it," Bart said. "One helicopter heading into the city at night. Not a humanitarian-aid mission, you can bet on that. More like they're going in to get someone out who is in their inner circle, and fuck the rest of the starving sons of bitches out there." He finished and took another sip of water while Jared remained silent, listening to the soft murmurs of Shannon reading to Essie.

"Maybe we should cover the OP with a tarp during the night hours and figure out some sort of camo for daytime shifts," Jared said.

Without looking over, Bart nodded.

"Can't those guys see people in the dark with some sort of heat sensors?" asked Jared.

"Some can, but if they're flying without lights, the pilots are wearing night-vision goggles." Bart waved a boney hand. "We can come up with a plan tomorrow...set up a safer OP." With that, Bart rose and ambled off to the back bedroom.

Shortly after Bart retired to bed, Jared and Shannon blew out the candles and put Essie to bed before lying down for some badly needed rest. Calvin came in around 2200 hours, woke Bart for his shift, and four hours later Bart woke Jared for his watch. Jared felt like his head had just hit the pillow when Bart shook his shoulder. The group was most vulnerable in between shifts.

They only had two mechanical watches and neither had an alarm function, so when it was time, the person at the OP would walk down to the house, wake the next person, then return to their post until the next person arrived. It wasn't the best scenario for pulling security, but it was the best the little group could do with what they had at their disposal.

Jared got up, rubbed his eyes, pulled his shoes on, and grabbed his rifle before donning his gear and numbly stumbling out into the cold towards the OP. Once he arrived, Bart briefed him on what happened, which was nothing. After the quick briefing, Bart left Jared sitting alone in the cold. This was the worst part of this whole thing, Jared lamented to himself.

He missed sleeping through every night while cops and other first responders took care that nothing bad happened to all the sleeping people. My God, he thought, just one full night of uninterrupted sleep would do wonders for my head. He looked down at the watch Bart had passed on to him and saw it was a little past 0200 hours.

Forty-five minutes later, Jared was freezing, his legs were stiff, and he was having a hard time keeping his eyes open. He had never fallen asleep while on post simply because Bart had threatened to kill him if he did, and he was fairly sure Bart had not been bluffing. Before the event, he wouldn't have seen the importance of staying awake while on a post. Post event, he saw what people were doing to each other and was in no way inclined to be subjected to the merciless violence humans were bestowing on one another.

He stood and stretched, which only served to make him colder. He folded his arms and did a series of squats in a futile effort to warm his chilled body. His knees screamed in protest and his lower back ached. On his fifteenth squat, he froze halfway up.

In the distance came the faint sound of beating rotors; the helicopter was returning. Suddenly, Jared wasn't cold or stiff as the noise of the approaching aircraft grew louder. He strained his eyes to see into the darkness, scanning for the helicopter, but saw nothing. He shifted his position, feeling suddenly vulnerable. Jared moved to a large rock, where he crouched in an attempt to hide himself from the approaching machine.

As he settled into position, Jared heard a distinct change in the pitch of the helicopter's engines. Jared was not a helicopter aficionado or even a helicopter enthusiast, but he knew something had changed, which most likely meant something was wrong, since the rhythmic roar of the bird had changed to something that sounded more distressed, even a little hysterical —if a helicopter could sound hysterical. Seconds later, he heard a loud crash, followed by a higher pitched whine from the engines, and then silence.

He crept forward, staring into the night, still unable to see a goddamn thing. His eyes were unable to penetrate the molasses-like darkness. *The fucking thing crashed,* Jared thought, standing as still as a statue while he digested this information. *Holy fucking shit, the thing just crashed and I heard the whole thing.* This was definitely something Bart would want to hear about pronto. Jared broke into a sprint for the farmhouse.

Jared hurried into the small house, blasting straight into the old man's room. Bart sat straight up in bed, pistol in hand.

"Don't shoot, it's me," Jared hissed.

"What the fuck time is it?" Bart asked as Jared fumbled around in the darkness before lighting a tiny candle on the dresser.

"The helicopter crashed out there somewhere," Jared said.

Bart squinted in the flickering light before swinging his boney and nearly translucent legs over the side of the bed. He didn't say a word as he pulled on his pants and then his boots. Jared stared briefly at the old man's bone-white legs, wondering if they'd ever seen the light of day. Weirdly, Jared's mind wandered as he speculated whether the old bastard had ever owned a pair of shorts. Come to think of it, Jared had never seen the man in shorts and, when they'd packed to leave San

Jose, he'd never seen a pair of shorts in Bart's possession. Once Bart had his boots on, he turned from Jared as he readied his gear and slung his rifle.

"Where and how far away?" Bart asked flatly.

Jared relayed what happened, then told Bart he couldn't be sure how far out the thing had been when he heard the crash. It was very difficult to gauge distance in the near complete darkness, not to mention the eerie quietness that had suddenly enveloped Earth with the sudden absence of anything electronic.

Finishing with his gear, Bart turned back to Jared. "Let's get Calvin up to man the post while you and I try to find the crash site."

Calvin was wakened, much to his chagrin, briefed, huffed a bit, and then headed out to the OP. Bart followed Jared off the property and into the hills in the general direction Jared thought the crash sound came from.

Outside, there was a fair amount of ambient light with the moon and stars overhead. Still, the going was slow as the two tried to move as quietly as possible while also keeping watch for any threats. After creeping through the darkness for two hours, both men were breathing heavily and slicked in sweat.

Jared caught the faint scent of something burning and pulled Bart close. "You smell that?"

Bart nodded, staring into the early morning darkness. After a moment, Bart leaned closer to Jared. "We stay here till light; then we can look for smoke."

They both moved to a cluster of rocks and settled in, each man facing in a different direction for security purposes. Neither man spoke, each lost in his thoughts as they waited for the sun to light their way. Oddly enough, the sun was the reason both men were huddled on the hard-cold ground next to each other, clutching rifles, with no access to all the amenities electricity had offered before the event. The sun they now needed for sight and warmth had recently evicted them from the comforts they had enjoyed, leaving them with only hardship.

Jared's watch read 0630 hours when the first inkling of light began to creep across the landscape, pushing the night slowly off the playing field. As the day grew brighter, both men caught sight of black acrid smoke curling skyward. The location of the crash, was clearly marked by the smoke and Jared realized they had passed the crash site during their two-hour hike.

The rapidness with which the night became day always amazed Jared. Within what seemed like a few minutes, it was bright enough to see everything around them clearly. Both Bart and Jared saw the body at nearly the exact same time. Bart's weapon came up, sweeping the surrounding area, a look of concern on his face.

The body was about fifty yards from their position and looked to be a soldier in full battle gear. The soldier was twisted in a very unnatural position, not moving.

"Cover me," Bart ordered, moving towards the body, weapon raised and at the ready. Bart reached the body then waved Jared forward. The man in the battle gear was a mess, broken and twisted in ways a human body was never meant to be positioned. Bart began removing the man's battle gear, but left the man's boots and clothes on.

"I don't know what happened, but I'd bet this poor bastard wasn't strapped in when the bird started crashing, and he just fell out," Bart said as he opened the man's pack, dumping its contents on the ground. The pack contained small radio batteries, extra socks, ammunition, a rifle cleaning kit, and a beautiful pair of night-vision goggles, which Bart held in his hand like they were the Ark of the Covenant.

"Holy fucking shit, look what we have here," Bart chortled.

After admiring his find for a few seconds, he continued

digging through the pack and found extra batteries for the goggles along with a small solar charging unit for recharging the batteries. He held the items up to Jared.

"Fucking score," he said, looking like he'd just won the lottery.

After going through all the stricken man's gear, Bart set aside several items he planned on taking; the rest he'd leave. There were two fragmentation hand grenades, four loaded rifle magazines, the night-vision goggles, along with the batteries and charger. The man's weapon was still strapped to him, but badly damaged. Jared saw the barrel was actually bent and the buttstock was missing. Bart pulled the bolt carrier group out of the Colt and stowed it with the rest of the man's gear he had set aside.

"Let's take this poor soul to the crash site and see if there are others. Poor son of a bitch, what a fucking way to go," Bart said as he motioned for Jared to grab an arm and help with moving the man. The two men struggled to drag the dead man along towards the crash site, with Jared glancing down every few seconds into the man's lifeless eyes and smashed face, thinking to himself how surreal it all seemed

Chapter 34

THE NIGHT WAS COLD, and John's joints were stiff and more than a little sore. He slowly flexed his muscles in an effort to get some additional blood flowing into his legs and arms. The flexing only seemed to cause him pain with no perceptible increase in heat to his tortured limbs. The sun was coming up and would soon bathe his tired, aching and half-frozen body with its lovely warm rays.

John froze as he caught movement at the edge of the clearing near the crashed helicopter. He fucking knew it, there were people living out here in the hills, and he had been right about them being attracted to the crash site. He focused the binoculars on the source of the movement and saw two armed men dragging the body of one of his team members.

John's temper began to flare until he realized the soldier was very obviously dead and the men didn't seem to be showing the fallen man any signs of disrespect. Sure, they'd stripped the man of his load-bearing gear, but they'd also left the man's clothing in place, including his boots, which John knew, from spending far too much time in shitty third-world cesspools, were the first to be taken from a dead body.

John watched as the two men laid the body a short distance from the still-smoldering wreckage. They moved near the downed aircraft, catching sight of the doomed crew chief's broken body still tethered to what was left of the aircraft's fuselage. The two men cut the body away from the helicopter, moving it next to the other soldier's body before going through his web gear.

The crew chief hadn't been wearing his pack, so the search went quickly and, again, the men left the man clothed and didn't so much as touch his boots. John watched as the men next pulled the two pilots from the wrecked cockpit and laid them alongside the other two deceased servicemen.

After the last pilot was laid on the ground, John watched the men sit and drink from water bottles. They talked for a few moments, stood, and began rummaging through the wreckage again. Both men worked on pieces of metal, which they freed from the airframe, and then used the metal pieces to start digging. *What in the fuck are these dudes doing?*, wondered John. Ten minutes later he realized they were digging graves for his fallen comrades.

None of this made any sense to him after what he'd seen in the world so far. He had fully expected to see his comrades stripped and discarded like trash when he first laid eyes on these two. John was pretty sure if it had gone that route, he would have wanted to kill both these guys, but then again, he was already behind enemy lines and didn't need anyone looking for the killer of their father or brother or whatever these guys were. He had enough trouble simply by being stranded.

It wasn't that John was scared of being killed; he just was of the opinion that when life serves you up a dick sandwich, you don't go making things worse with shitty emotionally based decisions.

Now he was doubly glad he hadn't moved on these two as he watched them toil in the hard soil. John watched for a few more minutes before packing his gear and slowly moving towards the two. He knew they would be digging for quite a while and felt fairly comfortable in being able to move close enough to follow them after the burial. He wanted to see where these people went and figure out if there were any more folks out in these hills. By the looks of the two gravediggers, John surmised they were well armed, mildly trained, and most likely a threat only to those who would threaten them and theirs.

Jared and Bart dug four shallow graves, placed the mangled and burned bodies into the graves, and covered them with dirt. After the bodies were covered, they piled rocks on top of the graves in order to at least attempt to safeguard them against scavengers. After placing the last rock on a soldier's grave, Bart groaned and straightened up, stretching his back. Jared wiped his brow with his sleeve, looking out to the surrounding hills.

"We really should have pulled some sort of security while we did this," Bart said, staring at the nearby landscape.

Jared just stared off into the hills, not saying a word, but getting the feeling suddenly they were being watched.

"Easy, don't let on. I got the same feeling," Bart whispered.

John watched as the two men took their break, drank some water, packed their belongings, and then began moving away from the crash site. John's plan was to track these two, not follow them. Following people oftentimes resulted in your being identified, ambushed and killed. These were just a few things John intended to avoid if he could.

John had set up ambushes on people following him and his mates in the past and knew how well it worked. Once a party knew it was being followed, they would round a bend or some other natural visual barrier, and part of the team would simply drop off the trail, concealing themselves in a hasty ambush position. When the following party arrived in that area, they'd be ambushed, and it would suck for them.

John moved laterally till he was safely out of sight, then began to run. He would leapfrog these two men, letting them come to him, pass, and then he would repeat. This way there was no way John was going to get ambushed since he wasn't moving along the same path they were. The trick to this tactic was for him not to get too far ahead in case they changed direction. If this happened, he stood a very good chance of losing them. Traveling ahead short distances and keeping them in sight as much as possible was going to be the way he handled tracking this little party.

John moved quickly for twenty minutes before arriving at a spot he felt would be a nice overlook position. He waited for another fifteen minutes before he began to get a bad feeling. *Where are these two dudes now?* From his position he could nearly see all the way back to the crash site and should have been able to spot the men with little effort. The cool morning air was absolutely quiet except for an occasional bird chirping.

John immediately checked his rear before moving his position to a large rock, where he felt he had the best chance of defending himself should he come under fire. He took out his binoculars and began scanning the hills in the direction he guessed the two men would have taken away from the crash site. Something caught John's attention about twenty yards up the side of an embankment, something just a bit off, a quarter of a shade different in color from the surrounding vegetation.

John focused the optics on the deviance, adjusting the visual aid so everything was crystal clear. The abnormality came into focus, revealing the younger of the two men lying prone, weapon trained back in the direction the two had come from—the same direction John would have come had he simply followed the two men.

"You sneaky fuckers," he muttered under his breath. Two minutes later he found the older man positioned another fifty yards straight down the path the two had been following. John didn't know if the men had intentionally set up an L-shaped ambush or had done it by accident; either way he would have been in big trouble if he was lazy and just trailed the two men.

John watched the two for the next hour and was impressed with their patience. He didn't know if they had a solid reason for doing what they had done, or if it was one of those things where people being watched sometimes felt an energy from those doing the watching. Either way, they had to be dealt with carefully now that he knew they weren't just a couple of dumb-ass city folk.

At the hour mark, the older man stood, waving to the younger fellow, who rose from his position, glanced about, then jogged down the hill, joining his older companion. They conversed for a few seconds, gave the surrounding hills one last visual go over, then turned and started off in the direction they were traveling before their security stop.

The two men set up an ambush two more times over the next two hours as they steadily made their way east through the hills. John was ready for this and easily avoided any contact with the two men. During one of the ambush stops, John never actually spotted the other two men until the older man rose and they continued on their way. During one of John's leapfrog runs, he stopped short when a small house came into view. He skirted the house, moving into a position where he could observe the two men's approach to the little domicile.

A short time later the two men came into view and were met outside by a woman who was accompanied by a small girl. The older man tousled the girl's hair, after which the younger man picked her up and gave her a hug. The woman spoke with the two men gesturing towards the crash site numerous times.

Five minutes into the conversation, the younger of the two men left the group, walking up the road away from the house and in the opposite direction they'd come from. Several minutes later the younger man returned with a third man, also older, but looking in better health than the original old man.

———

WHEN CALVIN REACHED the small group standing outside the house, Bart filled him in on what had happened, telling him he got the feeling they were followed even though they hadn't seen anyone or any sign of any survivors. Bart just kept shaking his head, saying something wasn't right.

"What were they doing flying into the city with just the crew and one soldier?" Bart asked the group. "It makes no sense at all. If they were gathering aerial intel, they'd have had at least a couple more folks, I'd imagine." Bart scratched his head and peered around at the hillsides. He didn't like this new turn of events.

After a bit, Shannon took Essie and moved to the OP so the men could grab some much-needed rest. Bart and Jared crashed immediately after eating a quick and cold breakfast. They both slept for several hours before rolling out of bed, getting dressed, and arming themselves. When Bart was finished, he moved through the house to the front door and exited.

Jared watched him leave, feeling the old man's struggle and pondering the man's future. He moved to a window where he could see the older man. Jared knew the night before had taken a toll on Bart, and he was beginning to see him weaken almost daily. Outside, he saw Bart hunched over in the side yard, coughing into a small kerchief. Bart didn't see Jared watching as he withdrew the kerchief, sucking in a breath while wiping a small rivulet of blood from his mouth.

Bart spat a bloody glob onto the ground, gathered himself, and then moved back towards the front of the house. Bart returned to the house, staring blankly at Jared as he entered. Jared wasn't sure if Bart knew he'd seen his coughing episode. Either way, Bart made no indication had and returned to his bedroom.

Calvin was still sleeping, so Jared wandered down to the OP to relieve Shannon. She jumped as he approached, clutching her rifle tightly in her hands.

"Bart's right, someone is watching this place. I can feel it, call it woman's intuition or whatever, but they're out there."

Jared tried to smile to ease the woman's tension, but he felt it too. Although Jared felt the same uneasy feeling, he just wasn't going to say anything with Shannon already obviously wound up over it.

"Head back and get something to eat. I'll sit out here till someone relieves me."

Shannon nodded and took one more glance around the countryside before she and Essie moved off towards the little house. Shannon's rifle was slung haphazardly across her slender shoulders, while Essie's tiny hand was clasped tightly in hers. Jared watched the two walk away, thinking what an outlandish sight this should have been. Two months ago, this picture would have been absurd, even alarming. Now it seemed bizarrely normal.

━━

JOHN HAD MOVED into a position where he could observe not only the house, but its occupants' little lookout position. He was mildly impressed by two things: first and foremost, that the tiny group actually had a lookout position and manned it twenty-four hours, day and night. Secondly John was impressed at what a great spot it was in regard to covering all the avenues of approach to their dwelling. This made his moving around the little ranch substantially more difficult than John would have preferred.

John watched all morning, not seeing the two men he followed from the crash site till close to noon. The older man looked haggard when John saw him emerge from the house. John watched the older man as he coughed, spit blood on the ground, wiped his face with a rag, and then walked back inside the house. Shortly thereafter, the younger man stepped out and made his way to the OP, where he conversed with the female for a few minutes before she took the child and returned to the house.

John rolled over onto his back, questioning just what in the hell he was doing out here. Why was he spying on these people? Was it because he was God knows how far from home base and his entire team along with the exfil group were all dead and buried nearby? Why hadn't he simply moved past these people and kept going to a point where he could establish comms with someone in the rear and get picked up? He thought about it hard for a full minute. The entire world had changed while he and a select few refused to admit it and worked tirelessly to pull society back together.

He had always been driven to the point of seeing his objective through a pair of drinking straws at times, losing all peripheral sight altogether. This had always served him and his mates well in the old world, where they didn't give a thought to the reason for a mission, instead focusing only on its completion. They simply got their marching orders, figured out how to achieve the objective, and then went to work.

Not one time did he or any of his mates question why they were kidnapping this guy or killing that guy. John and people like him were put on a task and they completed it, end of story, no questions asked. Sure, some of the good folks he'd sent to

Allah, or whomever they were being sent to, had it coming, and at times he'd seen firsthand why they deserved to be sent, but many times he had not a clue about a target's worth in the world.

Now lying on his back in the warm California afternoon sun, watching these people struggle to survive, it began to dawn on John that what he was doing was not only futile, but also a little selfish and possibly just plain wrong. He hadn't thought about it on any other mission since the people he'd been sent to retrieve were more than happy to jump in a working helicopter and take a ride to a place where they could get back to work, be fed, and have someone else worry about their safety and security. Essentially, they'd be putting their heads back in the sand, where they had most likely had them buried before the event.

Maybe Mother Nature had just hit some reset button and wanted some time to heal and cleanse herself of the human scourge who had really taken her to task over the past one hundred and fifty years. Who was he to go against that? He thought with a sly smile.

John took in a deep breath, leaning his head back till it touched the rock he was resting against. He stayed there clearing his mind, relaxing his body, attempting to void out any tension, stress or other negative elements from his mind, soul and body. When he opened his eyes, he felt so relaxed that he was a little concerned his bowels wouldn't hold. He took another breath, allowing his body to tighten ever so slightly, restoring faith in his ability to control his bodily functions, and then stared back at the group below him.

The younger man sat at the lookout post, his head sweeping side to side as if he was sure he'd be attacked at any moment. John thought back, trying to remember if he'd done something to alert them to his presence. No way they could know he was here, he'd been far too careful and, although these folks were on the right track in regard to taking care of themselves, they were not the pros he was used to tracking and hiding from.

On the other hand, a ten-million-dollar military helicopter had fallen out of the sky right in their backyard, killing nearly everyone on board, so they might have a sneaking suspicion someone had survived and was lurking about. John kicked himself for not contacting the two men at the crash site. It would have been easier than trying to walk into their base camp, where he was sure they would want to protect the woman, child and whatever supplies they had. Yes, it would have been far less dangerous had he just called out to them and done a good ole-style Special Forces meet and greet right there at the downed helicopter.

John stared hard at Jared as the younger man left his seated position, making his way along a small ridgeline not far from the OP. *What is he looking for, or is it just the crash that has them on edge?* John wondered.

He made a mental note to be careful, the human was a very difficult animal to deal with, and he had been amazed more than a few times at what his enemies had known, assumed, or been able to achieve through either luck or sheer willpower during battles he'd been involved in.

John knew the driving force in all human adversaries was the will to live, and that drive was stronger than any other except maybe the will to procreate. He'd seen some guys do some absolutely stupid shit in the past for a piece of tail. John remembered a mate of his who'd gone through a door in some hovel thousands of miles from home, been confronted by an armed man, and shot the man five times center mass.

They all watched the man crumple like a neglected mari-onette, and began searching the rest of the residence. John's mate who shot the guy should have been the one to make sure he was either very dead or secured. Instead, he took his eyes off the downed man and stared at a nude photo of a woman hanging on the wall. He hadn't taken his eyes off the doomed man on the floor for more than two seconds when the man produced a small pistol and shot the operator in the neck.

John understood how fucked up life could be, and that incident always leapt out at him as a life lesson. His mate, Francis Connor, was a beast of an operator, a mentor to John, and a close friend, and had died right then and there on the dirt floor of some shitty-ass mud hut, with only the man who killed him lying next to him. Their team medic worked on Francis while a second medic from their Ranger support element came in and worked on the downed Hajji. The bad guy lived and Francis died, a hard lesson but not one John ever forgot. Never underestimate your adversary and never overestimate your own capabilities.

John had lost other mates, but losing Francis hit him and stuck like glue throughout his tenure in the Special Missions Unit. He shook his head, clearing it of these thoughts from a time so long ago and so far away with respect to where the world was today. John pondered Barry for a moment. Why hadn't the guy jumped at the opportunity to be rescued from that hornet's nest he was living in? John marveled at how resilient humans could be, wondering if the guy had figured out how to survive in that environment only to have it demolished when John and his former team showed up. He swept the binoculars across the land for as far as he could see and had an epiphany.

The base he came from was tasked with all the work being done in Northern California, parts of Nevada, Oregon, and up into southern Washington State. The only reason they didn't have more territorial responsibility was due to aircraft limitations and, that was it. John knew there were likely more than forty million people in California, or at least there had been before the event, while the total number of personnel working out of his base was about one hundred.

His tier one mentality of "I can do anything, anywhere, anytime" began to crumble at this thought. They had two Black Hawks—check that, one Black Hawk and a hundred people—check that, ninety-five people, most of whom acted in support roles, trying to pull together the resources to get forty or fifty million people back online. America was gone and the foolish bureaucrats refused to see reality for what it was.

John came out here to pick up Barry, whether he went willingly or not, so basically, he'd been sent to kidnap a man from his house on orders from someone who didn't have the foresight to stop something like the event from happening in the first place. Instead of working to hoard societal assets like Barry, the government should have been working to distribute these assets along with food throughout the land in order to give people the best chance at surviving the fast-approaching winter that was sure to kill millions of his countrymen.

John's head hurt as he mulled over this new, yet moribund, world he existed in. He better start thinking like a new world man and not a man from the past. He did well and had talents that few men possessed, but he was still a novice at living in the post-apocalyptic world. John wondered where Barry was right now and if he was still alive, hoping his dislodging the guy hadn't resulted in Barry's death.

John looked back down towards the little house and saw the woman, accompanied by the little girl, sitting outside on the front steps, eating something. *What am I doing here?* These seemed like decent people who, out of curiosity, had come out to the crash site, found his dead teammates, and actually taken the time and energy to bury the poor souls. Turds wouldn't have done that; only decent people would go that far out of their way for the dead.

John wiped his hands across his face and almost stood up

and simply walked down to the house. The old tier one operator side of him reared its head, keeping him from something that could have resulted in getting shot or having to shoot someone who, at the present time, he had no interest in shooting.

John relaxed a bit, trying to come up with a way to make contact with these people. He had worked with Special Forces guys who specialized in linking up with locals, providing aid, training and actual on-the-ground fighting assistance, but he had never been cast in that forum. As a Ranger, he had pushed into plenty of villages and ended up talking to the elders, but it had always seemed to be preceded by some sort of raid or force of some type. Once he arrived at the Unit, he was assigned as an assaulter and, well, they didn't do a lot of PR work. They weren't who were called upon when the situation needed a humanitarian touch.

It wasn't that they were incapable of being people persons, it was just that the government spent so much goddamn money training him and his mates, that when something came up that no one else could handle, John and his friends handled it. The people they dealt with weren't the types to respond to the white-glove treatment, so they left the winning-their-hearts-and-minds stuff to the SF boys while he and his friends slaughtered those whose minds couldn't be won over by logic, reason or the notion of being a positive force in the world.

John laid on the ground as the sun passed overhead, commencing its slow descent into the west. He watched as the older man relieved the younger man on the OP and then, a few hours later, was himself relieved by the third man. John had come up with a plan on contacting these people in a way that would likely scare the holy-ever-loving shit out of them but hopefully wouldn't result in anyone getting shot.

As the sun was about to slip behind the hills, John saw the younger man emerge from the house, walking in the direction of the group's observation post. John pulled the binoculars to his face and cursed under his breath. The younger man was carrying a pair of night-vision goggles in his left hand as he trotted up the slope to relieve his partner. John watched the man relieve the third guy and then settle into the OP as the relieved man strolled back towards the house.

John was going to have to be extra careful with what he had planned that evening. He hadn't planned on these folks having the same night-vision capabilities he had and, quite frankly, didn't like the pendulum tilting in anyone's favor but his own. The use of NVGs by this little group concerned John, although he saw by the way the younger man handled the piece of equipment, it was foreign to him.

John made sure he wasn't clearly in the line of sight with the OP as night blanketed the countryside. He snapped his own goggles down over his eyes, scanned the area, then began cleaning his rifle. He did this by feel alone, like he'd done thousands of times in the past.

John and his Unit mates found they had battlefield needs that had to be met no matter what the circumstances. One of these needs just happened to be weapons maintenance. Like everything they did, it came after trial, error and a ton of round tabling within the Unit. Every man in the Unit carried a rifle and at least one sidearm. Many carried more than one sidearm along with an assortment of knives, small swords and hatchets.

John and his fellow operators oftentimes worked in small teams in very dangerous areas of the world. Several times John had worked in either two-man teams or even as a solo operator. In a two-man team operation, John would clean his rifle while his partner kept watch with a fully functional rifle. If the proverbial shit hit the fan, the two men would have a rifle and a pistol in the fight straight out of the gate.

This was all great, but the men took it to the next level,

teaching themselves to clean weapons by feel so there were always two sets of eyes on alert, watching for threats. This became even more important when John found himself working alone like tonight. If he simply broke his weapon down and cleaned it like most other military personnel did, he would have been taking a great risk, with no one watching his back, and relying only on his ears as early warning detectors. By cleaning his weapon at night, he triple-tasked by listening, watching with the NVGs, and cleaning his weapon by feel alone.

This little weapons-maintenance strategy was just one tiny way in which the members of the Unit were different from every other unit in the world. They constantly debriefed, critiqued, strategized, rehearsed, and then repeated that process. They went outside the Unit in order to see how others were doing things in an effort to find better and more efficient ways to accomplish their missions.

The sightless weapons-cleaning trick had actually been discovered by one of his mates who had been at a civilian range and seen a blind man who was visiting the range and, under close supervision, been given the experience of firing a handgun. Afterwards, John's mate had described how the man was taught one time how to break the pistol down before he did it on his own, using only his hands.

Members of John's unit round tabled the idea, contacted a representative from the Society for the Blind, and set up a meet and greet. They were put into contact with a former Air Force pilot who lost his sight after his plane was shot down in 1971 over Vietnam.

The man taught the operators in the Special Missions Unit more than a few things about operating in the blind, so to speak. The weapons cleaning ended up being the tip of the iceberg. They learned to pick locks while blindfolded, and one of John's mates even taught himself to read Braille. So, on a night somewhere in Northern California, Jared sat in an OP fiddling with the night-vision goggles, rifle lying next to him on the ground, while John sat, head moving back and forth searching stygian surroundings, his hands gliding over the surfaces of his rifle like Helen Keller reading a Stephen King novel.

Chapter 35

THE FOLLOWING MORNING, Jared opened his eyes to the early morning light streaming through the bedroom window. He stretched and wished so hard for the world to be back to normal that his head hurt. Alas, the world was still a fucking mess, so he threw his legs over the edge of the bed and sat up with his head in his hands.

After rubbing his temples for a couple of seconds, he stood, slid his feet into the Salomons, grabbed his rifle, and stepped out into the hallway. He heard the soft murmur of voices emanating from the kitchen and headed in that direction, hoping for a cup of coffee. Bart and the two girls were seated at the kitchen table as he walked in, immediately sensing something was going on.

Bart slid a piece of paper across the table in Jared's direction. "This was on the front door this morning," he said as Jared stared down at the paper.

The note read: "I WAS IN THE HELICOPTER CRASH AND FOLLOWED TWO OF YOU BACK HERE. DIDN'T WANT TO SCARE ANYONE, SO I'VE STAYED AWAY. I

WOULD LIKE TO TALK. NOON TODAY I WILL COME
DOWN. PLEASE DON'T SHOOT."

Jared read the paper two more times, then looked at Bart.
"When did you find it?"

"When I came in this morning after Calvin relieved me."
Jared's mouth fell slightly open and Bart held his hand up.
"There was no reason to wake anyone up. We get precious
sleep as it is, and I sure as hell wasn't going out to look for
some ghost who was able to get to the house without me seeing
him."

At 1130 hours, Bart and Jared sat on the front porch in two
chairs side by side, rifles leaning within easy reach of each man.
At Bart's request, Shannon and Essie remained inside the house,
and Calvin went out to the OP while they waited on the porch
for the mystery person to come waltzing down the road. As the
two men sat in silence, waiting for God knows who to pop out
and surprise them, a man appeared on the road leading to the
little house. He was about fifty yards out and dressed in full battle
kit, including a rifle, which he held loosely in his right hand.

"Easy," Bart whispered. "Let him come to us, act relaxed,
but be ready."

Jared shifted ever so slightly as the man began walking
towards the house. He had an ease about him, a long stride,
but a relaxed one as if he were stopping by for a beer and to
watch a ball game.

Bart slowly rose to his feet, rifle in hand. "Follow my lead
and, if any shooting starts, spread out so he has two distant
targets to deal with."

In response, Jared got to his feet, his rifle in hand as well as
he stepped off the porch and to the side.

John walked up the dirt road, seeing the two men sitting on
the porch. He knew the other man was out on the post and the
women were inside the house, so it didn't appear they had any

funny business planned for him. Still, he kept his rifle ready in his right hand, but not in a threatening way. He watched both men rise, weapons in hand, preparing themselves for his arrival.

John didn't like this, but he also didn't blame them for being cautious. They had a woman and a child, so he gave them a pass on being armed. Plus, why couldn't three armed red-blooded Americans meet and get to know one another without there being any shooting? As the man drew within ten yards of the house, Bart stepped off the porch.

"Why don't we all sling these rifles so no one gets hurt during the get-to-know-each-other period."

The man stopped and cocked his head; a half smirk reshaped his mouth. Then as suddenly as he had appeared in their lives, he slung the rifle to his back, shrugging his heavily muscled shoulders in order to situate the rifle comfortably. Bart immediately did the same, with Jared following a second after. Once the weapons were slung, Bart walked straight out to the man and shook his hand.

"Name's Bart and this here is Jared," Bart said.

The man shook Bart's hand and nodded to Jared before answering. "Name's John," he said as he looked around the yard, scanning yet fully engaged with Bart and Jared simultaneously.

"Well, John," Bart continued, "why don't you come inside and meet the ladies. Then we can get to talking about where you came from and what the hell has been going on in this country."

Bart turned on his heel, walking straight into the house, where Shannon and Essie were huddled on a small love seat. Essie clung to Shannon, giving Bart the impression they had been watching through a window, and fled to the love seat when the men turned towards the house.

"Shannon, Essie, this here is John," Bart said by way of introducing everyone with a single sentence.

John stepped through the door, nodding his head to the woman and child. "Nice to meet you two. Hope I'm not intruding."

Shannon seemed to relax, peeling Essie off her and getting to her feet. "Are you hungry, John?"

John replied in that easy way he had about him. "I am, haven't eaten in twenty-four hours."

Shannon rose and walked into the small kitchen, leaving the men in the main living room area of the house. Essie curled into a ball on the love seat, staring wide eyed at John, who smiled down at her.

Bart took a deep breath then motioned to a chair. "Sit and let's talk a bit."

John liked this guy, he was straight to the point on everything so far and, if John was as good of a judge of character as he fancied himself, he didn't see Bart changing anytime soon. John unslung the rifle and gestured towards the door. "Mind if I lean this next to the door?"

Bart thought about this for a moment. "I think we all should lean 'em there together."

All three men set the rifles next to the door, then sat in various chairs in the room. Bart leaned back, staring wordlessly at John. Jared thought he felt tension in the air, but quickly realized here were two alpha dogs sizing each other up. One was well past his prime and maybe not much longer for this world, while the other was in his prime, appearing more than capable. This wasn't a dick-measuring contest; it was more of a respectful and mutual evaluation of one another.

After about fifteen-seconds, which to Jared felt like an hour, Bart spoke. "Why don't you tell us who you are and what you were doing out this way?"

John nodded. "Fair enough," he said and proceeded to tell

Bart and Jared he was with some National Guard unit doing recon for survivors as well as a situational report for what was left of the government. John told them how the helicopter had some trouble, crashed, and killed everyone but him. When he finished, Bart leaned back in his chair and stared hard at John, who stared back just as hard.

"Bullshit," Bart barked, loud enough to make Essie jump. "That's a load of bullshit if ever I heard a load of bullshit." Before John could defend himself, Bart continued, "I was starting to fucking like you, John, whoever the fuck you are. Now you go and tell me some wild tale about how you're in some National Guard unit and just happened to crash, and now here you are sitting in our house, about to eat our food, which is pretty fucking scarce nowadays, if you hadn't realized.

"Bullshit," Bart said again, not so loud this time. "Bullshit, bullshit, bullshit, and shame on fucking you for lying to me like that. You should know better than to lie to your elders, boy." Bart was truly angry, but Jared sensed he was more disappointed than anything.

John, on the other hand, sat as cool as ever, watching Bart, letting the older man vent. Bart turned sharply, pointing to the rifle John had leaned against the wall.

"That goddamn weapon is not issued to National Guard units; it's an H&K 416. This ain't my first dance, John; specialized teams carry those weapons." He turned back and flicked his hand at John's clothes. "Those BDUs are made by Crye and cost too much to issue to every soldier. Hell, the Marines don't even wear Crye BDUs."

He shook his finger at John, who remained sitting, staring back at the upset old man, without so much as a flicker of emotion on his face.

"I was born at night, but not last night, John, so tell me, why would you lie to me about who you are and what you're doing out here?"

John listened to everything the older man had said without even blinking. The old fucker sure had a point, and he knew a little more about the modern military than John would have guessed. He was carrying an H&K 416 and was wearing Crye Precision battle dress uniform. He was probably carrying and wearing nearly ten thousand dollars' worth of gear, not the normal load out for your regular Army or Marine unit.

Just then Shannon brought a plate of food to John, handing it to him. He stood, thanked her, and then settled back into the chair. The silence deafened Jared as the two men sat, Bart staring intently at John while John stared intently at the plate of hot food. Finally, after what seemed like an eternity, John pulled the plate close to his face and drew in a deep breath through his nostrils, savoring the smell of hot food, then leaned back away from the plate, rested his head on the back of the chair, eyes almost closed, shoulders sagging for a few seconds. He exhaled and sat forward to stare back at Bart.

John nodded his head slowly in the affirmative, setting the plate of food on the floor between his feet. "Well, I can't lie to you and accept your hospitality without my conscience eating me alive."

Bart cocked his head, saying nothing.

"Truth is, there's not much left and, now that we are into this thing about five weeks, there are a lot of dead Americans across the country." John looked at Shannon and Essie, then back at Bart. "The government was warned many times about this sort of disaster, but the cost of hardening the entire military or, worse yet, the entire country just wasn't feasible to those ole boys in Washington."

Jared leaned forward. "Harden against what?"

John looked squarely at him for a second and then back at Bart, who raised his eyebrows as if prompting John to carry on with his tale.

"An EMP or a solar flare like the one that lit this whole thing off," John said.

Over the next hour, John told them he was in a specialized unit and filled them in on what had happened and how the flare had ignited a global EMP brawl with a sprinkling of tactical nuclear warfare just for good measure. Jared's mind was racing as he listened to John's tale. Not one thing John said could really be argued and, God knew, Jared went over every detail in his mind, trying to debunk what he was being told, thinking that in some way if he could disprove the story, then the whole thing hadn't happened and they could all go back to living their old lives with plenty of food, water, and other luxuries like baths, showers, and full nights of sleep. Oh yeah, and a lot fewer hostile people to deal with.

John guessed the population in California alone had gone from around forty-million people to about five million in the span of four short weeks. John assured them it would get much worse before anything started getting better. The fact that they were even alive was a miracle, in John's opinion.

After John finished filling in the small group on the demise of the world, he settled back and began inhaling the food Shannon had given him. Jared and his friends sat in silence, watching John, thinking about what he said. It wasn't anything they had a hard time believing. More than anything, none of them wanted to believe what John had said. They all wanted to wake from this nightmare that was at times overwhelming.

He knew if he hadn't met Bart, the likelihood of him lying dead on the side of some street in San Jose was somewhere between highly likely and insanely probable. Jared stared at this John guy sitting in front of him, clad in military garb, eating the food Jared and his group had scavenged for their future, and wondered where this relationship was headed.

Bart interrupted Jared's thoughts. "Why'd you come up to

the house and make contact? Why not just make your way back to your base?"

John took his last bite and smiled, his eyes twinkling like something was funny that only he knew. "I think I'm done with the Army. The work I've done in the past has been without a doubt far more violent and full of death, but this work post event has left a bad taste in my mouth, and I don't think I'm gonna bust my hump getting back to that life."

Bart just stared back as if waiting for John to finish and, when he did, he continued, "To be honest, I don't know why, I just did. In fact, for the first time since I can remember, I don't know what to do or where to go. I just had a feeling about you all after seeing you bury my men, and felt like reaching out to some people who seemed like normal folks just trying to make it through this tough hand life dealt everyone."

"You still hungry, John?" Shannon asked, interrupting the men.

"No, but thank you for the food. It was delicious and hit the spot."

They sat in silence until Bart spoke up. "Mind if we talk as a group in private?"

"Not at all," John said, getting to his feet and heading to the door, where he grabbed the rifle as he slipped through the front door. After John had vacated the house, the little group faced Bart.

"I think we ask him to stay with us," Bart said.

"I agree," Shannon piped in, just a little too quickly. Every head in the room turned as she spoke, causing her to flush red.

Bart came to her rescue, turning to Jared. "Well, how 'bout you?"

Jared thought about it for a moment, trying to evaluate this new situation in the same manner he evaluated everything in his previous life. He was beginning to see things as threats and assets but was still having problems sorting through how to make sound decisions that would ensure securing a positive future for the group and him. Bart waited patiently as Jared sat as still as a statue, lost in his thoughts until Shannon broke the silence.

"I like him, he seems nice, and I get a feeling of security being around him." All heads turned to her and, again, she blushed. "I mean, he's in the military, so he knows about guns and stuff like that," she said, fumbling for the words.

Jared took a deep breath before speaking. "I agree with everything you all said, but there's one thing that no one brought up."

Bart elevated an eyebrow as Jared continued.

"He is in some Special Forces deal, and I will be the first to admit I don't know a thing about what that means other than what I've seen on TV, but I believe it's safe to say he could take what he wants from us and there's not much we could do to stop him. Now, having said that, he did come to us in a peaceful way." Jared paused, staring at Bart and Shannon as if waiting for their input.

They remained silent, letting Jared work through his thoughts on the subject.

"I think we ask him where he sees himself fitting into this group and what he thinks we should do to survive the foreseeable future; then we make a decision. We used this same method where I used to work, and they said it could be applied to any situation or profession."

Bart slowly nodded his old head as Jared finished.

"In addition to that, I think we should involve Calvin in these talks," Bart said. "If he disagrees, he may have a reason that changes everyone's minds. We need to hear what he has to say before making a decision like this."

The group exited the house and awkwardly explained to John they were moving to the OP to discuss matters in private with Calvin.

John merely nodded, not moving from the chair he flopped into on the house's front porch.

Calvin heard everyone's thoughts and had little to add that the group as a whole hadn't already come up with.

When they returned to the house, Bart laid out the group's thoughts to John, asking him to elaborate on how he would fit into the group and identify what assets he brought to the table.

"Can we all be brutally honest here?" John asked the group.

"If you're not going to be honest, then this is a waste of everyone's time," Bart fired back.

John pursed his lips, nodding ever so slightly. "Well, this group is not going to last long in the world I've seen so far. Bart, you are not well, and that's not good for the rest of these folks since you seem to be the only one here who has the slightest understanding of how to handle yourself." John looked directly at Bart. "They know what's wrong with you? Coughing up blood is very serious and potentially lethal." John paused, staring at Bart. "How long do you have?"

Bart's nostrils flared briefly; then his shoulders sagged visibly, his eyes glazing over for a moment as he lost himself in his thoughts. "I had six months, seven months ago," he said without emotion.

John nodded, bowing his head reverently before continuing. "This guy is most likely the reason you're all alive, and he's living on borrowed time, so what are you going to do when he's gone?" John lowered his voice as he ended his last question, knowing this little group had five weeks earlier been shielded from the harsher things in life like death and evil. "Where do any of you fit into this group?" John continued. "Where do any of us fit into this life, for that matter? I'll tell you one thing, we as humans are a social animal and, that reason alone, is why you are all here together right now."

John further elaborated to the group, telling of his experiences within a very specialized unit in the Army. He trained all over the United States and had knowledge of food-storage locations as well as places to obtain ammunition and weapons. He told them how he was proficient in handling all types of weapons and explosives, which could be beneficial to them surviving the mess they were all calling the here and now.

After ten minutes, John was done relaying his career and life experiences to the group. In doing so, he divulged secrets he swore to keep on behalf of a government that was all but gone, making him really not beholden to anyone in regard to his sharing secrets.

"I'm not here to be your leader or dictate what you all do; I just want to be part of something and have my input heard and used by you all to make decisions on what you're going to do in the future. I think we will all agree that if any one of you wanted to strike out on your own, you could, and there would be no hard feelings. I just want the same afforded me."

The tiny gathering grew silent as John ended his address, leaning back in the chair.

Jared was the first to speak. "When were you going to tell any of us?" he asked, staring directly at Bart, who was wiping a bit of bloody spittle from the corner of his mouth, making no attempt to hide the act. The cat was out of the bag, so no use trying to conceal his illness now. Masking it had taken more energy than he had, and he was exhausted. Bart was tired of hiding his illness and damn near tired of living, if he were brutally honest with himself.

"Ah, I don't know, you all have enough to worry about already, and there's not a damn thing any of you all can do about it. I'm dying and that's that."

"And that's that?" Jared exclaimed, leaping to his feet. "We could have gone into town and tried to find medicine or someone who knew what to do."

Bart waved him off tiredly, wiping his mouth again before

inspecting the bloody rag. "They couldn't do a thing for me before all this, so there sure as hell isn't a thing anyone can do now. It's life and I've served my purpose, getting you through the first bit of this mess."

Later that night Jared sat in the OP, thinking about Bart and how alone he was about to be. He didn't like it, and this new guy didn't completely feel right to him. He trusted Bart, had fought side by side with him, been scared nearly to death, and survived with Bart. He had a strange relationship with the old guy, almost like a kid who didn't have a father, then some old man had taken him in to fill the void. To think it might be coming to an end was unutterable.

Shannon came and relieved him, leaving him to walk back to the darkened house lost in his thoughts of the old man who was the sole reason he was even alive. The entire thing was really just too much for Jared to wrap his head around. The event, the violence that followed, nearly being killed in the supermarket that, not seventy-two hours before, had been filled with smiling employees and soccer moms. Then his meeting this old guy, striking a deal with him, both men holding up their end of the bargain like some 1800s spit-in-the-palm handshake deal.

When Jared reached the house, he went straight to Bart's room and listened to the man's labored breathing for a solid thirty minutes. Finally realizing tonight wasn't the night, he turned and was about to walk to the kitchen when he saw John sitting on the couch, staring at him. As the men's eyes met, John gave him a wordless nod and just stared. Jared walked over and sat across from the strange new man who had simply appeared at their doorstep less than twenty-four hours ago. The two men sat in silence for several seconds. Jared didn't have the nuts to ice this guy for minutes like Bart had done. John saved Jared any further discomfort.

"I don't know what you're going through, 'cause I don't

know your relationship with the guy, but I'm here to tell you I've lost twenty-two close friends in the last ten years, and that sucked more than I could ever explain to you. I lost guys who were my peers and that hurt, but the worst were the guys I looked up to, my mentors, the older guys in my unit. I always looked at them as invincible, indestructible guys who were there as I came into the Unit and guys who would be there when I left the Unit." John leaned back, seeming to travel back to some faraway land where he'd lost his friends.

"They were a security blanket and I didn't even know it while they were alive. It wasn't until the first one got hit by an IED that I realized how much I was leaning on him. It hurt and it hurt for a good long time, but I pushed it down and came to realize I was them, I was the mentor to the new guys coming into the Unit, and I couldn't afford to be leaning on anyone since all the new guys were leaning on me. Circle of life, bro, it just keeps turning and we keep on pushing, day in and day out."

The two men sat in more silence, each pondering a thousand different things, both present and past.

THE NEW DAY brought with it a gruesome discovery as John found Bart cold to the touch, but with a look of peace on his face. It was as if the arrival of John was all it took for Bart to let go and move on. Jared would never know, but Bart thanked God every day that this wet-behind-the-ears kid had arrived on his doorstep and given him a reason to live the last five weeks of his life. Jared would never know that Bart felt he had lived more in the last five weeks than he had since his wife passed. Jared would also never know that Bart cared for him like a son. Bart genuinely grew to love Jared during the short and tumultuous time they knew one another.

When John told Jared the older man had passed, Jared went directly to the room and knelt by the bed, placing his hand on Bart's cold arm. At first, Jared nearly pulled away at the feel of cold flesh, but instead he kept Bart's arm wrapped in his hand until his body heat warmed the arm. He stayed this way for a bit before rising and pulling the covers over Bart's face. Jared walked out of the bedroom and into the living area, where everyone sat eating breakfast.

"We have to leave this place."

THE END

Continue Jared's journey with
Book Two
TEARS OF CHAOS

About the Author

Rick was raised in Napa Valley, California. In 1986 he joined the Marine Corps and served over four years with Third Battalion, 1st Marine Regiment as an anti-tank assault missleman and later as a scout with 3/1's Surveillance Target Acquisition (STA) platoon.

After the Marines, Rick went into law enforcement, where he worked for 28 years in numerous positions such as Gangs, SWAT, Patrol and Homicide before retiring in 2018.

Writing has always been his passion, which he now pursues full time. He draws on his experiences from law enforcement and the Marines to flesh out reality based apocalyptic novels.